S

The Legacy of the Lynx

Clio Gray

urbanepublications.com

First published in Great Britain in 2016
by Urbane Publications Ltd
Suite 3, Brown Europe House, 33/34 Gleaming Wood Drive,
Chatham, Kent ME5 8RZ

A CIP catalogue record for this book is available from the British Library.

ISBN 978-1-911331-44-5
EPUB 978-1-911331-45-2
MOBI 978-1-911331-46-9

Design and Typeset by Michelle Morgan

Cover by The Invisible Man

Printed and bound by CPI Group (UK) Ltd, Croydon, CR0 4YY

urbanepublications.com

Table of Contents

PREFACE
YOU HAVE TO KICK A MULE TO GET IT GOING

The secretary to the eighth Duke of Aquasparta was reading with great interest an open letter sent to the *Philosophical Transactions of the Royal Society*. The original missive had been printed a couple of months ago, it taking a while for the translations of the Transactions to filter through to the more far-flung parts of the continent such as Italy, and longer still before he could be bothered to flick through it and take a read. But this letter was enough to stop him in his tracks.

'*My name is Golo Eck,*' he read, '*descendant of Johannes Eck, one of the five founders of the first scientific academy in Europe, the Accademia dei Lincei, begun in 1603 by the extraordinary vision of Federico Cesi, Duke of Aquasparta, 2nd Prince of Sant'Angelo and St Paul, Marchese di Monticelli, Lord of Porcaria, Civatella Cesi, and Marcellina Poggia Cesium, Noble Roman and Nobile di Terni.*'

The iteration of the Cesi family's standing in society were for him unnecessary, but he could see how others might be impressed.

'*My intension, in short,*' the letter went on, '*is to restart the Lynx, resurrect Federico Cesi's primary intentions which were to disseminate knowledge and encourage further study of the world in which we live. Towards this end, I have been gathering information on the whereabouts of the lost library of the Lynx, as that society was commonly called. Following the death of Federico Cesi it was absorbed into the Paper Museum of Giovanni Battista della Porta, a staunch member of the Lynx, but when della Porta died his entire library was dispersed and it has taken many decades for me to track down where it went, and to whom, and where it might be now.*

'But I have made great strides recently, and I now believe that the greater portion of the Lynx Library lies in three separate places: a private collection in Wexford, Ireland; the Athenaeum in Deventer, and the Biblioteque Nationale de France. This last is of most concern, as I have learned that within the next few months it will be openly coming up for auction, and therefore the possibility is that it could be dispersed towards the four corners of the earth and never be reunited with the Lynx.'

So much, so true, the secretary thought, but what he read next was more perturbing.

'My plea therefore,' went on this Golo Eck, *'is that those of you who already understand my concerns, as well as those of you who are only just learning of them, be both vigilant and generous. This is a matter of principle for the entire scientific community of the world, for if we don't act soon then we will certainly lose the chance to bring back together our shared history, by which I mean the history of the Lynx, our stepping stone from darkness into light.'*

There was more, a lot more, about the importance of the Lynx not only as a physical body of scientists but as an idea, about the necessity in these times of uncertainty to collect together the lost library, give it the chance to breathe fresh air into its lungs and thereby invigorate the entire corpus of scientists scattered across Europe and beyond. It was also a well aired grievance that all the most prevalent journals had huge backlogs, that it could be months, often a year and sometimes two, before a submitted paper saw the light of day. If the Lynx was re-established – and with it it's notoriously forward thinking Imprimatur that could have a paper go into press within weeks – then the ramifications were huge, but still he hesitated.

The letter smacked of a scam, but if so it was a good one, this Golo Eck asking for any donations towards the purchase of the various parts of the lost Lynx library to go through the Royal Society in London, no obvious way for Golo Eck himself to profit from it, at least not directly. But someone could profit from him, that much the secretary realised as he read through the article for a second time.

He'd spent a while, when he'd first got here, going through the many documents kept by the Cesi family – which was his job, after all – and he knew all about the founding members of the Lynx: Federico Cesi, Francesco Stelluti, Anastasio De Filiis, the Scotsman Walter Peat and his great friend Johannes Eck from Deventer. He was also aware of the unsavoury scandals that had surrounded them – admittedly mostly originating from Cesi's own father who was as welded to the Church as a barnacle to its shell. Heresy, sodomy, exile and murder were the worst of them, not to mention the concomitant crimes of the more famous moths attracted to the Lynx's flame, those men it had nurtured and supported when no one else would. Like Galileo Galilei, for instance. And he could think of one family, and one person in particular, who absolutely wouldn't want Golo Eck dragging up the old history of the Lynx, especially not now.

Scam or no scam, Golo's letter sparked off the secretary's own little scheme inside his head. Knowledge, after all – as the founding constitution of the Lynx proclaimed with such fervour – was its own *raison d'être,* and he thought long and hard about how best to make it work in his favour. He was no fool, no everyday man on the make, and so he took his time before drawing out his quill, licking it, dipping it into his ink, beginning a not-so-open letter of his own.

The Lynx might be rising somewhere in the badlands of Scotland, but the secretary of the eight Duke of Aquasparta was about to set a hunter on its trail.

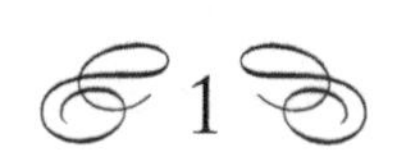

HALF A CENTURY IN THE MAKING

LOCH ECK, ARGYLLSHIRE, SCOTLAND 1798

'What the curse is he doing now?' Ruan Peat asked sourly, pacing the floor for the umpteenth time before coming to rest by the large window and tapping the glass impatiently with his fingernails.

'It's not going to help, you interrupting him every five minutes,' Fergus commented, regarding the younger man's back, the tense hunch of his shoulders, the bone at the nape of his neck moving between the shadowed hint of hairline and his collar as if it was a snake about to burst from his skin. Ruan took a step backwards and grimaced at his reflection in the window. Beyond it lay the grey stretch of the loch: the stunted birches and alders cowering at the base of the hillside rising up sharply from the farther shore. He knew how they felt, that yearning in their bent-low branches to stretch and grow, the urge they had to reach towards the sky despite the winter winds that always kept them down.

'But does he have to check everything three times over?' Ruan complained, turning back to look at Fergus, who didn't appear to have moved a muscle, sitting at ease on one of the several trunks they'd packed with the possessions needed for their journey.

'Now you know that's not entirely fair,' Fergus said. 'He just wants to make sure everything's locked up tight so it will be fine for you when you get back.'

'What makes him think I'll ever want to come back?' Ruan said loudly. 'I've been cooped up in this hole all my blasted life and as far as I'm concerned once I'm out, I'm out.'

Fergus smiled. His grizzled beard made it hard to detect but Ruan had grown up with the man and knew every twitch of him, or thought he did, and he bridled, started pacing the floor again.

'You think you know me,' Ruan said, stopping his pacing long enough to kick hard at one of the heavy sea chests. 'But I'm near of age now and my own man, and what gives Golo the right to think he's going to live out his life somewhere new and exciting and send me packing back here with my tail between my legs?'

Fergus didn't smile this time. Angry words were buzzing on his lips but he held them back.

'I'll go see how he's getting on,' Fergus said instead, pushing himself off the chest and standing up.

He was around the same height as Ruan Peat but had a good fifty pounds on him and it crossed his mind to give the lad the thrashing he deserved for his ingratitude but reined it in. This was Golo's big day after all, and he wasn't going to let the likes of Ruan Peat spoil it for the old man; but his blood was boiling and before he left the room he turned back.

'He's spent half a century aiming for this moment,' Fergus said, 'and God help me I'll swing for you if you try to ruin it. Why not think on what's he's done for you, for a change?'

Ruan stopped where he stood and stared at Fergus with open animosity.

'And why don't you?' Ruan spat out the childish retort, a hard gnawing starting in his belly. 'You'd be nothing but a couple of muddy footprints without him, you and your father. Ever think on that?'

Fergus stood in the doorway looking daggers at Ruan Peat. It hadn't always been like this between the two of them, but every time Ruan had the upper hand. He was family, after all, and Fergus was not, and there was the end to it.

'Just make sure you know what you've got before chucking it all away,' Fergus gave his parting shot, exiting the door and slamming it shut behind him before Ruan could get in another word.

Fergus didn't move away immediately but leant his back against the wood the second he'd closed it. He hoped to Heaven everything went to plan, and that this trip of theirs would force the boy to grow into the man he already believed himself to be.

'You know as well as I do that his head's halfway up a creel!' Ruan shouted through the wood, banging at it with his fist to make his point, realising that Fergus was just the other side. Fergus flinched at the accusation and closed his eyes. It took all his self-restraint not to fling the door open again and give Ruan a good kicking.

'All those times he's sent you off,' Ruan went on without remorse. 'Don't think I don't know what you were doing. Trotting off with his precious letters so nobody can interfere with them. And who the bloody hell would do that anyway? Mad as a toad with a stick up his arse...'

'Enough, boy,' Fergus growled, angered that Golo's minor paranoia should be described so crudely.

Certainly Golo was a little obsessed, as all great men were, but it was not the time to argue. They'd be off in the next few hours and, after they'd reached Port Glasgow, he and Ruan would be going their separate ways for a few months at least, and thank God for it. He cricked his head to one side, clenched his fists, wondering how it would feel to squeeze the life right out of the last line of the Peats, and nobody to cry about it but Golo Eck.

2
BAD DAYS, BAD FLEAS

WEXFORD, IRELAND 1798

Jesus and Mary, but last night had been close. Greta's skin felt like it was crawling with snails just to think on it. It wasn't the first time she'd been stopped, but those men were huge in their uniforms and iron-tipped boots and could have stomped her into the ground, crushed her bones into a thousand pieces, and no one any the wiser.

Peter would have noticed – eventually – that she hadn't turned up, but by then she'd've been nothing but a skinful of maggots. Plenty others had gone the same way, pouffed out of existence; who knew where and who knew when, but gone all the same.

She was stiff all over. She'd spent the night scrunched up beneath an overturned cart, the stink of its rot and mould rubbing off on her clothes, taken in with every breath. She supposed she must have slept at some point but it didn't feel like it. She stamped her feet to get her blood moving, but not too loudly, not knowing how far – or how close – she was away from the English encampment. Running blindly through the night was not the best method of judging how far you'd gone and in what direction. She shook her head, could feel the fleas skittering across her scalp, caught one of them as it made its way out of the thicket of her bound hair and onto her forehead.

'Bastard shitty bastard bastards!' she hissed between gritted teeth, capturing the escapee between finger and thumb, easing their pressure so she could see it.

Satisfaction, no doubt about it, at its capture. She squinted with concentration, manoeuvring her thumb, getting ready to sever its shiny body right down the middle with her nail. But her fingers were too cold for the delicate operation. She misjudged, and before she knew it the little brown bastard had leapt away before she could give it the execution it deserved.

'Bastard bastard, shitty, shitty little bastard...'

Greta was almost crying. She scratched madly at her head with both hands, dislodging all the scabs, finding some satisfaction in the mild pain this caused her, stopping every now and then to ease one scab or another along the length of her hair until it came free, looking at it briefly before flicking it away into the undergrowth. Enough was enough.

She savagely ripped her knife out of the sheath on her belt. She was lucky she'd been left with it. The soldiers had had no problem finding it when they'd searched her, patting her down a bit too thoroughly for comfort, and not just one going at it, but several more.

'Got to make sure you're just a lassie passing through to market,' they'd said, squeezing her small breasts as if there might be secrets hidden there – as if she was stupid enough to think that wouldn't be the first place they'd look.

It had only gone further once: stinky soldier fingers poking inside her. Vile that had been. More than vile, more like violation. Exactly like violation. Not that she'd told anyone about it. Not even Peter. That would have meant going through it all again, and she preferred not to think about it.

Preferred instead to crush every little bastard flea she could get her fingers onto. So this particular one getting away was a defeat she could not bear and she took hold of her knife and started chopping at her hair, hacking it away inch by inch, lock by lock, curl by curl, until all she was left with was a bare couple of inches of reddish stubble sticking up into the morning.

Take that, you little fecking eegits, Greta thought, putting away her knife. *And take that, the fecking rest of yous,* she thought as she kicked away the remnants of her hair until it was all disappeared into the grass around her so thoroughly it might never have been.

Maybe she was starved of sleep; maybe she was freed by the shearing of her hair; maybe it was because she had no need to hide that red hair under her bonnet anymore – a bonnet now stamped into the mud – but whatever it was, Greta had a sense of being free and alive again, and within a couple of minutes had snatched up one of those shitty fleas that had given her so much discomfort, caught it up and snapped it in half, leaving a smear of blood on her finger – her blood – the other half stuck to the ridges of her thumb, its tiny, tiny forelegs still scampering until Greta scraped it off against her jerkin, not out of pity but disgust.

GOODBYE RING, HELLO ROAD

LOCH ECK, SCOTLAND 1798

'At last!' Ruan exclaimed as they piled themselves and their luggage into the open cart and were away, Golo having finally finished his checks on the house and outbuildings, the last shutter closed and nailed, the last key turned in the last lock and secured.

Golo was smiling broadly but said nothing, and made certain to place himself between Fergus and Ruan for the first leg of their journey. Despite Fergus's belief to the contrary, Golo was well aware of the feud that had grown up between his two protégés. He was neither deaf nor blind, and although they'd both tried not to argue or posture in front of him there was nothing went on beneath his roof he didn't know about. He was sixty seven years old by his last count and this war between Fergus and Ruan had gone on far too long. Hence his eventual plan of action. Time apart would do them good.

Golo never had family in the conventional sense. He'd spent his life obsessed with his past, and with Ruan's, with resurrecting what their shared ancestors had started. The world was in darkness and it was high time it came into the light, and that was never going to happen until the doors of knowledge were flung open to every man and woman who had an inclination to learn. And this was his goal. He was an old man, he knew, but an old man with a mission, and he wanted Ruan and Fergus beside him when it came to fruition, to carry on his work when he was gone.

The cart bumped and joggled them down the road but Golo kept his eyes upon the house that had been built above the loch, steady and serene. He loved every contour of it, every board, every wall, every shelf that held every book in its library. The most important of these last had been carefully chosen and culled and packed into three of the sea chests whose bulk and weight were weighing down their cart. They were the kernel of what he hoped to achieve, and he had more. He had the ghost of the Lynx at his side. He'd been tracking their lost library for years and now knew for certain where the most part of it was – one third in Ireland, one third in Holland, one third in Paris. All he had to do was put them together and the Lynx would be reborn.

The cart stumbled around a bend, house and loch disappearing from view. Golo turned towards Ruan, wondering if he had the same small kick in his gut at leaving that Golo did, but Ruan wasn't even looking in their direction. His lips were parted and Golo realised Ruan was humming some small tune to himself. Golo winced and turned away. Fergus observed this small gesture and unexpectedly rose to Ruan's defence.

'He's young, Golo,' Fergus said softly. 'And he's off on that big adventure he's always dreamed of. He might not think it now, but never fear. One day he'll be back.'

Golo blinked. Fergus had been with him since Fergus and his father were fresh off the boat from Ireland, and ever since had proved himself a kindred spirit, never slighting Golo or his obsession, working with him man and boy to get them to the point they were at now.

‘There’s something I should have told you long ago,’ Golo said quietly, not wanting Ruan to overhear. ‘You’re as much my son as Ruan is, never mind that neither of you are my flesh and blood.’

Fergus was about to speak but Golo placed a hand on Fergus’s knee and stopped him.

‘If Ruan doesn’t want the house then it’s yours, every last nut, bolt and book of it. It’s already taken care of. Half yours, half his. Not that I’ve told him. Let the young pup find out about life when he’s ready.’

Fergus blinked. He’d not expected this,

‘So you’re not sending me to Ireland to be rid?’

Golo’s stomach turned a somersault.

‘My God,’ he stammered, ‘but of course not. Surely you didn’t think…’

Fergus’s beard parted slightly as he let out a small chuckle.

‘Of course not,’ he said. ‘Though I did wonder when you first proposed it. Are you sure this Mr Crook really has what we’re after? It seems such an odd place for any of the Lynx to end up.’

‘That’s precisely why I need you there, to verify it. He does sound a little…eccentric, shall we say,’ Golo smiled, stones and glass houses coming to mind. ‘But if it really is the case then the ring and khipu will be a small price to pay for his inclusion.’

Fergus patted the pouch in his pocket, remembering Ruan chucking his ring at Golo when the idea was mooted, saying he didn’t want it anyway, no matter how many generations of his family it had passed down through. Ruan’s ease at parting with his link to Lynx pained Golo, that much was plain, but Golo accepted it, as they hoped this Crook fellow would. Golo sighed, perhaps remembering the same scene.

‘And let’s not forget,’ he went on, ‘that this Mr Crook has offered to help with the French part. My contacts tell me Paris is pretty much closed to foreigners, at least to the English and that, apparently, includes the Scots.'

He grimaced, and took a deep breath. 'And that's if we can get the necessary funds. Letters of intent and promissory notes aren't going to be enough, however much I'd like them to be.'

'If I can get finished in Ireland soon enough…' Fergus began, but Golo shook his head.

'One problem at a time. That's the only way we'll get there. One step, one problem at a time.'

'If anyone can do it, it's you, Golo,' Fergus said after a couple of moments.

'You mean I'm the only one mad enough to try,' Golo replied lightly, patting Fergus on the shoulder.

'You and me both,' Fergus laughed. 'You do know there's a civil war going on in Ireland?'

'I do,' Golo smiled, 'but if anyone can do it…'

'I know,' Fergus said, but felt a small jiggle in his stomach at the thought of going near fighting of any kind, but then again how bad could it be? This was Ireland after all and Ireland was no France, a country at war not only with itself but apparently just about every other country in the world.

'Life would be so much easier if folk just got along,' Fergus said, looking briefly at Ruan, a look not lost on Golo.

'It will come out right in the end, Fergus. You'll see. It's like you said before, he's young, and this adventure? Well, it will be the making of him.'

'Of all of us, I hope,' Fergus said.

'Of all of us,' Golo agreed. 'A new chapter in all our lives, and by God, Fergus, I mean to see it done.'

ALMOST STOPPED BEFORE THEY'VE STARTED

The boulder came out of nowhere, tumbling down the hillside with the momentum of a bull on heat, dislodging a tide of smaller stones that plinked and jumped onto the track a couple of seconds before the main event. It gave the boy driving the cart just enough time to hie up the horses and swerve them off the track to one side before the massive boulder darkened the sky above them and thundered down a few yards ahead, spewing up great wafts of dust and dried mud as it landed, lurching forward into the stone wall on the other side of the track before bouncing back again, rocking like a madman on his heels.

'My God!' Ruan exclaimed, jumping from the trap that had come to a ragged halt. 'Where the beggeration did that come from?'

He was excited, and made no secret of it. They'd all been within a second of being crushed to death or bowled out of the way like skittles, yet Ruan was happy as a bairn in a sandpit. He ran up to the boulder and laid his hands upon it, as if it had secrets to tell to only him.

'Nearly did us all in!' he said, his eyes shining, no fear in them, only the exhilaration of narrow escape. 'Imagine the chances!'

Golo already had, and found them wanting. His heart was doing somersaults and he put his fingers by habit to his wrist to check his pulse. It was fast and erratic and he tried to breathe deep and slow as the doctor had instructed him, looking up the short incline from the top of which the boulder must have come. The sun was against him, and although he shielded his eyes there was nothing to be seen but the top of the hillside and the blue sky beyond, and several lines of dust trickling downwards in the boulder's wake.

He looked over towards Fergus, about to speak, but Fergus was already getting his way down from the cart, pragmatic as always, trying to figure a way around the obstruction that had so inexplicably landed in their midst.

'It shouldn't be too hard,' he was saying, 'we'll have to unharness the horses, lead them around individually. We'll need to shift the cart ourselves, take it and all the luggage around the wall. Get everything reassembled on the other side...'

He was cut short by the cart boy shouting out a warning as another smaller rock came hurtling down, missing Fergus's shoulder by barely an inch and only because Fergus flung himself behind the larger boulder at the warning. This second rock did not have the weight or mass of the first and hit the track and bounced once before flying spectacularly over the stone wall and going rolling on down the lower side of hill, continuing right down to the bottom of the valley the track was carved into, until it reached the river at the base a good two hundred feet below. It spooked the horses and they picked up their legs and began to run, taking the cart – and Golo – with them, Golo shouting wildly as he felt the heavy chests shifting in their ropes at his back.

The cart boy and Ruan charged after the cart and caught the reins only seconds before they attempted the insane leap over the wall to what they saw as their only path to safety. The horses were still frothing and rearing and pounding at the earth in panic when Golo stepped down on shaking legs and sat heavily on the ground, breathing hard, his heart racing out of control. Fergus ran towards Golo, glancing up the cliff, fearing a landslide might be in progress. Like Golo he was hampered by the sun being directly in that quadrant, but he saw the faint flit of a shadow that might have been a mountain hare or a deer. Or a man.

'Goddamnmit, goddammit, ' Fergus said over and over. 'Are you alright, Golo? Are you alright?'

Golo nodded weakly. 'How long to get round?' he managed to ask, as Fergus put an arm about his shoulders and helped him away twenty yards back up the road in case anything else might fall.

Fergus didn't answer immediately. He was badly shaken. Landslips were common enough occurrences on these roads, especially after the type of weather they'd been having – dry for weeks on end and then sudden downpours that could dislodge the earth around anything and set it falling – but he'd never been in such close proximity to it actually occurring.

'I'm not sure,' he said eventually, 'couple of hours maybe. Quicker if I can leave you and give the lads a hand.'

'Go,' said Golo, leaning back against the cliff. 'I'm fine,' he said. 'I'm fine.'

Fergus hesitated a moment but then went to help the others.

It took three and a half hours, Ruan and the driving lad – much to Fergus's annoyance – keeping up an unstoppable banter about badly things might have gone.

'One second more and we'd have been catapulted down the side of the glen;'

'Squashed into fish chum;'

'Had our skulls crushed like cobnuts.'

On and on until Fergus threatened to chuck the two of them down the side of the valley himself and finish what the boulder had not managed to do. He was not angered so much by their chatter as worried about the cause. He couldn't understand how a landslip could have dislodged that first enormous boulder and then a second smaller one, but nothing before or since. The whole incline was crenelated at the top with rocks of all shapes and sizes, none of which had fallen with them, and he thanked God for it or they would truly have been done for. But he was curious and took a few minutes before they left to take a proper look at the boulder that was blocking the middle of the track.

It was of no uncommon shape, slightly larger at the base than it was at the top, and had landed the same way up it must have been at the top, a tideline clearly indicating how much of the base had been in the ground and which above. What concerned him most was that the bottom couple of inches that were stained by soil and peat had several lines marked through them – not clear, not that straight – but it looked to Fergus as if someone might have put a couple of strong crowbars beneath the boulder to send it on its way and, however you looked at it, that could not be good.

Once back on their way Ruan and Golo were in good spirits.

'We should still make the boat,' Golo was saying. 'No journey ever goes as one would expect and I built in an extra day to make sure of it.'

Fergus was relieved to hear this news. He hadn't imparted his suspicions to Golo that the landslide might not have been all it seemed and was glad of it. Golo had enough to worry about, and his grounds for suspicion were thin – a few marks on the stone were neither here nor there. Nor, apparently, were the hours they had wasted because, as usual, Golo had planned well. Another day's travelling and they'd be at the top end of the Holy Loch where they would say farewell to the cart boy and load their stuff onto the ferry that would take them from the Holy Loch to Gourock, and from Gourock on to Port Glasgow.

But when they got to the Holy Loch their hopes took another dive.

'It's been holed,' they were told by the man who was supposed to shift their gear onto the ferry.

'What do you mean?' Golo asked, doing that thing Fergus recognised, taking his pulse with his fingers, as if that was going to stop the heart palpitations he'd suffered these past few years.

'You must have more than one ferry,' Fergus put in.

Their luggage was piled up high behind them, the cart boy already gone, filled with his stories, eager to get back and tell them loud and long to anyone who would listen. Fergus was not best pleased, and no more was Golo Eck, and he was about to speak again when the harbourmaster held up his hand and got his tuppence worth in first.

'Canna help it, gents,' he said, all dour looks and drooping jaws and a massive stomach sticking out over his drawers. 'We've only the one and it's holed good and proper. Ferry's aff til we can get it fixed. Might be one day might be two, but we'll fix it. Till then we've nought more to tell ye. Over land to Port Glasgow's a helluva way and'll take far longer than us'll need to fix the boat, and no more price, like.'

It was deeply frustrating to look over that short stretch of water and see the lighthouse at Cloch Point on the other side and know they weren't going to make it in time for their respective passages to Ireland and the Continent, but they had no choice.

'Cupla bonny stopping houses in Dunoon,' the harbourmaster offered. 'An I can tak care on yon chests so's you dinna need to move 'em.'

Golo waved a limp hand.

'So be it,' he said wearily.

Fergus looked at him with some anxiety. The travelling had seriously tired Golo and it might be no bad thing to be delayed. It would give Golo time to rest up before the boat journey he was dreading, hating confinement and proximity to other men, the lack of space, of having to eat and sleep with people he didn't know.

Fergus arranged transport to the nearest coaching inn, secured assurements that their baggage would be safely kept and a boy sent to fetch them the moment the ferry was fixed and sailable. Ruan, meanwhile, was clicking his heels on the flagstones as he stamped up and down.

'What the blasted hell are we supposed to do in a hole like this for two days?' he said with venom, spitting into the green waters of the loch. Fergus closed his eyes in irritation, busying himself with seeing to Golo, who patted his hand with his own.

'Don't worry, old friend,' Golo said. 'It's a setback, nothing more, nothing less. We'll be in Port Glasgow shortly and once there we can rearrange our passage onward. No journey is worth its goal if obstacles are not put in its path.'

Fergus smiled briefly. It was so like Golo to see the good in the bad.

'And a couple more days together,' Golo continued. 'Where can be the harm in that?'

None at all. Fergus thought. *Unless I kill your ward for being the most annoying person on the planet.* As if on cue Ruan picked up a handful of stones and began to pitch them at the heads of the oystercatchers who flashed up their red legs and beaks and took a noisy decision into clumsy flight to get out of his range.

He dreamt that night of Ruan throwing those stones at the oystercatchers, but this time Fergus – who had taken on the form of the rolling boulder – rammed right into Ruan's back and shoved him down into the green water, happy to see the panic and despair on his young and handsome face, and did not lift a finger to save him.

No point, Fergus had thought in the dream, *of pissing into the wind.*

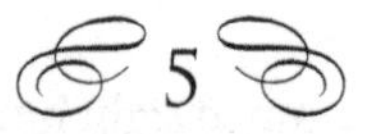

GETTING ON, AND LUCK ON THEIR SIDE

The harbourmaster's guess had been good, and two days later they were all delivered without further incident to Port Glasgow.

It was the busiest place Ruan had ever seen and he was goggle-eyed with staring at the enormous harbour that had been excavated into the river Clyde, at the warehouses, bond sheds and custom houses dwarfing the dwellings scattered behind them like seed thrown out for hens. Most of all he was hugely impressed by the gargantuan tobacco ships that plied between Scotland and New England and the intricate riggings of the barques, brigs and snau – mostly of Dutch design – that went out over to the continent.

'My God!' he shouted, as they pushed their way through the noisy and busy quays that were thronged with stevedores, passengers and traders and lined on the landward side by chandlers, rope makers, sail menders and all sorts of other wondrous wares he'd never seen before, certainly not in such profusion. The stink was appalling, a mixture of rancid fish and sweat, bilge-water spilling out into the river stale from thousands of miles of travelling. Ruan breathed it all in until his blood began to fizz and tingle in his veins.

My God! This is what life is all about, he thought: tumultuous and busy and filled to the brim with new things. Fergus tried to keep one eye on the lad whilst he struggled with Golo to keep the trolley they had bargained for from tipping over with the weight of their sea chests and baggage. They were looking for a boat called the Collybuckie on which Golo had booked his and Ruan's passage. By great good fortune – at least for them – it had not sailed on time but was still in dock owing to the captain having come down with some fever or other, and was due out on the morrow.

Golo was sweating. He hated the rambunctious noises and crowds, the shouting and smells, and was more glad than he could say that Fergus was still at his side, guiding their way through the throng of bodies, immensely relieved when Fergus shouted that he could see the gangway they were headed for.

'Just over there!' Fergus yelled, shoving a couple of small boys out of the way, the uneven wheels of the trolley bumping over the cobbles, setting the sea chests wobbling dangerously on its back.

The Collybuckie looked a mean and shabby craft compared to the great fleets that went over to the Americas, but then it did not have so far to go, nor such great and unpredictable seas to contend with. Once at the gangplank, a crew of men swarmed over to take their chests on board and stow them in the hold. Their papers were checked; Ruan leaving Golo and Fergus to this tedious duty, running up the gangplank laughing as he left them behind.

Golo was finding it hard to believe this day had ever come. He was brimming over with excitement and undeniable trepidation, hoping his heart could take it. He gripped hard at Fergus's hand before he took his first steps on-board and away from the pandemonium that was helter-skeltering around them both. Fergus's own boat over to Ireland had well and truly sailed, but they were frequent, and he was booked onto the next one available, due to sail that very afternoon.

Fergus was worried for Golo, and – though he hated to admit it – worried too for Ruan Peat. He'd not always been the thorn in Fergus's side that he was now and he prayed to God that Golo was right, and that this journey would be the tool Ruan needed to heave-ho him back onto a more even keel.

'A new chapter,' Golo said, Fergus bending his head down to hear him so his beard touched Golo's sparse hair. It was such a gentle, unbefore-made touch that Fergus was moved to rest his chin briefly on Golo's head. It only lasted a moment, this contact, before Fergus broke away.

'Be safe,' he said quietly. 'I'll come find you when I've done what you've asked.'

Golo nodded, his eyes wet as he gripped Fergus's hands hard in his own.

'You've meant so much to me,' Golo said. 'I feared you would go after your father died, and I cannot thank you enough for not leaving me alone with that young boil who calls himself Ruan Peat.'

The jest was timely, and Fergus smiled.

'Where would I have gone?' he said, and after a second Golo answered in all seriousness.

'Back to Ireland. I always thought you'd go back. And now you are going, if at my own bidding, and I wish it wasn't so.'

'As do I,' Fergus replied. 'But it's not forever.'

Two strong men teetering on the brink of emotion and not quite getting there.

'Look after Ruan,' Fergus said, realising suddenly how deeply he cared for the sullen boy, never mind he'd made his life a misery these past few years.

'I will,' Golo said. 'But who is to look after you?'

Fergus brushed at his beard and then tapped his finger against his chest.

'I've your tokens, and because they are with me I shall be invincible.'

They both smiled at the bravado, but with it were content. They hugged briefly, patting at each other's backs, and then Golo Eck went up the gangplank onto the Collybuckie, Fergus keeping watch until Golo reached the safety of the boat, when he turned and waved, Ruan suddenly appearing at Golo's side and also raised his hand before dragging Golo off to show him where they were berthed.

Fergus pushed his way back through the crowds of shouting men, running boys, the huge tottering pallets of merchandise being directed this way, the imposing piles of barrels waiting to be shifted seaward or landward depending on what they contained. He looked back only once but there was no sign of Golo or Ruan, only the small, shabby outline of the Collybuckie itself, dwarfed by monsters on either side.

'Be safe,' Fergus whispered. 'Both of you.'

WHEN A HANDKERCHIEF BECOMES THE SKY

Ruan revelled in their going. He couldn't wait to leave Scotland behind. He couldn't believe he'd allowed himself to be cooped up in that house for so long with no one but Fergus and Golo for company. No wonder he'd griped at them both like a scratchy burr. Anyone would have in his situation. He should have left years before, with or without Golo's blessing, with or without the paltry allowance that would revert to him from the Peat Estate the moment he turned of age, as he would do by the time this journey was halfway through.

He'd been a fool, he told himself, for this was what life should be: the salt and the sea and the anticipation of all that would come. He'd hardly spoken to Golo since they'd been on board. They shared quarters, but Ruan spent as little time in them as he could. It had pleased him at first when Golo took under his wing the young cabin boy, Caro, assigned to look after them, and then it had irked him, Golo apparently wanting to spend no more time with Ruan than Ruan did with him, and happy in Caro's company.

He'd broken in on them one day to find Golo brushing the young lad up on his reading and writing and had gone away shaking with some emotion he only later realised was jealousy. Not that it made him seek out Golo – rather the opposite. Let Golo fill someone else's head with rubbish for a change, for Ruan was sick to the back teeth with it, glad all that was behind him. Back in Scotland he'd been forced to be a part of Golo's obsession with the Lynx, but it was no longer his concern.

All had gone swimmingly as the cat-built ex-collier of the Collybuckie swept its usual rounds, heading from Glasgow to Aberdeen and from Aberdeen to Hull, stopping at both to unload and load up again. Ruan had the chance to roam more streets and towns, hardly understanding a word the natives said, so thick were their accents. He'd been excited when the winds rose as they rounded the Strait of Dover, and less worried than he should have been when those same winds drove them off course and then ceased abruptly, the fog coming down like a shroud for an entire day and night so he could barely see a few yards in front of his face.

The Collybuckie limped on down the channel towards its goal of Gravenhage, already a day late for their landing, and by the time the fog lifted they were miles further on than they should have been, the rising winds making it impossible to turn. The only thing to do was to head on and find relief in Vlissingen on the lea side of the Walcheren Peninsula. But the winds did not let up, instead got stronger with every hour, hammering at them from every side as if it had iron and malevolent intent in its fists.

Night fell, and even Ruan was thinking enough was enough. Excitement was one thing, but he saw fear in the faces of the crew and didn't like it one bit, swiftly obeying when everyone was ordered down below, told to hang on to what they could, make sure they were all together and accounted for.

The Collybuckie lurched like a drunk between the walls of a dark and narrow alley, the waves monstrous to either side, the storm giving no appearance of abating. Down below, loose cargo rattled and rolled in the hold, broken from their moorings. Trickles of sea water began to seep in through the caulking. Planks shrieked and rivets popped from their holes.

Ruan was gripping for dear life at one of the tables bolted to the floor when a chair flew loose from its bolts and knocked him free as a tooth from a rotten jaw, sent him rolling about the floorboards trying to grab onto anything solid and fixed, hands flailing in the darkness, every lamp and candle long since smashed or blown out. A hand caught him as he thought he might be crushed against the furthest side, hauled him up, kept him fast. He couldn't see his rescuer nor had any breath to thank him, for off the Collybuckie went to the other side, all that was left being to cling on in the hope that it would keep on righting itself after every horrid lurch and dip. Ruan couldn't help but think of the Corryvrecken whirlpool just off Jura where men and boats had been sunk and lost, their boards and bodies flung up months – and miles – later.

Jesus, don't let me die like this, he prayed, his clothes drenched with sweat and the sea that was coming in at them from every angle, sloshing around their feet, eager to swallow them whole. And where was Golo? Suddenly all Ruan wanted was Golo by his side to tell him everything would be alright, but he'd not seen Golo since the storm began to worsen so swift and sudden an hour or so earlier. He was sure he wasn't in this room with everyone else for he would have sought Ruan out, and had probably – like the idiot he was – not been able to bear the thought of being smothered in other people's sweat and fear and gone up on deck, despite all the warnings given to the contrary. And Caro? Where was Caro? Probably with Golo, and suddenly Ruan couldn't bear it any more.

'Golo!' Ruan shouted again and again, but his exclamations were subsumed by the awful noises of the boat beginning to come apart at the seams and the sea that was crashing and crushing them, and the wind that was screaming all around them, conspiring like a pack of wolves to bring this fleck of humanity down, forcing it closer and closer in on itself until it had nowhere else to go.

Ruan was right. When the call came to go down below into the communal space where passengers and crew gathered to eat, drink, play cards and pass the time, Golo went with them, though not for long. He was soon forcing his way up to the freedom of the over-world on deck, bent almost double as he struggled, half crawled, his way up the steps and across the deck, hanging onto halyards. Loose ropes whipped like cats-tails from the booms that swung without warning across his path, unsecured sheets flapped and cracked above his head. He felt his guts turning inside out and a sulphurous burn in his throat from the bile that made him retch and spit even as he sucked for breath against the terrible push of the wind.

He could hear the shouts of the crew somewhere on the other side of the boat as they fashioned rafts however they could. They lashed old rollers and spars together along with any buoys they could lay hands on, adding some uprights, weaving in safety lines so that survivors could tie them about their waists or wrists to haul themselves in, should they make it as far as the water. Golo knew then the Collybuckie was done for and would soon be swamped, going down like one of those whale pods he'd once seen as a young man, sinking themselves in circles, sucking everything else in behind them.

Golo had already resigned himself to dying, knowing all those rescuers with their makeshift rafts are on the other side of the boat and he cannot reach them without being tipped into the sea. But he doesn't want to go, God help him, not without seeing some small scratch of light again: a sliver of the moon, a hint of dawn upon the horizon. He's never felt such urgency for anything in all his life; he's always been so rational, such a placid and unexcitable man, but the strength of this need in him for a glimpse of light is overwhelming.

The tears stream down his face as he crawls along the deck to find only more darkness and a wind so strong it knocks him straightaway off his feet when he tries to rise. He wishes now he'd stayed down below with the others, found Ruan in the scrum, tell him he loved him, to carry on the task once he was gone.

The lad must be terrified, Golo thinks, glimpsing the white-tipped line of another massive wave about to crash down upon the Collybuckie, the dark lines of two masts already broken and snapped. And then, despite the skirling and screaming of wind and wave, he has the strangest conviction someone else is out here with him. He can feel it. He wraps himself around the nearest capstan, lets himself be pulled and pushed by the enormous waves, until extraordinarily, miraculously, he hears someone calling out his name. The words are harsh, as if screeched from the throat of one of those black-headed gulls he's always hated, but he hears them all the same.

'Golo! Golo Eck!'

Ruan, he thinks, *it must be Ruan, come to find me.* And he shouts back that here he is, when suddenly his seeker bumps hard into his back, inadvertently colliding in the darkness. Then there is the indescribable comfort of a hand clutching hard at his shoulder, someone crouching down beside him, shielding Golo's body from the appalling storm with his own.

'Golo! Thank God!'

Golo has no idea who is speaking – certainly not Ruan – the unknown voice rasping in his ear like sand scouring out a shell.

'They're lowering down the lifeboats!' the voice tries to shout though it is weak and ineffectual against the roaring of the wind and the crashing of the waves and the screeching of the boat's boards as they are torn asunder the one from the other. 'And they're throwing out the rafts! Everyone's to go, all into the sea!'

Golo opens his eyes, unaware he has closed them, and whispers his thanks to God as he is dragged bodily along the deck, clothes ripping as they snag on the boards, not that he cares. And then he understands he is not being pulled in the direction of rafts but right down to the danger zone. He's being taken to where the boat is almost dipping beneath the waves, and he starts to struggle, tries to free himself, but whoever is upon him has already wrapped his large body about Golo's own like a heavy cloak and has sliced a line of guy rope from the collapsing sails, pulling Golo's arms behind his back and binding them before Golo has time to react. He kicks out madly to get some purchase on the deck and push his assailant backwards, knock him flat, but the man is too strong and wily for such playground tactics and Golo is held fast, a prickling against Golo's skin as a face is held against his own, a few words growled into Golo's ear.

'Rafts are out there, but nowhere for you to go, old man, but down.'

A sharp shove against his back and Golo is sliding the last few feet of deck towards the broken rails as the boat dips once more, and over the edge he goes, banging on the wood, unable to break his fall. Immediately before he hits the water he sees a flash of white up above him and is absurdly grateful for it, mistaking the fluttering, fluting fall of his own handkerchief for the dawn. Then he's in the water, the coldness so shocking, so profound, that his body has no time to close itself off from salt and sea and in they go, flowing freely down his windpipe, seeping quick and seditious into his lungs.

Meanwhile the Collybuckie has dipped again to the opposite side and down go the two proper lifeboats, the makeshift rafts and the men tied to them by their ropes. Everyone brought thronging up from the lower deck and chucking themselves in afterwards grabs at the buoys, at the wood, at each other, at the safety ropes dangling from the rafts, hauling themselves through the waves towards the possibility of survival.

But none of those ropes were grasped by Golo Eck because he's already been swept fifty yards away from the Collybuckie and three fathoms deep. Just a glimmer of the light he has longed for as a troupe of phosphorescing medusa swim deeper and deeper to escape the pull of the waves, going down with Golo Eck as far as they can go.

Ruan gasped and flailed with the rest, scrambling for a place on one of the rafts, the coldness of the water terrible and the darkness almost worse. But he grabbed at something that slapped against his cheek: a barnacle-encrusted rope-end that scoured a red weal down the side of his face. He pulled himself along it, hands bleeding, almost at the moment of exhaustion when he heard a voice and felt the back of his jacket being tugged and pulled, and then he was up and onto a raft.

Scarcely was he there, panting for breath, shivering violently in his skin, when he saw a little scrap of blonde hair about to disappear beneath the waves. He lunged forward, gouging a deep and ragged line through the skin of his forearm on a nail as he grabbed his fingers through the hair and tugged at it with all his diminished might. Someone beside him came to his aid and together they hauled young Caro up beside them, bleeding and bruised, his face so blanched it could be glimpsed even through that blackest of nights.

Another two men were rescued in the next couple of minutes and Ruan did his share to bring them in, along with Caro, the last so fat he almost up-ended the raft as they manhandled him on board, spitting out his thanks with the water coming up from his throat. Moments later, the Collybuckie went down without a fight, presenting only as a small signpost of creaking wood and flapping sail.

By then the rafts had been blown too far distant for its sinking to suck them down with it and the survivors shook and shuddered against one another as the waves came down on them again and again, all holding their breath until they bobbed back up again. The salt scratched at their skin and great swathes of kelp slapped and wrapped about them. They wrenched themselves free of its extra weight so that it wouldn't sink them.

The sea was a violent and malevolent enemy out there in the darkness, intent on their destruction It flung them up onto the crests of waves and then back down into troughs so deep it seemed impossible they would not be swallowed up by the brine. The threat of imminent annihilation was a black hole in all their chests for the next few hours until at last, at last, the screaming of the wind abated and the sea returned to a less treacherous rhythm.

Even so, their chances of survival appeared bleak for they had no idea where they were nor where the wind and waves were taking them. They all had a dread in the pit of their stomachs that when dawn came they would look around to see nothing but sea on every side. What would happen then they had no idea.

Only one man among them – the last to be dragged in, mainly by Ruan and Caro – was differently minded. He was fat as a blubber whale, which no doubt explained why he'd survived so long in the water. Once the raft had rocked into something approaching calm, he kept their minds focussed with his incessant banter, cheerily leaning over to slap anyone so worn out they had nodded their chins down on their chest. He had a lively stream of anecdotes and stories that kept the rest clinging to their ropes, listening hard to every word, anything to tune out the fear that threatened at every moment to overwhelm them.

Ruan had no idea if this was the man's intent or merely his own way of coping, a survival mechanism to get him through that dreadful night. He remembered the fat man from the Collybuckie, having played cards with him on several occasions. He'd talked a lot then too, much to everyone's irritation but by Christ, Ruan was thankful for it now. He was terribly worried about Golo and whether he'd managed to get aboard one of the lifeboats or rafts, for he surely wasn't on this one. His eyes smarted with the assault and battery of wind and salt, but every time he thought on Golo the tears came spilling out, no matter how hard he tried to stop them.

'Think on me as buoyancy,' the fat Italian was starting off again. 'Sure I'm big, and far more corpulent than I've any right to be, but that just goes to show I've a good lifetime behind me. And I can assure you I've done my duty by family, friends and church so, if I go, feel free to utilise me anyway you can: as an extra buoy if that's helpful…a bit of meat and blubber if not. All grist to the mill for the continuation of human life and continue we will, my friends, in one way or another…'

He talked and talked like this, all through the several hours that were left of the night after the storm subsided and before dawn came and the sun began to move up from the horizon. It was then that they realised his optimism was well-founded; the sea they'd been so fearful of become an ally, delivering them within a quarter-mile of the shore.

'It's only fair to tell you,' the fat Italian said then, 'that I can't swim a stroke, so it's up to the rest of you to tug me in.'

And by God, they were more than glad to do that small service for him and those strong enough and able threw themselves into the water, pulling the raft and the fat Italian behind them. The tide was with them but still it was a battle, the waves strong and still huge, crashing chaotically all about them, rocks and reefs to left and right and no idea which way was best to get them in. And they maybe would have been defeated right at the last had there not been men on the beach, men who'd been up and early, raking at the weeds the storms were throwing gratis on their shores.

They wasted no time once they spotted the bedraggled company in the water – mostly due to the fact that a hugely fat man was waving his sodden coat above his head to alert them. They kicked off their boots and tore off their coats and chucked themselves into the water, swimming out until they reached the raft, taking over the ropes, hauling in every last survivor, depositing them shivering and shaking upon the sand, removing them back to life from the uncaring sea.

They were taken up the shore into their rescuers' cottages, placed about their fires to dry out a little, warm up, while a messenger was sent to the Servants of the Sick to come and take these incomers off their hands. Ruan was so exhausted and addled by all he'd been through he hardly remembered the journey from the village to the quiet oasis that was the monastery of the Servants.

But he got there somehow, and was stripped of his clothes, the welt on his face and the deep wound in his forearm cleaned and dressed before he was placed upon a narrow bed, where he slept without a break through the next forty-eight hours of his life.

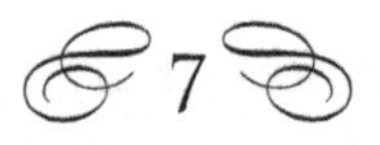

A BODY FOR THE BODY SWEEPERS

WALCHEREN PENINSULA, HOLLAND 1798

The waves rolled in, tall and grey, big with the wind of the last two days following the storm, but regular now and long, spindrift blowing up the beach from their breakers like dirty, sand-edged snow.

Wading through the knee-deep spume came George Gwilt, heading for the tide-line, picking his way with care, not wanting to stumble over any hidden rocks or boulders kicked in unexpectedly by last night's tide. The gales had brought the water much further up the beach than was usual, throwing stones and detritus right up and over the thin path that nipped and tucked its way along the tops of the low dunes, putting down a layer of stones at their feet maybe six inches deep and five yards wide.

Stranded below the dunes were great heaps of shiny brown seaweed – oarweed and kelp for the most part – ripped from their off-shore moorings. It had been swooshed upon the sand mostly by that last great tide, many still attached to the stones that had previously been their anchors, welded to their roots by white clumps of crustacean-drilled cement.

George stood for a few moments, the spindrift bobbing about his gaiters, its tops blowing off every now and then, taken away by the wind, cartwheeling up the wet sand towards the dunes like living things. He looked off towards the horizon, taking a quiet delight to witness the short moment needed for the sun to rise up from nowhere into day, a quick sharp burn of pink and gold upon the horizon as its herald before sun and colour were swallowed up by the overwhelming grey of the on-coming day.

He looked to his right, along the line of the bay, seeing all the other men from his village jumping down from the dune path onto sand and stone. They scattered themselves out across its length, kelp-forks slung over their shoulders, the hard metal tines of which were secured by lattices of twine-bound twigs, shafts strong and long, worn smooth by many years of being worked as they were about to be worked now.

A Godsend were these storms: all that kelp and oarweed ousted from the sea-bed, lying there heaped up for the taking – essential for fertilising their vegetable plots, more valuable still when they dried the surplus down, got it piled into charcoal pits and burned into potash, some of which they'd use, the rest they could sell on to the potteries and buy such stuff the village needed that they could not make for themselves.

George looked about him, going towards the place he'd allotted for himself, barging through the spindrift now, turning his back to the sea and the sun rising above it, his own fork upon his shoulder, ready to be deployed. Once at his spot he set to with his rake, dragging the stranded seaweed away from the stones and onto the sand from where it could be more easily hoiked up and loaded onto the donkey carts the women would soon bring down onto the bay. He slashed off the stone anchors with his bill-hook, pulling away the carcasses of birds and fish, separating those that might still be fit for eating, the rest chucked back into the weeds to enrich the fertiliser that would soon ensue.

Every now and then he stood back, looked along the line of the bay at his fellow villagers. He saw them setting to or leaning away as he was, hands put to the arch of their backs to ease the ache of the work, not that any of them rested too long. This seaweed was a gift, a bounty that might not be here at all after the next tide was in, taken away as easily as it had been given. There was an added hope too: the possibility they might find something useful buried in these tawny heaps; some unusual flotsam or jetsam from a boat upturned out there in the channel, always a few caught unawares every time a storm blew out of nowhere, as this last one had done. A couple of years back they'd found a chest filled with quills and parchments, inks and blocks of sealing wax of all colours. Not much use to a village that boasted only a few literate men, George one of the few. But wax was always useful for sealing cheeses, plugging holes in this or that, and the rest of the haul they'd sold off in dribs and drabs at markets all along the coast, bringing in a bit of extra geld. They'd found other things too: a couple of partly stoved-in barrels of what they'd taken to be fruit of some kind that the women had peeled, boiled up and pickled – you could never be too careful. It had tasted well enough afterwards, though they'd never learned the name of whatever fruit it was.

This latent thrill of discovery was always present whenever the villagers raked at the piled-up storm-weed; and trepidation too, for they might also find a few soft carcasses of sheep or goats wrapped in those wild wide strands of weed. Animals swept off the cliffs or dunes were always a loss, the meat usually spoiled and rotten by the time it was found and of no use anymore for eating, though sometimes it could be saved by salting and drying. And then there was that other kind of discovery: the bodies of sailors or fishermen – sometimes men they knew – who'd been tangled in their nets, or not quick enough back to harbour, broken up with their boats at the bases of the cliffs further down the coast.

Worst of all was when they found one of those skinny-limbed boys the big ships needed to go a hundred yards or more up into their rigging to release a sail or tie it fast. These boys were wasp-thin, plucked from their slender foot-holds on masts and ropes by winds that had already blown down full-grown trees, winds which this time had wrecked the roof of George's village's communal barn; winds so strong they took only seconds to tug up those rigging boys and send them out upon the cold water of the sea like seeds strewn on a field.

For all these reasons George Gwilt took his time when his fork hit something hidden within the weeds – something too large to be a fish, unless it might be a porpoise, whose stories were always written out upon their dulling hides: the soft, blank paleness of the very young; the pocks and scars of harpoons or disease on those who'd survived longer. So there was a hard scratching in George's throat and at the ends of his fingers as they gripped the shaft of his rake when he felt their tines hit something larger. He withdrew his rake immediately and studied the suspect area of seaweed.

He could see nothing immediately untoward but his gut tightened, and he used the toe of his right boot to delve gingerly into the mass, kicking it gently, trying to dislodge some of the seaweed, moving along the line a foot or so and repeating this manoeuvre several times. Whatever was there behind the curtain of weeds was at least five foot long and fairly pliant, and George knew this was no length of wood or hidden barrel. He took a deep breath before poking gently with his rake at the mass of seaweed, hearing a gentle tearing sound as its spokes caught at some material that had parted from its seams.

A body, then.

George knew it. A waterlogged sack of skin that must have been buffeting through the last couple of nights before it hit the breakwater, limbs tangling in the kelp until it was wrapped so tight it came in with the weed, rolling in with the tide. George sent up a silent prayer to the God that he rather doubted inhabited the great welkin of the sky above him. Deities held little sway in the belief schemes of men like George Gwilt. They served only to provide them with the faint possibility that there was an unknown order to the otherwise random piling up of disasters that framed their everyday lives, giving them a little hope that being alive was not just a measure of years to be got through and endured, that all they had gone through and suffered had not been done in vain.

It was a hard philosophy George lived by, and squeamishness was not in its remit, and soon he was pulling away the last vestiges of seaweed that were hiding the body he already knew lay within. He could see in his mind's eye the corner of the cemetery in which this new corpse would be buried, one of the many he and his villagers had raked out of the sea over the years. They were men and boys, for the most part, and sometimes women too, mostly gravid, the load within their bellies too heavy for them to bear.

Most of these unfortunates went unclaimed, buried without names, packed as close together as scones upon a skillet with all the others who had gone before them. Sea-bought souls, such people were called around these parts: sea-bought, village-buried, consigned to a communal pit with the scantest of blessings. Unless they were proven suicides, who had not even the grace of being placed in consecrated ground.

George Gwilt lay down his rake, got to his knees, started at the pile of seaweed with his hands. He wanted, by doing so, to be gentle and respectful and give this dead person some kind of normal human response when his face was brought into the light.

It didn't take long – two minutes to uncover the most length of the corpse – enough to show George which end was which, and only a couple minutes more to pull the weeds from the dead man's face.

And it was a man, square-jawed, stubble popping from his chin, neck and cheeks, the small growth of it exaggerated by the bloating of his skin; a man advanced in years, well dressed. These facts gave George an odd relief, for here must be someone who had already lived the most part of his days. He must surely have had the chance to take his best shot at life, done whatever he needed to get done. He was of an age to have not only children but maybe grandchildren too, and could be considered, therefore, to have passed the greatest milestones every lifetime hankered after, assured of some kind of hereafter if only in the children he had left behind.

And there was something else George noticed pretty much straight off, which was that this man had more flesh on his bones than any of the villagers he knew, a man obviously well nourished, well cared for. So, not a local man, and far more likely washed off one of the big ships that passed out there in the straits, a merchant maybe, or perhaps an ex-soldier. He was certainly someone who had lived a far longer, more prosperous life than any that was to be had around here.

Armed with this knowledge George pulled away the last of the seaweed with more curiosity than dread, hoping to find an obvious coat pocket that might reveal a wallet or papers, anything that would give this man a name or some sort of provenance. On closer inspection the man's clothes, bedraggled as they were, were of a far finer quality than George had ever seen in his life. And grand clothes meant grand lives, and grand lives meant money. If George could be the mechanism by which this grand man got home, if in name only, then so much the better would it be for George and his village, who might even reap some reward from it.

And so he worked at the seaweed and managed to uncover the elbow to an arm that was crooked across the man's chest, hiding him, holding him and his waistcoat down. George paused. There was something not quite right here. He couldn't pin it down, but the feeling was strong in him just the same. He wondered if he should stop, go fetch the priest, let the man do his usual mutterings, deliver his last rites and unction.

He felt peculiarly sullied by such close contact to this sea-bought soul and would have liked to have lit up his pipe and stand there leaning on his rake for a while, thinking things over. But he'd already caught a glance at the men working over on the bay to his left, and saw how they'd noticed his own rhythm pause and change. He knew that it was only a matter of minutes before they came crashing through the gates of his only chance at a pass to a better life than he and his boys lived now. If there was anything to be found on this body then by God George meant to find it before the rest of the snafflers got their noses in the trough.

And so he didn't baulk, but took hold of the arm of the man in the seaweed, its stiffness apparent even through the richness of its cloth, and he tugged at it hard until it came free from its shoulder. The snap was audible as the arm broke rigour and came back at George with such force it almost knocked him over. George swallowed down the bile and took a pinch of the sleeve between his fingers, moved the arm so he could study it with more ease. It was a big hand, George thought, with fingers puffed and hard as white puddings. The hand had the look of having been squeezed through the lacy cuff that was secured about his wrist, a stricture held in place by a small gold pin. George hadn't seen much gold in the course of his life but he knew it for what it was and, with fumbling fingers, he managed to turn the cuff so as to reveal the workings of the link, released the catch, fiddled it from its button hole.

He might have hoped for a fine gold fob watch, but he didn't have time to look, not now. Possibly the ring though, which was in-turned towards the man's palm on his signet finger, puffed as it was. And a large ring, probably for pressing a seal into wax. But it was protected by the ungiving curl of the man's fingers that rounded about it like a sea urchin denuded of its spines. George had his knife with him but could not bring himself to severe the swollen finger in order to secure it. Pocketing a single gold cufflink was one thing – it could have fallen off anywhere on this man's journey from sea to shore – but cutting off a finger was something else entirely. It was something that spoke of greedy intent, and that was an ignominy he would not have his fellows cast on him for the rest of his life.

He could have wished for more time to explore the strange country that was this rich man's body but he was a pragmatic man and was happy enough with a cufflink. Instead he rocked back upon his heels and waved to the men who were only twenty odd yards away from him now, eager for their take. He shouted out for one of them to run for the Body Sweepers, the Servants of the Sick, to whom this kind of laying out of the dead was meat and drink.

He stayed close by in the meantime to make sure that none of the others did what he had not been able to do, to treat this body like any other salvage from a shipwreck, to roll it out of its temporary grave and ransack it for all it was worth.

A CORPSE CAN BE A HEAVY LOAD

The Body Sweepers arrived within an hour of George sending for them. He had a passing familiarity with one of them, Brother Joachim, for Brother Joachim periodically visited all the villages hereabouts: lancing boils, setting broken limbs, pulling rotten or broken teeth, excising haemorrhoids, handing out ointments to alleviate men's most private ailments. He treated the ailments that men would prefer to suffer and allow to superate rather than go to one of the women in the village who would normally be able to treat such minor ailments, if they were asked.

Brother Joachim greeted George warmly, asking after his family, if his youngest son had found the going easier on his mismatched legs with the specially elevated shoe Joachim had provided George with last spring.

'He's going a regular treat, thank you,' George replied. 'Went at the fields last harvest so's yous could hardly see the scythe blade, so quick was he.'

Joachim beamed, his pleasure evident and genuine.

'I'm very pleased for it, Mr Gwilt. No need for his life to be hampered by being shorter on the one side than the other. We've all shortcomings, whether you can see them or no. But what have we here today?'

George didn't reply, merely cast his glance down at the dead man still half encased in his seaweed tomb.

'So no one local?' Joachim asked as he got to his knees, his cassock giving an ease to his movements that George, in his damp, salt and sand encrusted trousers, envied. He didn't answer, but shook his head, knowing as well as Joachim that if he'd known who this man was then he and the villagers would have seen to him themselves.

'Well there's some praise due to God for that, then,' Joachim said, as if George had spoken, his fingers automatically sketching out a quick sign of the cross as he did so

'Nicolas,' Joachim called over to the brother who had accompanied him.

The gathered men moved back to make way for him, shifting themselves a few yards down the beach where they had set up a small fire. They were soon sitting comfortably about it, smoking, watching the proceedings with interest, but making no move to participate. Nicolas hovered, looking as if he were about to bowk at any moment, and so it was left to George and Joachim to do what was needed.

Neither of them spoke as they went about their duties, clearing the rest of the weed from the body, rolling it towards the canvas stretcher Joachim had brought with him from the Servants. All the while, there was a small undercurrent of talk from the men about the fire as they made various guesses as to who this drowned man might be, from what ship he might have been blown off and where that ship might have come from or have been going to, given the time-frame, the currents, and the strength of the winds over the past few days.

The body was stiff as a board, which made it difficult for George and Joachim to get him properly out upon the sand. His legs were slightly crooked, one arm still folded across his chest, the other – the one George had yanked free – the only incongruity, being loose and broken at the shoulder. George coloured as Joachim noticed this, looking questioningly at George.

'I was just trying for a pocket,' the words stumbled out of George's throat, tight with guilt, wondering if this Man of God might not be able to see right through the threadbare pocket of his jerkin to the small lump of gold that lay within.

Joachim cast no aspersion, although had maybe made his guess, for his fingers lingered for a moment over the empty button hole in the wet lace of the dead man's cuff. George felt the sweat prickling in his armpits and at the back of his neck, felt an urge to blurt out the truth of his small theft. Before he could, Joachim looked up at George and smiled, patting him roughly on the back as they both squatted on the sand.

'You did quite right, Mr Gwilt. It is no easy thing to die a stranger in a strange land.'

And then there was nothing for it but for the two of them to cart the corpse off to the hospital of the Servants of the Sick. Had the man been less well dressed, or more well known, they might have taken him straightaway to church and cemetery for quick burial, but plainly this was someone of import, no anonymous sea-bought soul.

The corpse was a heavy load, for water always finds its way into a body too long immersed and his clothes were of the kind that sucked it in and held it there. Nicolas took the head of the stretcher, George and Joachim at its feet, George oddly glad of the duty, for he felt a debt to this dead man not only because of the pilfered cufflink but because George had been the one to find him.

Once up and over the scratchy, fifty yard spread of the dunes they got onto the track that led from George's village to the hospital and found the going easier. Joachim struck up some chat, asking George about his village's latest goings on – who had died, who was sick, who might be in need of his care. Once George had answered as fully as he was able Joachim fell silent for a while before starting up again.

'So what's your guess, Mr Gwilt, about where this man came from?'

George took his time answering, the same calculations going on in his head as had been doing the rounds of the small beach-crowd earlier, weighing up the intertwining influences of storm and tide, current and wind.

'Couldn't be sure, Brother,' he said finally. 'But most likely he's off of one of the ships going through the straits, blown off course. Maybe the trader that goes from the Scots' land to Gravenhage. Must've been due about now.'

Brother Joachim nodded.

'As it happens,' Joachim said, 'there was such a boat.'

The stretcher dipped suddenly as Nicolas stumbled on a stone, shifting the weight of the corpse back to George's side. George caught the weight and said nothing. He felt a fear creeping through his body quick as sea fog rolling in from wave to land after a warm day, so fast that one minute you spy it lying benignly a half mile out and the next it's upon you, its coldness clammy on your skin. He swallowed, his throat constricting at the strong smell of his own sweat through the salt and wet that was habitual in his clothes. It was a dampness that caused mould to grow upon their hem-lines and seams so that George sometimes had to hold the clothes over a low fire to burn away the mould that gathered there before rubbing them over again with wax. The process always made his clothes seem thinner every time, despite the added weight of the wax.

'We think it was the Collybuckie,' Joachim went on. 'Boat that got caught in the storm, blown off course just like you said.'

George made a sound in his throat but did not comment.

'As a matter of face there's a man back at the Servants,' Joachim went on after a moment. 'A Scotsman. Says he was on it, this boat, the Collybuckie. Said they broke up in the storm. Managed a couple of lifeboats and some rafts and saved a good many of the passengers and crew. But not all. Never all, as you know as well as I do, Mr Gwilt.'

A few moments quiet then, just the sound of their feet trudging along the path, the slight shift of the corpse within its sheet on the stretcher side to side as they went, George feeling every sway of it as if it was a living man they were carrying.

'One of the rafts made it in further up the peninsula,' Joachim said quietly. 'All survivors gone now, except this one man. Well I say a man, but he's hardly more than a boy. He's been sending folk up and down this stretch of coast ever since the wreck…'

Joachim looked over at George, whose heart had suddenly begun to race, his free hand moving awkwardly across his body to the pocket where the cufflink lay, the guilt heavy on him. But Joachim did not accuse him and went on with his tale as easy as if he were sitting around that fire George's fellows had struck up back on the beach.

'Well, you know how it goes, George. I gather a couple of other rafts and lifeboats made it in too, though none so close to here as his, but they've none of them found the man he's looking for. But he hasn't given up and maybe, given your find today, he was right to wait.'

George swallowed. He was desperately trying to locate the

damned cufflink in the sand that had accumulated at the bottom of the pocket he had hidden it in, his blunt fingers finding nothing. All the while he made a vow to himself that no matter what the temptation was he would never do such a thing again, would never ever steal from the dead, not when someone was so desperate to find him, whoever he was.

And then they were at the entrance arch to the Hospital of the Servants of the Sick, and a few minutes later they were in the chapel, rolling out the corpse onto a wooden bier that had been erected in front of the altar, Nicolas making haste to leave, George shuffling his feet, Joachim looking at George questioningly as George fumbled in his pocket once more. And then he found it, and he brought out the cufflink, held it towards Brother Joachim.

'I'd no reason taking it,' George said softly. 'And surely not from a man's been through what this'un,' he tilted his chin at the corpse, 'must've bin through. I'm sorry, Brother. I don't know what I was thinking.'

Joachim took the small cufflink from George's fingers and looked at it curiously, at the odd shape of it, the fine detailing on its decorative side that looked almost like a lion's head, almost, but not quite. And then he did the entirely unexpected and handed it back, although George held up his hands and would not take it.

'No one's going to call to you on it, George,' Joachim said, 'least of all this man you've found, and neither the one who's been looking for him, if anything is to go by. They'll not miss a small thing like this.'

But George refused absolutely, telling Joachim to reunite it with its owner and this time Joachim did not demur, leant over the corpse and threaded the small gold link back within its cuff.

Later, George would bless this small act of honesty, and for Nicolas leaving, both incidents leading directly to Joachim asking

George to remain for the laying out of the dead man. Had he not done that he would not have met the dead man's friend and instead would have gone straightaway back to the fire on the beach, listened to the crackles and pops of the seaweed the men put on it to augment its flames, the discovery of the corpse giving them grace to knock off from their labours for a couple of hours to gossip about it and shake their heads, and thank God it had not been one of their own.

And if he'd done that then George would never have found out anything more about the corpse that had been rolled up like a cigar in the seaweed. He would always have wondered who he was, would maybe have asked Brother Joachim about it when next he saw him. Maybe Brother Joachim would have answered, but it wouldn't have meant anything to George Gwilt and his life would never have changed as it did, starting with the invitation from Joachim to stay, and so was there when the young man seeking him had given him a name.

Ruan Peat was far younger than George had been expecting, maybe the same age as his youngest son, who'd just turned seventeen. There was none of the prosperity about him Joachim had spoken of, for his own clothes had been ruined by his shipwreck and desperate swim to shore. He was dressed now only in the cast-offs held by the Servants from other men not so fortunate, given out to the poorest during the winter months as George could well attest to, most of his own family's clothes having been acquired by such a gift.

Ruan was shaking as he approached the corpse in the chapel. The first thing he did when he'd woken was to ask about Golo, still a little feverish, finding it hard to make himself understood, but insistent that someone – anyone – carry on looking for Golo. He was most eager that word be spread so that Golo would know where Ruan had landed up. That Golo was dead didn't seem possible. He'd looked after Ruan since he was a young bairn. It was a common enough practice in the area of Scotland they came from, this fostering. Families often swapped children and brought them up as their own in order to strengthen the kinship between them. It was an ancient Pictish custom that had stitched one clan to another for centuries.

It wasn't quite like that in Ruan's case. His family – the Peats – had been rooted in Argyll for God knew how long. It was the Ecks who were the incomers, who needed to be established, and this fosterage between the two families had been the way to do it ever since. All to do with that damned Lynx, Ruan knew. But Ruan was the last of his line, and by his time the custom had all but died out until both mother and father had succumbed to some strain of pneumonia when Golo stepped up, re-invoking the old tradition and taking him in.

Jesus, get a grip, Ruan told himself, wrapping his arms about his body. *It can't be Golo. It just can't be Golo.*

He wished Fergus was here. He would know what to do. He would know how to handle all this. He would have told Ruan to go and sit down on his narrow Servant's bed and wait while Fergus got on and dealt with everything that needed to be done. But Fergus was away in Ireland doing Christ knew what on Golo's say-so, and Ruan was alone. He'd stood outside the chapel for a good while before he could make himself take the first step in.

It can't be Golo. It can't be Golo.

But no matter how many times he repeated the mantra there was a faint doubt at the back of his mind, for how else to explain why Golo had not come looking for him? He certainly wouldn't have gone anywhere without scouring the whole peninsula searching for his almost-son.

Ruan pushed open the chapel door and went inside. He took a few steps down towards the bier erected to take the dead man's body and had to stop. He had to hold his hand over his mouth to stop himself from vomiting, the smell was so awful. More awful still was that he recognised something of the clothes despite the bloated body distorting them, all the blood draining from his face like whey through a milk-sieve.

'Take your time,' Joachim said kindly, coming up to Ruan and putting his hand below the lad's elbow. 'But you need to let us know if this is him. If this is the man you've been looking for.'

Ruan swallowed back the acid that had surged up his throat, not daring to open his mouth, fearing how bad it would smell, fearing what else was going to rise up and take its place.

'I can't,' he whispered.

'I know,' Joachim coaxed. 'But if you don't look then you'll never know for sure, and that can only be worse.'

George Gwilt stood to one side of the bier, hands clasped on his thighs. This was too hard. Too hard. The boy was too young and this death too bad. He wanted to run over to the lad and tell him he needn't worry, that it was going to be alright; except that if this was his friend then it wasn't going to be alright, not for this boy, not ever again.

Ruan moved onwards, Joachim guiding him, keeping up a gentle pressure on his elbow to push him on. Ruan got within three yards of the bier when he suddenly bucked away to his right and threw up the meagre meal of soup and bread that he'd had for his lunch, retching and coughing as Joachim rubbed at the his back.

'It's him,' Ruan choked out between clenched teeth once the worst was past. 'I can't believe it's him. It can't be him. It can't be him. It can't...'

'It's alright, son,' Joachim said, gently turning Ruan around, nodding at George briefly before he led Ruan away back up the nave and out of the chapel into sunlight.

George stayed where he was, uncertain of what he should do, enveloped by the solemnity of the moment and the silence of the chapel, a cool darkness given by the thickness of its walls because the sun had moved on and was no longer shining – however weakly – through its single, east-facing, window.

He was unused to deep emotion, had no time for it in the continual hard graft that was his life. He woke up in the early morning, went and fetched his sons from their homes along the shore and together they went to work at whatever was needed. They went to work, they came back to one of his son's homes and ate whatever meagre meal his daughter-in-laws had conjured up for them. Then he took his leave, trudged back down the shore to his own little cottage and went straightaway to bed, utterly exhausted. He slept while the sky was dark and then, when it was light, he got up and repeated the whole exercise again, day after day, month after month, season after season.

The storm that wrecked the Collybuckie had been a welcome relief to the tedium, despite it having ripped off the roof of the communal barn – which would mean disaster over the winter for the entire village if it wasn't fixed – but they had the whole summer to carry out whatever shabby repairs they could manage.

In the meantime, there was the interruption to normal daily life necessitated by every able-bodied man going down onto the beach to rake up the weed. He'd not counted on finding a body, never found one before, and to be present when that corpse was identified was an absolute first. He doubted it could have been the lad's father, for the age disparity was too great; more likely Ruan was a grandson, but either way George wished he could have spared the boy the sight.

'How is he?' George asked when Joachim reappeared a few minutes later.

'Not too good,' Joachim said. 'But he won't leave. He's sitting outside. Says he'll not be completely certain until we've undressed the body. Apparently this Golo Eck wears a ring that's unique, and he refuses to believe this is he until we take it out to him.'

George nodded, looking down towards the body and that curled up hand, thanking every god that might be up there playing without care amongst the stars that he'd not taken out his knife.

'Is it his father? His grandfather?' George asked quietly.

Joachim shook his head. 'Neither, but I gather he might as well have been.'

And with that they said all that was needed and set about undressing the corpse with method and care. Joachim gave George directions to unbutton and unbuckle his clothes, explaining briefly that the cold of the sea must have delayed the rigour that should already have come and gone. It was not as bad as it had been when George first found him, some of it jogged loose by his travelling from the sands. George took great care to ease the man's limbs away from his body before tipping him almost into sitting so that Joachim could pull off coat, jerkin and shirt. Joachim next directed George to the foot of the bier and to lift up the legs so they could remove boots, trousers and undergarments.

Once every item of clothing was removed, they went through every pocket of the wretched material before folding the clothes up and laying them neatly on an empty pew. An unsteady drip fell from the stack like a metronome that has lost its rhythm and purpose, yet still carries on regardless. The removal of the ring was an unpleasant task, George having to rub grease from one of the tallow candles up and down the man's finger, squeezing the putty-like flesh until the ring finally slid away and came free.

Once done, George wiped his hands upon his trousers and then immediately regretted it. He felt the slime and stink of the wax and the dead man's skin seeping through the coarse weave like oil from fish-guts, and knew he would rather beg another pair from the Servants, no matter how ill-fitting, than wear these breeches ever again.

They also removed a well-wrought chain from about the dead man's neck that held a charm of sorts, with the same lion-like insignia Joachim had noticed on the cuff-links. There was a girdle-pouch too, the kind that travellers strapped about their waists beneath their clothes to keep money and documents safe. From this they extracted a soggy wad of papers that may at one time have been money bills or maybe letters. But it was of no earthly use to anyone now, being little more than a handful of sludge. There was no fob-watch, and for that George felt obscurely grateful, as if its non-existence somehow validated his reluctance to search for it in the first place.

All done now, and only a naked man upon his bier, a dark stain spreading out about his body as the last of the water made its way from skin to wooden grain. the grey hair upon his chest taking on a life of its own as it dried in the candle light, springing back into its accustomed curls. The man looked older than he had when he was dressed. His skin sagged, deprived of the musculature needed to give it substance, and the flesh of his face pulled away from eyes and mouth, giving the impression of the drop and droop of palsy. The skin was blotched, blossomed over chest and legs with yellow and purple bruises, the base of his buttocks a vivid purple where the blood had finally settled and coagulated once the body had come to rest on the beach wrapped up in his weed.

Joachim went off to the sacristy to fetch some shrouding and a sack in which to gather up the dead man's clothes and belongings. George had been tasked, in Joachim's absence, with folding the dead man's hands across his chest and closing his eyes. He could use candle wax if necessary, for they'd already tried to do this several times, and each time they had been unnerved to find the eyelids sliding back to half-mast, the clouded blue irises of the man's eyes staring right back up into the world they could no longer see.

George did as directed, dribbling on a little wax before gently easing the eyelids shut and holding them closed, feeling the pulse of his blood at his fingertips as he did so. The skin beneath his touch was thin and flaccid, reminding him of the new-born bat he'd once found fallen from the gable-end of the barn. He'd only known it was there because he trod on it and heard the crunching of its tiny bones beneath his boot. He'd looked down to see the slight, dark smudge of its blood upon the step, one tiny wing thrown free into the cone of light that came from his lamp. He'd leant down then and seen the wing, smaller than the length of his smallest finger, beating frantically against the sandy dust it was lying in, and a single claw – like the tendril of a plant – extending beyond, scratching at the dust as if it was trying to write some final message to George, its murderer. He'd felt such pity then, and such revulsion, that he'd picked up the tiny animal between forefinger and thumb and flung it as far away from him into the dark night as he could, his heart beating, beating, and wishing all the while he'd not been the one to do that stepping, to have obliterated such a fragile fight for life.

Only when he was sure the tallow had firmly set did George lift up his fingers, relieved the eyelids this time remained shut. The worst was over, George told himself, and only the lesser duty left of placing the man's hands across his chest. As he performed this final task George couldn't help but notice the unnatural bulge of Golo Eck's right shoulder where George had previously pulled his arm clean out of its socket. In trying to right it now, he suddenly understood what he'd already seen out on the beach and that something about this manner of the laying of his arms was all wrong.

He looked closer then, and saw how bruised were the man's wrists and forearms. And they weren't just bruised but abraded, and in a way he'd seen before when cattle, sheep or goats fought against the tethers they'd been put in for one reason or another. He'd seen such marks on men too – thieves and drunkards for the most part – locked into the pillory, restrained at ankle and wrist, coming out two days later rubbed raw almost to the elbows, unable to stop fighting against the wooden stocks that held them to their punishment. He knew there'd been lace cuffs about those wrists, had seen them first-hand when he'd taken away the cuff-link, and more recently at the undressing. But he understood they'd been not nearly tight or hard enough to cause this much damage, no matter that the man had presumably been jumping from a sinking ship, fighting for his life.

Joachim chose that moment to return and was already speaking as made his way from sacristy towards transept.

'Can I ask you to take this out to Mr Peat?' he was saying, beginning to pile Golo Eck's clothes and belongings onto a large pewter tray, having been unable to find a sack close to hand. He stopped abruptly when he saw George's face, the concern on it, the way he had stepped back from the corpse, pointing mutely at the arms he had just folded across the dead man's chest.

'George, whatever is it?' Joachim said, putting down the tray, his gaze following George's indicating finger. 'Is there a problem?' he asked as he came around and stood beside George who responded by lifting up the candle he'd used for closing up those blue and blinded eyes.

'It's his wrists and arms, Brother. Take a look at them.'

Joachim did, but only a cursory glance before switching back to George's face.

'Well yes,' he said. 'They're bruised and scratched. However else would they be? You know how a man's flesh swells when he's been in the water, and he'd shirt cuffs on, mind. And cufflinks.'

He'd been about to make a small joke about those cufflinks but George was shaking his head vigorously.

'No, no,' said George, his voice anxious and pitched too high. 'I mean, I know. I know about the cuffs, of course I do, but these here marks weren't made by anything like as skinny as them lacy doo-dahs.'

Joachim frowned, looking back down again at the purple circlets and scratch marks that went all about the man's wrists and partway up his forearms almost to his elbows.

'Them've been fettered,' George said quietly. 'Them've been tied. I'd swear it on my life, Brother. On my life. He was in the water but he was tied when he went in there, and alive long enough for them there bruises…'

George stopped abruptly, finding it too hard to comprehend what must have happened to this man who might have survived the shipwreck, just as his kinsman Ruan Peat had done, except that unlike Ruan someone had made damn sure that he did not.

'Are you certain?' Joachim asked, for it did not seem to him an absolute at all.

'Just look,' George said and turned Golo's left arm up, exposing its underside, an inch-wide bruise about his wrist where all the blood vessels beneath had been ruptured.

Joachim bit his lip and shook his head, seeing it too.

'Then someone has to tell the lad,' he said, 'because surely for him this will change everything.'

AN ISLAND NOT SO GREEN

DUBLIN, IRELAND 1798

Fergus got off the boat in Dublin and felt immediately and astonishingly at home, only fifteen when he'd left, heading away on his own great adventure. Getting down to Wexford was his primary goal, but first they'd decided it best for Fergus to make contact with an old acquaintance, who might be able to help him on his way.

Ever since the ultra-Protestant Puritan Oliver Cromwell had declared the union of England, Wales, Scotland and Ireland in 1649, there'd been a constant undercurrent of trouble. In the last few years – inspired by the Revolution in France – a new and more powerful group had emerged. The United Irish were attempting precisely what their name implied, their aim to unite a large portion of the populace – poor and wealthy alike – into their rebellion for Independence against English rule. Quite how bad it had got neither Golo nor Fergus had fully appreciated, all news being filtered through the myopic reports of the English press. They had, though, unearthed a few more spirited articles in an independent Scottish broadsheet more sympathetic to the Irish cause.

'Look at this,' Fergus pointed out to Golo when he first came across them. 'I know this name, Peter Finnerty. I was apprenticed to their Printworks for a few months before we left.'

'Is that so?' Golo replied with interest. 'So you were an aspiring journalist in your youth? Why doesn't that surprise me?'

Fergus smiled, for that had hardly been the case. He'd been shoe-horned into the job by his father when Fergus made it clear he wasn't going to follow his paternal footsteps into the law. Yet he remembered the Printworks with great affection, Jerome Finnerty being a kind and tolerant master, if a little eccentric. He had the apparently unique affliction of being born with freakishly elongated big toes which forced him to wear shoes far too large for the rest of his body. The waddle those shoes gave his gait conveyed an undeserved impression of oafishness and imbalance, which could not have been further from the truth. On warm days Jerome preferred not to wear proper shoes at all, opting instead for sandals, his two big toes heading out over their top edges like unexpected isthmuses, constantly being stubbed, grazed and stood on, so they no longer had any nails.

'I doubt Jerome is still alive,' Fergus told Golo with a pang of regret, 'but certainly his son was named Peter, a little younger than me to be sure.'

Golo smiled, tapping at the broadsheet and its article with the stem of his unlit pipe.

'Well then,' he said. 'I know we were discussing trying to get you passage further south and nearer Wexford, but it strikes me that Dublin and this Peter are better places to start. Information, Fergus, and knowledge. They are always the key.'

Fergus set out from Usher's Quay towards the north side of Dublin, where Finnerty's Printworks were located, a bubble of excitement in his chest. But when he got to the bridge to cross the Liffey he found his progress barred by a large and impenetrable crowd.

'What's going on?' Fergus asked of no one in particular, imagining maybe a feast day, when one saintly effigy or another was paraded through the streets of the city from church to cathedral or back again.

'Another hanging,' the woman to his right replied.

She quickly crossed herself as a temporary gibbet came into sight, rolled up from the curve of the bridge from the other side and pushed into place at its apex. Right behind it came a group of uniformed soldiers dragging two men so extensively chained they couldn't move without the soldiers' help, who were none too kind about giving it.

'For why?' Fergus asked, thinking thievery or murder, his eyes fixed on the gibbet and the soldiers shoving wedges against its wheels to stop it shifting when the inevitable came.

'You been hiding in a molehill?' asked the woman, incredulous. 'They're both ours, man, may God have mercy on their souls.'

Fergus didn't understand but had no choice but to stand fast. He was locked in on every side by folk pushing forward, craning for a better look. He'd no choice but to watch with the rest as the first of the shackled men was hauled up the steps onto the gibbet's platform, a black sack shoved without ceremony over his head followed by a noose the size and flexibility of a goose's neck. The crowd hushed, and from inside the sack came a muffled shouting, Fergus far slower to understand than everyone about him who swiftly took up the chant, repeating the man's words, stamping their feet in rhythm.

Erin go Bragh! Erin go Bragh! Erin go Bragh! Erin go Bragh!

The growing strength of the chant was loud and unsettling – to Fergus at least – an unpredictable wave surging through the crowd only to be pulled back at the last moment. It was replaced by a communal gasp and sigh when the trapdoor beneath the condemned man's feet was released. Down he went and quick, the rope thankfully performing its duty well, snapping his neck bones so one moment he was alive enough to shout out a last truncated *Erin go Br...*and the next was an empty vessel, the rope sliced through and down he went – out of sight, out of life – into the carapace of the gibbet, trapdoor swiftly put back in place to make a solid standing for the next man to take the fall.

The soldiers were discomfited by the animated hostility of the crowds, no matter they'd been expecting it, and wasted no time bringing the second man up the steps. The quicker it was done, the quicker they could get out of here, but the men and women gathered on Fergus's side of the bridge were only silent for the time it took the first man to drop, and that was no time at all. Now they were all starting up again, small noises from one and then another until, like a flock of swans alarmed by some strange shadow at the edge of their shared vision, every individual took courage from their neighbours and shouted louder and louder.

They continued until they were as loud as they could be, egging each other on with their incoherent yelling until the blond-haired, uncapped captain of the execution detail raised a warning arm. From where Fergus stood the man looked like an angelic choirboy, nothing threatening to his gesture, but the crowd knew different. They wavered but did not stop entirely, not until the choirboy gave a curt nod of his head and his soldiers raised their guns, aiming them indiscriminately towards the townsfolk gathered on the bad side of the bridge.

Fergus took a quick pace back in alarm, bumping hard into the man standing immediately behind him who did not take his cowardice well and punched him hard in the left kidney, shoving Fergus back into his allotted place. The danger was real and immediate, Fergus could feel it, and would have thrown himself to the ground if there'd been space, but was kept aloft by the people all around him, everyone packed together like bricks in a wall. The second man had a second black hood pushed down roughly over his face, a second noose flung about his neck, the crowd going quiet for just long enough for the condemned man to get out his own cry of rebellion.

'Christ save me and the gree...'

The last consonant cut off as the choirboy himself pulled the lever and the trapdoor disappeared beneath the man's feet and down he went. Utter silence then, only the eerily loud creak as the rope stretched and twisted as the man's body jerked, his death not so quick as the one that had gone before, and far too prolonged for anyone to have the stomach for.

'Christ save me and the green,' a single voice rose up from Fergus's left but the choirboy captain was having none of it.

'Level guns,' he ordered, and his men swung their guns around and aimed them at the crowd.

'Christ save me and the green,' another voice, wavering, coming from somewhere at Fergus's back, but there was no heart in it, not with the threat of bullets about to be fired without discrimination. The man on the gibbet was still kicking feebly, the black sack going in and out, in and out about his mouth as his body fought to bring in breath – or death – despite itself. Sweat prickled at the nape of Fergus's neck and then, without conscious thought, his hands went to his mouth, cupping his lips.

'Christ save me and the green!' he yelled, loud as he was able, sending the small woman next to him ricocheting to one side as he took a step to brace his legs as he shouted again, other men dotted throughout the masses joining in, only a few of them, but as loud as they could make it. It didn't last long, half a minute if that, until the first shot cracked through the air above their heads and smacked into the ground behind them. Another followed, and another, and then the crowd were picking up their feet and running, as was Fergus, who was tugged along by the man who had previously punched him in the back.

'Well done, son,' Fergus heard the man saying before they were parted, Fergus exhilarated, his heart thumping with fear and adrenalin as he scrambled out of distance of the English guns, soon far away, melting into the backstreets with all the rest.

Me and the green.

Lord knew why he'd been the one to begin the shout, certainly Fergus didn't, only that he'd been caught up in the moment, horrified by the inhumanity of that second hanging. Now his heart was pumping and his feet were running, taking him along the streets he'd known as a lad and they didn't go a step wrong, kept him going and going until finally he was where he wanted to be, walking now, hardly any breath left in him. Here he was, outside Finnerty's Printworks, only a knock on the door between being outside and going in.

10
SEA AND SALT AND BEES

WALCHEREN PENINSULA, HOLLAND

Ruan sat outside the chapel on a small stone bench, listening to all the noises produced by a hospital for the dead and dying. He heard the muffled cries and moans coming from the patients immured within its walls, the soft sounds of brothers' sandals hurrying – always hurrying – across the courtyard from one part of the building to another. He heard the shuffling of cattle and goats within their outhouses and byres whilst they waited to be fed or milked.

He'd known nothing about the services these Servants of the Sick provided when he'd arrived, and hadn't wanted to know any more of them. However, the Brother who periodically arrived to redress his wounds insisted on filling the silence. He told Ruan how they were an Italian-based order founded by St Camillus in Rome in the 1580s, active ever since, spreading slowly across Europe, primarily through fields of battle where they aided the wounded and buried the dead, the Walcheren Peninsula being as far north as they'd so far got; the place everyone nearby was brought to when they were sick or on their last legs; or after a shipwrecking, as in Ruan's case.

He cowered against the stone that was hard at his back, below his buttocks, the skin of his hands white about the knuckles as they gripped the thick slab of the seat. His black hair was matted and fell maddeningly across his forehead but he didn't want to move a muscle, not even to shove it away. He found some relief in the dark veil it was drawing between himself and the afternoon that had no right to be so bright.

He deliberately slowed his breathing, hoping that by doing so he could maybe doze off. With luck, if he did, he'd slip off the bench and bash his head, then at least he'd be able to remain here a little longer. He toyed with the idea of re-opening the wound on his arm, but it had already begun to scab over beneath its bandage. Maybe if he rubbed a little dirt in it…

Come back, fever, do your worst. Keep me here a little longer, keep me here until someone arrives and tells me what to do.

He withdrew into the carapace of his youth and ignorance like a hermit crab diving into an empty shell, dreading that at any moment someone would come and winkle him out. He wanted to stay until he had external direction. He didn't want to have to think about what he was going to do if that really was Golo inside the chapel. Maybe he'd made a mistake. Maybe he still had too much salt in his eyes and it was making him see things that weren't really there. It was true his sight was a little blurry at the edges, and that was enough to convince him that of course it hadn't been Golo.

The body on the bier was hugely swollen – enough to burst several buttons on the coat and the shirt below it, and Golo had never been like that. His skin had never had that ghastly green translucence like holding up a bone china cup to the sun. Certainly the clothes looked like Golo's, but what did Ruan know? He'd hardly seen Golo those last few days on the boat, happy to let that little tic of a boy see to his needs. Maybe Golo had dug out something new to wear. Lord knew, everyone else was stinking with the voyage and Golo was very particular about keeping clean. He used to swim in the loch every morning for a few minutes until he got bronchitis a few years back and Fergus forced him to stop. Yes, Ruan thought. That must be it. It looked a bit like Golo, that body, but it surely wasn't. Golo wouldn't just leave him. Golo wouldn't do that. Ruan couldn't be left marooned here with nothing and no one. It just wasn't possible.

He released his grip slightly on the stone seat, convinced that he'd truly been mistaken. All he needed to do was stand up and go back inside the chapel and tell everyone he'd made a mistake and that would be that. He'd stay on a little longer here at the Servants and then Golo would suddenly appear. He'd maybe have a beard and his clothes would probably be ragged from being in the water. Ruan would make a joke about how unkempt he looked, and then they'd laugh about how ridiculously frightened Ruan had been – not that Ruan would admit to it, not to Golo's face. But Golo would know it anyway, because Golo knew him inside out and back to front, like one of his precious books from which he could recite every page without even having to look at it.

That was how it would go, Ruan decided, and at last he moved a hand up and brushed the hair away from his eyes, only to spot the black cloud of George Gwilt bearing down upon him, holding a tray in both hands piled high with the clothes and belongings of the dead man in the chapel. Whoever he was.

'Brother Joachim asked me to give these to you,' George said, standing awkwardly by the young man on the bench who looked like he'd been drained of blood, his thick black hair accentuating the fragile features of his face. Ruan looked up and smiled, which was so unexpected that George's mouth, which had been dry and scratchy, suddenly flooded with saliva, because he knew what was coming next, the lad's expression clear to see.

'You can take them straight back,' Ruan said. 'I was just about to come and tell you. That's not Golo in there. I made a mistake. I've been sitting here thinking about it, and I'm certain I've made a mistake.'

George understood all too well the nature of grief and what it does to a person. Grief is its own new world, a strange place that had you believing the opposite of what was true. It made you see mountains where there were none or, conversely, and like Ruan was believing now, that there were no mountains at all. All he had to do was blink and he would wake up and the world would be exactly as it had been before. George didn't move. This was Brother Joachim's territory. These were the Servants of the Sick, after all, who administered not only to the dead and dying but those they left behind. This was not George's remit and he didn't know what to do.

'It isn't Golo in there,' Ruan repeated. 'I just need to stay on a few more days and he'll turn up. He must have got separated from everyone else. There's still one raft unaccounted for. It must have got blown further down the coast, but they'll know to send him here. Everyone comes here, so I've been told.'

George swayed slightly. He had the same disparity to his legs his youngest son had, though nowhere near so bad, but standing stationary too long was hard work, making his neck and back ache as his body was forced to lean to one side. And who knew? Maybe the lad was right. There was a raft unaccounted for, and there was the outside possibility it had been grounded towards the neck of the Peninsula, one side or the other. Even so, surely they'd have heard news of it by now.

His back was really aching, getting ready to spasm, and he had to take a step to one side. It made the tray tip, dislodging one of the cufflinks that was pushed over the edge and sent plinking onto the ground by Ruan's feet. Ruan stared at it, then bent and picked it up, holding the small dab of gold between his fingertips, smile gone.

'No!' Ruan shouted, leaping to his feet and, in the same movement, striking the tray from George's hands, all the while keeping that little tip of gold within his closing fist. 'It's not him, dammit!'

Ruan's voice was hoarse and petulant, belief and disbelief fighting a battle he could not win. He stamped his foot. He bit his lip until it bled. He clenched his fists tight and then opened them up again, the small shine of falling gold caught by the sun, glinting like the malevolent yellow eye of a goat, the only animal George knew that had an iris shaped like a square, who could stare you down the length of a field, it was so unnatural.

'It can't be him,' Ruan's voice crumpled back, as did he, into the boy he no longer believed himself to be.

He collapsed onto his bench and all the air came out of him in a soft kind of howl, the sort of noise a bitch will make when she knows her pups are being taken away before their time. George was horrified. He had no words. He could do nothing except slowly bend down on one knee and start to gather the spillings from the tray.

'Stop, I say,' Ruan wanted to sound commanding, to hold back the tide.

His throat was strangled by his tears so the words didn't come out right, came instead as a blur, a plea that George was desperate to obey, but could not. His knees creaked as he lowered himself further and carefully began picking up each garment. He folded them carefully, retrieving the girdle belt that had gone below the bench, the pendant, the ring, the scattered cufflinks, placing them gently to one side where they could easily be seen and recognised. He left the tray on the ground and made no further move to touch it. Using the bench he levered himself and his aching back and knees up again, and sat down next to Ruan Peat.

He'd been hoping that by now someone, anyone – preferably Brother Joachim – would have heard that howl of despair and come to aid this boy who so evidently needed their help, because wasn't that what they did, these Servants of the Sick? But no one came. Joachim must have heard the boy's cry but ignored it, his duty to the dead outriding his duty to the living, leaving the situation to George. He was as ill-equipped to deal with it as the time he'd had to tackle his uncle's beehives when his uncle fell sick and no one else about to see to them but George.

'Just use the candle to smoke them out,' his uncle had advised. 'Then you can lift the honeycombs and slip in the new slats without them noticing.'

George had done as he was told, lit up the candle and set it burning beneath the hive. Out had come the bees as they were supposed to do, and in he'd gone, nimbly lifting the lid and removing the combs, shoving them into his bucket; but apparently he'd not been quick enough because before he'd time to put the new slats in the bees came back. There was no smoke in the world that was going to keep them off the interloper and they covered him head to foot in a moment even as he took to his heels and ran all the while from the village to the sea, the only place he could think to go, them being on him and stinging him and getting into his mouth and ears and up his nose.

It was a miracle he survived at all, saved only by the salt, coming out with a face like a cauliflower and hands that wouldn't function properly for almost three weeks. Sea and salt and bees. He'd been fond of none of them since, but would have taken his chances with any of them over what he had to do now.

'God knows, I wish it was otherwise,' George said quietly, 'but I think you know it's him.'

Only stillness at his side, only this boy Ruan Peat, so suddenly deprived of everything he thought he could depend on. There was a gasping noise from the boy as he leant down and picked up the large gold ring that had been on the finger of the dead man in the chapel which, thank the Lord and his own good sense, George hadn't taken when he'd had the chance. Ruan cradled the ring in his hand. Evidence he could neither ignore nor deny. He leant over and placed his head on George Gwilt's shoulder and wept like the child he was. No rage anymore for the world that had done him wrong, only this silent weeping that broke George's heart, the tears soaking right through his thin coat and even thinner shirt so that he could feel their warmth upon his skin.

'It's alright, lad, it's alright,' George said, knowing full well that it wasn't.

But the boy had the ring, the cufflinks and the pendant. The rest of his belongings might be at the bottom of the sea, but the jewellery he could pawn or use as leverage to get himself back home. And the Servants wouldn't abandon him. They'd look after him. That was what they did. George could have taken the boy home with him, but the moment he thought of it he disregarded the idea. Nothing there but a cold and empty cottage; no fire struck up since yesterday because George had been down on the sands raking in the weeds for the past few days. And no food. Or nothing like what Ruan would have been used to.

George twitched. Not enough to dislodge the weeping boy, but he twitched all the same because he'd not told Ruan the worst of the news, the details of how Golo had – or had most likely – died.

George wondered if he should just walk away and leave the job to someone else. But no. That was not a road he chose to take. He'd started with dishonesty with the cufflink and meant to finish in the opposite way. George gently lifted Ruan's head from his shoulder, holding his chin in one hand, brushing that thick black hair away from his swollen cheeks with the other.

'There's more, I'm afraid, lad,' George said. 'But let's go back inside to Brother Joachim and we'll tell you all.'

ARRIVAL AND ARREST

DUBLIN, IRELAND 1798

The Finnerty Printworks was exactly where it had been in Fergus's day, on the corner of Stoneybatter and Arbour Hill. It looked as he remembered, although its stonework exterior was smoke-blackened and pitted, no doubt because a blacksmith's had opened up just down the road where previously – if he remembered rightly – there'd been a glove-maker's shop. The outside glass of the windows was covered with a thin film of dusty grime but the door was as it had been, standing open a few inches to let out the stench of the fixing agents used to stabilize the ink.

He could hear the presses working within, the rhythmic thump he'd always found so comforting. He didn't bother knocking, knowing no one would hear him if he did, and instead pushed the door wide open and stepped inside. Two people were standing by the presses, talking animatedly – a young girl, with hair the colour of bright red sandstone, who was thrusting a piece of paper at a man who absolutely had to be Jerome's son, Peter. He had the same features as his father, the slightly squashed nose, the wide forehead, but patently not the affliction of the long toes because he was wearing ordinary sized shoes.

'Hello?' Fergus asked into the noisy interior.

Neither of them heard him but went on talking just the same, the man he took to be Peter Finnerty waving his right arm to indicate the presses, the girl shaking her head violently, patently telling Peter something he didn't want to hear. She turned suddenly and pointed at the door and then did a double-take to see Fergus standing there. She immediately grabbed at Peter's elbow, trying to push him away from the presses, throwing herself bodily against him in order to get him to shift his ground. But Peter did not go. Instead he took the girl's shoulders in his hands and gently pushed her away from him, gazing now directly at Fergus with such a look of defiance that Fergus stopped short.

'You're too late!' Peter shouted above the din of the presses. 'The news is already out and soon everyone will know that William Orr is innocent and should never have been condemned to hang!'

Fergus was too startled to move, but he held up his hands in a gesture of submission.

'My name is Fergus Murtagh,' he spoke loud and clear, hoping he would be heard, or that at least the man could read some of the words upon his lips. 'A friend of your father's.'

Peter Finnerty let the girl go and immediately put out a hand and pulled a lever to pause the presses. The wood groaned as it ground to a stop and then Peter was moving quickly across the room and taking Fergus's hand within his own.

'My God! My God! It's really you! It's Fergus Murtagh,' Peter said. 'But by God I recognise you. You used to work for my father when I was a bairn.'

Peter's face cracked open in a wide smile that was as welcoming as it was unexpected and Fergus returned the fervent handshake, happy to reciprocate.

'You weren't exactly a bairn, Peter,' he said, 'only a few years younger than me.'

'Oh indeed, indeed,' Peter said, 'but those few years made all the difference.'

The red-haired girl was looking daggers at Fergus, her face puckered in consternation and evident worry.

'But you have to go, Peter,' she said, casting a dark look at Fergus. 'I've already told you. They might be on their way right now. They could be here any minute. Seditious libel, they're saying, and that's going to mean gaol.'

'Wheesht child,' Peter said warmly. 'It's going to take at least another couple of hours. I've only just put the first of the news run out, so how are they going to get here so soon?'

The girl thrust out her hand again, flapping the piece of paper she was holding.

'But it's here, Peter. It's all here. They've been waiting for the chance of it, just like Father Kearns said they would, and...'

'Greta, enough. We can spare a few minutes for our guest here, and then I promise you I'll be out of that door and away over the hills before you can spit.'

The girl did not look happy but she subsided for the moment, and Peter led Fergus past the now quietened printing presses into a small room beyond. Inside, there were a couple of chairs ranged around a large table that was scattered over with pieces of paper that looked to Fergus to have no order at all.

'Why don't you go outside, Greta,' Peter said, as he motioned Fergus to sit down. 'Keep a lookout. If you see any soldiers coming then let me know. And now,' he continued, speaking directly to Fergus, 'tell me why you're here. You sound like a Scotsman, dammit! Whatever happened after your father was exiled? Dad ran several pieces on him and his case, but I'm afraid we never got enough support to bring him back.'

Fergus subsided into his allocated chair, flabbergasted at this last information. His father had committed career suicide when he began taking on cases that pitted Irish against English, digging out documents to support land claims going back hundreds of years, some long before Oliver Cromwell came over with his parliamentary army to exterminate dissent against foreign rule. He'd no idea anyone had tried to get his father's sentence of exile quashed so he could come back home, sure his father had never known it either and that saddened him greatly, making it difficult for him to know where to start.

'Thank you,' was all he said, casting his eyes over the papers strewn about the desk, picking out several oft repeated words and phrases: *United Irish, Revolution, against the English, unsupported accusations...*

'So you're back?' Peter began easily, apparently unable to allow a silence to grow now the background noise of the presses was in abeyance.

'I'm back for a reason,' Fergus said, a little hesitantly.

The talk of approaching soldiers and seditious libel alarmed him but Peter seemed relaxed enough and so Fergus took a chance.

'I'm back because I need your help, Peter,' Fergus went on. 'I know it seems an odd request, and we'd no idea what I'd be facing when I got here, but I need to get to Wexford...'

Peter let out a breath.

'That'll not be easy. Don't you realise the entire country is practically under siege?'

Fergus shook his head. 'We only knew what we could glean from the papers, and that hasn't been much.'

'It wouldn't be,' Peter replied hotly. 'The English don't want it known what they're doing, the crimes they're perpetrating to keep us under their heel. We've one great name on our side though, and someone you'll no doubt remember. Recall that young ragamuffin you used to run with on your street? The one your father got interested in the law?'

Fergus thought for a moment and then widened his eyes in surprise.

'You don't mean Wolfe Tone?'

Peter smiled. 'I do indeed. He went on to great things. Called to the bar in '89 and wrote several rather inflammatory pamphlets on behalf of the Catholic cause. You may not know it but he was in right at the start of the United Irish. Had to leave in '95 to avoid being strung up for treason.'

'My God!' Fergus said, astonished. 'What happened to him? Where is he now?'

Peter tapped his fingers on the table.

'Still fighting for the cause. Went to America and then to Paris where he was welcomed with open arms. He's rallying troops right now in France to invade Ireland on our behalf, and has even started an Irish Legion to take in all the exiles who've had to flee from our shores if they want to keep on breathing. We've kept in touch, him and me, as you obviously haven't.'

Fergus shook his head. 'No chance of that,' he said. 'We went over to Scotland, ended up in one of the remotest corners of that country, and I've been there ever since.'

Peter narrowed his eyes and leaned forward, crossing his arms on the table in such exact imitation of his father that Fergus could almost see Jerome sitting there in place of his son. Time to lay his cards on the table, and the fact that Peter was still in touch with Wolfe Tone was stirring up the beginnings of a great idea in him. Like Golo said, information and knowledge always the key.

'The man I work for,' Fergus began, 'is called Golo Eck. His great aim in life is to resurrect a society started by one of his ancestors, a democratic, sharing society to promote new science right across Europe.'

'That's some aim,' Peter said slowly, 'and one sorely needed. If we could get rid of even half the superstition I've come across it would be a great start. But where do I come into this? Surely you didn't come here for the good of your health.'

Fergus's turn to smile, and he took a deep breath, trying to formulate what to say next.

'I came to you,' he said, 'because we knew we'd need information about what was happening across the country. I've read a few of your articles. They got into the Scottish press if not into the English.'

'Well God bless Scotland!' Peter said. 'Quite a few Scots have come over to Ireland specifically to help us in our fight. I thought at first you might be one of them, but obviously not.'

'No,' Fergus flinched at the accusation. 'But I'd no idea how bad things were. I saw a hanging on my way here, on the bridge…'

'That would have been William Orr and his brother,' Peter sucked in a breath and shook his head. 'And they're not the only ones. Men have been executed left, right and centre. Dragged out of their houses and hung from their own eaves, burned then to the ground and their families with them. I'll not lie to you, Fergus, things here are bad, and it doesn't look like we're winning, not at the moment. Wexford is one of our strongholds, but how you're going to get from here to there…well…'

Peter sighed, leaning back in his seat, crossing one foot over the other, another echo of Jerome that Fergus could not miss. His great idea was slipping away from him practically before it began, but no harm in giving it a shot.

'If I wanted to get a message to Wolfe Tone,' Fergus asked, 'would you be able to do it?'

Peter snorted.

'It would be hard, my friend, no doubting that. My correspondence gets checked before it leaves the end of the street. It's a miracle those few articles got through to your Scottish papers, but not for want of trying. But there is one other person he's in touch with…'

The moment dragged as Peter studied Fergus and Fergus studied Peter.

'And who's that?' Fergus asked eventually.

'Man named Mogue Kearns,' Peter finally said. 'One of the commanders of the United Irish, was in France during their Revolution. It's to him Tone promised he'd get the French to invade on our side. You know the French – never liked the English, as no more have the English ever liked the French.'

Fergus saw with slight alarm that Peter was beginning to tap his fingers on the desk, just as Jerome used to do when he was about to squash some story or other.

'This society I told you about,' Fergus said hurriedly. 'It's called the Lynx. And Golo, the man I work for, is very keen to get its old library back together. That's why I'm here, to get to the part of it that's in Wexford. But another part is in Paris, about to go up for auction, and we can't get there. We can't get the permits to get into France, but from what you say it seems that Wolfe Tone might be able to help us gain access to it…'

Fergus trailed off when he saw the look in Peter's eyes.

'Is this a joke?' Peter asked slowly.

Fergus closed his eyes. It certainly was no joke to Golo and yet here in Ireland, with men being strung up on bridges and others, like Peter Finnerty, apparently about to be arrested for doing nothing more than his job, the entire idea of the Lynx seemed irrelevant and mediocre. He felt embarrassed for Golo and mortified for himself. He opened his eyes, shook his head.

'I know it seems like nothing to you, Peter,' Fergus said, 'but it's Golo's life's work, and outside of all that's happening here I know it's important. It's information and knowledge, and free access to both for all. And I swore to him, I swore to him I would not fail.'

Peter was quiet for a moment as he weighed the situation up.

'You do realise that this…errand,' he wanted to add the adjective trivial to his sentence but restrained himself. 'Well, that it might cost you your life? Nothing is certain here, Fergus. Nothing at all. Just mentioning the name of Wolfe Tone in the wrong place will be grounds enough to get you arrested.'

Fergus hung his head. Peter had not exactly ridiculed his task but even to Fergus it seemed paltry, given the circumstances Peter was obviously in, it no doubt seeming that Fergus was chasing shadows of no consequence, a child running after bubbles when so much more was going on in the world. Strangely it was Peter himself who came to his rescue.

'But I do understand, Fergus,' he said. 'I really do. I know what you mean about knowledge and information. If we'd more of it here then we'd not be in the clinch we're in now. If everyone was allowed the pleasures of being able to read and write then everything would be different, but it's not. It's not. Half our population lives in hand-to-mouth poverty and are illiterate to boot. They can't even communicate properly because of it, despite the fact they're trying to fight a war to make things better for their children, if not for themselves. So I'm asking you again, Fergus. Why exactly are you here?'

Fergus put a hand to his pocket, the one that contained the ring and khipu, and suddenly saw a way out, and a good one.

'I've something might help with that,' he said, 'something from the Lynx. A way of encrypting messages, passing along information, devised by a people with no written language themselves.'

Peter leaned in towards Fergus, a spark of interest on his face.

'Now that, my friend,' he said, 'is something truly worth a trade. Something we are in sore need of. We've cadres of United Irish right across the land, but passing information is our Achilles heel. It's been impossible to mobilise in coordination but if we could, well, things might go very differently.'

Fergus smiled though his beard, and thanked his inner Golo he'd managed to drag something from the Lynx that had some workable value. The more he thought about it the more convinced he became that the khipu could do just that. It was tailor-made for the type of hidden communications Peter and his underground network needed. Get stopped with a letter on you and it was neck-in-a-noose time; get stopped with a khipu and no one's going to be any the wiser. All he had to do was pass on what he knew about how it worked, let Peter adapt it to suit their needs. He was about to do just that when the red-headed girl came suddenly bowling back into the room, shouting for all she was worth.

'It's them!' she yelled. 'Soldiers! They're on their way, Peter. Oh my God, you have to get out!'

Peter Finnerty was on his feet in a moment.

'Greta,' he commanded. 'Take Fergus out the back. Take him to Father Kearns. Don't argue!' he added, as the girl started pulling at Peter's sleeve as she had done before. 'Enough, girl!' Peter said, though not roughly. 'Please Greta, do as I ask.'

Greta's face was white as a seashell abandoned on the shore but she obeyed and let go her grip on Peter and instead grabbed at Fergus, propelling him towards a small door that lay just beyond the paper-scattered desk.

'Quickly!' Peter shouted, but did not follow them, and instead pushed the lever of the presses so they all started in unison, almost drowning out his last command. 'Get Fergus to Mogue Kearns,

Greta. Tell him to tell Kearns what he's just told me. It's important, Greta, or I wouldn't ask it!'

Fergus's heart was in this throat. He wanted to stay and argue Peter's corner. He was not the lawyer his father had been but had picked up some of the jargon down the years, but Greta was not taking no for an answer and pulled him on with a strength her small body should not have had.

Moments later they were tumbling out the back door of the Printworks onto the cold surface of the Stoneybatter, Greta forcing Fergus to run with her, hard and fast, pausing only once to rub away the tears that were pouring from her eyes and blurring her way. Ten minutes later she was shoving Fergus into a little ginnel where they could stand at last and take their breath.

'They didn't ought to have done that,' Greta said, smiting her face with the back of her hand several times to stop herself from crying. 'They didn't ought to have done that,' she repeated as she released Fergus.

He flopped down to his knees, cracking them against the hard stone of the vennel, wild thoughts racing through his head like the deer that ran so elegantly over the moors above Loch Eck. Events had overtaken him and were moving too fast. He still had to get to Wexford, and could not ignore the possibility of getting some kind of message to Wolfe Tone, but everything else was scrambled. What was going to happen to Peter? Jesus Christ, he might even hang like those men on the bridge earlier.

'You have to come on,' the red-headed girl was saying to Fergus, angrily prodding him in the ribs. 'If Peter says you're to get to Mogue Kearns then I'll get you to him, but we can't stop here, not for long.'

Fergus looked up. The girl appeared thinner than she'd done before, maybe because she'd shoved a boy's cap over her head, hiding her hair, this simple ruse drawing a person's eyes away from her face and back down to her scrawny frame, making her look astonishingly like a boy. Her features were not too fine, combining with stubby eyelashes and brows that were so fair they could hardly be seen. An elvin, intersex creature of indeterminate age, lying anywhere between eleven and eighteen, Fergus could not decide.

'I said, come on!' the girl said, kicking Fergus hard in his side.

Fergus obeyed, emerging out the other side of the ginnel into a squalid street of run-down houses, washing slung out between them like paltry sails. A few pieces of paper floated down out of the sky and Fergus grasped one as it came within reach and paused to read it, squatting down to grab a few more that had landed in the puddles between the cobbles.

The Inhuman Treatment of Prisoners of War, he read, and in particular of one William Orr.

And then he understood why Peter Finnerty hadn't come running out of the Printworks behind them as he'd fully expected the man to do. He'd spent his last few minutes of freedom fetching up as many as he could of the fliers he'd been printing, flinging them out in handfuls onto the street so the wind would take them as far as it could, an act of such defiance and bravery it made Fergus feel sick. Greta wasn't so affected.

'Get off your arse, man,' she whispered hoarsely. 'If Peter's fool enough to let himself be arrested then I'm sure as damn not going to let you go without spilling out everything he thinks you've got.'

'It's the khipu,' Fergus managed to breathe out, but Greta wasn't going to wait for any explanations.

'The kimu, kimsoo, whatever you said,' Greta spat at him, 'had better be worth its weight in gold for what I'm about to do for you. And if Peter hangs, if Peter hangs…'

But this was a line of thought Greta could not bring herself to follow. Instead she got her hand twisted in her new companion's collar and hoisted him to standing.

'We've a way to go,' she said. 'And if you're coming then you'd best look lively, for I'm not one who waits.'

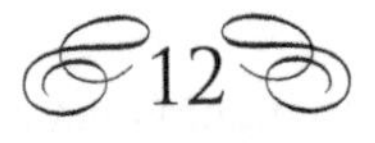

12
SERVANTS AND SUBHUMATION

Walcheren Peninsula

'So what are your plans?' Brother Joachim asked Ruan Peat, as they sat straight-backed at the refectory table the morning following the laying out of Golo Eck.

Bowls of honey-sweetened brose stood before them; both were untouched. The rest of the Brothers had swiftly eaten, eyeing Ruan all the while, talking quietly about the unenviable position he was in. Here was a foreign lad, shipwrecked, now alone in the world, with nothing left to him but the clothes upon his back and whatever he'd been carrying in his pockets when he'd chucked himself overboard from the Collybuckie. More precisely, he had what he'd managed to hang onto during his night of being battered about on the dark ocean before being eventually dragged into shore. Even they, the Brothers of the Servants, must surely own more than Ruan Peat did now, but he apparently had Joachim fighting his corner and so they soon departed, leaving the two alone in the near empty room.

Ruan cleared his throat, glad the rest were gone. He hated the way they'd slyly glanced at him as they shoved their porridge into their mouths. He had, more than once, fought down the desire to spring to his feet and shake his fist at them all, shouting to the world that he didn't deserve any of this, and what the hell was the world going to do to make it right? Last night he'd been so angry, so despairing, he'd not been able to think straight and the night hadn't done him any favours, falling asleep only to wake what seemed like a few minutes later, panic in every cell of him, sweat soaking from the nape of his neck to the tips of his toes.

The darkness gave no comfort, made it hard for him to grasp what course of action would be reasonable and what not. All that went through his mind as he stared up at the ceiling of his cell was that all those lessons studying logic and philosophy with Fergus had been a waste of time. Why weren't they helping him sift through his memories so that he could get at what he needed? And what he needed were names, and a place to start.

He'd no money, no way of going anywhere, forward or back. All Golo's letters of introduction and banking arrangements – that wad of papers kept in his girdle pouch – had been mulched into nonexistence by the sea. He'd the pendant, ring and cufflinks, all made of gold, but how that could translate into proper currency and bartering material he'd no idea. He was as useless and vulnerable as a snail that had lost its shell. And here, under Brother Joachim's scrutiny and the bright light of morning, he felt more vulnerable still.

'You will, of course, be welcome to stay here for as long as you need,' Joachim's soft voice said, though this was not strictly true, not unless Ruan elected to become a lay brother, which seemed to Joachim unlikely in the extreme. 'And we need to decide what to do with your friend's body.'

Ruan swallowed, and swallowed again. Joachim, who'd been in similar situations with other relatives of other men and women brought up dead within his bailiwick, understood the indications and offered a solution.

'Mr Eck will be very welcome to stay here with us. Buried with full service, and remembered every week in our prayers.'

For a moment Ruan was perfectly still, for oddly what to do with Golo's body hadn't occurred to him. He knew Golo was dead, his dark night of the soul had seen to that. What were uppermost – when his mind alighted on that truth – were George's assumptions that somehow or other, in the middle of that brutal storm, Golo had not been given a fair chance of survival, some unknown person going to great lengths precisely to make sure that he didn't. It seemed incredible. Literally beyond belief. A fancy dreamt up by someone who hadn't known Golo. For what had Golo ever been but a self-sustaining scholar, a book-gnome clinging desperately to his stupid family history to give himself worth, and trying to make Ruan do the same? And none of it worth hiccupping over let alone killing for, and all of it anyway gone down the plug-hole now Golo was no longer here to keep shouting about it. Ruan was free of the yoke Golo had placed upon his shoulders early doors, and thank Christ for it.

Or so he had thought last night.

This morning he was wondering if it might not be the ladder that would help him out of the hole he'd landed headfirst in. The last thing he wanted was to go back to the former dregs of his life in Scotland. He assumed the house and lands there now belonged to him, and worth a small fortune. If he could figure out how to get his hands on it then he could spend the rest of his life free-wheeling, go wherever – and for as long – as he wanted.

The initial shock of Golo's dying was wearing off a little and Ruan's head was beginning to spin with all the possibilities that might lie ahead of him because of it, if only he could leapfrog over this initial step of being without anything in a place he didn't know and where nobody knew him. He couldn't bear that his great adventure should come to an end before it had even started. He was so disgusted by the thought that he suddenly put out his hand and pushed away the bowl of porridge before him as if it was the most poisonous thing on earth. He had no plans about what exactly he was going to do, but making contact with some of Golo's cronies who corresponded with him about the Lynx would be a definite step in the right direction.

But first he needed to make a decision about Golo, and really he had no choice. Ruan didn't like himself for what he was about to say, and knew it was the last thing Golo would have wanted, that Golo would have preferred at all costs to have his body repatriated and buried on the shores of Loch Eck. Maybe later, when Ruan managed to secure the monies he knew the Eck Estate would confer on him, but no more possibility of it now than landing a man on the moon.

'He'll have to stay here,' Ruan answered in a dull monotone to Joachim's question. 'And I need to find a way out. Get away.'

He was about to say more, sound out his vague ideas with Joachim, thinking maybe he could jump from monastery to monastery until he found someone who could help him out, but his train of thought was disrupted by the refectory door being suddenly flung open, one of the Brothers coming in, dragging a small boy behind him, holding him tight by the ear, kicking back at the refectory door to keep it closed before placing his large body between the ragamuffin and escape.

'Says he know you, Mr Peat,' said the Brother.

The lad, now released, ran towards Ruan like an iron filing towards a magnet, as unkempt a specimen of boyhood as Ruan had ever seen. Except that through the detritus covering him Ruan saw something he recognised. Surely this was Caro, the boy from the Collybuckie, the one Golo had spent so much time with, who Ruan himself had plucked from the water and dragged onto the raft. He stood up abruptly as Caro ran towards him and Caro would have thrown his arms about Ruan's waist if Ruan hadn't stepped sharply to one side. Jesus, man, but the boy stank! Ruan involuntarily pinched his nose shut with his fingers.

'Found him in with the goats,' the stout boy-bringer announced, as if in explanation of the smell and the rips in the boy's clothes that exposed rough bumps and rashes on his bared arms and legs.

'Is it you, Caro?' Ruan asked, letting go his nose just long enough to get the words out, pinching it tight shut again afterwards, because now the boy was nodding vigorously and making once more for Ruan, letting out another noxious wave of rotting vegetation with high notes of manure and urine.

'Why don't you sit down?' Joachim asked kindly, pulling out a chair that was as far distant from him and Ruan as it was possible to be without the boy being completely out of earshot, dismissing the Brother who'd brought him in with a wave of his hand.

'But I thought you already left?' Ruan asked, for surely the boy couldn't have been all this time at the Servants, unnoticed and unseen, could surly not have spent all this time in with the goats, despite the stench.

'I did,' Caro piped up immediately, thankfully sitting down on the chair Joachim had pulled out for him. 'Went with Mr Ducetti, but came back again.'

He was eyeing the abandoned porridge on the table with such longing that Joachim couldn't help himself.

'Hungry?' he asked.

'I'll say!' Caro replied, Joachim pushing a bowl across the table towards him that Caro attacked with the same fervour Ruan remembered he'd always done on board ship – quick and greedy – snaffling up what little was left after everyone else had had their fill.

Before Caro finished the first bowl Joachim was already pushing forward the second, finding it pitiful to see such a rag-thin boy so desperate for what he could get. Joachim wondered why the boy had come back at all.

'So you went away,' Joachim commented mildly .'But why on earth have you come back?'

Caro swallowed, wiping a gloop of porridge from his chin.

'I went away,' he agreed. 'Took Mr Ducetti to Middleburg on account of him not knowing the area and me having been here before. Afterwards I was supposed to go on to Vlissingen to meet up with Mr Froggit and the rest of the crew, but Mr Ducetti met a fellow at Middleburg and asked me to bring him at least some of the way, and I was coming back anyway on account of having another obbelligation, and so here I am.'

Ruan scowled. He couldn't give a tiny blue-arsed fly shit about what this boy had been doing, and the way he'd put an extra syllable into the word obligation irritated him beyond measure. He was as fluent in Dutch as he was in English, the former being Golo's family language – and God forbid they should ever lose even a tiny part of Golo's back-history so as to only speak the language of the country in which they actually lived.

'And exactly why would you do that?' Ruan asked shortly, wanting to get this over with so he could get back to his tiny cell and start making his plans.

His plans, not Golo's. His plans alone. He'd been dredging through his memory to conjure up some – any – of the names of the people Golo had corresponded with and where they lived. He didn't need details, just a name and a city, because he knew the kind of men Golo hobnobbed with were of a very specific type, always congregating in the same places, usually a coffee house or library. All he needed was a place to start. He was no longer pinching his nose, and had the pleasure of looking down it at this annoying interloper, reckoning the lad to be maybe twelve or thirteen, recalling how Golo had enthused about him.

'He's been jumping from ship to ship since he can remember,' Golo had said of Caro, plainly impressed. 'So think on that, Ruan, when you think your own life has not been all you've wanted it to be.'

Christ, that had hurt, like Golo had seen right down into the depths of Ruan's soul and shoved in a knife, given it a twist. Golo had the need for everyone to see the good in their situation and be grateful for it, even if what they'd got was being stifled to death in a draughty house on the indescribably desolate shores of Loch Eck.

Caro had fit Golo's do-gooding attitude like a glove.

'Italian originally, he thinks,' Golo had burbled on to Ruan the second night out on the Collybuckie. 'But his Dutch is excellent, his English not far behind, and,' – another twist of the knife – 'I'm going to tutor him in a bit of reading…'

Ruan's bitter reminiscences stopped as Caro shoved the last spoonful of the second bowl of porridge down his gullet and spoke.

'I'm so sorry I never found Mr Golo,' he said, looking beseechingly at Ruan who had sat down again at the table on the opposite side. 'But I did look, Mr Peat, I really did.'

Ruan could not have been more surprised if the lad had leapt across the table and bitten him on his condescending nose.

'What do you mean, you looked?' he asked, infuriated by the sudden pitiful look the boy was giving him, even more annoyed when Caro shrugged his skinny shoulders before responding.

'Well I saw him go up, and I went after him. But it was so dark up there, and the boat was pitching like a bitch in heat with the storm, and there weren't no lamps and I couldn't find him…'

Caro looked like he might be about to throw up all the porridge he'd so eagerly consumed, face pale as a shaving of pine, but Ruan was angry now, and would not let it go.

'You were out there with him?' he demanded, lips pinched into thin grey lines, an image flashing across his mind of what George had said, how Golo's wrists had been bound. But surely this Caro couldn't have been responsible, much as Ruan might have wanted him to be.

Caro hung his head.

'I looked, honest I did. Went where I thought he would go, where the others were roping up the rafts, but a wave came over and knocked me off my feet. Next thing I knew I was in the deep. Almost got my head caved in when the first raft came down.'

Even Ruan flinched at this news. He'd been out there himself and knew how utterly disorienting and terrifying it had been and if the boy's testimony was true then he'd hit the water long before the rest had done, alone in the unfathomably deep and malevolent ocean for ten minutes, maybe more. It was an absolute miracle that his skinny body hadn't frozen into an icicle in that while before Ruan had raked his fingers through Caro's hair and pulled him out. Even so, Ruan wanted to squeeze every last drop of information from the boy.

'So who else did you see out there on deck when you were there?' he asked.

Caro shook his head.

'Honest, mister, it was terrible dark and everything was moving all around and there was stuff being thrown up out of the cabins and the holds and everywhere..'

'You saw no one? You must have seen someone, anyone...' Ruan persisted.

'No one,' Caro said, and then lifted his head and opened his mouth in apparent surprise. 'But there was someone came up behind me when I went to find Mr Golo. I could feel his feet on the steps when I was almost up.'

'And you didn't think to look?' Ruan was angry all over again with this boy who most likely had Golo's murderer right at his back and hadn't had the nous to turn and take a look.

He felt a sudden pressure in his head telling him to desist, that he was being unfair, that he should stop, but he couldn't. The momentum of his rage was pushing him on, and not just the rage at Golo's death, but the rage that Golo's death had put him in such an untenable position. He would have gone on grilling the annoying boy had he not felt a painful pinch on his arm, right above his bandage, Joachim picking his spot carefully, enough to know it wouldn't harm him, enough to make it hurt and make Ruan stop.

'The lad has told you all he can,' Joachim said firmly, 'so let him be. He certainly needs a wash, and thereafter a change of clothes.'

Ruan pulled his arm away from Joachim, his anger unspent.

'You don't understand,' Ruan started to say, but Joachim interrupted.

'I understand exactly, Ruan,' Joachim said calmly. 'But I think you're missing the point. Don't you want to know why young Caro here has come back?'

Caro looked up gratefully at Brother Joachim but held his tongue, and Ruan subsided, for he had to admit he was mildly curious.

'So why then?' Ruan said loudly, though not as loud as before.

He blinked rapidly several times to dismiss the images flashing through his mind of poor old Golo, out there on the dark and thrashing deck, someone coming upon him and binding his arms before chucking him into the boiling sea. Assuming that was what had really happened. Another twist of the knife, because where had Ruan been in all this? Looking after his own skin was what, no thought of Golo at all. The guilt was sharp and sudden. The little tic Caro had done what little tics do, and clung on to Golo before Ruan even registered he'd gone.

The bell for eight o'clock mass rang out just then, Joachim twitching involuntarily, his body wanting to head off and start his working day as it always started, his head eager to stay and resolve the problems of these two young and desperate people. Time to wrap things up, and quickly.

'So why come back?' Joachim repeated Ruan's question, standing up, gathering the emptied bowls, placing one inside the other in hope that the two lads would understand he was keen to be away.

Caro answered by putting his hand between shirt and trouser belt and extracting a small package that he slid across the table towards Ruan Peat.

'Mr Golo told me that if ever I got sick of the sea he'd give me a position,' he said quietly. 'And after what happened, well, I'm sick of the sea.'

The statement was so bald and disingenuous it took Ruan aback.

'But you know he's dead,' Ruan said. 'That Golo is dead.'

Caro nodded. Caro looked up. Caro's eyes were wet with tears.

'Heard it when I got in early doors last night, but I'd nowhere else to go. Froggit and the rest will have gone from Vlissingen by now, but I heard you were still here, Mr Peat, and I thought, well, I thought that maybe…'

Caro's words dried up, but not his tears, and this lack of control aggravated Ruan, mainly because he'd done the same with George and was ashamed of it.

'So what do you expect me to do about it?' Ruan's words were hard and spoken sharply, and Joachim grimaced at his lack of compassion. 'And what the hell is this?'

Ruan poked a finger at the small package Caro had produced. It looked like a book wrapped in a scrap of oilskin, tied up tight with string that had been tarred, though not too well, globules of pitch spattered across the package's surface like a spray of blood.

'It's his book,' said Caro, sniffing back his tears.

This wasn't going anything like he'd imagined. He'd been so certain Golo would do him right, lift him out of his life spent jumping from one ship to the next. He lived in the hope that on the next ship he would seem old enough for the seasoned sailors there to give him leave and not do what seasoned sailors always did to young cabin boys. Caro had wanted out, and Golo had been his promise for it.

'No more running,' Golo told him. 'When we land, you're coming with us.'

All finished now.

Ruan Peat obviously disliked him, and nothing left but for Caro to get to Vlissingen and find another ship that would in all probability be worse than the last. When he'd started out, the younger Caro had been by disposition optimistic, but all that had been knocked out of him in his first few years at sea. Golo finding him, looking after him and teaching him had given him a glimpse of a whole new possible world. Going back to the old one was going to be worse than falling headlong down a flight of stairs into a scary unknown cellar, but it was the only way Caro knew to go.

One last chance, he thought and so, with shaking fingers, he undid the string, unwrapped the oilskin and shoved the book across the refectory table to Ruan on the other side.

Ruan frowned. He was sick of all this, sick of the interruption of Caro. He wanted away. Golo was dead, and he'd dealt with it. Golo was dead and his body would be interred here on the Walcheren

Peninsula and Ruan free to go and get on with the rest of his life. What he absolutely didn't want was this millstone of a boy around his neck.

'What of it?' Ruan said as the boy pushed the book at him.

'He said it was his favourite,' Caro replied quietly. He'd lost all hope in Ruan Peat, Golo's promises of a better life disappeared like diarrhoea down a pan. But against his expectations Ruan did, at the very least, put out a hand and pick the book up.

'*Behemoths, and other Wonders of the Deep*,' Ruan read out loud the title etched in worn gold-leaf upon its leather cover. An involuntary choke of ironic laughter came from his throat after he'd got the words out. So this was the only book to have survived their voyage on the Collybuckie. This one, and no other. Ruan felt sick.

Whatever Golo had told Caro this was certainly not his favourite book, and in fact was possibly the opposite. Golo's paranoia was such that all his most important volumes had been carefully stashed, at his request, cocooned and carefully packed away in straw in the sea trunks that were now presumably at the bottom of the sea.

'And he gave this to you?' Ruan had his own knife out now and could dig and twist with the best of them. 'But it's worthless! It's the worst of the bunch, and no wonder he gave it away without a thought.'

He was being deliberately cruel, he knew it, but Jesus Christ, what in hell was he supposed to do? And who was the victim here? Not Caro, who could go join another ship at any time. Ruan was the one who'd been stopped in his tracks, the one who needed help, and this damn fly production of a book that Golo never gave a damn about wasn't going to wash with him.

'So you stole a book,' Ruan said. 'And you think that gives you the right to come back here to me crying for penance?'

Caro said nothing. He'd nothing to say. He'd gone head to head with brick walls all his life and recognised another one when it was right in front of it. As did Joachim.

'I'm sorry,' Joachim intervened, 'but I really have to be going. I'm already late for mass. But I'll not be gone long, and there are certain things I'd like to speak to you both about afterwards. Caro,' Joachim said, pushing his arm beneath the lad's own. 'Why don't you come with me? We can say a prayer for Golo Eck together and then get you washed; and I'll speak to Ruan later, if that's alright with you?'

Joachim looked Ruan Peat bang in the eye and Ruan Peat looked back, but only for a moment. That look from Joachim was not one Ruan wanted to see again and despite his bravado he knew that one way or another his time here staying with the Servants was done. Time to get his head on. Time to figure out what next he was going to do. But despite himself he picked the book up the moment Caro and Joachim had departed. It had been Golo's, after all, and no harm keeping a keepsake.

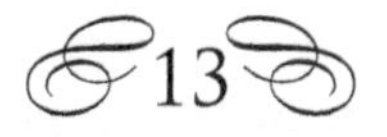

MORDECIAH CROOK IS NO MORE

IRELAND

Greta barely spoke during the few hours it took her to take Fergus to the small cadre of United Irish camping on a wooded hillside eight or nine miles south of Dublin. The outfit was a scraggy lot, thin men in thinner clothes regarding Fergus with suspicion until Greta explained that she was detailed to get him down to Wexford and then to Mogue Kearns.

Fergus was in a daze as they travelled south. He'd like the grown-up Peter and was shocked by what had happened at the Printworks and what might befall him. Greta didn't speak to him about it, nor engage in his trite attempts to talk to her about his and Peter's shared childhood. She was terrified Peter would already have been put up before the courts and found guilty, certain he must be in gaol and nothing she could do about it, frustration leaking out of her like a second shadow.

For his part, Fergus was alarmed by the extent of what was going on in Ireland, travelling with the cadre who apparently only moved freely at night, always slowly and with great care, no lamps or fires ever lit that might give away their position. The only person who had some degree of freedom during daylight hours was Greta. She scampered here and there to various previously established safe houses to garner their meagre supply of food, whilst the rest sat back in whatever hollow or glade they'd selected to hide in.

Conversations were few, the men obviously used to boredom and playing quiet games of cards or dice, ignoring Fergus completely. He found the whole experience alienating and claustrophobic, and was beginning to smell as bad as the rest. He didn't sleep well, unable to nod off like the others the moment their night tramp was done and dawn scratched at the horizon.

It was eighty odd miles to their destination, always hugging the coast and Fergus found the pace gruelling. Greta and her companions were able to cover fifteen miles or more at one hike with ease, despite the darkness. They knew their way, had done it many times – Greta at least – but as they neared the larger encampment of men outside New Ross that was their goal, Fergus was spent and exhausted.

They couldn't just march in and announce themselves, Fergus and the others having to wait an uncomfortable couple of hours packed between several ricks of straw while Greta went on ahead, winding like a slithery piece of seaweed through the rocks and tussocks that separated them from the oak knoll of the camp proper, a mile or so ahead. How she coped with such fortitude and survived a life like this, constantly on the move, left Fergus bewildered and filled with admiration. He was mighty relieved when the clump of men began to move forward, and Greta returned, despite her sudden materialisation at his elbow that had him jumping like a sand shrimp.

'Come on,' she said, gripping Fergus's cuff, the darkness so acute Fergus couldn't see a yard in front of him, Greta clicking her tongue every time he stepped on a twig or stumbled over a stone. But at last he could make out the tiniest glimmer of light between the trees up ahead and a few minutes later Greta led him into a large circle of men, two of whom immediately grabbed Fergus and shoved him roughly down on a fallen log which at least had the merit of being as damp and dirty as Fergus was himself.

'This here's Mick Malloy,' Greta said, pointing to a man standing with his hands tightly gripped behind his back, obviously suspicious of Fergus and wasting no time in small talk.

'So you're here for why?' the man said without preamble.

Fergus's escort hadn't left him and the weight of them at his back was intimidating. He was dog tired, finding it hard to think straight, let alone formulate any words. The man Greta had indicated as Mick Malloy spoke again.

'Greta says you've been sent from Peter and that's all to the good, but you need to tell us why.'

He was from the north and spoke fast and furious, but Fergus caught enough to understand what was being asked, Greta chiming in before he had time to speak.

'Still don't know what you and Peter were talking about so's you'd better tell us now and it better be good.'

Malloy nodded at Greta's intervention. He was short and wiry, with eyebrows joining at the middle, making him look like a man who could do a few rounds with a bear and come out the better.

'Got that, Greta,' Mick said. 'And we're still waiting for the answer.'

Fergus cleared his throat, trying to get the words straight in his head. Before he could start he was interrupted by Mick Malloy kicking hard at the log just to the left of Fergus's leg and leaving his boot there, trapping Fergus in.

'Don't want to start wrongly – Fergus, is it? But Jesus, we don't have time here for going around the houses. Just spit it out, an' we'll go from there.'

Fergus blinked, but did as he was told.

'I'm needing to get in touch with a Mordeciah Crook from Wexford on personal business. I'm also needing to get a message to Mogue Kearns to give to Wolfe Tone. That's the long and short of it…'

Malloy let out a snort of laugher before Fergus finished speaking, moving his boot and stamping it down onto the grass.

'Mordeciah Crook, is it? Well that's going to be difficult, seeing as him and his house were sent up in flames last two weeks back and nothing left of either of 'em but a big pile of ash.'

Fergus wobbled on his log at this information and Malloy noted it before going on.

'And Mogue Kearns or Wolfe Tone, is it? Well don't aim low. But I got news for you, Scotsman, that man Tone ain't been within hide nor hair of this place in years, and Mogue Kearns is well out of your reach.'

His derision was echoed by the men at Fergus's back, one of them thumping Fergus hard between the shoulder blades, sending him forward so he almost toppled off his log.

'Gonna need to do better than that,' one of them said.

'Aye right,' said the other, punching Fergus in the shoulder the second he'd righted himself, at which point Greta jumped up and squared herself in front of Mick Malloy.

'But Peter vouched for him!' she said with vehemence, her spiky hair jittering in the light of the fire that was hidden somewhere back in the clearing between the trees. 'And that should count for something.'

'And I've something to trade,' Fergus put in quickly. 'Something Peter thought might be of use to Greta and your cause.'

Malloy squinted, looking from Fergus to Greta, her earnestness, her loyalty so evident on her face that he lifted a hand so his comrades fell back, still laughing quietly. They left the three of them alone, for which Fergus was immensely grateful.

'Right enough,' Mick said, holding up his hands, offering placation. 'Sorry, lass. We knows how much you does for us and how genuine grateful we are for it, and for Peter too. But you,' he turned back to Fergus, 'you have some explaining to do.'

Fergus's stomach had dropped down a hole when Malloy said that Mordeciah Crook was gone, as was his house and presumably his library, including the Lynx part of it – assuming it was really there – nullifying his reason for being here. But there might, he reasoned, still be some rescue to the fiasco; his past relations with both Peter and Wolfe Tone might save him from being summarily killed and shovelled down the nearest hole as a spy.

He rubbed his hands together and spoke, editing his story of all the parts that would no longer make sense. He knew that he needed to make himself valuable if anything good was to come from this trip, and his skin goose-pimpled with Malloy standing above him like a stone as he tried to think fast and logical.

'The fact that Mordeciah Crook is dead certainly alters things,' he began, 'but I grew up with both Peter and Wolfe Tone before I had to leave with my father.'

'And why was that?' Malloy asked curtly, at least displaying a modicum of interest.

'He was a lawyer, Edgar Murtagh, started chasing landrights for Catholic claims. Got us both exiled back when…'

'Edgar Murtagh,' Malloy repeated quietly, perhaps recognising the name, though Fergus couldn't be sure and ploughed on regardless.

'The fact remains that I'm here, and it strikes me that my mission is not entirely lost, not if I can get word to Wolfe Tone about what me and my master are trying to do.'

'And what's that, Scotsman?' Malloy asked, unmoved and unmoving.

'It's no great thing to you,' Fergus admitted, 'an attempt to rekindle a society to push forward the views of the Enlightenment but the point is this...'

Fergus brought out his pouch and the khipu from it, laying it on his knee.

'That's some gewgaw,' said Malloy with unhidden disdain, 'but what the feck is it, if you don't mind me asking?'

'It's a means of communication,' Fergus went on, a little gratified that Greta was leaning in towards him to take a better look. 'Good for people in your circumstances. Able to encode a lot of information but no earthly way for your enemy understanding it, and there are a hundred ways it can be adapted to your needs.'

Malloy looked briefly at the strange ropey contraption Fergus had produced. He wasn't literate, nor was he good with numbers, and could make nothing of it. He turned his gaze to Greta.

'You're the one'll have to work with it, so what do you think?'

Greta hesitated. She'd never seen anything like it, but was keen on anything that might prove better than word of mouth or messages written on paper that could get the person carrying that message – herself included – arrested and hung.

'How does it work?' she asked, prodding her fingers at the strings on Fergus's knee.

'It's all to do with the knots and beads,' Fergus began to explain, 'and these divisions on the belt itself...'

'Enough,' Malloy interrupted. 'I don't have time for this but I'll tell you something for nothing, Scotsman, you've got here at a hell of a time. But because of this...this stringy thing, I'm going to give you a chance. We're due up in battle tomorrow. Should be a bit of a walkover but nothing's ever done until it's done, so here's the nub of it. Walk away with Greta and your gewgaw before it all kicks off or step up shoulder to shoulder with your countrymen and prove that you can fight. Do the first, and I'll keep you in mind if Wolfe Tone ever makes good his promise to get over here with his fighting Frenchies; do the second, and I'll back you to the hilt, take you to Mogue Kearns if it's with the last breath I've got blowing between my bones.'

He stomped away, leaving Fergus blinking and blenching behind him and Greta tapping on his shoulder.

'I'll go with that,' Greta said. 'But right now I need some shut-eye and I suggest you do the same. Big decision, Mr Scotsman, and thank your lucky stars you've got Peter on your side, because as long as you've got him you've got me.'

14
THE GRIMALKIN CLAUSE

Servants of the Sick, Walcheren, Holland

'He's not going to take me with him, is he?' Caro said to Joachim as the two of them moved away from the refectory. The lad was so downcast that Joachim decided to excuse himself from mass. There were times when people came first, and this was one of them. He was angry at Ruan for treating the boy so badly, and was trying to figure a way he could make it right. He had the glimmering of an idea how that might be done, but no point in offering the boy false hope, not just yet.

'Take heart, Caro,' was all he said for the moment. 'Let's get you washed and dressed in something other than goat urine and see where we go from there.'

He took the boy's hand in his own and gave it a small squeeze. It was not reciprocated. He wasn't even sure Caro was listening. The boy hung his head like the proverbial lamb going to slaughter and Joachim closed his eyes. He shook his head, disgusted – not for the first time – at how cruelly one man can treat another, let alone a child like this.

He was right. Caro wasn't listening. He was regretting letting go of Golo's book in his last ditch attempt to secure Ruan's favour.

That book was the only thing anyone had ever given him, at least anything good. He was remembering Golo Eck on the boat and how kind he'd been, and how eager to share his knowledge and how once – only once – Caro had been able to teach Golo something in return. It was in the bit about the whales, when the book had been describing those weird dolphins that had horns growing out of their heads.

'They call them narwhals,' Golo had said. 'And I've certainly never seen one, and indeed many people believe they don't exist.'

'Oh but they so do!' Caro had countered. 'I've seen them up there off of Greenland. We chased 'em for miles, but they got away, went charging up a split in the ice and then under so we couldn't follow.'

'Is that so, my young friend,' Golo had said, ruffling the hair on Caro's head. It was a touch he would have shrunk from if it had come from anyone else, but not from Golo. 'Well that makes you the wiser one of us two,' Golo added, and that was what Caro was recalling now, Golo and his words and the flash of light Golo had given him that all could come out right.

The wiser one of us two. Hardly the case now. Caro was defeated. Promise given, promise gone. Only thing left was to shrink himself back into the shell he'd already begun to construct about the deepest core of him, shrink himself up until there was nothing left.

Joachim, though, was not defeated, and the glimmer of that idea came to the fore. It was certainly a flimsy plan but he doubted Ruan would turn his back on it, not if it was delivered as a package. After depositing Caro with the brothers who would wash and bath him, put some salve on his sores, give him some better clothes, he went straight back to the refectory and intercepted Ruan who was on his way out.

'I can help you,' Joachim said.

'Help me how?' Ruan asked without enthusiasm. He didn't want any prayers said in his name and couldn't see what else might be on offer.

'With a place to go,' Joachim said, dismissing the urge to give the young man a slap, 'and a place to start. You said your Golo had all your letters of introduction in his waist pouch and we both know they're ruined beyond rescue, but I do know of one man of science who'll likely provide you with every assistance, once he knows what you're about.'

This was a bit of gamble on Joachim's part but he trusted in His God, and he trusted in the son he had abandoned when he'd joined the Servants. And the more he thought about it the more convinced he became that the probable outcome could only be good, and far better than Ruan deserved.

'Oh yes?' Ruan asked, though plainly wasn't expecting anything much, his face closed and sulky and belonging to someone much younger than his years.

'I have one proviso,' Joachim went on.

Ruan sighed deeply in response and it was all Joachim could do not to just walk away, abandon this young cuss to his fate and instead give his information directly to Caro who at least might make better use of it. But he didn't like the idea of sending Caro out, penniless and unprotected, to trek the length of Holland on his own, and so he bit his tongue, took a breath, divulged the relevant information.

'I want your guarantee that when I give you the details you will take Caro with you.'

'For God's sake,' Ruan muttered under his breath, but Joachim clearly heard him.

'Your absolute guarantee, Ruan,' he said. 'I want your sworn word that you won't ditch him halfway there because if you do, and if I find out...well.'

A few moments of silence then as Ruan weighed the odds. A place to go was something, and a name to head towards even better. If he could get that someone to guarantee him at a bank or with a lawyer then he'd be able to get hold of some funds to see him further. And he would need proof of Golo's death before he could lay hands on the estate, and he didn't have a clue how to go about that. But he saw his chance. Tit for tat, and all that.

'I'll take the little tyke with me,' Ruan said, 'but I'll need something in return.'

Joachim clenched his fists. It was an awful long time since he'd been so angry. Who the hell did Ruan think he was? Didn't he understand how lucky he'd been? Didn't he grasp the importance of what Joachim was offering him?

'Which is what?' Joachim said, rather shortly.

'A signed deposition from you and your Abbot that Golo Eck is dead and buried.'

Joachim sucked in his breath. He could have remonstrated, but in fact this was the first sensible thing to have come out of Ruan's mouth and had the unexpected upside that he could extract something further from Ruan at the same time.

'I'll have it for you first thing tomorrow. And at the same time I will have drawn up a document saying that you're taking Caro on as your indentured assistant, for as long as he agrees to the terms. And I want you to give George something for finding Golo and determining how he died. The cufflinks. Nothing more, nothing less. Will that suit?'

Ruan narrowed his eyes. He didn't like it at all but he really had no choice, and Joachim had a little knot of joy in his heart to see Ruan nod.

'We're agreed, then?' Joachim asked.

'We're agreed,' Ruan said with some reluctance, but he thrust out his hand and Joachim took it, and the two of them shared a hard and unpleasant handshake that had no good grace on either side.

'Until tomorrow morning, then,' Joachim said, turning abruptly on his heel and walking away before Ruan could change his mind.

He needed now to get to the Abbot before Ruan did, make sure all was above board, that the Abbot would hear Joachim's side and get the depositions drawn up so no one could dispute them.

When did people become so callous? he was thinking as he strode quickly away. But always, he knew, always had men been so. It was the reason he'd quit his previous life and joined the Servants in the first place. All he could hope now was that his son had not become one of them in between Joachim's going and his sending these two young souls to his door.

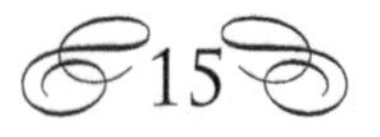

THE BATTLE OF NEW ROSS

IRELAND, 1798

Fergus hadn't thought for a moment he would sleep. Patently he did, because he awoke an hour or so before proper dawn, his back propped up against his log, Greta's voice speaking quietly to Malloy as they stood a few yards away from him.

'It's the English,' Greta was saying. 'There's more than we thought and already moving out from Waterford.'

Malloy's face was scrunched in annoyance. Until yesterday his scouts had told him there was only one garrison in the vicinity of New Ross and Malloy had upwards of three thousand men scattered here beneath the trees. But if another force of Loyalists got here too soon then the taking of New Ross was not going to be as easy as he'd previously supposed. And it was a place he wanted. A stronghold they had sore need of.

'Are you sure?' he asked, sounding more dismissive than he'd meant, disliking himself for blaming the messenger, especially when that messenger was Greta, who had never yet steered them wrong. 'My lads told me they were sticking to Waterford like flies on shit,' he felt compelled to say nonetheless, 'and that was only two days past. And we need New Ross. If we can get our hands on the town and hold it then the ones who've already gathered on Vinegar Hill will at least have somewhere else to go.'

Greta nodded. She knew as much, how the remnants of various bedraggled and demoralised cadres had retreated to the high ground of the hill above Enniskillen in the hope of getting enough of them back together to make a stand, if the worst came to the worst. She'd not been in Dublin long but it appeared the situation down here had deteriorated sharply. She was not one to bite her tongue. She'd been at this game as long as any of them, maybe not fighting directly, but just as integral a part.

'I'll stick around, give you warning when they're close.'

Malloy shook his head. 'No, Greta. We can't go changing our plans now. I need to get inside New Ross and you know you're needed down in Rosslare.'

Fergus couldn't help but overhear. He was twitchy. He was no master strategist but could see Malloy was right. If there really were a load of English soldiers on their way here then surely it would be better to be garrisoned within a town's walls than isolated out where they were, with only a few trees for cover. And any minute now they were going to ask him for his decision – run with Greta or stay and fight.

Everything in his head was telling him to run, that this wasn't his fight – except for that fact that it was. It really was his fight. He'd been away from Ireland for so long he'd lost touch with what was going on here. His father had fought in his own way, and maybe it was time Fergus did too. And it shouldn't be hard. Not from what he'd gathered from the mutterings of the men and what Malloy had said to Greta: only one garrison of Loyalists somewhere to the west of New Ross, and upwards of three thousand Irish rebels gathered here under Malloy's command. How hard could it be?

If he fought then Mick would take him to Mogue Kearns and Kearns would get him in touch with Wolfe Tone and maybe a way to help Golo get at the library in Paris before it was too late. His blood was jittering in his veins with awful anticipation. He was no fighting man, never had been, and oddly found himself wondering what Ruan would do in this same situation and was in no doubt what that would be. The thought that Ruan might be a braver man at his core than Fergus didn't bear consideration.

'Made a decision?' Greta asked without preamble.

Fergus looked up sharply, unaware that Malloy and Greta had approached, Fergus hesitating only a moment before he spoke, an audible tremor to his voice.

'I'm staying,' he said and Mick Malloy chuckled from somewhere deep in his throat, a noise more like a raven's caw than anything else, setting Fergus's nerves on edge.

'Very good, Scotsman,' Malloy said, 'and I'd ask a favour of you for Greta before we go in for the push.'

Fergus hauled himself to standing.

'Anything,' he said, attempting a smile at Greta that did not come out well.

'Folks here ain't that good with reading,' Malloy went on, 'and Greta gathered a few broadsheets on her travels. Would be a great help to her if you took some of 'em to the men, read out the good bits, give 'em a bit of encouragement before we head on in.'

His words were so casual that Fergus found himself nodding; the fact that they would be going into a pitched battle any moment receding into the background now he'd a task to do.

'Alright, of course,' Fergus said, Greta shoving a bundle of papers into his hand.

'Thanks,' she said, her face covered in muck and fire-soot, directing him towards one part of the camp. 'And they'll maybe want you to write some letters,' she added, giving him a pencil and a sheaf of dirty paper. 'Just in case, like.'

Fergus did as he was bid, and Greta was right. Most of the men weren't that interested in the news sheets he was bringing them but quite a few wanted letters they could carry in their jackets in case they never made it out. They were all of a kind, all addressed to wives, sons, fathers; all minimal, all stating the bare bones of what needed saying – that they loved them, that they were fighting for the cause they all believed in, that they would try to get home if they possibly could.

The few who had no family were in the main more interested in having actual news stories read out to them. Fergus picking carefully for the good, avoiding the bad. A short while in he was brought up short by a tiny article coming under the heading of *Lloyd's Register of Ships* that Fergus almost passed over.

'Oh my God,' he whispered, a name jagging itself off the page like a splinter. He struggled to focus on the tiny print marching across the paper like a colony of ants and had to use a shaking finger to keep his eyes going in a straight line. But the name was there all the same, and it cut him to the quick.

'Lost, the Collybuckie, departed from Port Glasgow and thence to Aberdeen and Hull and for the Continent. Caught thereafter in a storm off the coast of Holland. Said the captain, James Ferguson, from Vlissingen, 'We lost several passengers and crew, but thanks to God's Grace, and the villagers of the peninsular of Walcheren, and also to the Servants of the Sick who bide there, a great many more of us were saved than would otherwise have been done. My personal thanks must go to one Brother Joachim who was so instrumental in bringing me back to health after I was found, and who is even now caring for one of our passengers who did not fare so well as I did.'

Fergus read these lines several times over and felt sick, and then was sick, spewing up the viscous coffee made from ground acorns he'd been given earlier and the pieces of bread from the night before that were too hard and stale for his stomach to assimilate. It was impossible for him to believe that Golo and Ruan might be dead, that he was the only link left in the chain. The article gave hope, for obviously very few of either crew or passengers had been lost, but dread was rubbing through his bones and grinding at his heart. He took a few steps in one direction and then another, clutching the paper to his chest, trying to shake off the fear.

Time now to write his own letters, time now to put down everything he had so far encountered in Ireland in black and white. If, God forbid, neither Ruan nor Golo were still alive then someone somewhere might be caring enough of their cause to take up cudgels on their behalf, make sure all they'd worked for did not come to nought. He moved away from Malloy's soldiers and began to scribble his scrappy and paltry messages, hoping he'd got everything into them that needed saying.

Once done, he sought out Greta, his head a massed confusion like a thicket of brambles grown wild. He was committed to the fight, but if anything happened to him he needed these letters delivered. Greta was nowhere to be seen as he picked his way through the silent simmering crowds of prostrate men back up to the old log he'd slept next to. Still no Greta, only the burly outline of Mick Malloy standing with his back to Fergus and his men, gazing through his glass at the town of New Ross.

'I need to speak to Greta urgently,' Fergus said, grabbing impetuously at Malloy's shoulder as several church bells began to chime in the surrounding villages.

'Gone,' Mick said brusquely, brushing Fergus off like a wasp from a plate. 'Sent her off a couple of minutes back. If you've changed your mind, Scotsman, then you're too late. We're about to move.'

He turned then and pushed a hand hard at Fergus's chest where he was still clutching his batch of broadsheets.

'Jesus, man! Don't you know anything?' Malloy sounded exasperated, kept jabbing at Fergus with a calloused finger, perhaps not so sanguine about the coming battle as he'd first seemed. 'Get that lot buried beneath a load of leaves or branches. You want to tell everyone where we've been? Jesus!' Malloy repeated, shaking his head. 'Just get it done, then join the boys and tag yourself onto the lines.'

Malloy stomped away, barking out quiet orders to his men who had stood up at the sound of the bells and were loading their few muskets, taking up the shafts of their huge pikes in their strong hands, leaning the weight of them against their strong shoulders. Fergus looked quickly about him, spied the log. It took all his strength to roll it but he managed, thrusting the bundle of papers into the hollow beneath before releasing it, sparing time only to rip out the little paragraph on the wreck of the Collybuckie and scribbling a few words in the margin before tucking the paper into his pouch alongside ring and khipu.

Brother Joachim/Walcheren. Grimalkin/Deventer. Golo Eck & Ruan Peat/Loch Eck, Scotland.

Not much, but enough of an aide memoire in case his precious letters never got delivered, or he suffered some blow to the head that rendered him incapable of reasonable thought. And then a miracle happened. Greta emerged from the trees and appeared at his side.

'You looking for me?' she asked casually. 'Thought you might change your mind. Thought I'd better hang out a few minutes more for when you did.'

Fergus slipped back on his heels in his surprise, sprawling into the mud.

'Greta. Oh thank God!' Fergus scrabbled, blessing every inch of the girl who had so fortuitously materialised at his side.

'So, coming with?' Greta asked, raising a knowing eyebrow. Fergus righted himself, trying to muster some dignity.

'Actually no,' he said, brushing ineffectually at the mud on his clothes. 'No. I'm going to stay and fight.'

Greta took a step back and studied Fergus with interest.

'Really?' she asked, as if Fergus had said the most surprising thing she'd ever heard.

'Really,' Fergus confirmed, his head in a scramble, still teetering on the brink, knowing here was escape if only he chose to take it but, seeing Greta, knowing what she'd been doing the last few years, hearing the scepticism in her voice, he did the only thing he could.

'I'm sticking in with the others,' he said boldly. 'But will you do something for me before I go?'

Greta's smile wavered and she looked at Fergus with something approaching concern.

'You do know this means fighting, right? I mean real down and dirty fighting? I know Mick thinks it's going to be a pushover and he's usually right, but even so...'

'Just do this for me,' Fergus said, taking his letters, holding them out to Greta. 'Just take them. If you can get them to someone who can send them on then so be it. If not, you've lost nothing.'

Greta took the letters and looked at them.

'Ain't no people nor places I've ever heard of,' she said.

'I know that,' Fergus said. 'But please. If anyone can get them where they're meant to go then it's you...'

He got no further, Greta melting away into the trees as a burly hand shot out of nowhere and took Fergus by his collar.

'C'mere, you,' the man said, forcibly dragging Fergus into the lines getting ready to march from their glade, a pitchfork shoved into Fergus's hands once he was stood back upon his feet.

'Can't 'ave you going into battle without summat,' the man said, almost kindly. Fergus stared in disbelief at the paucity of the weapon he was to fight with, sweat prickling his skin, legs shaking as Malloy's voice rang out into the dawn.

'Men to the ready! You know what to do. Get to the gates, those who've been tasked. The rest to the square. Time's up, lads. Let's give those bastards a good thrashing!'

A soft roar rose from the crowd in acknowledgement. No going back now and Fergus fell into step with the rest, hands gripping at his pitchfork. Everything else fractured and slipped away so he hardly noticed where he was going or how he was getting there, nothing about this scenario seeming real. Surely he, Fergus Murtagh, secretary and scholar, could not possibly be going into battle – a real live battle – from which he might never return.

'Jesus and Mary, protect me; Jesus and Mary protect me...'

He whispered the words in time with his marching away from the oak copse and down the short hill and along a muddy lane, everyone jostling as ten men abreast were forced into five, other lines of men diverging away to east and west, starting to jog now, levelling their pikes. Fergus pushed along with one lot through the east gate of the town, running through the streets, more men splintering away to left and right as they went, disappearing down ginnels and lanes, not an English soldier in sight.

'First gate taken!' shouted a scrawny boy who ran up beside Fergus, shoving him out of the way to reach the man in command of Fergus's section, the news spreading quickly, passing from mouth to mouth, man to man, the mood swiftly becoming buoyant and excited, especially when another shout reached them:

'Second gate taken!'

The cry was up, Fergus pulled along by the victorious crowd into the square at the centre of New Ross, everyone bundling and tumbling in together so that it seemed less like a battle than a badly planned day out at a fair. Malloy himself suddenly appeared, hoisted onto the top of the pump at the centre of the square, kept aloft by men on either side.

'Third gate!' Malloy shouted in triumph. 'Third gate secured!'

Fergus closed his eyes. If this was fighting, it was a doddle.

'Thank God,' he breathed. 'Thank God.'

All gone to plan. Only one gate left to take and the town was secured, everyone locked safely inside its walls, any actual hand-to-hand carried out by other men in other places, enemy routed, only thing left being victory parades or whatever the United Irish did to celebrate a town brought under their command. Fergus's heart began to calm, his mind to settle like leaves after a storm. It was all going to be alright.

Until suddenly it wasn't, until suddenly other men in proper uniforms began spilling like angry hornets from every side street and ginnel into the square, emptying their guns into whoever was standing closest. Malloy suddenly tipped from the top of the pump as he began yelling, getting his men into a defensive circle. Fergus's bladder emptied of its own accord as he levelled his pitchfork like the men around him were doing with their eleven foot long pikestaffs.

Following their example he began jabbing randomly and without conscious thought into the maelstrom of absurdity that had overtaken him. Elation and horror surged through his veins when he actually hit hard enough to get his pitchfork into an enemy chest. The ensuing spurt of blood was immediate and shocking but not enough to stop him bracing his boot against the fallen man's ribcage, feeling the scrape of enemy bones against the tines as he pulled his pitchfork free, nothing in his head but the raw need for survival and the conviction that he did not want to die, not here, and not like this.

The world Ruan encountered after leaving Walcheren was unlike anything he'd seen. There were no mountains, not even hillocks, only the flat rolling out of a land that seemed to have been constructed entirely of straight lines. The waterways had no curves or meanders, the upbuilt banks on either side wide and flat enough to take a walkway, each carefully lined with trees to form an orderly corridor along which people walked in their square-toed clogs, or rode within their square-boarded wagons. The only height in this flat and waterlogged landscape came from the windmills, composed of more straight lines.

He wasn't happy to have Caro hopping along beside him, and early doors they'd made a tacit pact that neither would speak to the other unless it was absolutely necessary, and it seemed it wasn't necessary at all. Ruan had a few coins with him but he begrudged spending them, especially on Caro, so they spent their nights sleeping rough. The weather was in their favour, warm and balmy, little wind once they'd cleared the peninsula and come inland sufficiently to escape the fog that rolled in from the sea the first two nights when all they could see were the tops of the trees that marked out the lanes beside the waterways they were following. Some of these had lamps strung on lines between the trees and Ruan took some pleasure – when he encountered them – in forcing Caro to keep pace as Ruan chose to walk on into the night because of them. He was hoping Caro would give up the ghost and flit himself off to Vlissingen before they left the peninsula, but Caro was made of sterner stuff. Nor had Joachim entirely abandoned Caro to Ruan's less than robust sense of care, explaining in detail the contract of indenture he and the Abbot had drawn up that was levied in Caro's favour. Joachim had taken the unusual step of giving Caro his own copy of this contract, and a personal letter from Joachim himself.

'If you can stick it out to Deventer,' Joachim told Caro, 'then I want you to present your copy of the contract, along with my letter, to Hendrik Grimalkin. He's the man I'm sending you both to. Hendrik is my son – was my son, still is my son – and he's a good man, Caro. He'll see you right.'

And so Caro stuck it out, not that Ruan was making it easy. Ruan was taller and stronger and made certain to keep his pace a little faster than Caro found comfortable, so that by the end of every day Caro had to take a sudden sprint – just when he was most tired – as Ruan ducked himself out of view a couple hundred yards ahead to bivouac beneath some hedge or barn for their night's rest, and no companionable fires or chats once they bedded themselves down.

The one thing that surprised Caro was that each and every night Ruan would take out Golo's book, *Behemoths, and other Wonders of the Deep,* and read through its pages until there was no more light by which to see. Caro didn't know why Ruan did this. He hoped it was for the same reason Caro would have done, and that Ruan was missing Golo. He hoped this because a glimmer of his former optimism was threading its way back into his bones, because if Ruan really did miss Golo then maybe he wasn't bad through and through, and maybe one day Caro would wake up to find that Ruan had turned into Golo, and then everything would be as alright as Caro had always hoped it would.

The town of New Ross thundered and thrashed with the clash of metal on metal and boots on the ground and muskets blasting, yells and screams from every side, the shouting of orders and counter orders. Every citizen still in abode barricaded themselves into home and hearth, hands held against their ears. Malloy's men were corralled inside the square, victim to better armed men, better strategists who despite being far fewer in number had out-thought them to a humiliating degree.

Red jackets were waiting for the moment to pour in through the fourth unsecured gate at the other end of town in a fast and predetermined order designed to trap the rebels in the centre of New Ross before opening fire. First line down on one knee letting rip while the line behind them took aim, first line falling back to reload while the second took over; a murderous wave that was terrifying and deafening, rolling on like an unstoppable tide, cutting down Malloy's men who were standing behind the huge length of their pikes that were useless against an enemy armed such as this; the smoke from English muskets so thick that the men in the square soon began to choke, unable to see properly, pikes levelled but no idea who they were levelled at, everyone panicking, unable to understand how their victory had so suddenly spiralled into obvious defeat.

'Hold fast!' Malloy was shouting at his ruined lines of men, all of them forgetting how to keep formation, the outer circle already shot down and bleeding out onto the streets making it more difficult for the ones behind them to attack. Malloy kept up his shouting, tried to keep his men in order, reposition them so that those with pikes were on the outside, charging into the streets and ginnels with their weapons held horizontal and dangerous. He saw his men tripping and falling over one other, skidding and slithering on the blood and guts of the comrades who'd already had their stomachs, arms, necks and brains blown off or out. The stench of sweat and fear and gunpowder was in his nose, in his throat, so much smoke his eyes were burning. Only one garrison of English against his three thousand men, but pikes and pitchforks could not face down massed English muskets, and certainly not when more were coming on behind.

'Retreat!' Malloy shouted. 'Everyone retreat!'

The order couldn't come soon enough for Fergus, who was pulled back with the rest like a pebble on an ebbing tide, the only reason any of them getting out at all being that the first gate they'd taken was still secured. Barely one hour after they came in the Irish were stumbling back out again, scrambling and running for their lives, abandoning the cumbersome pikes that kept tripping them up. They were useless now, dropped alongside their useless dead as the survivors ran for the hills, Fergus with them, clutching at his chest, two ribs broken. The pain was desperate and sharp but not as desperate and sharp as his need to get away.

Estimated rebel deaths at the Battle of New Ross: almost half their number. One thousand, four hundred and sixty eight, by Malloy's later count; all left to rot in the early summer sun on the streets of New Ross.

Some were later buried, most kicked into the waters of the River Barrow that obligingly carried off their carcasses, clogging up the one against the other at its bends, snagging on tree roots and boulders, straddling over weirs and shallows. There were a few loyalists too – but only a very few – dotted in amongst those of the insurgents, stinking and rotting all the same.

A small chance of survival for the wounded who managed to drag themselves out, or were dragged out by their bloody collars by their bloody comrades, quickly ensconced in a makeshift hospital in a nearby barn, the end of last year's straw making do as pallets. There'd been nothing to give them but encouragement and water and tying up the holes in their bodies with strips of their own clothes. Surviving then, until the English coming in from Waterford got word from their scouts what they were about, and the barn swiftly barricaded and set alight, the smoke and flames of the communal funeral pyre funnelling up into the afternoon air, singeing the wings of the rooks and crows who blackened the sky, drawn in their thousands by the delicious scents of so many dead and dying in so small a place. It was watched from the oak knoll by Malloy, Fergus and the other survivors, sickened to the heart by such cruelty and waste, men wanting to fling themselves down the hillock to attempt a pointless rescue had not Malloy's barking held them back.

'It will not go unpunished,' Malloy said later, his anger as hot and vicious as the flames that were eating his men alive half a mile distant and nothing he could do to save them. By Christ and His Holy Mother, Malloy swore they would be avenged.

There was no victory here, and his men would need to be redeployed the moment night came down to hide their going off to Vinegar Hill to join the rest of the defeated. But Mick would not go with them. He had other ideas, none of them good, and Fergus – though he didn't know it yet – would have his part to play.

BEHEMOTHS, AND THE WONDERS OF THE DEEP

WALCHEREN, HOLLAND

It came as a surprise to Ruan, though not to Caro, that the complicated network of ostlers and horse-rent so common in Scotland was in little evidence here. Rivers and canals took the place of roads, folk jumping on and off the many flat-bottomed barges that coursed their slow and ponderous lengths. Nothing like Scottish rivers, that tumbled hurriedly down the sides of mountains to empty themselves gratefully into the peace of a loch before spilling on just as eagerly out the other side.

Three days in, and hardly a word had passed between them. Ruan bought bread and the strangely smooth and waxy stuff they called cheese hereabouts, shoving some of it at Caro, who nodded his thanks. Caro, for his part, steered Ruan right when he was about to go in some catastrophically wrong direction. Ruan knew the language, but spoke with an antiquated accent that many of the folk he asked directions from completely misunderstood. Whenever Caro pointed out a mistake Ruan would sigh deeply.

'Do you think I'm an idiot?' he would say, Caro keeping his mouth zipped because yes, he did think Ruan was an idiot, but at least he was an idiot who took Caro's directions, not that he ever thanked him for it.

Once they'd passed Zutphen, Caro mentioned casually that they could probably save themselves a deal of time by taking one of the vessels going up the Ijsseldyk River that went directly into the heart of Deventer.

'Don't you think I know that?' Ruan replied testily.

The fact that he didn't know it irked him, not that he was going to let Caro see it. But he took up the boy's suggestion and managed to hail one of the fishing boats that plied its length, happy to take passengers for a few coins. Even then Caro hadn't been able to resist butting in. The fact that Caro managed to bargain the price of their passage down to half of what had first been suggested didn't impress Ruan a whit. Effectively he'd saved Ruan the same amount Ruan had had to shell out to keep Caro in food on their journey, so that was enough to call it quits. He did reward Caro with a short nod of his head, which Ruan deemed generous in the circumstances.

The barque they alighted on had two triangular-shaped sails, one huge – draped like a theatre drop-curtain drawn in at its apex – the other much smaller, narrower and taut, leaning in towards the centre of the boat. Ruan had never seen the like, and he toyed with the idea that maybe he should start writing some of these experiences down. Travel books did well these days, and if he went on as he meant to do then maybe there was a book in it for him to write.

He was aware of Golo's copy of *Behemoths, and other Wonders of the Deep* that was nestled inside his pocket. He'd been looking at it ever since they'd left the Servants, not for its actual content but because of the notes Golo had obviously spent his days at sea scribbling feverishly into its margins: an abbreviated history of the Lynx. Ruan knew it the moment he'd started flicking through its pages. Not that he cared about the Lynx. As far as he was concerned that chapter of his life was over and done with, and thank God for it. But he studied it anyway because, for all his truculence and bad humour, the pain of losing Golo was becoming greater with every passing day. He didn't understand why, nor did he particularly want to, but he found that by trying to interpret Golo's miniscule writing in the margins of Caro's book he was comforted, as if Golo hadn't gone away at all but was merely waiting around the next corner; that someday soon he would leap out and tell Ruan it had all been a big mistake and here he was again, and no matter Ruan's short-fallings he was proud of what Ruan had, or would, become.

It was ridiculous, Ruan knew. Golo was never going to be proud of him. Golo had only known this blighted Caro for a week but in that time the boy had obviously wormed his way into the place Golo had previously kept for Ruan. His nature was disinclined to harbour regret but regret was there all the same, and the only way Ruan knew to accommodate it was by accusation. How dare Golo write all his secrets in this little book and then give it freely to a nobody like Caro? The more Ruan read of the notes the more incensed he became. This was the Lynx, for Christ's sake! Golo's abiding passion, a legacy rightly Ruan's and no one else's.

He was also regretting giving up the ring that had belonged to his ancestor. Ruan had never worn it, never valued it. He'd allowed Golo to give it to Fergus as part of his monumentally stupid plan of sending Fergus to Ireland to meet a man who might or might not have a part of the Lynx library, and who might or might not be able to help in securing the part that was France. He had Golo's own ring, taken from Golo's dead finger, but it was too big to fit onto any of his own, even if he could have brought himself to do so.

The water of the river flattened out, and the boat soon had them the last few miles towards Deventer where they disembarked at a small landing stage beyond a bridge. The barge didn't actually stop, only slowed down long enough for its two passengers to leap from barge to jetty, saved from a ducking by the men on the landward side catching at their outstretched arms and pulling them in, depositing both like ungainly fish.

Exhilarated, Ruan began to laugh and, before he could stop himself, he lavished a great big smile upon his companion and Caro began to laugh too, a little manically, as if this was the start of something new. His newfound joy diminished somewhat once they were back on their way, Ruan resuming his sullen attitude, his too fast walking, Caro having to jog most of the length of a lane called the Zandpoort to catch him up. But once they'd reached The Brink, the huge plaza that pulsed away at the heart of Deventer, Ruan finally stopped and sat down on one of the stone benches there and Caro sat down beside him, catching his breath.

They were surrounded by market stalls, bustle and noise. Ruan looked around him, spotting the ancient Weigh House opposite, a squarish building – of course it was – with a square outside-staircase leading to a square balcony above its solemn gates. Most impressive was the massive copper cauldron that hung from the Weigh House wall, the large scroll emblazoned beneath it declaring that here was where counterfeiters would meet their end, their living skin boiled right off their bones.

Now that would go well in my forthcoming publication, Ruan thought, and also made a mental note of the tall, flat-faced buildings on the opposite side of the plaza. They had the weird property of seeming wider at the top than at the bottom, all bearing large rectangular windows, several overhung by strange signs – *The Three Golden Herrings*, for one, though no explanation given for what it might mean. Other houses carried curious inscriptions upon their blank facades in the form of mottos or pithy, playful sayings. It was all so strange that Ruan broke his customary silence.

'Ever seen anything like this?' he asked the air, though it was Caro who answered.

'Never!' Caro replied with enthusiasm. 'And look over there, between the fish seller and the dumpling monger. Isn't that Korte Bischopstraat, where Brother Joachim said we should go?'

Ruan's good humour soured back into his habitual irritation with the boy. Why did this blasted Caro always feel the need to take the upper hand? Ruan shook his head and stood up abruptly.

'Well then, Mr Man, who always has to wear the cleverest clogs,' Ruan said, injecting every word with such venom that Caro winced. He couldn't seem to get anything right. Just when things had been going so well he'd gone and spoiled it again.

From now on, he told himself, *just button up.*

They exited The Brink and walked in silence up the narrow ginnel that was Korte Bischopstraat, turning right and left according to Brother Joachim's instructions. Finally they emerged onto The Singel – a promenade with a lagoon-like canal on its farthest side marking the boundary between the oldest part of the city and the new. The Singel was wide, the houses on The Brink's side tall and narrow, several thin storeys going up into the sky, crowded but neat, like teeth in a well-kept jaw. None of the houses had names or numbers, so it took them a while to find the one they were looking for.

'It's got a bell outside,' Joachim had told them, 'like off a ship, and a bell-pull in the shape of a lion's paw.'

Enough description for Ruan and Caro to go by, and they went up The Singel looking at every door until they found the one they wanted. Ruan was unaccountably nervous, made more so because

Caro was jiggling behind him like a flea on a hot plate.

Goddamn children, he thought. *Why is it not a one of them can ever keep still?*

He was unaware of the extra letter Caro was carrying, nor that it might release the two of them from the contract Joachim had forced Ruan to sign. If he had, he too would have been jumping for joy, as Caro was now. Instead he was irritated all over again and tugged so hard at the lion's paw that the ship's bell rang and reverberated as if it was about to bring the house down. Ruan involuntarily went back down one of the short steps that led from pavement to door.

After half a minute the door opened to reveal a small woman tightly wound in black, her hair scraped back from her face and bound in a neat mignonette at the nape of her neck. The only relief given to this stern exterior came from the bright white pinafore edged with two inches of intricate lacework at its base.

'Can I help you?' she asked, and Ruan went back up the step, took off his tattered hat and bowed briefly, not considering for a moment that he looked more like a rag merchant than the highborn person he considered himself to be.

'I'm here to see Mijnheer Grimalkin,' Ruan said in his oddly formal Dutch, taught to him by Golo, already by then fifty years out of date. 'Sent by recommendation of his father, Joachim.'

The woman looked at Ruan blankly, and then a sudden colour suffused her neck above her high-buttoned collar and she raised a hand, waving them in.

'I'm so sorry,' she said. 'But of course, you are very welcome.'

She led them into a hallway that was pleasantly cool, if a little dark, every wall panelled with polished wood, and the floor likewise. She motioned them to a pair of chairs that sat near the base of a narrow staircase.

'Please sit, please sit,' she said. 'Let me get you some bread, and I've mutton stew too, if you'll give me leave to heat it through.'

Ruan threw a puzzled glance at the woman but she was already turning away.

'We've no need of bread, Mevrouw,' he said hurriedly. 'I'm here rather to see Mijnheer Hendrik Grimalkin. It's of some importance, or I would not ask.'

The woman stopped her quick sweep towards her kitchen domain and turned back.

'Are you not mendicants of the Order, then?' she asked, surprised. 'In need of repast?'

Ruan creased his brows, shuffled his feet, looking down as he did so to see his dirty, salt-rimmed boots, the poor quality of his trousers – cast-offs from the Servants, his own ruined by the storm and the rescue from the Collybuckie – and suddenly understood.

'Oh no, Mevrouw, you misunderstand. We're not from the Order at all. We were shipwrecked by Walcheren and sent here by Brother Joachim, to his son.'

The woman didn't move, except to lift a hand to her throat.

'Brother...Joachim...sent you here to meet his son?' she asked with obvious hesitation. Ruan clicked his tongue. He couldn't understand why the woman was being so obtuse. It was an obvious enough request, and here she was treating them like beggars at her door.

'Grimalkin,' Ruan said loudly. 'I'm not mistaken. This is where I was sent, and this is why I'm here, and I will not leave until I see him.'

The little woman in her black dress and white pinafore blinked. She wasn't sure she liked this interruption to her calm kingdom and took a few moments before she spoke, her voice hardened, knowing she had the upper hand, whatever this upstart in his ragged clothes thought was going on.

‘Well then,’ she said, after a few moments. ‘I will thank you to bide here while I ask my husband if he is able to entertain visitors.’

Ruan bristled and she noticed it but was not inclined to pander to the brash young interloper taking up room in her lobby. Instead, she cast a brief glance at his younger companion who had sat on his seat at her command and was now swinging his legs back and forth, as if he was bursting to add something to the discussion, but didn’t have the nerve.

‘I presume you have names?’ Mevrouw Grimalkin asked, looking not at Ruan but at Caro.

‘Mine is Ruan Peat,’ Ruan spoke up in a moment, needled by the woman’s inability to grasp how important his visit was. ‘And I’ll thank you to remember it.’

The moment these last words left his lips Ruan knew he’d made a strategic error. The woman appraised him without warmth, before turning her gaze back to Caro.

‘And you. What is your name?’

Caro stopped swinging his legs now he’d been asked a direct question. He glanced at Ruan, saw the thunder gathering on his brow and knew this was not someone he could bide with any longer that he had to. Abuse on ship was one thing. He hadn’t expected it when he’d started out but was somewhat inured to it after several years, and by Christ he wasn’t going back if he could help it, but all this shite with Ruan Peat ignoring him and bullying him was about as much as he could take. Sea or poverty had been his choices up until now, but he had Brother Joachim’s letter of endorsement in his pocket and here was the woman to whom it should be delivered, and she’d already noticed he was a person, an actual person with a name.

‘Caro,’ he whispered. ‘My name is Caro, and if it’s not too late to ask, I’d really like some of that mutton stew. I’ve a stomach hollow enough to swallow an ox.’

BURNING BARNS, BURNING MEN

Fergus never understood what it was about this particular battle of New Ross that led to such brutality, but brutality there was, and of a type he'd never before experienced. The battle itself had been bad enough, and he'd done things in the awfulness of the moment that he'd never believed he was capable of. Less than twenty minutes after they'd run for their retreat they heard guns firing in the square, the Loyalist garrison tidying up and shooting dead any of their enemy still breathing on the streets of New Ross.

When an escapee from the town joined their forces they learned that things were worse than they'd supposed and that many of those shots did for the remaining inhabitants of the town, condemned as collaborators by the mere fact of their being there when the battle had taken place. Nor did it take them long to understand what soon happened to the makeshift hospital that was housing the sick and injured rebels dragged from the field of battle. They all saw the barn going up in flames, every last person in it caught like hedgehogs in a woodpile, no possibility of escape. It was cruelty beyond compare and had the inevitable consequence of Malloy's men retaliating in kind, executing the few captive prisoners they had at their disposal as well as returning the favour and burning alive several Loyalist sick housed in their own little hospital in nearby Scullabogue.

Too much for Bagenal Harvey, short-time Commander-in-Chief of the United Irish, a man co-opted and never in love with the cause - sprung from Wexford gaol by Malloy's men partly in response to the unreasonable execution of Mordeciah Crook and the burning down of him and his house - Bagenal Harvey resigning his commission a bare two weeks after being gifted it, taking to his heels, fleeing the whole mess as fast as he could, the repercussions of New Ross too much to deal with, leaving Malloy and his men – and the whole of the United Irish – without direction or a nominal leader.

Malloy received the news with equanimity. The only hint on his face of his seething anger at this betrayal was the unnerving worsening of his squint, his bad eye drifting a few millimetres left of centre and staying there. He'd already instructed his men to get out as soon as darkness fell.

'All of you off to Vinegar Hill,' he told them, holding up his hands to stop the inevitable protests. 'We need to consider our options, consolidate our troops, and Vinegar Hill is the place to do it. Set off as soon as you're able. Small groups, going different ways. Keep clear of any roads south. Don't want any of you bumping into the rest of the Loyalists coming up from Waterford.'

'What about you?' someone asked. 'Where are you going?'

'I'll be with you shortly,' Malloy assured them, 'just as soon as I've taken care of a small matter here that you've none of you to be minded with.'

'If you're staying then I'm staying,' piped up one voice, followed by several others mimicking his intent.

'No,' Mick said with absolute decision. 'You're not. The only men I want staying with me I've already told.'

There was a small ripple through the crowd at this command but no one openly dissented. Despite the havoc and devastation of New Ross everyone trusted Malloy implicitly and the moment night fell groups of men began slithering from their knoll, breaking away in twos and threes into the dark countryside. Fergus was not amongst them. He tried hard, but no one wanted an unknown stranger hanging on their tails and would surely kill him if he tried to follow.

His only option was to head off alone, with no idea of which way to go or whom he could trust. He knew he most likely wouldn't last twenty four hours without being arrested or murdered. He needed a plan and he needed it quick and an idea began to form when he inadvertently overheard Mick's conversation with the few men he'd chosen to stay behind, discussing the Bagenal Harvey situation.

'We should have left that bastard lawyer to rot in gaol,' Malloy muttered through clenched teeth. 'Who else knows about this?' he asked the burly man who had brought him the news, the same burly man who had shoved Fergus so viciously in the back when he'd first arrived.

'No one, Mick. Just us few and the man from Three Rocks who came straightaway once he knew Harvey had crept off with that pal of his, Colclough. Gone half a day already, heading for the Saltee Isles if no one stops him.'

'Right then,' Mick said. 'Let's keep it that way. Last thing we need is this getting out. Fecking lawyers. Got more slip than eels.'

Fergus hadn't intended to listen, far more concerned with how to extricate himself from this pile of shit he'd inadvertently dug himself into. It was all too hard and precarious. Wolfe Tone be damned. As much as Golo loved the Lynx he surely wouldn't want Fergus risking his life for it, certainly not more than he'd already done. He'd write another letter telling Wolfe Tone all that had happened, tug on childhood sympathies, give the letter to Mick Malloy to do with whatever he would, but that was as far as Fergus was going.

What he needed now was out and soon as he was able. The most pressing concern for him was not what was going on with the United Irish but finding out whether Golo and Ruan were still alive. Jesus, he felt alone, a lost pigeon looking for signs of home who would have given anything, anything in the world, to be back there again. And then he saw his chance. Malloy was talking about Bagenal Harvey, that he was a lawyer and on the run.

Fergus stood up, took a few steps through the trees, but he was no silent forest creature and within moments he was manhandled to the ground, his ribs moving an agony in his chest so he could hardly breathe.

'Jesus hell,' Malloy was bearing his teeth as Fergus tried to lift his face into the small circle of light cast by several candles shoved into the earth. Mick indicated to his henchman to let Fergus go, which he did. Fergus gasping greedily at the air.

'What the feck are you still here for, Scotsman?' Malloy asked. 'This is a private conversation we're having.'

Fergus blenched, discovered before he'd had time to properly think his one plan out.

'You said if I fought then you'd help me,' he croaked, 'and now I think I can maybe help you too,' at which pronouncement Mick's bad eye did a further swerve to the left, so much so that Fergus was unsure whether the man was looking at him or someone over his shoulder.

'And what the feck do you think you can do?' Mick growled.

Fergus's blood began to hammer in this throat, his head telling him this was a really bad idea, his blood telling him it was the only way out. He found his voice, began to speak.

'Bagenal Harvey's a lawyer. My father was a lawyer. Maybe I can reason with him.'

Malloy snorted, though whether in approbation or disbelief Fergus didn't wait to find out.

'I'm just saying,' Fergus went on quickly, 'that I know lawyers through and through, and maybe I can bring this Bagenal Harvey back to you before anyone knows he's gone.'

'And how on earth could you do that, Scotsman?' Mick's voice was sceptical. 'The man's obviously got a liver yellower than a side of cheese, and nothing you can do about that.'

'You don't understand,' Fergus said. 'Surely when he became your Commander-in-Chief he signed some papers to that effect, and maybe that's enough for me to coerce him into returning.'

Mick Malloy's entire body visibly tensed and Fergus thought all was up. Mick's swiftest, surest course of action would be get shot of him once and for all, strangle the life out of him and leave him behind. But Malloy did the unexpected and gave Fergus a chance.

'You're right enough on both counts. I promised you help if you fought, and you did, so what are you asking me to do?'

Fergus swallowed, answering as succinctly as he could.

'I'm asking you give me leave to go after him. After Bagenal Harvey. Maybe I can catch him up, maybe I can't. But if I do then I'll make damn sure he comes back again. In return I want directions, places I can go, strategies to keep myself safe.'

It sounded weak, even to Fergus, and Mick Malloy was not taken in.

'And how do I know,' Malloy asked, 'that you're not just running away because things have gone badly?'

Fergus hesitated, but not too long, and then took out his pouch and offered it over.

'Because of this,' Fergus said. 'You know what I offered Greta to help with your cause. She doesn't know exactly how it works but she's smart, she'll figure it out. Get it to her or your Mogue Kearns and we'll call it quits.'

Mick stared at the pouch and then at Fergus.

'And just what is it?' he asked, making no move to take the pouch though Fergus continued to hold it out to him. Fergus shook his head.

'I can't explain it to you, not now, not in the dark. But Greta knows enough. Get it to Greta.'

Malloy narrowed his eyes, his men shuffling their feet behind him.

'We need to get moving, boss,' one of them said, casting an anxious eye about him. 'Darkest hour's almost on us.'

Malloy weighed up the odds and added his own rider in his head. He and his men had work to do and he saw that Fergus could indeed be of help, if not of the sort he was offering.

'Agreed,' he said, taking the pouch and tucking it carelessly into a pocket, Fergus letting out an audible sigh of relief.

'And you'll give me directions? Safe places to go?'

'I will,' Mick said. 'We know Harvey is heading to the Saltee Islands and if you're true to your word in finding him then I can steer you right.'

'Alright then,' Fergus said, and after a brief discussion - Fergus making a rudimentary map in his head about where he should go - he was ready to depart.

'You'll be needing to start by going through Scullabogue,' Malloy said, nodding his head towards the tiny village that lay a mile or so to their right.

Fergus frowned. 'Isn't that where…'

'It is,' Malloy cut him off, 'but it's the quickest way out, and there's only one or two soldiers there. You still up for it?'

Fergus swallowed but nodded, Mick giving Fergus a hard slap on the back that was the closest thing to encouragement he could muster. He wasn't going to tell Fergus the real reason for sending him unprotected through the dark streets of Scullabogue, no more would he have told a terrier he sent into a badger set to sniff the brockies out. War was war after all, and more often than not the terriers got out the other side alive.

Caro's belly was round as a pumpkin, Louisa Grimalkin taking discreet pleasure in seeing the ragged boy fill himself full. He was respectful, didn't dive in like a beggar, but took each spoonful slowly, closing his eyes, licking his lips, complimenting her on how well it tasted.

'Ain't eaten mutton stew in I don't know how long,' Caro said, Louisa smiling, which was more than could be said for her husband upstairs once she'd finally consented to take Ruan Peat up to see him.

She gave no introduction except to announce Ruan's name, and couldn't help enjoying the immediate look of discomfort on the whippersnapper's face when her husband looked up from his desk in obvious annoyance. He was a scholar right down to the marrow who hated having anyone invade his private chambers. Fine at the library – there it was expected – but not here, not in the private sanctum of his home, as well she knew.

Hendrik had been born to the part, being tall and thin, with a face that might have been mistaken for the business end of a hatchet. Sharp and stern were the words most often employed to describe her husband's features, stern and dry as a sea-bleached stick. He looked so incredibly unlike his father that Ruan had difficulty seeing any resemblance at all, and was so unnerved he couldn't get his words out.

'What the devil do you want?' Grimalkin was quiet spoken, with an undertow of authority that meant he hardly ever needed to raise his voice to get himself heard. Indeed, he had never shouted in his entire life, not since he was a boy.

Ruan cleared his throat. He'd been expecting to be welcomed with open arms, from father to son, assumed everything thereafter would go smoothly: off to the bank to get some money; off to the lawyers to formalise the declaration of Golo's death and then away he would be, free and clear. The reality was so different that Ruan's skin prickled with trepidation.

'Your father, Joachim, sent me,' Ruan managed to get out through the constriction in his throat, his previous bluster dissipated like dandelion seed on the wind. The silence that followed this announcement gave him to understand what people meant when they spoke of quaking in their boots.

'My father,' Hendrik Grimalkin finally said, his voice hard and brusque, hands clenching into tight white fists on the table before him. 'Well, boy? What of him?'

Another short silence as Ruan tried to pull together the words he needed. He'd never felt so intimidated, nor so defenceless. He needed this man's help. Jesus, he needed all the help he could get. He'd not quite grasped the enormity of the plight he was in, not until now.

'I was…shipwrecked off of… Walcheren,' he began slowly, hesitantly, trying to fit together what he needed to say. 'And Joachim's a brother at the Servants of the Sick there, as I'm sure you know…'

Ruan's little speech trailed off because it was obvious even to him, who was no connoisseur of other people's emotional reactions, that this was news to Hendrik Grimalkin. Hendrik stood up so suddenly that his chair scraped back across the wooden floor, two sharp lines of varnish scratched out in its wake.

'He does many good deeds there,' Ruan ploughed on. 'He looked after me and my…' Ruan searched for the word. He wanted to say father but that was not quite right, and it was palpably obvious that getting it right in this situation was what he needed to do. '… my guardian,' he grasped the word. 'His name is Golo Eck, and I believe…it's possible certainly…that you may have corresponded with him.'

This last he'd plucked out of the air for he'd no idea who Hendrik was or whether or not he was part of Golo's extended network of supporters. Hendrik Grimalkin gave no clue. He merely stared hard at Ruan Peat before moving towards the window that looked out over the Singel and the slow-moving waters of the lagoon beyond. He turned his back on his visitor for such a long silence that Ruan dared not move. His future life was hanging in the balance. He'd no idea where to go if things here didn't pan out. He had a terrible itch on his nose but didn't want to disrupt whatever was going on by scratching it. He distracted himself by casting his eyes over the many books on the many shelves in the room, noting how similar they were to the ones in Golo's library. There was the map of the world made by Aaron Arrowsmith a few years before, volumes of the latest works of eminent philosophers, philologists and mathematicians in Dutch, English, German and Latin; other tomes on natural history and botany.

The room was so like Golo's that Ruan's eyes unexpectedly welled up with the memory and, without conscious thought, he put his hand up to brush away the drops that were forming on his eyelashes, blurring his sight. The sudden movement was apparently sensed by the black streak of Grimalkin at the window who chose that moment to turn back to his visitor. Who was the most discombobulated was hard to say, both recognising, at the same moment, this shared weakness at remembrance of times past.

'Sit,' Grimalkin said succinctly, taking his own advice, moving his chair back to its accustomed place behind his desk, grimacing at the thin lines scoured into the varnish of the wood and choosing instead to sit himself down in one of the two leather armchairs placed about the cold and empty fireplace.

'You must excuse my rudeness,' Hendrik Grimalkin said, as Ruan subsided into the opposite chair. 'Only it's such a long time since I've heard any mention of my father. He joined the Order almost a quarter century and half a lifetime ago, and I wasn't even aware of the name he'd taken, let alone where he might be now. If truth be told, the Order served him as a coffin as far as the family was concerned and to hear of him now, well, it has been a bit of a shock.'

Hendrik was not a man given to agitation, nor to drink, but the sudden occurrence of the first demanded the second. He stood up briefly and went to a cupboard, opened it, removed a bottle and two glasses, placing all three on the small table beside his chair, pouring out a hefty swig of grappa for them both.

'To the renascence of those lost to us,' he said in toast, drinking the spirit down in one, refilling his glass before Ruan touched his own. 'Let's start again. Your name, you said was…'

'Ruan Peat,' Ruan gladly supplied the information.

The tide had turned, he could feel it, and all because he'd allowed a few tears to drop in memory of Golo Eck. He breathed deeply, and out it all came: their leaving Scotland in search of the lost library of the Lynx, the shipwreck, his survival, Golo's death. He didn't add any details, didn't mention Fergus at all, nor George's suspicions about how Golo had died. But he did talk a little of Joachim, Grimalkin's father, and how diligently he'd cared for both

Ruan in his sickness and Golo's body, arranging the burial of the latter before directing Ruan to his son for the help he so obviously needed.

'He always was a caring man,' Grimalkin said, swilling his third grappa around his glass. 'Your Joachim. My father. He almost ruined the family business by doing other people right. We have a printing impress, still do, no thanks to him. He was forever giving away the merchandise to scholars who couldn't rub two groats together. Hang the money, that's what he used to say, the pursuit of knowledge is far more important than lining the coffers of dull men who already have too much.'

Hendrik Grimalkin let out a short bark that might have been laughter, but Ruan didn't interrupt. He wasn't much interested in what this Grimalkin man was saying. His mind was wandering to the mutton stew whose warms scents had drifted up the stairs behind him. His stomach was already growling and was not being helped by the small sips of grappa he was forcing himself to imbibe, which went down his throat like paint stripper.

Let the man talk, he was thinking. *Let the man talk all he wants if he'll give me the help I need.* He supressed a sigh as Hendrik Grimalkin proceeded to do exactly that.

'Sadly those dull men, as he called them – the shareholders – didn't see it that way, and the moment I came of age they forced my father to resign his office of directorship in my favour, and how glad he was to hear the news!'

Ruan could sympathise with the shareholders. He'd have done exactly the same in their place. Whether the son agreed with this decision was undecided, as Grimalkin made no more pretence and removed a large handkerchief from his pocket and wiped his tired grey eyes before starting up again on the apparently interminable story of his family history.

'Precisely three days later,' Grimalkin continued, his tongue loosened by the alcohol and the sudden influx of memories this visitor had brought in with him when he stepped over the threshold, 'my father vacated the family home – this home – taking nothing with him but the clothes he stood up in, leaving behind a bundle of documents signing all his interests over to me and a short note telling us he was off to join the Servants of the Sick.

'And that was the last we heard of him, from that day to this. Twenty four years ago that was. He left us on the feast day of St Camillus. My mother always said we should have seen it coming, and she was right in her way. He always held that feast day in the highest regard, revering Camillus above the other saints of the pantheon. It came from his time fighting in the Seven Years War, although he was only at the very start of it, on the Austrian side, stationed on the sunken road between the Morellbach brook and the village of Lobosik, when the Prussians attacked. He never told us much, only that it was a terrible day, one born in fog and dying in fire, along with uppermost of five thousand men.

'That more didn't go the same way was due entirely to the monks of the monastery of St Camillus near Lobosik who came out of their walls the whole day of the battle, despite the constant firing of artillery from both sides. Their men went in under cover of the dense mist that never left, dragging away the wounded, no matter their allegiance, to their hospital. My father amongst them.

'He always had a soft spot for mist and fog, did my father, precisely because of it, and so it seems fitting in some way that you're telling me he now resides on the very edge of the Walcheren Peninsula, where fog and mist must be a daily occurrence...'

Hendrik Grimalkin's voice trailed away, to Ruan's profound relief.

It was an endemic trait of his personality that he didn't care greatly about other people or their feelings unless they impinged directly upon himself. He had begun to fidget during Hendrik's talking, not that he was aware of it. His left leg was jigging up and down and he was winding his thumbs around and around themselves in circles where he had interlaced his fingers upon his lap.

Hendrik noticed, blinked in annoyance, embarrassed and humiliated that he'd spoken out his deepest secrets to someone who so plainly didn't give a damn. The only reason he didn't chuck the young tyke straight back out into the Singel was because of Golo Eck, because it was a name he knew well and had the highest regard for.

'Well,' he said curtly. 'Get yourself down to Louisa. She'll arrange food and a bed for the night and we'll discuss your situation in the morning. Good afternoon, sir.'

Hendrik stood up, went back to his desk and sat down, turning his attention to the papers neatly laid upon its surface. Ruan was out of his seat with an alacrity that bordered on the rude, and Hendrik felt his teeth grinding together as he clenched shut his jaw. Frugality with words had always been his way until today, and he would not let the lad go without a last parting shot.

'I will help you, but only because of Golo Eck,' he said to Ruan's retreating back. 'And I hope you will remember that.'

Whether Ruan Peat would remember it or not was moot, for he was already stepping out into the corridor and starting for the stairs, not bothering to close the door behind him.

SUNKEN ROADS AND PEOPLE DYING

Greta Finnerty was cursing herself for waiting so long before leaving Rosslare. Certainly she'd had her orders from Mick Malloy but Christ, she should have realised she'd waited too long. Wolfe Tone might well be coursing over the waves with his French soldiers to come to their rescue just as promised, but he was going to be too late.

She'd heard other news on her way from New Ross to Rosslare and it wasn't good. General Gerard Lake was amassing his Loyalist forces, getting ready to attack Vinegar Hill. How he knew about Vinegar Hill she didn't know, but he knew it all the same; the last of the United Irish gathering there for the past few weeks and a chance to get rid of the lot of them for good. The moment she heard the whisper that Lake's forces were on the move – twenty bloody thousand of them – she uncurled herself from the harbour wall and set off.

Only one thing for her to do now and that was to reach Vinegar Hill before Lake and his men did, tell the United Irish that no French reinforcements were coming their way, at least not in time, and to run like hell while they could.

There were no heartfelt goodbyes, just Fergus slipping from the knoll and setting off.

'I'll be watching,' Malloy said as Fergus looked back once, saw Malloy tapping at the telescope slung from a piece of string around his neck.

Fergus glanced up at the sky. A moon just passing from the full, flattened on one side like it had fallen on its face and got up again. Clear skies, a few silver-etched clouds scudding silently across a bat black night. Let him watch all he liked. He could hardly believe Malloy had agreed to his plan, but that was all to the good. Fergus had no intention of tracking Bagenal Harvey, but now he had names and safe places to go. Soon as he hit the coast he'd be off for Holland.

The moment he set foot on the streets of Scullabogue he took off his boots and strung them about his neck. There were curlicues of smoke coming from the chimneys of several houses, possibly actual inhabitants, possibly the odd Loyalist here and there, though Malloy had assured him there were only one or two. High rankers, he said, who didn't want to muck in with the rest who were camped out somewhere to the south.

Fergus kept to one side of the street, creeping through the moon shadows. He could hear men talking in the cottages and the shuffle and clinking of several horses. His broken ribs were making it hard for him to move as quick as he'd have liked and the wheezing of his breathing was loud in his ears. He had a distinct burning sensation in the small of his back and imagined Mick Malloy up there in the knoll of oak trees sighting him in the cross hairs of his telescope. He'd assumed there'd be a quick scamper through the village, keeping to the back lanes, but there were no back lanes, only the one main street, cottages on either side.

He went quietly and slowly down the street, stopping every now and then, his blood pulsing in his throat. He had the most God awful headache he'd ever had in his life and it was getting hard to think because of it. And then a thin sliver of light widened a few yards from him as a door opened and the bulky form of a man lurched out onto the street.

'Gotta take a piss, lads,' the man said, unmistakably English.

Fergus froze, pinioning himself against the nearest wall, trying to make himself small and dark and unseeable in the too bright night.

'Watch out for them native rats!' came a voice from inside the cottage.

'Got a thing for English cocks,' came a second, which was met with much merriment and ribald laughter.

'So much bigger than their own,' the burly man replied jovially. 'I know, I know.'

He turned the corner of the cottage, his back to Fergus, and put one hand out against its wall to brace himself as he unbuttoned his trousers, sighing as he let go a stream of urine, steam rising up into the night. Fergus didn't move. It was clear to him that the men inside the cottage had been drinking and maybe weren't at their best, but obviously they were soldiers and Fergus didn't move except to slowly, slowly slide himself down the wall until he was hidden in its deepest shadow. The man finished his business, did his trousers back up, turned around and, as he did so, caught a slight movement on the other side of the street.

Seven hundred miles away, Ruan considered he was having a hard night of it. The bed he'd been given was too soft for him to sleep easily. Louisa Grimalkin had begrudgingly given him the remnants of the mutton stew Caro had already apparently feasted on, for there'd not been much left. He'd had to fill himself up with bread, which wasn't ideal. In fact none of this set up was ideal. He got the distinct impression that Hendrik Grimalkin hadn't exactly warmed to him, though he'd no idea why, especially given that special moment they'd shared of collective tearing up. But tomorrow was another day and the one Ruan firmly believed was going to solve all his problems.

He turned himself over in his bed and sighed, gazing out of the window at the moon that hung like a pallid coin in the night sky. Money was what he needed most at the moment and Grimalkin his only means to it. He was trying to think of the best strategy to follow, and that was undoubtedly Golo and the Lynx. Grimalkin was like every scholar and tutor he'd ever come across all rolled into one, and Ruan had one ace up his sleeve: Caro's book, so liberally sprinkled with Golo's words and thoughts; *Behemoths, and other Wonders of the Deep* the bait on the hook, with a few tantalising facts to trade about the Lynx that no one knew apart from Golo, Fergus and himself.

And where are you now, Fergus? He asked of the cold and uncaring moon. *If you were with me instead of that boil Caro, this would all have gone so much easier.*

He sighed again and closed his eyes, and a few moments later was asleep.

Fergus was spotted.

'Hie!' shouted the man, his hand still fumbling with his trousers. 'Get out here, lads, and quick. There's a rat on the move!'

And Fergus was on the move, running as fast as his stockinged feet could take him down the lumpy, bumpy street, stubbing his toes numerous times, not that he noticed. The thumping in his head was like a sledgehammer and he was gasping for air as his heart beat out his increasing panic in his chest against his cracking ribs.

For a brief moment a cloud passed over the moon and all was darkn and Fergus believed all might yet be alright. Mick was watching. He'd see what was going on and send help. Just a little further. Just had to get to the trees on the other side of the village, disappear into the undergrowth, just had to…

The first shot hit him in the shoulder like a thunderbolt and down he went, face slamming hard onto the cobbles, chin bone snapping in two, right hand crumpling up below him, a shard of broken rib pushing into his left lung. The pain was immediate and overwhelming, a great whooshing sound in his ears as if he'd been plunged below the waves of a raging sea. Only gradually did that sound separate into the thudding of several pairs of boots crashing down the street towards him, on him before he properly understood what they were about, kicking and stamping, joined by the hammering on his head of the butts of their guns. Quick and brutal. Just like everything else about that day in New Ross and Scullabogue, Fergus's last thought flitting through his mind like a leaf in an empty forest:

Why didn't I keep my boots on? I don't want to die without my boots on.

So silly and inconsequential, but no time for more. One of the men fixed a bayonet and struck Fergus through back and belly, slicing his guts betwixt and betwain. His ragged, stockinged feet twitched feebly as he lay there pinioned to the ground like the victim of a shrike stuck by a thorn to its tree.

Mick Malloy slammed shut his telescope and let it drop.

'Well feck, there goes nothing,' he muttered, his squinty eye throbbing from being pinched closed all the while he'd had his good eye fixed to the glass. The Scotsman had only been in his purview a little over twenty four hours but Malloy was not without compassion. Fergus had done exactly as Malloy had supposed and been caught, and now Malloy had the information he needed – which cottages the Loyalists were in and which ones they were not.

Now he and his men could get down there and finish the job, burn out the bastards in one last cock-a-snook before they legged it for Vinegar Hill. Tit for tat and back to tit again. The Loyalists had burned the rebel hospital and Mick in turn had burned down theirs. Only this last cremation to go, just to let the English know the United Irish weren't beaten, not by a long chalk.

One last stand, boys. One last stand.

SECRET SOCIETIES, SECRET NAMES

DEVENTER, HOLLAND

Ruan was keen to put his plan into action, but by the time he crawled himself downstairs Hendrik Grimalkin was long gone.

'He'll be back later this afternoon,' Louisa told him. 'Do you want something to eat?'

Ruan did. He'd been hungry from the moment he'd woken up and was looking forward to something good, only to find that Caro had beaten him to it once again and not much left of the skilleted scones and eggs Louisa had cooked up. Ruan ate what was left, slopped out cold upon a plate. He was angry all over again because of it, and more so that he had to kick his heels for the best part of three hours before Grimalkin finally reappeared, Caro skipping along behind him having apparently spent the morning with the man.

'You should see the library Mr Grimalkin took me too!' Caro was beside himself with excitement. 'It's enormous! Belly of the whale kind of stuff!'

Grimalkin smiled coldly at Ruan Peat.

'I'd've taken you too, if you'd been awake at a suitable hour,' he said, Ruan frowning, not understanding why the world was treating him so badly, yet again. It was as if Fergus had taken over their bodies, put his words into their mouths, his expression upon all their different faces. The only man he'd met who'd treated him with a little respect and kindness had been that man back at the servants…George, whatever his name was. Ruan was aggrieved, but pleased with the scheme he'd made the night before and now was the time to put it in action.

'Can we have a little talk?' Ruan asked, politely.

Grimalkin lifted his eyebrows enquiringly.

'Certainly,' Hendrik replied. 'Caro, why don't you go along with Louisa and see what she's got prepared in her kitchen for you.'

'Righto, sir, thank you sir,' Caro piped, to Ruan's immediate and visceral disgust. Apparently toadying was what got you on around here. He moved his neck as if he had a kink in it, resolving that it would not kill him to do the same.

'I think I may have something that will interest you… sir,' he tacked the last word on as an experiment but it was a moment too late and didn't sit right, and that was the way it was understood.

'Do you, now?' Hendrik replied, a little too sarcastically for Ruan's comfort, but heroically swallowing his pride.

Just get it done and over with, and in a few days you'll be out of here forever. Neither spoke any further until Hendrik led Ruan up to his study and motioned Ruan to sit on the same armchair he had the night before.

'I'd rather stand, if that's all the same to you,' Ruan said, Hendrik closing his eyes briefly, wondering why nobody had never had the nous to beat common civility into this boy.

'Let me start…' Hendrik began, but was immediately interrupted.

'No, no,' Ruan said hurriedly. 'Let me. I believe I've certain bargaining points in my favour.'

Hendrik bit the inside of his lip with irritation, at least until Ruan extracted the large gold ring from his jerkin pocket and held it out towards him. It had a huge lapis lazuli at its centre and even from the yard or two that separated them Hendrik could see it was engraved.

'Let me see,' he said, taking out the magnifier he habitually kept in his pocket, used to examine the various manuscripts he encountered during the course of his working day. 'But that's a very fine stone you have here,' he stated, intrigued by the engraving. 'A quarter moon, and maybe the sun,' he said, studying it with care, 'with a triangle of light going from the one to the other.'

'It means the Enlightened One, *L'illuminato*,' Ruan stated, confident his plan was in the off and bounding helter skelter towards success. 'I don't know how much you know about the Lynx from Golo...'

'Not much,' Hendrik interrupted, still looking at the ring, 'but maybe you can, ah ha, illuminate me.'

Ruan winced. A scholar then, like he'd thought. No doubting it now, not with a pathetic pun like that.

'Well,' he said, like the seasoned bargainer he believed himself to be. 'This ring is just the start, but there's so much more I can tell you. All the secrets of the Lynx laid bare. Imagine all the papers, the books you could write about it, the first Scientific Society in Europe...'

Ruan stopped abruptly, Hendrik having shifted his intent gaze from the ring to Ruan's face.

'You mean to trade? Is that what you mean to do, young man?'

'Um, well,' Ruan faltered. 'The shipwreck and all. I need help...'

'And you're intending to blackmail me with the knowledge your...guardian,' Hendrik remembered well Ruan's own grasping for the word the night before and employed it to its full force before he went on, 'with the knowledge that your guardian, Golo Eck, the man who presumably has clothed and fed you your whole life, clearly meant to gift freely to the intellectual universe?'

Ruan swallowed. He'd not anticipated this reaction for a moment.

'I just didn't think you'd help me…' he stammered, and for the first time in his life Ruan blushed, going the deep red of dock-seed in autumn that children so often pull up with their fingers and scatter like a trail of crumbs upon the ground.

'I think, Mr Peat,' Grimalkin said sternly, 'that we need to start this conversation again.'

Ruan nodded miserably and Grimalkin softened somewhat. Ruan might be rude and full of bluster but it had to be admitted he was having a bad time of it. It wasn't every day a person was shipwrecked in a foreign country and found himself without guardian, money or direction. He'd come to Hendrik for the help he was too young to procure for himself, and Hendrik was not without sympathy.

'Alright,' Hendrik said, commanding as he'd done before. 'Sit down.'

And this time Ruan did.

'No more pandering,' Hendrik stated, 'and no more lies, young man. And if you can be civil, I'll thank you to start again at the beginning…'

20

THE RISING OF THE MOON

VINEGAR HILL, NEAR ENNISCORTHY, IRELAND

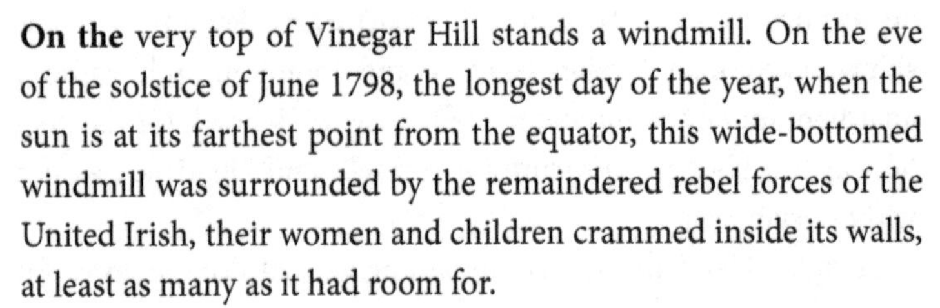

On the very top of Vinegar Hill stands a windmill. On the eve of the solstice of June 1798, the longest day of the year, when the sun is at its farthest point from the equator, this wide-bottomed windmill was surrounded by the remaindered rebel forces of the United Irish, their women and children crammed inside its walls, at least as many as it had room for.

Outside the windmill the menfolk sit and talk, their pikestaffs and meagre gun-stocks gleaming in the sparse evening light. The sun is a few degrees above the horizon to the west as they grit their teeth grimly at what the following day might bring. There are, among their numbers, Catholics, Protestants and Dissenters altogether, labourers, landowners, even priests, all wanting the same thing: all wanting the English gone.

The night, when it comes, is pale with the solstice, and they can see each other's bodies, smell each other's sweat, each other's fear, all taut and tense as they hunch side by side upon the mist-dampened grass. Down below them, from the valley, come the sounds of the twenty thousand men-at-arms the Crown Services have sent to defeat them, barricaded into the small village of Enniscorthy, its native inhabitants having long since fled.

These forces are under the command of General Gerard Lake, Loyalists to a man, eager for the fight that will come with the morning. The thought of it lying no heavier upon their shoulders than the weight of their coats and capes, for they know how vastly they outnumber their opponents on the hill, both in terms of men and weaponry. They want nothing more than to wipe the last of these squalling rebel Irish from the face of the earth.

The victories of the United Irish have been paltry, sporadic and few, at least by General Lake's reckoning – Oulart, Ballymena, Larne and Carrickfergus among them, and the holding of Antrim town for several inglorious hours. But by the early months of 1798 the rebellion is on its last legs, retreated all to Wexford to regroup, and from Wexford to the Hill, where the rebels have been holed up in its precarious protection since the back end of May.

There'd been several battles since – New Ross notable amongst them, both for what had happened during and after. The tales that went the rounds of that particular confrontation had been ferocious: of the summary executions and the burning of hospitals on both sides, but mostly of the lone man who had been bludgeoned and bayoneted to death on the streets of Scullabogue, the man who hadn't had his boots on and whose bloody body nobody came to claim. His suicidal mission had been apparently to let the enemy know in which cottages a large part of the Loyalist Command in Wexford had been holed up in. Holed up, and then burned out.

It was just the sort of legend General Gerard Lake had been sent here to stamp out, along with all the other incursions against the Crown forces hereabouts. Most of leaders of the Irish opposition had already been captured, arrested, exiled or hung, but a few still clung on, including Father John Murphy, nominal commander of the forces on Vinegar Hill, and his fellow ex-priest Father Mogue Kearns. Not to mention the squint-eyed Mick Malloy who had caused them so much bother at New Ross.

Time to sweep them all away like the lice they were. One last push, one last extermination, and all would be over. Time to take a last glass of wine in anticipation of the glories the morning would bring, General Gerard Lake the most fêted man in Ireland since Cromwell himself.

All three of those named leaders of the United Irish were there that night outside the windmill, alongside the nine other men who made up their command. All were worrying about how little chance there was of victory when they engaged in battle the following day. All were clinging to the desperate hope that the French would get here in time – as the message from France had promised, a message from Wolfe Tone himself.

He'd tried it before: fourteen thousand Frenchmen sent out in December 1796 to invade Ireland, and several more times since, with no incursion as yet successful, beaten back by bad planning, storms and winter seas swirling up against them, lashing at their sails, breaking their masts. Or by too many English being nearby or too narrow a harbour to negotiate, too difficult a coast-line, too little local knowledge on board to guide them in.

But right now it was the height of summer, the weather calm for weeks, and Wolfe Tone had given them his word, had sworn it. The men on the Hill were not entirely without hope, believing there was still a chance that three thousand French soldiers were on their way at that very moment to help them out, if only they could hang on a little longer.

The night was warm on Vinegar Hill, low clouds settling on its summit with the partial going down of the sun, hiding the windmill and its men from the eyeglasses of the Loyalists gathered down below. They'd no fires lit up top for there were no trees with which to fuel them, the few thickets of whin and juniper skirting its lower slopes not fit to provide timber and only wide-bladed grass here on the flat plateau where they were encamped. They counted out the minutes, marking down the hours until the sun would rise again, a bare half mile of scrubland dividing them from their enemy.

Their clothes were heavy and uncomfortable from the mizzle, and scraps of sounds came up at them from the valley below of men moving, leather creaking, horses' tackle jingling in the windless night. A few bars of English song reached them, which unnerved them all the more, hinting of men so relaxed, so convinced of their coming victory that they thought nothing of indulging in so commonplace an activity as bawling out a few ballads around their camp-fires as if they were all on a weekend jaunt, instead of being seven or eight hours away from massacring every last man, woman and child garrisoned above them on the Hill.

Eleven of the twelve-strong committee of the United Irish commanders up there tried to block out the sounds of those merry English songs, tried to focus their energy and attention instead on making plans, devising strategies. Already they had earmarked several escape routes from the westerly side of the hill primarily, they'd agreed, for the women and children, and any wounded, whose numbers they anticipated would not be few. Such escape routes would also serve the rest if things tomorrow went as badly as seemed likely.

Only the ever-optimistic Myles Byrne, the youngest of their crew, protested at these plans, insisting they would not be needed, that victory would be theirs. Whether or not the rest of them agreed they were loath to begin evacuation under shelter of the night, conceding that to do so would be to admit to defeat before it happened, and would only serve to demoralise the several thousand fighting men who were gathered about them in the thinness of the night.

'No news of the Frenchies, then?' asked Murray O'Dowd, hardly expecting an answer, and no one immediately replying.

'Nothing,' Gerry Monahan finally said. A small shuffle of movement followed this single word as they all involuntarily pulled in their boots and shoulders a little, as if by doing so they could make themselves less vulnerable to what must come.

'Has Greta Finnerty not got back from the bay?' O'Dowd asked, meaning the bay outside of Rosslare just below Wexford. It was where the French – according to Wolfe Tone's missive – should already have landed from Brest several days before, and if not then, then any minute now.

'Nothing,' Gerry Monahan said again. 'But she's a good lass is Greta, a staunch one. She'd've come here soon as she could if she'd any news.'

'So,' stated Harry Doherty, 'it's not good.'

Silence.

The mist shifted about them of its own volition. There was no wind, only their collective bodies' exhalations, the warmth escaping from their damp clothes and the smoke of their pipes drifting out about them. Then up spoke Myles Byrne again, young maybe, but already a hero of Bunclody and Arklow who'd seen worse odds than this and was not about to give up now, a boy young enough to have no real notion of dying or defeat, who saw his future only as one bright victory piled upon the next, as only the youngest can.

'It could be worse,' Myles said. 'At least if all goes badly,' – although plainly, from the jaunty tone of his voice, he did not expect this to be so – 'then Greta's her cousin to tell all that's happened, remember our names, if nothing else.'

Mick Malloy coughed.

'Peter Finnerty's been arrested,' he said gruffly, 'no one knows what's happened to him yet. No news out of Dublin with Greta in Rosslare.'

There was a collective sigh. This was not what they'd wanted to hear, which was why Mick had left it so late in the telling. Peter's success in getting out what was going on in Ireland had been of great cheer to them all ever since he'd set up The Press in his father's print works. He'd managed the seemingly impossible, getting some of his articles into the Scottish broadsheets, and several into the English ones too. The most recent exposed the public executions of thirty-four rebel men of Dunlavin to the banging of English drums back in May. Probably the precipitating factor in Peter's arrest, Mick thought gloomily.

It was a bad blow, Mick hating that he'd been the one to give it out, harbouring the same claustrophobic fear they all did – excepting Myles Byrne – of being trapped inside a body that was shutting itself down, its blood getting thinner with every successive attack, its extremities being lopped off one by one by their enemy, digit by digit, wrist after hand, elbow after knee, shoulder after hip. Despite such blows Mick felt the thrum of the blood of their rebellion in his sinews, in his veins, within this heart of them, still having the urgent need to fight and survive.

They heard approaching footsteps and saw the dishevelled figure of Father Mogue Kearns appearing from the mist. He'd long since abandoned religious garb, as had John Murphy, who both looked the same as the rest – like old potatoes dragged up too late in the season from the ground, all tufts and tatters, mud and scrapes. But Mogue Kearns was a different kind of man altogether, and the tale going the rounds at the moment was that when he'd been studying his vocation in Paris, during the Frenchies' Revolution a decade before, he'd been seized as a traitor by the raging mob for the crime of being English – which he most certainly was not. He'd been strung up from a lamp-post until the weight of his body bent the post down enough to allow his toes to touch the ground, giving him just enough breath to survive until some passing Samaritan cut him down and brought him back to life. Just how true this was no one knew, but it bucked them up just to think on it, for a man who could survive that could survive anything.

'What's up, friends?' Mogue Kearns asked, sitting himself down between Malloy and Harry Doherty, laying a hand briefly on each of their shoulders as he did so, his knees cracking audibly as he got himself cross-legged to the ground.

'Myles here was just telling us how we'll all be heroes by tomorrow,' Harry said, uplifted by Kearns presence as if they'd been a failing arch whose keystone had just been pressed back into place.

'Ay, but only once we've all been gutted like herrings,' O'Dowd added, his voice a cheery antidote to his words.

'Ah but,' Kearns said, joining in the casual banter that is all a man has left between himself and the abyss he knows he is about to fall into, 'the jig's no up yet, not until the last man takes his dance.'

His comrades smiled grimly in the shallow darkness. Mogue was the man everyone wanted by their side in battle, a man who'd been with them from the outset and somehow survived to be with them now. And sure enough Mogue went on to say what they'd all been trying to formulate in their heads but not had the words to do so.

'Hold fast, friends,' said he, his voice strong and clear despite having spent the last couple of hours administering the Eucharist in the form of scraps of stale bread and some muddy water pretending to be wine to any of his rebel flock who would accept it, no matter their creed.

'We'll maybe fall tomorrow,' Kearns went on, 'as we've fallen before, but there'll always be others who'll rise up to take our place.'

He nodded briefly in the direction of young Myles Byrne, whose smile could be discerned from the glinting of his teeth – a boy, Kearns reminded himself, who'd come through worse than this. He rubbed his hands together, a familiar gesture to the others, before lowering them to his knees, began to knead his battle-swollen, damp-eaten joints with his finger-tips. No one spoke, all aware of the pain Kearns was hiding, the weakness to his body he never mentioned, not wanting to trouble anyone, yet which everyone knew about from his lop-sided gait, his uncomfortable manner of sitting and trying to remain still.

A few moments passed until Mogue stilled his fingers, until he lifted his head and looked about him, looking above the heads of his comrades towards the tall black stillness of the windmill that stood against the slow-wheeling stars of the sky. It seemed to Mogue as if it had been anchored to the ground for the specific purpose of pointing upwards to God's greater creation, reminding them just how small they were in the grand scheme of things.

'There's still the small matter of the Scotsman's Bauble,' he said into the darkness, mainly for a bit of light relief.

The rest exchanged furtive glances as Mick Malloy stiffened but did not flinch.

'I'll not apologise for what happened,' Malloy said quietly. 'We're at war, and I only did what needed doing.'

Everyone knew about New Ross and the burnings and the lone man who'd died in Scullabogue – the Scotsman Mogue had mentioned – Malloy having had the grace to give Fergus a good backstory despite having practically sent the man to his death. The little package Fergus had given Mick he'd passed on to Mogue a couple of hours previously, just after Mick himself arrived on the hill.

'So let's have at it, then,' Myles Byrne spoke eagerly into the darkness, his voice untrammelled by the cynicism the rest had adopted. Mogue Kearns smiled to hear his enthusiasm, his lack of fear, could see the lad's straight back silhouetted against the dark grey of the mist beyond, the strength coiled within his young limbs. They might lose tomorrow's battle, Mogue thought, but if lads like this could be relied on then he had spoken truly when he'd said they'd not yet lost their war.

'Well, my young friend,' Mogue Kearns rejoined. 'Why not indeed?'

He nodded to himself, then bent down and undid the satchel that contained everything he now owned: a couple of crumpled, unclean undergarments, a handful of mismatched laces for his boots, his beloved bible – several of its pages ripped and splotched with the blood of men he'd given last rites to on other fields of battle – his portable monstrance, empty of anything but a few crumbs of consecrated, if mouldy, bread; and also what had been christened the Scotsman's Bauble. He lifted out the small leather pouch, grimy with dust and dirt, but with its buckle tightly locked and closed.

'Very well,' Mogue said, laying the pouch on his knee. For a moment it seemed the world had grown quieter, as if everyone about him had taken stock of some important moment, as if the rest of the men and their families encamped on the hill had all of a sudden subsided into sleep. Even the English and their loyalist lackeys down below in the valley had ceased their songs and the only sounds he could hear were the faraway grating calls of a couple of competing corncrake somewhere in the distance, the slight shuffling of his fellow commanders as they moved forward, and then the slighter rasping of the metal tongue as he slid it from its hold.

Nothing then but the creak of the leather as he slid his fingers inside the neck of the pouch and withdrew a waxed-paper bundle. It was soft and light and he unfolded it carefully, bade young Myles bring closer one of the shuttered lanterns they had lit so he could see the object more clearly. It lay there, limp upon his knee, and he looked at it curiously, unfolding its edges to reveal an object that was like nothing he'd ever seen before. It appeared to be some kind of belt made for the smallest of waists: an inch-wide strip of embroidered material from which strong yarns dangled from its length, all different colours, most of them beaded and knotted once or several times, some not at all.

Gerry Monahan sighed loudly, and spat in disgust, but Mick Malloy beside him sat quite still.

'What the feck?' Myles Byrnes said succinctly, but Kearns had no answer. He looked at Mick curiously, and Mick's squinty eye wandered off to the left as he offered explanation.

'Just said it was something we could use, that Greta knew what to do with it…' Jesus, he wished he could remember exactly what Fergus had said about it in those last garbled minutes before Fergus left the knoll. 'Something about codes, lines of communication… uncrackable,' he offered the random words before trailing off again. Mogue Kearns nodded, although couldn't see how it could function as such.

'What do you think, John?' Mogue asked, seeing Murphy's pale fingers moving with practiced speed as if he thought it might be a rosary of sorts. Murphy shook his head, but now Mogue had thought of rosaries he also thought of beads, and a sudden thought occurred to him, something he thought he'd seen in France way back in the day.

'It's just a bloody load of nothing,' Doherty said, speaking for all the others, all except Malloy who was looking intently not at the object itself but at Mogue Kearns, knowing that if anyone could work it out then it was he. Sure enough Mogue held up his hand.

'I don't think so,' he countered, 'but I need to think on it. It reminds me of something…'

'What else is in there?' Myles asked, dismissing the cats-cradle on Mogue's knee as the rest had done.

'Well, let's see,' Mogue said, going back to the pouch and tipping it up. Out came another smaller package, rounded this time, that fell straight to the ground, the paper unwrapping as soon as it hit, a large gold ring rolling out of its own accord with an enormous emerald at its centre.

'Jesus and Mary!' Myles whispered, bringing the light closer as he bent in for a better look, making the green stone glare back at them like the eye of a malevolent fox spotted in the middle of the night. Kearns picked up the ring and brought it level with his eye.

'But there's some engraving here,' he said. 'I can't make out what…'

He passed it to his left, to Harry Doherty, aware of the shiver of anticipation that was thrilling through the gathered men at this new discovery. Doherty handled it deferentially, took his look but passed it almost straightway to O'Dowd, whose hand was already eagerly outstretched to take this more easily understood part of the Scotsman's so-called bauble.

'Looks like it might be worth a bloody fortune,' murmured O'Dowd as he took the ring and held it up. 'I done some work with goldsmiths afore I went into smithing proper,' he continued, his voice rising with excitement as he tilted the ring this way and that, 'an' I seen some stones then, but this is the biggest bloody emerald I ever seen!'

The ring went the rounds then, every man taking their look before passing it on to the next.

'A result at last, then,' Malloy said lightly, relieved. But even as he spoke his attention was sliding back to the many-tasselled belt and Mogue saw that look, rubbed at the stubble on his chin. His movement dislodged the pouch and, as it fell, a small scrap of paper fluttered out. He picked it up. It was newspaper article, the print far too small to read, but there were also a few larger words blocked out in pencil in the margins. He'd broken his reading glasses several months previously but could just about make them out, faint as they were.

Brother Joachim/Walcheren. Grimalkin/Deventer. Golo Eck & Ruan Peat/Loch Eck, Scotland.

The linkage of words meant nothing to him except for Walcheren, for that place was well known to the United Irish. It was the first port of call on the established escape route the exiled rebels had established from Ireland to France, there to carry on the fight by joining Wolfe Tone's Irish Legion. Walcheren, home of the Servants of the Sick whose Abbot was Irish and sympathetic to their cause.

He was about to hand Malloy the article for explanation, before remembering that Malloy was practically illiterate, barely able sign his own name in a wiggly line. Malloy saw the motion that was quickly withdrawn and took advantage of the others being distracted by their quick-fired argument about how much the ring was worth and how many muskets it could buy them for the next battle, even if it could not provide for this.

'It's the stringy bit that's the thing,' Malloy said quietly to Kearns, screwing up his face in concentration, making the black line of his eyebrows even thicker and more menacing than usual. 'I just can't remember exactly what he said about it, only that it could pass on messages, messages no one else could read. But he said he told Greta. We need to get it to Greta.'

Mogue Kearns shrugged slightly and picked up the khipu – not that he had any idea that was its name – folding it gently back inside its piece of paper.

'Well then,' he said, just as quietly, 'if that's the case, then that's exactly what we must do.'

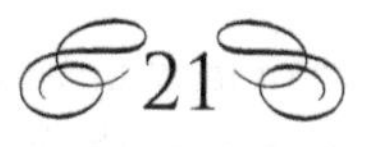

TO THE WINDMILL ALL

The small figure of Greta Finnerty was walking fast along the narrow lanes and byways that roughly followed the passage of the River Slaney. She'd already passed Killurin, Ballyhogue and Brownswood and knew she'd not far to go.

She would have been running if she'd been able, if she'd had the breath, if her legs didn't feel heavy as quern-stones; if only her boots had been better fitting and hadn't rubbed up an army of blisters upon her heels and toes making every step an agony, making her grit her teeth every time she came down upon a stone. She was thankful it wasn't raining, that the night was but a shadow of what it could have been later or earlier in the year, that her way was still faintly visible by the fading light of the summer solstice sun.

She was terribly anxious that she wouldn't get there in time, no matter how fast she went and cursed herself for not leaving sooner, for hanging on so long in Rosslare right until the last moment. She'd wanted to have good news for the men on Vinegar Hill that the French really were coming, the masts of their battleships thick as a forest and in sight of shore. But they hadn't been, and now she was panting with the effort of moving so fast, the blood and water from her burst blisters gathering in the heels and toes of her boots, soaking through her socks, an unpleasant squelch with every step.

She glanced up at the sky, saw that the true darkness of the night would soon fall. She could make out the glimmerings of pale stars against the welkin and felt suddenly insignificant and tired, wanting nothing more than to rest up, snooze for a few hours in a ditch, beneath a hedge or hayrick. She did not, for she knew that stopping would be the end, and so she grimaced, eased the straps of her backpack with her fingers, regretting the bare fact that she couldn't risk taking out her shuttered lamp, not with Crown Forces in the area, closing in even now upon the Hill, when a person could be shot down or bayoneted for the small crime of carrying a light through the night.

Oh God, but her feet really hurt now, and although she clenched her jaw and balled her fists she couldn't stop the tears from running down her face with the pain. Yet still she went on, could just about make out the thread of the track as it wound its way between hedges, alongside farmyards, her heart pounding every time a pig stirred at her passing or a cockerel thought to spread its wings at the lightness of the night, or some sheep moved out from the mufflement of its flock as her foot kicked a stone as she scurried their sleeping by. And then at last, at last! She saw the flattened hump of Vinegar Hill in the distance where it slouched its small height above the village of Enniscorthy, the tall black line of the windmill on top.

Just a little farther, she kept repeating in her head. *Just a little farther.*

She wasn't entirely sure what would happen when we she got there bringing the bad news that the French weren't coming after all, or at least weren't coming quick enough to give them any aid.

But surely, she thought, if she got there good and early they'd have time to skidaddle it away from the Hill. They must have escape routes planned and surely would understand that to run away and fight another day was better than to stand and fight a hopeless fight.

Greta was no newcomer to the rules of battle and knew a bad bet when she counted up the odds, and Vinegar Hill was the worst of the lot. Greta thought suddenly of Myles Byrne, up there on the Hill, the boy she and her brother had grown up with in Ballylusk, working alongside him in the tattie fields every October, her tagging along as Myles and Joseph went fishing in the rivers around Monased; young Myles, who had become a man and the hero of Bunclody to boot, even if he was only eighteen. The same age Joseph would have been if he'd not been killed.

Greta looked up once again at the sky and saw it had changed, become lighter instead of darker, and realised with dismay that the sun must already be nudging its way back up from the horizon. She must have been walking, walking, walking, right through the blackest part of the night without her knowing it, wondering if it was possible that her head had fallen asleep and been dreaming while the rest of her body had just gone on, plodding its way one more yard, one more furlong, one more mile, without her being aware of it. It must have been so, because when she looked up again she saw that she was really close, and only a spit away from the hill, only a few more miles to go.

And so she pushed herself on, pushed herself harder than she'd ever done before, closing every yard with grim determination, counting them out in her head to keep herself awake, keep herself focussed. She counted out the yards, counted down the miles, going from four miles down to three, from three down to two, two down to one, when she was almost on the straight lines of the farmers' fields as they fenced their way up the back slopes of the Hill, clearly seeing the paths that snicketed through the gorse and scrub-line at its base emerging out the other side, all heading to the same place, all leading towards the top and the flatland and the windmill stretching up into the sky.

She stopped, some unknown sound catching her ear. She cocked her head and listened: soft sounds all around her, carried on the slight breeze of the coming morning, an enemy army sleeping just the other side of the hill from where she stood. She could smell their fires, the oil they'd used to lubricate their muskets and guns, the rank odours of too many men and horses gathered together in a single place. And worse, the sounds were changing as she listened, for this army was beginning to yawn and stretch; there was the splashing of water, the pissing of men, the gentle snorting of their horses responding to their masters' touches, the soft snicks of metal as saddles were lifted and strapped, uniforms straightened, weapons loaded, canons checked.

Panic now, Greta understanding that soon they would begin to mobilise in earnest, begin to swarm around the base of the hill, cutting her off from above. Only a few precious minutes left for Greta to break from the path and forge her way straight up the Hill towards the rebel forces the fastest way she could; only minutes left to pass her message on; only minutes left for any of them up there to have any chance of escape.

All on her.

All on Greta Finnerty, and she was heavy with the weight of it, tears prickling at her eyes, fear moving her small legs in her boy's trousers and her too big boots, on and on and on.

22
DECISIONS MADE

DEVENTER, HOLLAND

At the very top of Hendrik Grimalkin's tall, thin Hollandish house were several small rooms sited beneath the eaves, Ruan assigned one, Caro another. Needless to say, to Ruan's mind at least, Caro had got the better one, the one that looked directly over the wide promenade of the Singel and the slow moving loop of the lagoon beyond. Not that Ruan complained. They'd been here a few weeks now and he'd learned to kow tow with best of them.

After their little talk in Grimalkin's study Ruan had come wise to the man: treat him like a schoolmaster, like the one in charge, and Hendrik was happy. It didn't come naturally to Ruan, but he stood in front of the small mirror on his small washstand and practiced ingratiating expressions. Apparently it had done the trick, with Hendrik at least, who had finally consented to traipse him off to several of the banking companies and lawyers in Deventer, one of each agreeing to do the necessary.

Ruan had been expecting to walk into Deventer a man in dire need and walk out the next day as one with the world laid out at his feet; but that had been far from the case. The letter from the Servants stating Golo's death had to be verified; more letters sent to confirm its authenticity; yet more pushed out to Golo's lawyers in Glasgow asking for a copy of his Last Will and Testament and to his bank to see if they could meanwhile free up any monies for his ward. Nothing for Ruan to get his hands on until the entire charade was performed and executed to the lawyers' satisfaction on both sides of the water.

Until then he was stuck with the Grimalkins and at their mercy. One word from either could see his entire venture sunk like a stone. He might have Hendrik on side but Louisa was another matter entirely. The little sneakit Caro had only the previous day produced a letter of his own, signed by the abominable Brother Joachim and his blasted Abbot, asking that Caro be released from Ruan's service into their own, if they saw fit to take him on. And of course Louisa – the dried up, childless, old stick of a woman that she was – grabbed the chance with both hands.

Caro was the absolute bees knees as far as she was concerned, as loaded with goodness and promise as those bees' knees were with pollen. Caro was like a pig in shit, and wasted no time sucking up to the woman, spending most mornings with her in her kitchen helping out, carrying her bags back from market, tasting everything she cooked and declaring it as nectar beyond compare.

It made Ruan queasy to think on it. On the plus side it meant that when his money came through, when Golo's estate was finally ceded to him lock, stock and barrel, he'd be as free of Caro as he would be of the Grimalkins, the only thought that kept him going. Until then he had no choice but to bide here, compliment old Louisa as best he could, pretend interest in Hendrik's work at his blasted library where Hendrik spent the most part of his time.

If mirrors on washstands could speak, Ruan's would have had a great deal to say about his practiced ingratiating smiles and platitudes, but also the invective – if inventive – speeches he would pour out onto the Grimalkin household once he was finally able to leave.

⁂

Ruan was entirely right about Louisa's dislike of him. She tried to hide it, would not stoop to being low and mean while he was a guest in her house, but he got under her skin nonetheless. Every smile he graced her with seemed like a simulacrum, every compliment accompanied by a snide backhander.

These potatoes with cheese are wonderful, Mrs Grimalkin. They're not quite like we had back at home, but they're good all the same.

You keep your house so clean and tidy, Mrs Grimalkin. I'll bet you know every mouse by name.

He didn't seem able to help himself, and the moment she thought of him she began to grind her teeth: so smug and self-righteous, believing he had the moral high ground because he'd been dealt a bad hand. She had to concede that it undoubtedly was a bad hand – no one would wish such disaster on anyone – but he had his way out. Her husband would make sure of it, if only to get the excrescence that was Ruan Peat out of their household as soon as possible.

Young Caro had been through the same experience on the Collybuckie as Ruan had, and far, far worse in earlier years, as she was beginning to understand through unguarded comments, unspoken fears, like when he jumped every time a large man in the market covered him in shadow. What that lad had suffered hardly bore thinking about and yet here he was, in her home, still the brightest pipkin in the apple barrel.

Ruan was right about another thing too, and that Caro was fast becoming the child she'd always wanted but never had, not in all the eighteen years she'd been married to Hendrik. It hadn't been a bad marriage by any means, Louisa being of the firm belief that the welfare of her household and husband were her sole duties in life, and one she had never deviated from. She went to market every morning – a duty now enlivened immeasurably by Caro coming with her – and to her church for early mass on Fridays and Sundays. It was a habit her husband never tried to discourage, despite his belief – privately held, but widely known – that God, if any such Being existed at all, would surely not choose to confine Himself to designated buildings but would spread Himself instead throughout every nook and cranny of His Glorious Creation without need of being pinned down by the likes of Louisa and her priest.

He lived his life his way and allowed her to do the same, which was far more than many husbands would concede, and Louisa was truly grateful for it. Her one failing to Hendrik being that she'd not produced a child to carry on in his footsteps – many false starts, followed by as many miscarriages, not a single one going to term – her body now past the age when that failing could be corrected. And then Caro dropped into their lives – a startling, staggering child – sent to them by Joachim, Hendrik's father, of all people. A gift from the Servants, and therefore a gift from God. Finally an answer to the prayers she had been sending up with the incense at her church for nigh on twenty years.

A gift from God.

Since Caro and the despicable Ruan Peat had been beneath her roof Louisa had neglected attending her weekly Sewing Circle, when she and several other women met up at her neighbour's house two doors down along the Singel for a chat, a few cups of tea or hot chocolate, maybe even an alcoholic beverage or two if one of them had a birthday or something special to celebrate. And by God she had something to celebrate. A few days previously, when she and Caro had been chopping vegetables to put into the pickle pan, he had laid down his knife.

'Can I ask you something?' Caro said.

'But of course you can,' Louisa replied happily, going on with her chopping. Just having the boy here at her table invigorated her, made her feel ten years younger.

'Do you like having me here?' Caro asked. He didn't raise his face, couldn't meet her eyes, kept staring numbly at the shreds of cabbage and cauliflower lying next to his abandoned knife.

'Caro, of course I do! Don't you know that?'

The beating of Louisa's heart moved up a pace, fearing he was missing his life at sea – no matter how bad it had been – or worse, that he maybe wanted to go with Ruan off on the adventures Ruan could hardly stop talking about, once he was free. They'd had word that very morning from the Scottish lawyers saying they accepted the veracity of Golo Eck's death, his Last Will and Testament on its way. The coincidence was too much to bear. She put down her knife and looked over at Caro, his head still bowed.

'You're welcome here for as long as you like,' she said quietly, 'and I want you to stay, Caro. I truly do.'

She held her breath. Caro didn't move for a moment, then pulled a crumpled piece of paper from his pocket, trying unsuccessfully to flatten it out before holding it out to her. She took it and read it through, one hand going to her throat, fingers taking hold of the small cross she wore about her neck, for here was proof her God existed, right here. She dropped the contract of obligation Joachim had so carefully drafted to release Caro to the Grimalkins' care if he so chose and they agreed, moved around the table and hugged Caro to her, feeling his skinny arms clasping about her waist in return.

'You and me,' she whispered, kissing the top of Caro's head. 'You, me and Hendrik. A family. We'll be unstoppable.'

BATTLE SWORN

The darkness did not linger, nor the insubstantial dawn as the longest day of 1798, the 21st of June, came on too fast for the men on the Hill, their fear growing with every inch the sun slid up from the east. The stink of sweat was all-pervasive and they spoke in hushed tones as they checked their few hundred working muskets again and again, and that their paltry gunpowder stores were dry and easily accessible, their pikes evenly weighted, their pitchforks and bayonets sharp and bright.

The only sounds came from the grinding of soapstone against blade and tine, and the gentle susurration of linen and wool as the women hugged their children to their skirts in and around the windmill, listening to the incongruous gaiety of the larks scattering themselves high in the sky above them without a care in the world. Their men rounded their shoulders, rolled their necks, ears straining for the slightest sounds of movement from down below. Waiting was all any of them could do now, their resources far too limited to assume direct attack, defence their only option.

Several men had it on their minds to disembark early, take their women and children down the back-slopes of the Hill, get them to safety or at least the possibility of it. The women proved stronger than the men who were bending and would not hear of it, believing in the cause just as surely as did their menfolk and instead kissed their husbands, made their husbands kiss their children, then tried to squeeze themselves further inside the windmill, hide themselves within its sturdy walls, praying altogether that all would turn out for the best.

And then the enemy awoke.

Those garrisoned on the Hill heard it first as a rustling, as if the wind were sifting through a pile of fallen leaves. It was the sound of many men moving, of splashing water on their bodies, getting into battle-dress, breaking down their makeshift tents. A different, more menacing kind of sound came soon after: a jingling that lifted into the air as horses were saddled, guns and canons mounted onto carts, the hitching of harnesses.

Looking down through the morning, and the slight mist that still clung in gentle swathes to the lower slopes of the Hill, the remnants of the United Irish could see only hints and glimpses of the English lines as they began to snake out to east and west away from their barracks in Enniscorthy and began their encirclement of the Hill.

Through the mist they could make out the dark outlines of heavy cannons upon their carts, heavy men upon their huge horses, and their hearts began to pound within their chests and throats, their skin begin to prickle, the women pushing their children further into the windmill, those children crying now and whimpering as the anxiety of their mothers passed through their young skins with the ease of water falling through a sieve.

The bells of the surrounding parishes began to sound, signalling first six o'clock, seven, and then eight, the tension on the Hill almost unbearable until Mogue Kearns got to his feet, as did John Murphy, Myles Byrne, Harry Doherty, Mick Malloy and the rest of their twelve-strong council, shifting themselves to their allotted strategic points, a rustling murmur following them as they arose and moved as men began to suck deep breaths into their lungs to calm themselves, steady themselves, ready themselves for whatever was about to come.

Strong hands tried not to shake upon their pikestaffs and the few guns they had at their disposal. The comrades looked to one another, nodding their heads in mutual encouragement and support, each hoping that the cousins, brothers, friends braced on either side of them felt stronger and more optimistic than they did themselves. They stood shoulder to shoulder, rank by rank, hardly able to bear the waiting now, all wanting to get on with the fighting, get it done, adrenalin burning in their veins. They all felt the need to get up and going before the exhilaration of expectation was overtaken by a fear so abject it would paralyse them all.

And then it began: all hoos and hoys from the horns of the massed ranks of loyalists below as they encircled the hill, their trumpet blasts and clarions ripping the morning up and down. Then they came: the enemy racing up towards the rebel stronghold in a simultaneous five-pronged attack, cannons at the fore, blasting out huge gobbets of earth that billowed black smoke and hid the lines of artillery surging on behind them like beetles from a woodpile.

They fired as they ran, the cavalry rearing up the gentle slopes on their heels, having the advantage of height, firing their volleys into the midst of the United Irish who had no cover, no armour, no answering Irish guns. They could do nothing but launch themselves into a mad attack, yelling and shouting as they ran blindly down their hill, everything suddenly an obscurity of men tumbling into other men, hand-to-hand combats lit up by the flashes of discharging weapons and the smack of shells dispelled from English canons that blew every fourth man from his breeks, separating him from his legs, holing out a cavity in his chest so he could not breathe, the mist disappearing of a sudden as if dismayed, giving every man a better view of what he had to face.

The hooves of the English horses slid and stumbled, their riders swinging and lunging from side to side to avoid the boulders and stones that were being rolled and thrown down on them from up above. They came on inexorably up the slopes with the horses' legs buckling only a little now they'd found firmer ground, their hooves throwing up hard lumps of sun-dried earth to give the foot soldiers who came on behind some purchase for their boots. And down upon them came the United Irish, no match at all, stumbling beneath hooves and flanks, tripping over pikes, muskets firing randomly and without aim.

Within three quarters of an hour of the first assault three hundred men of the United Irish were already dead and another hundred soon followed. Barely two hours after it had begun this last-stand battle was done and dusted, only one tiny thread of escape left for the survivors who started running down its line fast as ever they could, women and children first, then those carrying the wounded with them, who screamed and cried out in pain as they were jolted down the slope, the able bodied men flanking them, still fighting to the last, all high-tailing it back for Wexford and the Wicklow hills.

Only one person of the rebel forces was running up and not down at that moment, and that person was Greta Finnerty. No weapons, no defence, no sleep, arriving a few minutes before the Crown Forces entirely encircled the Hill and attacked. She forgot everything in her life that had mattered up until now: the pain in her feet, the tiredness in her limbs and lungs and instead she ploughed up the side of the Hill to join her fellows as if it was the last thing she'd left to do in this world.

She grabbed a musket from a fallen comrade on her way up and held it clasped to her chest like other lasses her age might have clutched a child. She'd no idea how to fire it, had seen the man who'd been standing next to her a moment earlier holed out, exsanguinated, degutted by an enemy. Still she went on, screaming into the morning, unable to see what was only a few yards ahead of her, everything blotted out by the sulphurous black smoke coming up at her from the enemy lines. It burnt her eyes and was bitter in her throat, men's blood splashing hot and thick upon her jerkin, upon her face, the taste of it like iron and saltpetre on her tongue.

Within several minutes of Greta's charge her stolen musket was empty – not that she'd the faintest idea how she'd even fired it – each discharge flinging her back upon her haunches. But she got up again each time and went on, flinging the useless musket aside, attempting instead to raise up a pike that was lying beside yet another dead man's body, but it was too heavy for her to even lift properly, let alone get it tucked into her armpit to give its blade any proper purpose and down it went to the ground.

Greta charged on regardless, stopping only when something caught at her ankle with such force she assumed she'd been caught by some unseen shot or shrapnel. Face down she tumbled into the mud, breath knocked out of her, body unable to scramble itself back up. And then she saw the hand that was wrapped about her ankle and the face of Mogue Kearns, terribly distorted by pain and dirt, but Greta knew it all the same.

'Father!' Greta gasped urgently. 'Are you hurt?'

She moved her fingers clumsily, trying to find Mogue's neck, feel for a pulse, rewarded by Mogue releasing the tight hold he had upon her ankle as he moved his hand and clasped at Greta's own.

'I am that, lass,' Mogue Kearns gasped, 'and Praise God, but you're a sight to see.'

The words were fighting their way from the bloody spittle that was hardening at the corners of his mouth. Greta's heart lurched to see her hero so fallen, the heat of battle slipping away as if the pendulum that had supplied its energy had been gripped and stopped. She was suddenly aware of the awfulness of what was happening that she'd previously ignored: the agonised calls of dying men, the terrified screaming of women and children fighting to escape the windmill that had gone up in flames a few hundred yards above. They ran like frightened hares now its protection had been half blown away, its bricks and blocks tumbling from its blackened sides as it was struck again and again by enemy shells.

Beneath her knees Greta felt the heat and burn of unspent gunpowder that had set the dry grass to smouldering, steam whispering from the spilled guts of the fallen man to her left, became aware of the arrhythmic blasts of the enemy shells that were landing far too close for comfort, the last only a few yards from where she was crouched.

'But it's a miracle you're here, Greta, a miracle,' Mogue Kearns croaked, his words as stuttered and staccatoed as the artillery that was blasting its way through their shared day. 'You've got to go,' he spluttered on. 'This isn't a battle to be won or lost today and there are more important things to think of now than you or I. You have to get out, and you have to take this with you.'

Greta looked down then and, without realising it, by doing so she turned Mogue Kearns a little to his side and was appalled at the undisguised cry of pain that came from him and saw the blood that was gurgling from Mogue Kearns' belly, blood dark as tar.

'We need help!' Greta shouted out into the mayhem of legs and men that were tangled all around them, yelling out her words into smoke and maelstrom, unable to believe that a man like Mogue Kearns could die in such a way, couldn't understand how anyone so strong, so fierce and loyal to their cause could perish in the mud and shit that Vinegar Hill had become. And then Greta felt that grip again, this time upon her arm, stronger than she'd thought possible from a dying man and heard Mogue's quiet voice talking to her. Each word was slow and measured just as it was when Mogue talked to his troops, as he must have spoken to the congregation in his church before this war overtook him, before Mogue's bishop kicked him out of the ranks, ripping away his dog collar, leaving Mogue to replace one faith with another.

'I'm not going to die, Greta,' Kearns was saying, 'at least not yet. But neither must you because you're Heaven sent. I'm passing back to you a duty only you know how to use to our advantage.'

Mogue fumbled at a pocket in his jerkin, finally bringing out a leather pouch that was slick with blood. Greta feared Mogue was about to quit this life but Mogue's voice denied it, strong enough to swear Greta to an oath as he handed the pouch to her.

'It belonged to the Scotsman Fergus,' Mogue said quickly, 'and I need you to figure it out, and I need you to be safe, so take it on the Road to Exile…'

'But no, Father!' Greta interrupted, aghast at the idea. She knew how long that road was, had set many men on its path and couldn't understand why Mogue was sending her that way too.

'This is no time for argument, Greta. You must do as I ask. You must be safe and so must the Scotsman's Bauble. And there's something else with it, a scrap of paper…it says Walcheren…'

Too much pain then. Mogue broke off and started to cough – a deep, chest-racking spasm he couldn't stop – and saw Greta looking about her, saw the panic surging through her young body, that she couldn't think properly, that she'd been too long on the road before she'd got here and thrown too quickly into battle. He thrust the pouch into her hand and closed her fingers about it.

'Swear to me, Greta,' Mogue murmured. 'Swear you will do me this duty.'

Greta nodded, anchored back on Mogue's eyes. 'I swear.'

Mogue patted her hand.

'Alright then, now away. Right now.'

And then the situation overtook them both as several men skidded to a stop beside them, settling about Mogue Kearns like flies to a wound, starting to drag their fallen leader back up the slope, his groans soon lost to Greta as they went, leaving her alone and stranded and utterly unsure what to do. She wanted to be with Mogue Kearns, stay with him until the end and for just a moment she remained kneeling in the blood-soaked mud until she heard another sound, one that rendered all others mute: the whistle of a canon-ball.

Down it came a second later and would have taken off her foot had she not had the wit to curl herself up and fling herself back down the slope of the hill like a hedgehog in free-fall. Her head and body banged against rocks and stones as she went on rolling down the scree, the Scotsman's Bauble tight in her fist, Mogue's words of exile and duty ringing in her head.

She came to a stop thirty yards below, lodged in a whin bush, sick and dizzy with her going, head bursting, feeling a pressure against her ribs she knew didn't belong there. She wondered if she'd been hit before realising no, it was only her fist, the pouch, the Scotsman's Bauble in it where it did not belong. Still she wavered, wanting to go back up to Mogue's side, wanting to fight and fall with the rest and not slink away like the useless girl she was. But Mogue had sworn her to an oath and she had agreed to it and would not let Mogue down.

She began to slither her way down the remaining slope of the hill, snake-like upon her belly, keeping below the haze of dark smoke that took the place of the early morning sun. She sifted herself into the scrub, a band of panic tight across her chest when she realised she'd brought herself within a spit of the enemy, only a few yards between her and the English line.

She lay still then, hidden in the gorse with the fallen prickles hard against the soft arch of her belly, digging into hips and thighs. The pain of her blisters began to come back at her whilst the yellow scent of the gorse was incongruously sweet in the midst of the stink of the battle that was trammelling and roaring its way further back up the hill. The fever of fight had burned itself out, but not the need for escape. She raised herself up on her elbows. She couldn't see much from her hidey-hole, peering through a tangle of twig and branch that served as untidy bars to her untidy cage, but she could make out the shapes of men and their horses stumbling back down the battle-worn slopes.

The irregular thumps of large hooves made the ground shudder beneath her, the horses' hides slick and greasy with blood, sweat and spittle, their movements clipped and jerky with excitement. The returning men began patting down their steeds, strapping bags of oats about their necks, before sitting themselves down upon the ground where they started stripping and cleaning their muskets, rubbing the blood and fat of dead men from off the leather of their coats, coagulating into small groups as Greta watched.

They were quiet at first but soon beginning muted conversations, boasting out their near misses, counting out their kills. The volume of their voices rose with relief, some soon laughing, others smoking and drinking, a few standing up to piss into the bushes just above Greta's head. Hundreds of men a few cubits from her hiding place, milling aimlessly around their makeshift camp, awaiting orders.

The fighting had lasted two hours only, enough to fulfil their objectives just as General Lake had predicted.

'Hit 'em fast and furious, hard as you like,' he'd told them, and that was exactly what they'd done.

All over for Greta's fellows on the Hill, and most likely for the whole of Wexford now the Hill had fallen. And no option for Greta other than to stay hidden for the while. She spied on the victors braying out their victory, gathering themselves together, clapping each other's shoulders, throwing buckets of water over their heads and their horses, pouring out beakers of rum to toast their success.

And so she waited in her prickly bivouac until the last of the Loyalists were gone, taking their canons, their horses and their triumph with them. And only when the last had retreated to Enniscorthy did Greta uncurl her shivering body and look back up at the devastation on the Hill: deserted by the living, replaced instead by several hundred yards of burn and scorch and heaps of bodies. Some were whole, but many more were scattered limb from limb, all left to rot out the rest of the day they'd not had the luck to see the end of. Greta wanted to crawl her way back up to the windmill, wanted to march and stamp and scream her way right up to the summit of the Hill and shout out that at least they had defended their cause to the last.

The stub of the half-blown away windmill stood smoking like a pyre, a marker of a communal grave that would never be dug. Greta began to drag at some of the stones that lay about her on the grass and from underneath the whin and gorse. She pushed them altogether, scraping her hands, ripping her nails to jagged shreds. Only when the cairn was one foot round and one foot high did she stop, and then she carefully unclasped the small chain that hung about her neck, and with it the tiny silver cross that had been her mother's, dropping it right into the centre of the cairn, topping off the hole with a few more rocks, a few more pebbles to fill up the gaps. She took her own oath on top of the one Mogue Kearns had given her, that one day – no matter how far away that day might be, no matter if she was an old woman by then with legs like sticks ready to be broken up for the fire and a back that groaned beneath the weight of its years – that one day she, Greta Finnerty, would come back to this very spot. She would find this cairn and from it she would take up the cross and the slope and the path, and walk her way to the summit of Vinegar Hill, a woman as free as the wind.

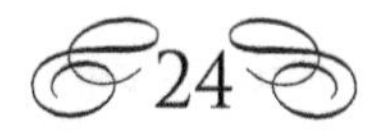

THE SMALL INIQUITIES OF THE SEWING CIRCLE

DEVENTER, HOLLAND

Louisa was so full of her astounding news about Caro that she couldn't wait to say it out loud to anyone who would listen. That night she went to the first Thursday meeting of the Sewing Circle she had attended in weeks. She didn't want to blurt it all out in a second and took her time to build the moment.

'We've a couple of new lodgers,' she told the other women of the group.

Usually they weren't particularly interested in the dry old men the Grimalkins frequently played host to, all come to visit the Athenaeum Library that was – not that they'd any inkling of it – one of the best of its kind in the world. But it hadn't passed unnoticed that a rather dashing, raven haired young foreigner had recently taken up residence. His presence in the Grimalkin household had caused something of a stir, especially amongst the women who had daughters eager to be married off to someone of consequence.

'Well, it's about time you broke your silence, Louisa,' chided Theresa, the matriarch of the group and in whose house they were now gathered. 'My dear, we've all been simply gasping for news.

How good of you to bring it to our door.'

Louisa ignored the slight, her cheeks pink from the attention and the audible cessation of work being put on pause while everyone waited for her speak. She wanted to get straight to the subject of Caro but recognised the order the story must be told in.

'Well,' she began. 'The first is named Ruan Peat. He's from Scotland. Shipwrecked off the Walcheren Peninsula. Everything lost but the clothes upon his back, including his master.'

'He's very handsome,' offered one of the ladies, a couple of others giggling at the observation.

Louisa winced. She'd never really thought about it. As far as she was concerned a person as odious on the inside as Ruan Peat could never be considered in any other way than being ugly through and through. This description of him caught her off guard.

'Well, I suppose some might...'

'Is he single? Betrothed?'

Louisa was flustered by the interruption, making her tongue looser than it might otherwise have been.

'I really have no idea. But I can tell you that he lost his guardian in the shipwreck and is of the bizarre belief that this guardian was murdered while the shipwreck was going on, if you can imagine anything so ludicrous.'

It was not ludicrous in the slightest to Louisa's companions, who were avid readers of the penny dreadfuls that went the rounds; a handsome, unattached young foreigner shipwrecked and his guardian murdered...what could be more romantic?

Louisa was losing patience. She'd hadn't even got to the best of her news, the part about Caro, and realised that even if she did it was going to seem an anti-climax to these women. She looked about her, at doughy, bossy Theresa who was so fat she had difficulty moving from one chair to the next, at little Lisbet sat next to her, the human incarnation of a mouse – if ever God would allow such a thing. Suddenly she loathed them all, loathed their gossiping and tattling that could never be of any consequence.

She would never come back to the Sewing Circle again. She had Caro and that was all that mattered. Let them think what they liked. If they chose to chase after Ruan Peat, well, they were welcome, would soon learn what she already knew about how self-centred and opinionated he was. But she'd read the same penny dreadfuls the rest of them had done and decided to go out with a bang. They wanted a story and she would give them one, one they would swallow down like cormorants do sand eels.

'It's a tale and a half,' Louisa started, tacking together in her head all the little snippets Hendrik and Ruan had spoken of these last few weeks at table, 'all beginning a couple of hundred years ago with a secret society called The Lynx. It involves murder – not just of Ruan's guardian, whose name, by the way is Golo Eck, the same Ecks who originated here – and the unnatural love that can sometime arise between men of a certain disposition. This Golo Eck had been about to start the Lynx up again and Hendrik and Ruan Peat – once he's inherited the Eck estate and all that goes with it – mean to do the same…'

A bit of a lie on that front, but by now Louisa was off, talking for a straight eleven minutes without interruption, telling all she knew about what her husband had uncovered about the Lynx after Ruan handed over Caro's copy of *Behemoths, and other Wonders of the Deep.* And it was good stuff: a father's condemnation of his son for starting up a scientific society against the express wishes of the father's Church, a disinheritance in the making, the murdering of a pharmacist by the Eck ancestor, the way the Lynx had managed to get him freed from prison by a cardinal's intervention, the persistent rumours of unnatural relationships between the society's members, their prolonged connection to Galileo, especially once he'd come under investigation by the Vatican and condemned as a heretic…

It was lurid stuff, Louisa threading it altogether like the competent seamstress she was, her companions enthralled. She even managed to bring in Golo's intent of rescuing the part of the Lynx library that was in France.

'And we all know what the French are up to,' she said darkly, for of course they all did, it being common knowledge that the Revolutionaries were godless and without rule, chopping off heads with the same abandon these women chopped up herbs to put into their pots. Common knowledge too that the French were hovering on the hinterlands of Holland's borders with the aim of making its citizens as godless as they were themselves. Not that anyone in Deventer, let alone in Louisa's Sewing Circle, had noticed any substantial change to their daily lives because of these incursions. However they were uncomfortably aware that the Francophiles among them were already declaring themselves citizens of Batavia, as the French had decided their country should be called, and that this invading army of heretics might come marching through their streets at any moment.

It was an exit anyone would have been proud of and Louisa Grimalkin chose that moment to go.

'Oh, but sisters,' she said, standing up suddenly, a smile on her face like a cut of Edam cheese. 'I'm going to have to leave it at that. I almost forgot to tell you in all the excitement, that I now have my own ward to look after. Young Caro, our second lodger, and a better lad you've never met.'

And with that parting shot Louisa went down the stairs and left her Sewing Circle for the very last time, immensely pleased with herself, quite unaware that the words of her story were about to embark out into the world alone, their whispers and echoes seeping away from their source like water from a leaky well.

If only she'd understood the consequences, if only she'd realised how freely those words would soon be winding and wending their way through the streets of Deventer, reaching out to ears that were never meant to hear them – from wife to husband, from husband to apprentice, from apprentice to the foreign Guildsmen who congregated in the tavern of the Golden Globe, Louisa would have taken up her needles and threads and sewn her lips tight as a cockle, keeping itself safe from the storm that was about to come.

FEVERS, AND BAD OLD MEN

Greta Finnerty took herself away from Vinegar Hill quick as she could. She had a welter of bruises down both arms and thighs from her rolling, and her feet were in a bloody mess from tramping up from Rosslare. She'd no idea of the true extent of the losses brought on by the battle, nor what the English would do now that they had the Irish routed, blood-lust leaking from every pore. All she knew was that she had to do as Mogue had directed, and get away as fast as she could.

She listened at every wall and door she passed, eavesdropped outside taverns and farmyards without daring to approach any of them directly. This was not the time to be finding out the hard way who was a friend of the cause and who was not. Hard times could make a traitor of anyone desperate enough and there were reports of betrayals and subsequent arrests around every corner.

She did learn that every port in the south was being watched, every village harbour – no matter how small – now manned by English guards and no way through the cordon they'd cast about the coast, drawn tighter with every day like a salmon net whose holes got smaller with every pull. No way onto a boat then, not this far south, so not the usual routes to the Road to Exile, and no point either in hoping that Peter could help her for she still didn't know what had happened to him. There was one way further north she knew she could go, and she had no other choice.

A girl dressed as a boy, one with bad feet, left to travel her road alone, she feared at every crossroads, every turn, every path she took, every village boundary stone she passed, terrified she'd be recognised for her past services for what she was: a messenger for the United Irish who had lost her purpose, there being hardly any Irish United left.

She slept below hedges, in the lea-side of barns and hayricks, curled up against the boles of trees, waking in a fright at every sound, every snuffle of the foxes who smelt on her something of their own – blood and decay – coming far closer therefore than they would otherwise have done. Her dreams through those nights were dreadful and recurring: terrifying tableaux of the battle on Vinegar Hill, of Mogue Kearns' grip around her ankle dragging her down, pulling her slowly but inexorably below the surface of the earth, her mouth clogging up and gagging on the gore-soaked mud as she went.

She tore her shirt into strips and wrapped them about her feet, slicing her ill-fitting boots' uppers open with her knife to accommodate the bandages. Despite these rudimentary measures to alleviate her pain, the walking went harder than she'd ever thought possible. She hobbled along like a cripple, hands gripping two sticks of blackthorn she'd hacked from a hedge. She pulled up potatoes from their fields, gnawing at them as she travelled, plucking the dark green heads of fat-hen, taking freely of the wild raspberries that had fruited early.

She passed into Moone at the end of June, just over the border of County Clare, her body so tired that every time she stopped, or leant her back against a boulder or tree trunk, she almost instantly went to sleep. She woke only when her body slid to the ground with a thud that jolted her right back into waking, hardly able to remember where she was or how she'd got there. It wasn't long before the overriding loneliness and the impossibility of the task Mogue had set her became so overwhelming that sobs broke involuntarily from her throat and her feet started up their insistent throbbing in recognition of her despair.

Harder and harder became the necessary job of clutching at her blackthorn staffs to propel her on. One particular night she sat down against the bole of a tree and decided enough was enough. No more walking or hiding for Greta Finnerty. No more clinging to her oath when plainly it couldn't be fulfilled. Even if she managed to reach the safe house and over the water, it was all going to come to nothing. All she'd heard on her travels was of defeat, of the United Irish finished, Vinegar Hill the last nail in the coffin.

Enough for Greta Finnerty. Her struggle was over. Peter was most probably dead, as were Mogue Kearns and the others from the Hill. She'd no business living anyway, not now the rest were gone. She closed her eyes. Time to lay herself down to sleep and if she never woke up again, well, that was alright with her.

George Gwilt was a happy man. He woke before dawn, opened his door and straightway smelt the new wetness of the dust, saw the droplets clinging to the long meadow grass and the leaves of the vegetables in his plot. The previous night's rain had cleansed the air, taken away the stink of the pigs he and his sons had helped bring in from the scrub woods the day before, now corralled in a couple of fields that had been early harvested of corn, to snout and snuffle their way through the gleanings, churn up the soil, make it that much easier to pile on the rotting seaweed they'd gathered after the storm, harrow and plough once the time came right.

Because it was a Sunday, George was up earlier than usual, gratified to find no one else yet abroad. A single robin began to trill from an outgrowing tip of the quick-thorn hedges laid about the pig paddock. He saw the flash and flitter of a flock of goldfinch dipping in and out between the feet of the somnolent pigs and settle on the teasles. He made his way towards the sea and began walking the stretch of the bay towards the Servants, where he would take early morning mass.

His life had changed since the wrecking of the Collybuckie. Previously, he'd never spent a moment at the Servants, nor inside a church or chapel if he could help it, but now he grasped every opportunity to be there. And all because of the two gold cufflinks Ruan had shoved his way. Plus Brother Joachim had approached the shipping company at Vlissingen and had managed to squeeze out a small reward for the men who'd been responsible for rescuing the survivors of the Collybuckie who would otherwise have drowned, even if they were in sight of shore. How Brother Joachim had achieved this latter George didn't know, but it was to George that Joachim brought the news.

It had become their habit after Golo Eck to meet up every few days at the small wayside chapel dedicated to Saint Drostan, a small erection of timbers covering the spring flowing out of the earth as if from nowhere, bubbling from the ground and gathering instantly into a shallow pool before winding its way down to the sea. They'd sit on the benches there and talk about their days, the business of the village, what was going on at the Servants, and it was there that Joachim had met him several weeks previously.

'Ah, George! Just the person I was hoping to meet...'

As if anyone else would be sitting there a half hour after dawn. George smiled.

'Hello, Brother. Anything new?'

'Well,' Joachim said, returning George's smile. 'Quite a lot, as it happens. We had a visitor arrive late afternoon yesterday, come from Vlissingen.'

George frowned. This could hardly be considered momentous news, travellers arriving at the Servants all the time. Joachim interpreted his confusion and tipped his head slightly.

'He came direct from the shipping company that owned the Collybuckie.'

George shivered. It still brought a chill to him, that push and poke of his rake and what it had found.

'And he brought something with him,' Joachim went on, 'that I am now going to give to you.'

He produced a small bag and laid it down on George's bench, George hearing the unmistakable clink of coins and looking over sharply at Joachim.

'But what's this, Brother?' he asked, perplexed.

Joachim laughed.

'It's for you, my friend, for you and your village. Didn't you tell me a while back that your barn's roof blew away in that storm?'

George nodded. It was no secret. The Collybuckie had not been the only thing wrecked in that storm. It had been a terrible source of worry that they wouldn't be able to fix the barn before the harvest was in, for that communal barn was all they had to protect their stores over winter. Ruan's cufflinks had been sold but hardly raised enough, tiny as they were. The roof had taken all the top timbers with it and the whole structure needed pulling down and rebuilding.

'Well then,' Joachim said. 'Here's the answer to your problem.

You saved them, and now they are saving you. What could be more fitting?'

George clenched his jaw as his throat spasmed. He thought for an awful moment that he was going to cry. Brother Joachim saw it, and laid a gentle hand on George's shoulder.

'It's only right,' he said quietly. 'Those men would have died if it hadn't been for you and yours.'

And that was how it all started, George progressively passing off his duties to the village to his more than capable sons, spending more and more time at the Servants. At George's request, Joachim began to teach him about the laying out of the dead, how to tend the sick and dying, how to treat the diseases that plagued the Peninsula that was riven with swamps and mires and the filthy black mud that oozed great clouds of biting, stinging insects every summer.

Joachim, and now George, greatly relied in this respect on an ancient pamphlet entitled *On the Plague, and why it has particularly spread through the Low Countries, and how to treat it.* The author was one Johannes Heckius of Deventer, who styled himself on the title page as a Lincean Knight. Who or what a Lincaen Knight was neither knew, but the fact remained that the advice the author gave for the treatment of fevers was both appropriate and efficacious, and Joachim had come across nothing better. The advised medications might have been devised a couple of centuries before but if they worked, they worked. Ruan Peat was direct proof of that.

Greta did not die that night. She awoke with a start to find she was not alone, an old man sitting a few feet away from her, a small fire blazing between them within a ring of stones. Greta blinked, swallowed, scrabbled backwards against the tree trunk, her hands going for her knife only to find that her backpack had dropped from her shoulders and fallen like a noose about waist and wrists.

'Some emptiness in that stomach of yours,' the old man said, unperturbed by her evident panic. 'Heard it almost ten yards distant, grumbling like a fog horn, so it was.'

Greta said nothing. She was trapped. She moved slowly and carefully, trying to ease the backpack up so she could move more freely.

'No need to fret, lad,' the old man said, poking away at the small fire with his stick. 'Not dawn yet. Plenty of time to leave, and no one coming anyway.'

Greta's heart was thudding. She switched her eyes from left to right looking for possible danger points, saw only the grass of the unkempt field, grey in the gloom, spreading away a hundred yards and more towards the river's edge. She saw the silhouettes of forty, maybe fifty sheep, slumped upon its banks, huddling into one another, heads upon each other's flanks as they slept, the night still warm. Beyond them the river's water gurgling gently over its stones, the white wings of moths hovering in small disparate clouds from off its banks.

'Want a slurpy?' the old man by the fire was saying, holding out a beaker towards Greta who took it without thinking, started drinking greedily before choking, spitting out what was still in her mouth, green and purple flames jumping where the liquid hit the fire, the old man laughing softly into the dawn.

'That's poteen, lad,' he said, 'water of life, so they say, so don't be wasting it. Sip it gentle, sip it right, and it'll give you the best sleep you've ever had and Lord knows, you looks like you could use it.'

Greta was angry, on the verge of tears, couldn't take the old man's laughter, and tried to stand. Her legs gave way and down she went again, and the old man looked at her a moment, then shoved another cup towards Greta.

'S'only water,' the old man said, no laughter this time. Shamefaced in fact, for it had been a mean trick he'd played with the poteen and he knew it.

'Take it,' he said again. 'Take it from one who's already pissed a river away and knows its worth. Good enough for sheep, good enough for the likes of you and me.'

Greta took the beaker, sniffing first, sipping second and sure enough, just plain water this time, sweet with the taint of peat and all the more slaking because of it. The old man in the meantime raked at the ashes of his fire and drew out three charcoal-skinned potatoes, pushing them expertly onto a flat piece of bark with his stick and handing them to Greta, along with a knob of rancid-looking butter and a little pile of salt.

Greta was so hungry she took the trencher and broke open the hot tatties with her fingers, feeling the burn of their heat upon her skin without caring. She hadn't died. She was alive, and she needed to eat and did so, dipping each blackened piece of hot potato into the stale butter and salt, swallowing eagerly, sucking quickly at the water to cool the heat of them in her mouth and stomach.

'Don't mind me saying this,' the old man commented, once Greta had eaten and drunk her fill, 'but you was saying a coupla things in your sleep back then.'

Greta stiffened, fumbling once more for her knife and felt its hilt, wondering whether – if the worst came to the worst – she could really do another man to death in a situation like this, in a field with the river running at its feet and the muffled coughs of the sheep sleeping on its banks. Back on the blood-and-gut splattered slopes of Vinegar Hill she could have massacred an entire army, the roar of the fight swallowing her in its sea, directing her with its tides, her blood on fire. But maybe not here, in the early morning calm, not unless the man gave her provocation. He looked past the age of pounce and pin, dip and thrust, but you never knew, so although she leaned back against her tree she was on guard, ready to strike if struck at.

'O'Malley,' said the old man. 'My name's Owen O'Malley, case you want to know.'

Owen looked across the fire at the lad who had been so bone weary he'd carried on sleeping even when Owen came up beside him, knelt down, placing his calloused fingers against his wrist to see if he was dead or alive. It wouldn't have been the first one he'd come across. Several times over the past eight years of the United Irishmen's struggles he'd stumbled across some man or boy who'd escaped the fighting in one place, only to die in another of infected wounds or the constant drip, drip, dripping of their blood as they'd staggered on. It was a tragedy, was what it was.

If he'd been ten, fifteen years younger he'd have been with them, side by side, but he'd not the knees for it now, nor the will. Let the young do the fighting was his philosophy. After all, they had the most to gain. This lad, though, was younger than most and it had seemed criminal to leave him all on his own, so Owen had retreated a few yards and gathered together some fallen boughs and twigs to make a fire and sat there tending to it, waiting and watching, curious as to this boy's situation, and more so when he caught the few words mumbled out in his sleep.

'Them names,' Owen said, seeing the guard go straight back up in the boy's eyes like an axe-blade from the stump. And what eyes they were – green, like new born grass, the kind that always brought on an unwelcome twitching in his trousers ever since he was young. Not that he'd ever acted on it. Never had the guts. Always knowing it was wrong, but knowing it never made it go away. Sixty five years of dealing with it, but the impulse stronger now than ever, especially when it was so obvious this boy was going nowhere and no one to go to, just another casualty of the struggles, someone no one would ever miss.

It took all his willpower not to just leap across the fire and have done with it once and for all. Small burial mound out here in the sticks – no one would notice it, no one coming anyway, as he'd earlier observed, not with what was going on, all the unrest in the country. Oddly, it was precisely this that stopped him, because he recognised the names the boy had mumbled in his sleep. He looked longingly at his flask of poteen but didn't dare pour himself out another shot. Too much, and who knew how long his willpower was going to last.

Best thing was to get the temptation away and then he could drink as much as he wanted, imagine everything that might have happened. Those green eyes…that small compliant body…that small compliant body that could be his. Owen swallowed, his mouth flooded with saliva at just the thought of the transgression. It had always been like this, but he'd conquered it before and could do so again.

'You've nothing to fear from me,' Owen said, licking his lips, unable to deny himself this one small pleasure. 'But I'm guessing you're maybe friends with those people you were talking on, from the way you spoke them.'

He watched the boy closely. Do or die time. Literally. If the boy was part of the Cause then Owen would let him off with a free pass. If he was on the Loyalist side then things were going to go a different way. Sixty five years of repression was a long time to be waiting, and he'd no love for Loyalists, no matter how young. One gone would be a blessing to his country, no matter how they went.

'Mogue Kearns was the first of 'em,' he said quietly, and caught the small flicker in the boy's eyes at the mention of the name, the unmistakable look of yearning and regret in them that made Owen let out a sigh.

So, one of ours then, he thought with bitterness. *So close, and yet no turnips.*

He stabbed hard at the fire and lowered his head. Time to get the boy away from him before he changed his mind.

'Ain't dead yet,' he said, 'or so I've heard.'

He was rewarded by a smile from the boy that had Owen pulling his legs rapidly together to hide the small spurt of ejaculate he'd not been able to keep in. Jesus, but this boy looked good. A ripe plum begging to be picked, and if a smile could do that for him… Christ, he urgently needed to get out and away and see to himself before he really lost control.

'Guessing you're needing direction to a safe house,' he managed after a few moments, 'and there's one not long yonder; my daughter's home, maybe hole you up for a few days.'

Please Christ, take me up on it.

He couldn't get the images out of his mind – him leaping across the fire, doing what he'd been wanting to do his whole life. And then Greta spoke, the first she'd done so far.

'Thank you,' Greta said. 'I would be much obliged.'

Jesus and Mary, Owen O'Malley near broke his breeks. The boy's voice was so pure and unbroken, and his wanting of that voice and that body so great it was all he could do to speak.

'Shauna,' he said, he wasn't quite sure how. 'Her name is Shauna Clooney. Part of the safe house route. Lives up the road maybe ten, eleven miles. Follow the river, and if you'll take my advice you'll get to her soon as you can and she'll see you right.'

So close then, so close he came to snapping, but thankfully the boy got himself to standing then.

'Shauna Clooney,' Greta repeated. 'Thank you.'

Owen blinked. He thought of offering his hand, but the touch of that cool, pale skin against his own would have boiled him over. Instead he muttered out a few more directions and Greta nodded and went.

The moment the green-eyed boy began walking away, hobbling on his sticks, Owen took a few large swigs of his poteen, undid his trousers, and began to tug away for all he was worth. Jesus God, how had it come to this?

26

AND SHE SEES MAGGOTS IN HER TIDY HOUSE

Near the East Coast of Ireland

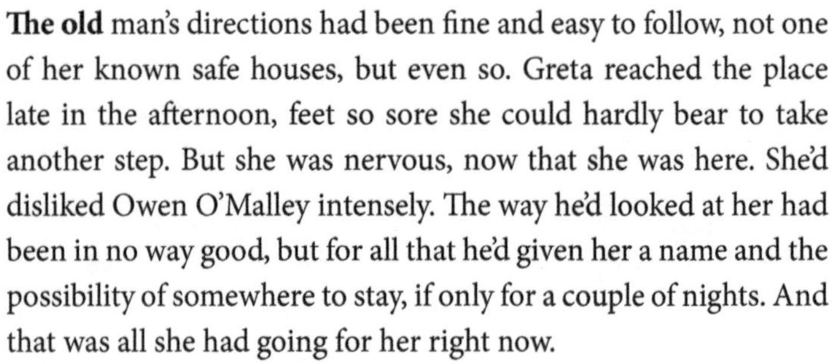

The old man's directions had been fine and easy to follow, not one of her known safe houses, but even so. Greta reached the place late in the afternoon, feet so sore she could hardly bear to take another step. But she was nervous, now that she was here. She'd disliked Owen O'Malley intensely. The way he'd looked at her had been in no way good, but for all that he'd given her a name and the possibility of somewhere to stay, if only for a couple of nights. And that was all she had going for her right now.

Her previous despair had dissipated a little. Owen O'Malley, no matter how despicable he had been, had told her that Mogue Kearns was still alive, and if he was alive then Greta still had a purpose. An oath was an oath, and no way around it. Even so, when she chapped at the door of Shauna Clooney's cottage there was a small tremor to her hand as she shooed away the several chooks that gathered themselves straightaway about her ankles, pecking at the maggots she was unaware were spilling in abandon from the cuffs of her trousers and the torn-up folds of her boots.

When there was no answer to her knock her heart sapped of a sudden with the contradictory anxieties of both relief and disappointment. She leant her shoulder against the wood of the closed door and closed her eyes. She might have gone to sleep again with sheer weariness if she'd not previously registered the white corner of a sheet fluttering from a line somewhere to her right. She forced herself to take a few more steps, took the couple of yards to the corner of the small cob-and-wattle building, seeing then a lean, freckly woman hanging out her washing on the drying green.

The woman turned at Greta's approach, shading her eyes, taking from her lips the last peg she needed to finish hanging out her sheets. She moved towards Greta, and if there was a threat there then Greta was in no fit state to see it, and for herself all Shauna Clooney saw was a raggedy-arsed boy hanging by her wall, noting the way he limped and stepped so gingerly in his boots as he took a single pace out onto the drying green. Shauna raised her arm in acknowledgment to let him know she'd seen him and for him to stay where he was.

No threat, Greta thought, as she saw that pale arm raised up into the late afternoon.

No threat, Shauna thought, as she raised it, for God knew she'd lived through enough of them over the years to know one when she saw it.

Nothing like being brought up a Catholic in a Proddie enclave for understanding danger, especially not when she'd a da like she had, who'd a mouth that didn't understand how to shut itself up even when the enemy were camped up just outside of town. Old da, she thought. Hadn't seen him in months, not since he'd taken himself off with the sheep down the drove roads, fattening them up on the riverside grass as he went, selling the best off at the markets he fastened on to, buying up others he could bring home to increase the quality of the flock. Always a sheep man, never one for arable. He maybe wasn't far away, but would never be back until the harvests were brought in and every last grain of corn gleaned from out of every field by his sheep and the newly arriving geese – share and share alike – and only then would he come home.

No threat then, she thought again, but was still surprised when she got close enough and the boy spoke out all hesitant, quoting her da's name right after she'd been thinking on him, offering up old Owen as his explanation for him being here at all.

'Your da Owen sent me,' was all he said, Shauna looking more closely at her visitor, alerted by the light pitch of the voice, the faint bulge of breasts beneath her jacket. She had the advantage of full light as Owen had not and realised with a shock that this was no boy but a lass in lad's clothing, and none too well fitting at that.

All threat gone now in that simple act of perception and two minutes later Shauna was welcoming this lost lassie into her cottage, into her fold. She had her sat by her range, presenting her with a bowl of warmed brose and her taking it as if she'd never had a better meal in all her days.

After Greta had downed the first bowl she placed it gently on the floor beside her feet and was about to introduce herself properly, thank the woman for her kindness, tell her who she was and how she had come here and why, when a few fat maggots rolled themselves out from her boots onto the floor. She watched their small white wrigglings with astonishment, unable to figure where they'd come from or what they meant.

When Shauna bent to pick up the bowl to give it a re-fill she saw those maggots, the blood draining from her face, appalled that such things should be found in her own home and in front of a guest, even a guest as ragged and battered as this young-comer. And then she saw another roll out beside its siblings and understood.

'Off with those boots!' Shauna ordered.

When the girl didn't react Shauna knelt down beside her and gently broke away the frayed knots of string that were holding the paltry scraps of leather together about her feet, horrified when she eased them off entirely as she saw and smelt the remnants of the lass's socks and the dirty strips of material stuck to her skin with sticky pus and drying blood. Straightaway she fetched a bowl of warm water, a small blizzard of soap flakes scattered upon its surface, and down she knelt again, picking up each of the girl's feet in turn and placing them in the water, socks and all, tutting, not in admonition but sorrow. Greta sucked her breath through her teeth as Shauna worked, wincing as the warm water seeped and broached the broken layers of her skin.

'My lord, girl,' Shauna Clooney spoke softly as she dabbed with the utmost care and gentleness at Greta's feet, peeling back what was left of her bandages, easing away the many strands of wool that had embedded themselves into her soggy-scabbed wounds. She skimmed away the maggots that fell into the blood-stained water of the bowl, throwing them expertly into the small fire that burned in the grate, their soft white bodies sizzling and exploding as she carried out her work with the efficiency of a mother who has spent many hours of her life tending to the bruises, bites, grazes and cuts presented to her by her own children – not that she'd ever seen anything as bad as this.

After she'd cleaned Greta's feet as best she could Shauna went into her pantry, bringing back bottles of lavender-infused oil, honey and goose-grease, then nipped outside for a few moments to pick some fresh wood-sage and comfrey leaves. Once returned, she applied all her medicaments in the specific order she deemed necessary before bandaging the girl's feet in a swaddling of clean rags.

'My Lord, girl,' Shauna said again once she'd finished, Greta having remained quiet throughout her ministrations, biting the insides of her lips when Shauna had run her nails through one or other of her sores to remove a last maggot, a last fly-egg or casing, some stubborn piece of earth that had been lodged inside her burst blisters from the first, moved not so much by the pain as this woman's efficient kindness.

When Shauna was finally done, and Greta's feet were mummified in her ointments and bandages, she threw the last aspects of those stinking socks and the pathetic scraps of what remained of her boots onto the fire, left them flashing and sizzling like bad sausages as they quickly disintegrated into the nether-realms of wood and peat. Shauna straightened up from her kneeling, wiping a hand across her brow, tidying back the strands of hair that had come loose during the hour or so of her nursing, drying her wet hands upon her apron and in doing so noting that it was bloodied and stained and would need boiling for at least an hour to get it back to righteous white.

'But what have you been doing in those fly-farms you've been calling boots?' Shauna asked as she levered her way to standing, started picking up her bottles and liniments and began to move away. And Greta couldn't have said whether it was this finishing or this moving away that triggered it, but suddenly she started to cry.

It was weeping like she'd not done since she was a bairn, if she'd ever done it then. She'd never been a complainer or a moaner, the sort of child who fell out of a tree and knocked herself out, woke up, brushed herself off, embarrassed by her momentary weakness, hoping her brother wasn't witness to it, wherever he was. This silent kind of weeping came as much of a shock to her as it did to Shauna and overtook them both completely.

Greta's entire body convulsed, making her feel like she was collapsing in upon herself, her throat completely choked like an eel-trap that has been left untended over winter with no way for anything to get in or out. She despised herself for this crying, but couldn't stop it. She wanted words to spill out of her mouth like those maggots had spilled out of her boots, wanted to tell Shauna all about the terrible things she'd seen, how she'd been responsible for the slaughter on Vinegar Hill because she'd not got there in time to stop it, how she'd grabbed at escape when offered it and turned her back on the one man she most admired in the world with hardly a second thought.

'Wheesht, wheest,' Shauna Clooney murmured, trying to calm the girl, hurrying herself back to her side once she'd replaced her bottles to the press. She dragged up a stool, sitting herself beside Greta, rubbing at her back, alarmed at the depth of the girl's distress.

But sent here by my da, she thought, and that's a gift worth preserving.

She eased the lass up from her chair and led her to the box-bed built into the wall nearest the fire; led her there and sat her down, pushing gently at her shoulders until the girl subsided onto its length, Shauna covering the shaking child with blankets, despite the summer's easy warmth and the extra heat from the fire, because she was shivering so. Then she placed a flagon of water by the side of the box bed, leaving the girl only when she saw her eyes close in sleep, despite the tears still rolling sporadically down her face.

Shauna left her, made her way to her own bed, listening to the girl's quiet weeping that just went on and on, Shauna's hands cupped around her chin as she lay back on her pallet, waiting until she heard the girl's breathing regulate into a softer rhythm meaning she was at last at rest, for a time at least.

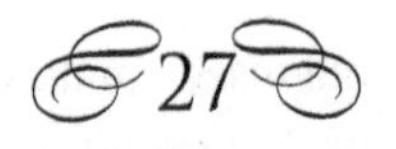

ST DROSTAN FORGETS TO COME THROUGH

WALCHEREN PENINSULA

George got to their meeting place before Joachim. It was an unusual state of affairs, George having started from his home a good half hour early, the day gloriously fresh and inviting. He didn't bother with breakfast and instead headed straight out, getting to the spring and crouching down, dipping the pewter mug – hanging from chain and hook – into the clear, cold water and taking a long draught before settling onto his bench. From here he could see the long bay below his village, and pondered on how different his life had been since those days following the storm and the gifts of both Ruan's cufflinks and the coins from Vlissingen.

Joachim had told him of a clock in his home town built into the tower in the central plaza, how whenever the hour struck, the figure of a woodcutter would come out of a hatchment at one side of the clock and move itself slowly to the other. He would chop at his never diminishing pile of wood as he went before disappearing once more, the circle of his existence spent half in darkness, half in light. And this was precisely how George saw his own life: the dark half having already passed, the new part, in the light, having only just begun.

He heard a noise in the nearby copse of alders and willows that grew along the line of the burn tumbling down past the Servants onto the polder line where it met the sea, at least when the sea was at its highest.

Woodcock, he thought, imaginings their fat bodies sizzling on a spit above an open fire. *Soon time to do a bit of hunting. Get the lads with me and pull in a few fat fowls before they turn into winter scrawn.*

He hummed softly and closed his eyes, enjoying the warmth of the rising sun on his skin and the sharp smell of stranded seaweed in his nostrils, the taste of sea salt on his lips. By Heaven, but it was good to be alive, and even better when he heard Joachim calling out his name.

'Hi there, George!'

And there he was, this Brother in his pale habit George had grown so close to, coming down the slope from the promontory that housed the Servants, stepping gingerly over the polders past the little copse where the woodcock lay. George stood up to meet his friend, raising his hand in greeting, when something flashed across his line of sight – a hawk, maybe, something fast, a peregrine maybe, or a merlin.

At almost the same moment Joachim lost his footing, went headfirst into a large mound of thrift. It wasn't hard to do. The polders were pocked through and through with small holes scoured out by the sea. George waited a few seconds, but Joachim didn't get up. The upper part of his body was hidden from George by the pink and green haze of the thrift he'd gone into. George leaned his body forward, shaded his eyes, but could make out only the tips of Joachim's boots, slowly registering their spasmodic kicking up and down, up and down.

George ran, best as he could with his uneven legs, Joachim maybe forty yards away, then thirty, then twenty, and still not getting himself up. George was panting hard by the time he reached Joachim, who was still prostrate, but he'd managed to roll himself over on one side and George was appalled to see both ends of the arrow that had gone in at Joachim's chest and out again the other side. One of Joachim's hands gripped about the ingoing shaft, the other flailing in the sand, and a broad dark rivulet of blood spreading obscenely across his habit both front and back.

'My God!' George murmured going down on one knee, immediately placing his own hand around Joachim's to stop him plucking at the arrow, the only effect of which would be to pull the barbed end of it deeper into the flesh on the other side.

'Don't move, Brother,' George said quickly. 'Keep on your side exactly as you are, and be as still as you can. Can you breathe?'

Joachim's face was pale as reed pith, but he moved his head a fraction in acknowledgement.

'Very well,' George went on, keeping his voice steady and calm. 'In a few moments I'm going to move you just a little. I'm going to pack some mud about your back and chest to slow the bleeding and then I'm going for help. Do you understand?'

Again Joachim gave a barely perceptible movement of his chin.

'Alright then. Don't you worry. We'll have you fixed in no time.'

George went quickly at his task, scooping up handfuls of the heavy, clay-like mud that made up the polders, building it in mounds about Joachim's chest and upper back, packing it tight and hard, grimacing when Joachim groaned as he shoved each one home.

'I'm away to the Servants now,' George said. 'Don't move. Concentrate on your breathing. Pull it in, push it out, and I'll be back in a flash.'

This was a little optimistic he knew, but he was only five minutes away from the Servants at full tilt and if he could get someone younger than he then they'd be quicker back. He was off then, lolloping up to the promontory, cursing as he passed the small copse, cursing even more as he caught a glimpse of someone leaping like a hare over the polders away to the west, well in the distance now, and no hope of being identified.

Goddamned hunters. Goddamned lousy hunters. Never mind that he'd only moments earlier been thinking of going out of and doing the same.

So, no woodcock then, just some young boy who probably had one of those new bows that were all made of metal and no easy things to master, so easy to aim one way and shoot another. Nothing in the copse now but a couple of starlings bickering about the bullace flowers and a wren chittering loud, low and hidden as he passed. He ground his teeth. No time to think on that now.

Afterwards he'd track down every last boy and bow within two square miles to find the nit-witted coward responsible, who'd not even bothered to check the damage he'd done before fleeing to save his own skin.

Time now to get to the Servants, and with any luck save Brother Joachim's life.

Shauna did not sleep well, but rose at the usual hour, her body honed by habit and common usage. Five o'clock, and always much to do in the hours that were spread out before her every waking day before she sat down to breakfast.

First there was the stove to see too, next she had to lay out her man's clothes, polish his boots, rub wax and goose-fat into every seam of them, into every crevasse, to keep his feet dry as she could. She had to skim the buttermilk for the soda-bread dough, mash up the bran-mix for the chickens, milk the cows in the shed before leading them out to the field behind the house, taking the time on her way back to pick any mushrooms she could find or gather any fruits, nuts or herbs, according to their seasons.

But this was a morning with a difference.

She knew it the second she opened her eyes and gazed up towards the small porthole built into the wall across from her bed that allowed in a small shard of light as soon as the sun passed a certain degree above the horizon. A clock of sorts, one that never lost time if you knew how it worked, going slower in winter, speeding up and then winding down again. Usually she would lie a while, just a few minutes, watching the sun slanting down the walls, guessing the weather outside from its intensity.

She would wait until its rays hit a certain point when she would sigh and creak her way up off her mattress, trying not to wake her husband, and move bare-foot across the cold flagstones and on into the next room. Here her clothes and clogs would have been left the evening before to warm themselves by the fire, her dress and undergarments hanging out their creases on the folding clothes-horse she erected every night by the grate.

But not this morning. For a start, there was no husband to mollycoddle, for he was away to the coast with a host of other men – at least those who hadn't gone south to take part in the Rising – because a pod of whales had beached themselves on the sands on some bay outside of Dublin. There was good money to be had in stripping down their carcasses, boiling out their oil, get their acres of skins scraped and stretched for leather, any ambergris collected, refined and filtered, the best sold to perfume-makers for a fine price, the worst to the soap-makers for a little less.

Her man had spent a good few of his early years, before they'd married, on the Scottish whaling ships up north and so knew what he was about. There was a possibility he might bring home more money than they could otherwise have accrued throughout an entire year of scrimping and saving on the farm. Be that as it may, the fact was that Donal was not here.and there was no need for her to set out clothes for him or get his boots seen to, and she was still wearing most of her own clothes from the night before, having lain down directly in singlet and stockings, stripping off only the outer layers. More importantly there was a young girl sleeping in the box-bed by her fire, and so Shauna dallied a little, not knowing whether her getting up would wake the girl, wanting her to sleep for as long as her body needed.

Shauna reflected that she could count upon the fingers of one hand the mornings she'd woken up alone in this bed since she was married, the few exceptions being when she'd been as beached as were those whales outside of Dublin, her stomach a gravid mountain rising up before her. Her successive children even then hadn't let her sleep too long, kicking – as they all had – with a relentlessness that told her each was over-eager to get out before their time.

Two of them had done just that, and in consequence died before opening their tiny, blood-smeared eyes onto a world that should have been theirs. Of the other four who had bided inside her a little longer, three had gone on to survive – hardy little beggars all – all now grown and gone, the two boys to the fighting, the girl marrying into a neighbouring farm. Only her and Donal left at the homestead, and her da Owen, when he was back for the winter from the droving.

She tried to relax, closed her eyes, tried to drift back into sleep, but her body was having none of it. Within a few minutes she was too restless to remain lying idly on her bed, needing to get up and doing. She dressed quickly and quietly into yesterday's clothes, but took a clean pinafore from the shelf below the wash-stand before splashing some water onto hands and face. She opened her door and tiptoed across the flagstones of the main room of the cottage, where the girl was in the box-bed.

She could see from where she stood that the fire had enough red life left in its embers to last another while and so she let it be, did what she had never done before – feeling strangely exhilarated to be breaking the pattern of almost every single day she had spent in this house for the last twenty-seven years. Instead of going to fire or pantry she stepped straight for the door that led outside, putting her stockinged feet into her boots but not doing them up. Before leaving she looked back at the girl, who was sleeping soundly.

The blankets Shauna had placed over her the night before had been pushed down below her waist, but Shauna could see the gentle rise and fall of the girl's chest, her small breasts more evident now that several buttons had been loosened on her singlet, hands curled liked a baby's beneath her chin. One bandaged foot hung over the edge of the box-bed, a dark brown stain spreading from heel to ankle.

She looked so very young and vulnerable that tears began to leak from Shauna Clooney's eyes as she stood there immobile, gazing at this wounded child she didn't know the name of, feeling an echo inside her of when her own children had been young, like she hoped she'd feel again if they ever provided her with another generation to mollycoddle and worry about.

But there were other things needed doing now, other animals needing her care and protection and so she slowly, slowly lifted the latch of the outer door and disappeared into the pale light of dawn.

Joachim was taken up to the Servants. Once there, George supervised the removal of the arrow, clipping off the barbed end so it could be removed, clipping off the feathered end for his own purposes, arrows being feathered differently, each to their own, and here was a way to find out who had done the actual deed. No doubt it would never come to anything as far as the law was concerned, but George was intent on discovering who that early morning poacher had been who'd hit a man instead of a goose or a woodcock or whatever else he'd been firing at. And hewas going to make damn sure he never did anything like it again.

Joachim was lucky, or God blessed, as the Brothers would have it, the arrow having grazed his heart but done no permanent damage. A lung had been punctured, but he would be able to get along with the other until it healed, as long as pneumonia didn't set in. There was no sign of it yet, nor two days later, which was a good sign. Of the person leaping over the polders and away George could give no adequate description, but once he was certain Brother Joachim was out of danger he spent every waking hour going round every house in every village strung out on the edges of the peninsula asking questions.

Who had been at home on the morning of such and such a date? Who had access to bows and arrows? What kind were they? Could he see the feathers they used to make their flights? Did any one of them possess a crossbow?

More and more George was thinking crossbow. So much harder to aim, so much easier to maim. He was convinced he could uncover the guilty party, but the more people he asked, the more they seemed to exclude themselves. He was not discouraged. He would not rest. He would not sleep easy ande would not desist, not until the culprit was caught.

Greta didn't hear Shauna go, passing quiet as the shadows did across the port-hole dial of Shauna's room. Greta wakened only when the cattle out in the shed began to low and clatter and cough as Shauna sat upon her stool, pumping out their milk into her pail.

Shauna had already seen to the chickens, giving them the last scraps of yesterday's mash and brose, scolding them as they were scolding her for not giving them anything fresh and new. She had tried to lead them away from the house and to the back of the yard so their noise wouldn't wake the girl, tempting them with a few handfuls of almost ripened corn she snapped from the field onto which one side of her yard was backed.

She'd found eleven eggs in the roost-house and was well pleased with that, didn't chide the chooks for long for their noise, was thinking instead on what she could make for breakfast. She'd still a few links of beef sausage she'd traded for down in the village the week before, and they'd been hanging in the smoke from the fire long enough since and would be truly tasty. She'd been saving them for Donal's return from the whales, but a good breakfast for the young visitor seemed a better use. Add to that some drop-scones made yellow by this morning's eggs and milk and there'd be a bit of a feast when the lass finally awoke.

Shauna was startled by a slight rapping at the door of the milking shed, and looked up to find the girl herself standing there, propped on two of Owen's old sheep staffs she must have found by the boot-box by the door.

'Can I give you some help?' Greta asked, Shauna so surprised she gave an inadvertently hard tug at the teats she'd been working, making the old cow low and give out a feeble kick that nearly overturned the pail. Shauna grabbed quickly at its rim to keep it still. She looked towards the girl and saw the feet she'd bandaged with so much care the night before now fortified by several strips from her ragbag, tied on with some of the knotted strings from the girl's mangled boots that Shauna had neglected to burn with the rest the night before.

On any other day than this her reprimand would have been sharp and quick – using dirty string on clean bandages, indeed – but not today, and not with the girl leaning there so pathetically, looking like an old woman fifty years before her time, thinking instead how hard it must have been for her to have hobbled across the yard on her makeshift crutches, feet protected from the cobbles and their dew by only those small scraps of dirty cloth.

'My Lord, girl,' Shauna said, putting a milk-spattered hand to her forehead, 'but what a fright you gave me. How are you not still sleeping by the fire?'

Greta smiled, and now she had no bonnet on and no oversized boots she looked so small and fragile and feminine that Shauna couldn't believe she'd mistaken her for a boy for even half a second. And that smile: it was radiant. No other word for it, no matter how filthy the girl's face was, how stained and puffy from last night's tears.

'But it's morning,' Greta said simply. 'And this is a farm, and I know there's much to do on it and if I can help, then so I will.'

There was such defiance to her answer, making it seem like she was expecting retaliation and was ready to counter it that Shauna smiled. She'd been just like this when she was young, and would have bet money – if she hadn't considered betting a mortal sin – that this girl had grown up in a family of boys. And so she said nothing, merely stood and gestured at the half-filled pail and the three-legged stool she'd just vacated.

'Any good at milking?' Shauna asked, and in answer Greta hobbled over and took Shauna's place on the stool, leaning her sticks against the side of the stall, taking the old cow's teats in her young hands with a tenderness that almost broke Shauna's heart.

'Any good?' Greta said, grinning up at Shauna, the milk already splashing white into the pail. 'Only been doing it me whole life.'

Later, they sat in the kitchen together, eating fried eggs and smoked beef-link sausages and the griddle scones Shauna had cooked up in the fat left by both. She quickly learned Greta's name, but it took far longer to drag out of her the rest of her story, Shauna assuring Greta that anything she said would go this far and no further. Greta became quiet and sad as she recounted her part in the struggles, but Shauna would have none of it. What this girl had done for the Cause was truly astonishing. She'd risked her life every day for getting on three years, working as a messenger, moving from cadre to cadre, from Dublin down to Wexford, dressing sometimes as a boy, sometimes as girl, whichever suited, slipping her way between chinks in enemy lines, gleaning information as she went that would have had her strung up from the nearest tree if anyone understood what she was about.

When Greta finally spilled out her guilt that she'd not got to Vinegar Hill in time to let them know the French weren't coming, and so precipitated a massacre, Shauna put her foot down.

'That was never going to happen, Greta,' Shauna said decisively. 'No matter what time you got there or did or didn't do, those men were always going to fight that fight.'

Greta didn't looked convinced, not until Shauna spoke again.

'My oldest son,' she said, 'went off to join the Rising last year, and my youngest fought at Bunclody with Myles Byrne. They both survived, the Lord be praised, and got to Vinegar Hill with the rest of them since the end of May. And I can tell you this, my girl, that no matter what the Frenchies were doing, or had intentions of doing, or whether or not they or you would've got there in time, those men at Vinegar Hill were always going to make their stand there. It was long ago decided, and I had word of it myself from my youngest. Nothing you or anyone else could have done to stop it.'

Greta tried to absorb what Shauna was telling her, her face scrunched up in concentration. She closed her eyes, shook her head.

'So why?' she said quietly. 'If they knew there wasn't going to be any reinforcements, why did they stay?'

'Hush yourself, child,' Shauna said. 'These are men you're talking about. If you or me had been in charge it would have gone differently a long time ago. Women always look to the future. We know what it means to invest in a child. Men don't. You're young yet, but you'll find out. Men only see the here and now. And those men on the Hill? Well, they always meant to do or die. It's all in the moment for them. It's all about power and keeping face. I've two sons, lass, both on the Hill, so I know what I'm talking about.'

Greta frowned. She'd never heard anyone say anything quite like this, but it all made so much sense: why Peter hadn't legged it when he'd had the chance, why Mick Malloy had done what he'd done, the things Mogue Kearns had said to Greta, who would have laid down her life for his. He'd the chance to get them all away and hadn't acted on it, and now Greta was beginning to question those decisions, seeing them from the outside instead of from the in, which was something she'd never done before.

'Do you know where your sons are now?' Greta asked, after a few moments absorbing what was for her a revelation.

'That I don't, Greta,' Shauna answered. 'I've heard nothing. But what I do know is this: if they died there on the Hill then they died for you and me and for the Cause we are not alone believing in.'

Greta nodded. This much she understood. Her older brother, Joseph, had taken up arms soon as he was able, her father next, both dying early doors, the reason she'd got involved in the first place, for if they believed then so did she. Far better to have a function than hang around an empty homestead and a mother who took refuge from her grief by denying that any other world might exist than the one that kept playing out in her own head, where father and brother still existed and went on with their lives.

'It may not be my way,' Shauna said, after a brief silence, 'or the way I might have chosen them to do it, but it's a truly righteous thing they're doing, those men, my boys. And you Greta. You too. Never forget that.'

Both quiet they were then, the middle-aged mother who might have lost her last remaining sons, and the lost young girl, thinking their own thoughts, hands clasped together sitting by their fire. They listened to the sounds of normal life going on all about them: the cattle grazing out in the fields, the occasional low bellow that came from a dam to her calf when they became separated by the throng for too long, the chooks pecking away at the stones in the yard for any seed that might have fallen into the hollows between the cobbles, the softer sounds of collared doves calling from their cot, the rise and fall of lapwings as they whirred haphazardly over the cottage and its surrounding meadows.

'Is there anything I can do? About your boys, I mean?' Greta asked. 'I could go back…I could…'

Shauna Clooney sighed, squeezing Greta's hand, her shoulders sagging without conscious thought.

'No, darling,' she said. 'There's nothing you can do. If it's done, it's done. Same as it's been since this whole thing started. Nothing to do but sit and wait, same as every other woman the country up and down.'

And that about summed it up: Shauna sitting here, waiting to hear if her sons were dead or alive, if they'd survived the latest battle and – if they had – whether or not they'd gone on to, and died, in the next. No adequate means of letting her know one way or another. Letters getting through occasionally but only if they knew how to write, and only if they had trusted channels to send them through. Greta thought back to the Printworks and the morning before New Ross and Fergus and to Mogue Kearns and her oath.

Christ almighty! How had she never seen it before? She had the means to help Shauna right here with her! It wouldn't take much. No need for complication. Knots and beads, Fergus had said, how hard could it be? But first, a proper look at the stringy doodah before she got Shauna's hopes up. She looked around wildly, suddenly remembering Shauna flinging not a few of her clothes on the fire.

'My jacket!' she exclaimed. 'Where's my jacket?'

Oh Jesus, please don't say you've burned my brother's jacket.

She snatched her hand away from Shauna's and put it to her mouth, because if it was gone then so too was the Scotsman's Bauble and her journey was at an end.

THE LEAPING OF THE LION

DEVENTER, HOLLAND

Several weeks after Louisa's last meeting with her Sewing Circle, which she had not attended since, she went about her duties with not a care in the world, because Caro too gets up at the crack of dawn every day to help her. Together they riddle the stove, fill the water buckets, wash the previous night's dishes, wipe the muck from everyone's boots and polish them into a decent shine – four pairs now, instead of two. They clean all the lamps, trim their wicks, change any linen that needs changing, then set to bashing at the bread dough, shaping it, winding it into plaited buns or sprinkling it with poppy or sesame seeds.

Then down comes Hendrik and the three of them sit together for breakfast, Ruan Peat always staying in bed the longest with no desire for a communal meal so early in the day. He spends no more time with any of them than he has to. He's lost interest in anything except the arrival of Golo Eck's Will so he can be released from their company entirely. He is polite and deferential, but refuses to accompany Hendrik to the Athenaeum and pays no attention to anything Hendrik talks about afterwards when he's come home. Hendrik had become fascinated by the history of the Lynx ever since Ruan gave him Golo's book, or rather the book that Golo gave Caro, deciphering Golo's scribbled notes in its margins.

And this morning is no different, except that Caro isn't here. Hendrik has discovered that the Athenaeum possesses quite a few of the Lynx papers – not so surprising, considering it is one of the foremost libraries in Europe, exactly the sort of place they would have ended up in, buried down in the stacks for decades on end. One of them has pointed to another possible deposit in a private collection in Arnhem and Hendrik knows the owner well and has sent Caro off to collect them.

He should be back tonight, or if not tonight then tomorrow morning, so Louisa has saved some of the bread dough and plans to make something special for his return. A stöllen, she's thinking, something sweet and delicious he'll never have tasted before. Yes, she thinks, that's what she'll prepare for him. Something to make him smile in wonder. She can already see that smile in her mind and is joyful because of it, even though it is only a promise of the real thing.

Greta's world was back on its axis, her Road to Exile still intact. Shauna had not burned her jacket. Gone were her boots, socks and the bottom half of her trousers, but not the jacket.

'That much leather?' Shauna laughed just to think on it. 'Of course not, child! It would have smothered my fire into nonexistence, and why would I burn the one thing you were wearing that could still be of use? I meant to talk to you today about replacing all the rest of your clothes, or rather the ones you're still wearing because my word, I don't know if you know it, but you look and smell a fright.'

The words weren't said badly and Greta didn't take them so, and before long she was kitted out in hand-me-downs of varying shapes and sizes, topped off by her brother's jacket. She would stay with Shauna Clooney only as long as it took her feet to heel and then she would be off again.

They got on well during the weeks Greta was at Shauna's, quickly settling into a routine. Shauna inspected Greta's feet every morning, removing the bandages, washing the sores, lathering on more medicaments before bandaging them back up again. And then the both of them went to the stock or the dairy for a few more hours, or weeding Shauna's vegetable plot, collecting fruit from the orchard, boiling it into pickles and jams, tying up bundles of herbs to dry near the fire, pressing down mushrooms with salt into a ketchup that would last far longer than either of them could hope to live.

By the time seven o'clock of a night came, Shauna and her young helpmeet had gained enough hours to afford them both the rare pleasure of having time to spare, and in the quiet times of the evenings they played card games or read to each other from one of the few books Shauna's mother had left her – books not opened for maybe fifteen, twenty, years. They also allotted half an hour a night to try to figure out a way the stringy belt – as Greta called it, for she couldn't remember it's proper name – could be put to use for the United Irish or, more specifically, for Shauna and her sons.

The first time Greta took out the pouch she was dismayed by the dark brown flakes that fell from its surface: Mogue Kearns' blood. Shauna understood, and swept every last fraction of them into a small handkerchief and handed it over to Greta, who took it with gratitude and placed it inside her jacket pocket. Then she turned her attention back to the pouch and tipped out its contents. Shauna was dazzled by the ring, but as soon as Greta explained how the belt might put to practical use she ignored it, the ring put away and never spoken of again.

'So where's the what of it?' Shauna asked, completely confounded by the khipu. Greta was puzzled too. She was an observant girl and was certain it looked different now than it had done when Fergus first showed her it, although this was the first time she'd looked at it up close.

'He said it was all to do with the knots and beads,' she answered slowly, biting her lip, unsure where to start.

She wished she'd bothered to go back to Fergus at the time and get the specifics out of him, but it was too late for that now. Still, over the following nights they had time and spent it well. Shauna had no writing paper in the house but fetched a beet bag from the pantry and ironed it flat and it would have to do. They began by Greta copying down the patterns of the differently embroidered squares that made up the belt – some looking like stylised depictions of trees and water, others taking the form of abstract symmetrical designs. All tiny, all beautiful, and while Greta copied Shauna looked at one or other and came up with several ideas of what they could signify.

'I suppose this one here,' she said, pointing at a group of little lollipops of differing heights standing together, 'this might mean family, or maybe a tribe or a clan. When I get lads coming through here on the Exile Road I'll often ask them where they come from and who their forebears were. Can't never be too careful, and if one answers wrongly we'd be maybe thinking spy, and testing them some more. Ooh, and this one here. This might be sheaves of corn, maybe means a farmer or rebirth or something like…'

Greta nodded each time Shauna spoke, jotting down her ideas beneath each illustration. When they'd finished that task to their satisfaction Greta moved on to drawing the positions of each knot and bead on each string dangling from each little square so that when done they had a complete depiction from beginning to end

– a random beginning and end to be sure, but a completion of sorts.

While they worked it became clear that it really could be used to encode information, though had no clue what the original information was. But that didn't matter. What was needed now was how they could use it to convey information, of more importance than ever since the disaster of Vinegar Hill that had scattered the surviving cadres completely. If they were ever to reunite and mount another successful uprising then the key to it was going to be everyone knowing where everyone else was and everyone acting in consort.

'Let's say you knit a band like a skinny scarf,' Greta proposed, Shauna nodding. 'We need to keep it simple, so maybe we have it in squares of different colours and from those squares we thread several plaited lengths.'

Shauna raised a finger and interrupted

'That's easy done. I can make a fair few of those a night if they're needed.'

'They'll be needed,' Greta said, with conviction. 'And the colours? Can you manage that?'

'Well,' Shauna twitched her mouth as she thought. 'Onion for brown and black, tansy for orange, Dyer's rocket for yellow and green, elder for blue, madder for pink…yes. I think if I think some more on it I can maybe get ten. Might have to shear the sheep early for the wool and raid my herb store right enough, but that's by the by.'

'Alright then,' Greta said, 'Let's say ten. So ten different coloured squares, a couple of plaits from each, a couple of knots or beads on each plaint and we could make an alphabet easy, knot at the top for one letter, knot at the bottom for another, maybe one square for direction, south or east and so on…'

'And then squares meaning yes or no depending on the placing of the bead, another for wounded – good or bad, another for alive or…dead.'

Shauna spoke these last words quiet and slow, Greta looking over at the older woman knowing she was thinking about her sons.

'That will do it,' Greta said after a few moments. 'That will do it.'

And so it did. They spent their last few nights together figuring it all out in detail, keeping it as uncomplicated as possible so it could be used by literate and illiterate alike, until they could produce a working prototype, one Shauna would put into action as soon as she had made it. They made plans for its dissemination, moving from one safe house to another with its rudimentary instructions, passing it from link to link, from chain to chain, moving slowly but certainly across the land.

Too soon for Shauna came Greta's leaving. No sign yet of Donal coming home from the coast.

'He'll be lording it up after the whales,' Shauna said. 'That's ay been my Donal. Stick a bit of money in his pocket and he'll step into every public house he can find from anywhere to here, and Lord knows there's a good many of those.'

It seemed wrong to Greta that he should do such a thing, and to a woman like Shauna who spent all her days working so hard, but Shauna herself did not appear concerned. She instead relished this time she'd had alone on the farm with her young Wexford Warrior, as she called Greta – in her head if not to her face.

It was a quiet night, the last one Greta and Shauna spent together, darkness a gentle shadow that hugged itself about the cottage; a night with no wind nor rain, no furrowing of clouds. It was late, far later than either of them were used to, but neither wanted to part nor sleep until it was absolutely necessary.

They sat outside, the stars bright, everything seeming safe and just as it was meant to be. They listened to the chooks shuffling themselves and their wings to sleep in the hen-house, and the doves snuggling down inside their cot, the cattle pluffing in their byre. Owls were on patrol, swooping down the long lines of wheat and rye in the meadows not yet harvested, calling softly to one another every now and then until they hooked their efficient claws into the backs of the mice and voles that ran along their hidden paths.

Shauna was dismayed that Greta would be gone the following morning for she had lit up her life and she was feared to go back into the darkness when Greta left.

'Don't forget what I told you,' Shauna said into the night. 'I know you know the route and that each place will direct you to the next, but stick to it Greta. And keep your voice low as you can. And I know the bands will hurt,' she added, referring to the strips of muslin she'd advised Greta to bind about her chest to hide the small budding of her breasts. Shauna had also cropped Greta's hair, for it had grown since Greta had first chopped it.

'And be wary. You'll not get on any boat at all if they believe you're a girl,' she went on, 'and Lord knows you don't want them discovering it part way out. For starters those old fishermen think women are the worst kind of luck and will chuck you overboard if they decide to blame you for their bad catches. And for seconders… well, I'm not even going to talk about that, but be warned, Greta. Men at sea are lonely, and there's a different law out there. Makes them less accountable, makes them take what they want, not what they're given.'

Greta didn't reply but leaned in toward Shauna and rested her head upon Shauna's shoulder, a gesture so casual and intimate that

Shauna closed her eyes, wanting to hang on to the memory of it for as long as she lived.

'I don't know how I'll ever be able to thank you,' Greta said, reaching out a hand and taking Shauna's freckly fingers in her own, trying her best not to cry.

'Only by coming home safe, darling,' Shauna replied. 'And by coming back to tell me all you've done and of the great adventures I know you'll have, which will be a hundred times more than any woman I've ever known.'

They went to their beds then, and the following morning Greta took her way down the path and Shauna went back into her house, ignoring the chickens that were clamouring for attention, ignoring the cows who were so desperate to be milked. Shauna instead went directly to her kitchen and swept up all the locks of Greta's hair she had shorn off the night before, securing them in a small bag that she hung on a nail directly opposite her bed just below the round window so that every morning afterwards she would remember her young Wexford Warrior and send up a prayer that she was safe.

Caro was eager to be off, eager to be home to Louisa, overjoyed – still a little stupefied – that he actually a place he could call home. He'd made good time so far. The two boxes of papers from Hendrik's friend in Arnhem were strapped to his back and he was just about to step on board the barge that would take him the last leg to Deventer when he heard a loud voice booming behind him.

'Well if it isn't my old friend! Wait up, wait up!'

Caro turned to see the broad smiling face of Signor Ducetti beaming down on him.

'It is you, Caro, why I thought it was, but my, you've changed!

You were a slip of a lad last time I saw you and I swear you've grown an inch since then. Do come up here and let me buy you the biggest lunch you've ever seen! I owe you much, not just for dragging me onto the raft but for leading me from Walcheren, and I am not a man who likes to be in debt.'

Same old Signor Ducetti, words pouring out of him like smoke from a chimney. A man who had never seemed able to keep quiet, not on the raft, not on the way from the Servants. Donkeys looked to their hind legs when he passed them by. Caro didn't really want to wait, certainly didn't want to miss this barge, but it seemed ill-mannered not to pass the time of day with a fellow survivor from the Collybuckie, and no sooner had they shaken hands than Ducetti was leading Caro back up the way to an inn, his big hand cradling Caro's shoulder.

'So you're still in Holland? You must tell me all about it. And I want to know everything!'

He laughed so loudly that people turned and stared, not that Ducetti noticed. He was too busy inveigling Caro to sit, choose whatever he wanted from the sparse menu.

'And wine! We must have wine and lots of it, and nothing but the best for my young friend. This is a celebration! An accidental celebration maybe, but they are always the best kind. And let me tell you, young Caro, that I have as much to tell you as you must have to tell me. I'm on my way to Amsterdam, to my shop there, but this happy coincidence has stopped me in my tracks!'

On and on he went, Caro subsiding beneath the wave of his words , sitting as commanded, choosing at random various foodstuffs, Ducetti demanding more, and before Caro knew it several hours had gone by, and then another hour, and another. He wasn't used to drinking wine and by early evening was sleepy, at which point Ducetti declared he needed rooms for the night.

'The best you have!' he demanded with his usual exuberance.

'I really must get going,' Caro tried to protest. 'You've already been too kind, and I've no money to stay another night away. There must still be a last barge that can take...'

'Nonsense, young Caro,' Ducetti interrupted, a flamboyant wave of his arm bringing the innkeeper running with yet another bottle of wine, Ducetti pouring yet another glass for the both of them.

'This meeting was meant to be. You did me a great favour and now I am giving you one in return. Life is too short,' Ducetti said, 'as we both, to our chagrin, know. But what we have must be lived to the full, Caro. Enjoy it, I say, and damn the consequences.'

Damn the consequences, Caro thought blearily. For what could be the harm?

'And I insist on giving you a gift,' Ducetti went on. 'Here, take this.'

He produced a large hunting knife and sheath from his baggage.

'A gift for my young friend, so that you will always have something to remember me by.'

Louisa heard the knocking at her door and went to it, opened it, her heart in her throat thinking it might be Caro. He'd no need to knock, she'd already told him, not anymore, but he was the kind of lad who would do it anyway. She was nowhere near finishing the stöllen she was in the middle of making for him but decided it might be even more special if Caro had a hand in making it himself, and so she quickly strode down the hall to the door. Disappointingly it wasn't Caro, nor was it the fish-seller's regular delivery boy who was due later that day. Instead stood a man she'd never seen before, a pony behind him with a dray on which sat two kegs of what she supposed must be beer.

'I'm sorry,' she said, rubbing her hands in and out of her apron. 'But we've ordered nothing. Our delivery for ale isn't due for another two weeks.'

'Nothing to do with me, Missus,' said the man, a slight accent to his words she couldn't identify. He had the wiry build of someone who regularly threw casks of this and that down as many chutes as there were days in his life. 'Been told to bring 'em here, and that's that. All paid for too, if you're the…' he looked down quickly at the piece of paper he was holding in his strong hands, 'the Grimalkins on the Singel.'

'Well yes,' Louisa said. 'That's us, but we've ordered nothing.'

'And yet,' the man said with a grin she found entirely inappropriate, 'here it is. Gotta shift it, lady, got my orders right here on this form.'

He thrust the form at her and from the quick glance she gave it could see he was correct. There was the name and the street and after a few moments she relented, supposing that Hendrik must have ordered an extra supply now they had Ruan and Caro with them.

'Well then,' she said. 'Best get it down to the cellar.'

Apparently the man agreed, for he snatched back the order from her hands and went straightaway to the dray, hoisting the first keg on his shoulder as if it weighed no more than a goose.

'Which way?' he grunted, and she led him through the door towards the cellar stairs, not wanting the beer to be spoiled, or the barrel burst, by this man rolling it haphazardly down the delivery chute at the back.

'Follow me,' said Louisa, leading him on, casting a quick glance into the kitchen at the roll of dough on her table, thinking yes, cherry Stöllen for sure. She'd several jars of wild geanies in the pantry in the cellar and she might as well fetch them while she was down there.

The man came on behind her, but the moment they reached the bottom of the stairs he put the cask down, extracted a leather-covered cosh from his belt and gave Louisa a smart smack with it on the back of her head. She couldn't understand it – one moment she was standing upright thinking about Stöllen and cherries and Caro, the next she was down on the earthen floor of the cellar, the taste of its damp soil in her mouth, her eyes unable to focus on the boots of the dray man walking away to one side of her, placing the cask of ale on top of one of the two hay-bails they kept down here for use as kindling when the wind gusted too hard down the chimneys and blew out the range.

She was trying to lever herself up, trying to make sense of what was going on, trying to crawl her body a few inches forward when the man returned from his labours. He went up for the second barrel and, passing her by, gave her another hard thwack with his cosh, a sound in her ears like the damp snapping of rotten wood and back down she went.

She wasn't aware of him leaving nor returning with the second barrel, nor that once done he unwound a line going from the first barrel to the next, and from that one to the base of the stairs where he lit its end with his flint before scarpering quick as he could up and out, onto the dray. He drove the pony with his whip so he was off down the Singel and turning a corner towards the Brink when the lit fuse reached the barrels.

FIRE, AND BURNING AMBITION

Greta went from Shauna's farm on her newly healed feet without a doubt, without a tremor. She was off on the route she'd been directed: first to the coast and the boat Shauna had told her would be waiting. Once there Greta did as Shauna had advised and pitched her voice low as she could, Padraig O'Rourke – the skipper – more sympathetic than she'd expected.

'A tad young, aren't you laddie?' O'Rourke commented, noting the boy's slight frame, the voice that had not quite broken. His first impression of this Joseph Finnerty was that he was somewhat out of the norm of the usual escapees over to France. He was a straight-backed boy, well featured, well fed, a well-packed knapsack on his back, boots that looked serviceable but rather too large for the rest of him.

There'd been a certainty to the lad's request for passage that few of the other rebel Irish had, asking specifically for Walcheren when most just threw themselves on his mercy, knowing he was their only way out. It hadn't escaped his noticed that this Joseph had the same surname as the famous Peter Finnerty and the boy admitted the relationship when asked. So, all in the boy's favour as far as O'Rourke was concerned, but he recognised a pretty boy when he saw one and knew what that could mean, warning his men off in no uncertain terms. Never tangle with a journalist or his relations was what he'd learned over the years.

Although the Finnerty kid was the only one on this transport he needed to land at Walcheren, he found he'd been done a favour once he got there, discovering quite by chance that the load of wool he'd been intending for the Spanish market was now in high demand by every merchant going since the French had got wind that the English were using it to insulate the bows of their warships against foreign cannons. Those merchants were paying top money for it, and three hours after offloading Joseph Finnerty he was counting out double the cash he'd been expecting to make in Spain, stashing it in his safe, and telling his men:

Back to Ireland! There's sheep to be shorn and wool to be shovelled into our holds!

Hendrik Grimalkin wasn't a man who took gladly to change. The intrusion of Ruan and Caro into the usual order of his life had been unsettling, to say the least, given the faint murmur of his erstwhile father they'd brought with them and the questions he longed to ask. How was he doing? Was he happy? Did he regret leaving his family so peremptorily? Hendrik's mother had received a few letters from the self-styled Brother Joachim over the years but Hendrik had never been permitted to see them, or to know his name.

He had spent his entire adult life dealing with the day to day concerns of the press his father had left in a financial shambles, and also with his mother's undoubted relief that she was at last being allowed to get on with her own life, and damn the consequences.

She was dead now, and perhaps just as well if Joachim was about to reappear in their lives.

Then there was Louisa, and the situation with the boy Caro. It was years since Hendrik and his wife had shared a bed once they'd realised they were unlikely to have children, a great regret on both sides. He'd gone to his work and she to her kitchen, and at night they went to separate rooms by mutual and unspoken agreement. But since Caro had arrived Louisa had re-emerged, starting to glow right in front of him, just like when she was a young girl and they'd first met. Their eyes would meet over the table while Caro chattered amiably on about this and that.

Once, only once, Hendrik had gone later to her room and knocked quietly on her door, waiting awkwardly, breathing fast. She'd opened it a crack, and then wider, and led Hendrik in and they'd lain together between her sheets, side by side, shy and embarrassed, his hand moving gently to her shoulder, then hers to his chest, taking their time, no need to rush, no need to do it all at once, both understanding they would need to learn how to explore each other's bodies anew. Enough for the moment to simply wrap themselves together in the darkness, a whole lifetime of nights left to see what would become of this renewed intimacy.

This was not the only spark Caro had unwittingly brought to life. Hendrik had forgotten what it was like to throw himself into a project, to cast aside the quotidian duties of administration, taking stock, greeting scholars who were exploring the Athenaeum for their own purposes. And now he was exploring it for himself, alive with curiosity about the Lynx, eagerly looking forward to every new day and the promise of new discoveries.

Every moment he wasn't thinking about Louisa and the time they'd wasted was taken up with the Lynx. He'd learned so much already, thanks to Caro's elfin speed in going through the stacks at his direction and the notes Golo Eck had made in Caro's book. It was all there – about the starting of the Lynx, of Federico's Cesi's obsession with secret names, secret symbols, the rings he'd given to the five founding members, the great risks they took right from the start in publishing daring new scientific theories, including the one that had Galileo nailed to the door of the Vatican by his heretical interpretation of the world going around the sun and not the other way round.

They'd had papal protection from one of their earliest supporters – Cardinal Maffeo Barberini, later Pope Urban VIII – otherwise the whole lot of them would no doubt have been locked up or excommunicated, their worst enemy being Federico's own father, who'd done his best to get them all exiled, and succeeded to a certain degree with Johannes Eck.

So here was Hendrik in the Athenaeum, humming with anticipation. He'd been leafing through the latest sheaf of papers Caro had ferreted from the stacks, before he set out for Arnhem, when he came across a pearl beyond compare: a long letter, written and signed by Federico Cesi himself, addressed to the other four founding members of the society, this one apparently belonging to Anastasio De Filiis, to establish the provenance of his ground-breaking ideas. He'd crafted it like a story, shifting from first person into third when he deemed it necessary. Hendrik had already read it through once and was now going back to the beginning to pick out all the information he could.

'On the day of my eighteenth birthday' Hendrik read, *'I, Federico Cesi, took a wander away from the celebrations my parents were throwing for me, away from the glitterati of Roman society, away from the people invited to the estate of Aquasparta, brought in by litter and horse-carriage the few miles out from the city.*

My father had not stinted on the occasion, and the previous day the courtyard was ringing like a blacksmith's anvil, its walls reverberating with the strikes of hammers on nails, erecting tables that were later covered with fine Luccan silk. It was adorned with huge silver platters of roasted meats, tiny songbirds on their spit-sticks, heads and feet still attached as is the custom, the suckling pigs sliced nose to tail to reveal the hares' flesh that had been hidden inside them, the rich, dark meat soaked through with fat, and all the more edible because of it. There were salads too, fruits and olives of every colour, bread plaits flavoured with poppy seeds, peppercorns and caraway.

It was the best of everything that could be concocted in the estate's kitchens by a team of cooks brought in from the city, and on the day of the celebrations the courtyard was a hubbub of people eating, drinking, laughing and talking, many of them clustered about the vast ice-sculpture that towered at its centre, hewn from a huge block of ice that had been kept in the ice-house throughout the winter. It had been augmented every day by servants throwing on successive buckets of water so that it grew thicker and stronger with every week, every month, all so that it could be finely chiselled, in the several preceding days before this celebration, by the famous sculptor Bernardino Bernardini, into the intricate form of Laocoon and his sons struggling with their snakes, the whole tableaux cast adrift upon an enormous wooden bowl of wine, cooling and watering the best the estate's vineyards have to offer, guests scooping up the deep, dark wine into their fine Merano-made glasses.'

Hendrik was beside himself with excitement. This was all so up close and personal he felt like he was there. He was already imagining how Louisa and Caro would react when he read it out to them the following morning, assuming Caro was back by then.

'It was the social occasion of the year,' he read on, *'not that Federico cared for any of it. He'd done the rounds, spoken to every*

last invitee but now, after several hours of early afternoon sun, and the rich food and wine, many of the guests had gone to cool themselves off in the grandeur of the Palazzo's rooms, ostensibly to admire the many tapestries and paintings that were hung upon the vast plastered arena of its walls, and who soon subsided onto chairs and chaise-longues to take a snooze or canoodle, or strike deals they could not make in the public glare.

'Federico understood that all of this day had been planned down to the tiniest detail, engineered for just one purpose: to give him the connections he would need to get on in Roman society, secure a good place in politics or commerce, give him the social network that would serve him well for the rest of his life. That this path his father had marked out for him was not the one Federico had chosen to follow was neither here nor there, not this afternoon, for Federico had his own decisions to make, and today was the day to make them.

'He'd come of age now and had his own money devolved upon him from his mother's side of the family, and although he'd undertaken to take these first few steps upon his father's track, starting with this big gathering of high society, he had partaken of them only out of duty. He knew fine well he would go no further down its road, for there were other places, other goals, Federico had the calling to pursue. And his road, unlike his father's, did not entail clinging like a grub to the Holy Roman soil his father had spent his life burrowing himself deeper into. Federico's aims were entirely converse.

'He longed instead for the open air, for the spaces and landscapes that existed outside the narrow, mercenary streets of Rome. He had a yearning to learn everything he could of the world that was all about him, and how it worked: the mechanics of its clouds and rocks, mountains and plants, the moon and stars beyond it, and the sun. It had never been enough for him to note their existence, but had an urgent thirst to understand the realities of how they had come to

be, how they grew, how they moved and changed and interacted, of what they would one day become. Somewhere deep inside the young Federico Cesi there had always been an unnamed realisation that the earth itself had a rhythm, a set of rules by which it lived, and it was to understanding these rules that he, that same day, decided to dedicate his life.

'And so he absented himself from the celebrations as soon as he decently could, late afternoon and the sun partway descended from its zenith, moving down its arc, heading for the same hills Federico was going towards now – those barren cliffs, white and bleak, that hemmed the western edges of his father's lands of Aquasparta. He'd been to the same spot more times in the last few years than he could count and yet still could not come up with an adequate explanation for the strange forest that grew from them, could not account for the trunks and branches of the trees that were evidently emerging horizontally from the otherwise stubbornly fruitless slopes. Only boles and branches – never leaves, nor either twigs nor buds – yet every fissure and crevasse of their bark so clearly demarcated. And when he touched his fingers to them they felt like stone, warmed by the sun maybe, but stone all the same. Lichen and moss grew upon their knots, but there was also a different kind of growth in their deepest parts that was metallic, and not a living kind of thing at all.

'A few weeks previously, Federico had got one of these anomalous trees – for certainly they were trees, no matter how strangely formed – dragged out of the cliff so he could study it, get at its root system, determine once and for all whether it was alive or dead. Despite the crumbling nature of the cliff, and the looseness of its composite shale, it took eight pairs of oxen half an hour to haul the selected trunk just a few inches from out of the place where it had apparently taken root, and two hours more to get it removed completely

'Froth had boiled from the oxen's noses with the effort like milk

from an overheated pan, their efforts disturbing a great hive of bees that swirled up into the air like an angry rush of leaves, hanging in a shimmering golden globe for a few moments before their migrating queen led them on. And when it finally came free there'd been even more of a puzzle set for Federico Cesi, for the five yard length of trunk they'd dragged clear seemed not to be attached to anything at all, was a mere stump at its buried end, just as it had been at the other.

'Federico was as baffled as he was amazed, and could not decide if these trees, on the very edge of Aquasparta, were vegetation that was somehow turning itself into stone, or – just as mysteriously – if it weren't the other way around entirely. If, by some unknown, anti-intuitive mechanism, they were stones turning themselves into something living. This was the conundrum that finally made up his mind: this would be his life, pursuing the answer of this puzzle wherever it would take him, like a shepherd will drive his flock through a difficult and alien terrain to reach the lush green fields he knows are hidden in the dark mountains beyond.

'This day was the start of his journey towards its understanding. He had sworn it when he'd woken up that morning, and he swore that oath again now, standing as he was at the foot of those contradictory cliffs, looking up towards the blackened boles of the trees that reared like hungry animals from its shale: trees that were trees and yet were also stone, and no way – yet at least – to tell which one was turning into the other.'

Such words! Here was the beating heart of the Lynx. Hendrik was thrilled by the wonder in them, the same pulse that drove all scientific enquiry on. And he was certain he'd read something before about trees turning into stone, or stone into trees. The Della Porta box maybe? And the bees, they jogged a memory too, but he couldn't quite put his finger…

'Mijnheer Grimalkin,' Hendrik didn't look up. It was Friedrich, one of the young scholars who assisted at the library, but Hendrik was far too intent on the Cesi document to reply.

'Mijnheer Grimalkin,' Friedrich said again, his feet dancing awkwardly on the wooden floor, Hendrik distracted by the movement and looking up.

'What is it, Friedrich? I'm in the middle of something important here.'

Hendrik's tone was brusque, dismissive, and although the young assistant flinched he didn't back away. Hendrik threw a glance at the large clock on the wall of the library. A while past three. He should have been home a half hour since. It had become their custom for Louisa, Caro and Hendrik to meet for lunch at two thirty before separating again to their afternoon's allotted tasks. Unexpectedly he smiled, looked up at Friedrich, about to make a light-hearted comment about being a brow-beaten husband these days, until he saw the grim look on his assistant's face.

'Is something wrong, Friedrich?' he asked, and was answered with the worst of news.

'It's your house,' Friedrich whispered. 'Your house is on fire...'

Hendrik blinked, and blinked again.

'My house is... on fire? My house is...'

He put a hand to his mouth until the shock of the news kicked him into action.

He stood up abruptly, his chair clattering noisily to the floor, as he started running like a maniac through the main body of the library, bumping into one person and then another, knocking their books out of their hands. He didn't apologise, kept on crashing through them all until he bowled his way out onto the street and up the road.

He could see smoke and flames curling into the sky, could see it was possible they were coming from his house but couldn't quite grasp that this could be the case, until he turned the corner and came running onto the flat promenade of the Singel and there it was – indisputable – his home blazing like a bonfire on New Year's Eve, a wiggly line of men going from the river to the house, casting useless buckets of water onto the flames about the door in the vain hope that if anyone was in there they might be able to get out. Someone was snaking the hose-pump – one of many kept curled up below the jetties for just such an emergency – from the water, another banging at the other end with his fists, trying to open the rusted valve.

Hendrik saw his whole life disintegrating in that awful burning and then suddenly the shouts crescendoed and everyone renewed their efforts as the flames began to creep along the jambs of the window-frames from Hendrik's house to the one next door – empty, thank God, its owner a single merchant, often abroad on business. The flames leapt and licked and increased their intensity and were soon jumping from roof to roof, their direction bent by a westward breeze.

The glass of the windows in both Hendrik's house and the one next door exploded altogether, shattering into a thousand splinters that rained down onto the men below who dropped their pails, flinging arms and coats above their heads, everyone praying this empty house would somehow swallow the fire, keep it contained within its bricks.

All along the Singel people were spilling from their front doors, alerted by the shouting, dragging excited children behind them. Women held their pinafores before their faces, men yelling for everyone to get back down to the water with their buckets and for someone, anyone, to get the hose-pumps working. At last they did – a man with hands the size of shovel-blades physically ripping the rusted valve clean off the hose-end so that at last the water began to bulge and course along the length of the pipe, coming out in a great and hopeful gush. Then the same man fought to keep it steadily pouring into the open windows of the house beside the Grimalkins – for there was no saving that one – others taking turns to operate the pumps, heaving the handles up and down with all the force their shoulders and backs could muster.

'Louisa! Louisa!' Hendrik ran towards the crowds, searching for his wife amongst the clamour of people, but no matter how many times he shouted, how many shoulders he grabbed at and spun around, he saw no trace of her.

Tears were running down his smut-blackened face, skin smarting with the heat and smoke and his despair. And next to the empty house was Teresa Arnolfini's, she of Louisa's Sewing Circle, and inside was Teresa, who had tipped herself off her chair and tried at first to stagger and then crawl towards the window, using the floor and then the wall as her support, smoke billowing in through every crack and crevasse from the adjacent empty house.

She could hear the commotion outside, could hear Hendrik's high voice keening for his wife and she began to shout and shake with fear, calling out for someone to come and help her because there was no one in the house but her, the maid having gone down to the boat-docks to fetch the flounder for their tea and no one down below coming to her rescue. Her legs would not support her weight but she managed to drag herself to the window of her second floor sitting-room where she fumbled with the fixings to get it open. Her fingers weren't working properly – too much smoke in throat and lungs, too much dread, too much heat in the fixings.

In the end all she could do was heave her heavy body up onto the sash-seat where she began hitting at the window with her fists, hammering at the glass with all the strength she had left so that eventually the glass gave way. Everyone looked up then and saw her, and could hear her wordless shrieking as she forced the top half of her body out over the jagged shards of the window as if she was about to fling herself out.

The breaking of that window sent some unseen signal that suckled the fire from its low creep and lick across the neighbouring roof towards her own as if it had been waiting for this moment. It gained a new surge of life, whooshing and swooping, pouring straight towards the open window where it swallowed Teresa Arnolfini whole.

'Oh my God, oh my God,' Hendrik covered his mouth with his hands as he craned his neck up with all the rest, and although he felt those words in his throat no sound came out.

There was a collective silence for a brief moment as everyone saw the flames engulf Teresa, everything catching alight at once – hair, clothes, skin – and that part of her they could see thrashing and mewling like no one had ever seen or heard before and prayed God they would never again. And barely a minute later, Teresa Arnolfini – gossipy, gout-ridden old Teresa – was burned right through at the middle, the fire releasing the top half of her torso with her head still attached, mouth still moving as it tumbled right down into the street, burning and smoking, writhing faintly like a snake that has been sliced through by a scythe until someone had the wit to pour a bucket of water over the part of her that had landed at their feet, sizzling and spitting and then – thank God – was still.

Many said later it was Teresa's life that had satisfied the fire, for after her falling it shrank of its own accord, withdrew towards its source, removed itself from the Arnolfini house and from the intervening neighbour's, pulling itself back to its primary source where it burned on and smouldered, singing itself quietly to sleep as the Grimalkin house collapsed about it, going on long into the evening and then the night, seemingly content to stay there, contained and restrained, slowly consuming every last particle of that abode that it could find.

Most of Deventer turned out at one time or another during those last hours to gawp and sigh and thank Christ it had been someone else's bad fortune to have their life reduced to ashes for no apparent reason. Ruan arrived, a little drunk, on the scene two hours later, having finally heard the news that was going the ups and downs of every tavern in Deventer. He was of no use to anyone by then. The men at the pumps and buckets had desisted their unequal fight and Hendrik Grimalkin slumped in one of the seats that lined the Singel's wide promenade.

'What's happened?' Ruan asked of the first man he saw, though it was obvious even to him that the Grimalkin house was no more.

'Burned down,' the man replied shortly, before turning away and throwing up for the fifth time that night, the same man who'd chucked the bucket of water over what was left of Teresa Arnolfini, unable to get the taste of her out of his mouth, didn't think he ever would. Never ate meat again, throughout the whole of his long life.

'But what's happened?' Ruan Peat persisted, accosting the next person he stumbled into. 'I don't understand. How could this happen?'

'Happens all the time, mate,' said the man who was dispiritedly rolling up the pump-pipe that had proved so worthless when put to the test. 'Could happen to any of us. Just be grateful it hasn't happened to you.'

FROM SEA TO SERVANTS

Greta was not intimidated nor made sick by the rolling waves, she was instead astonished. She'd always had the concept of its enormity in her head but once out of sight of land she found it hard to grasp the reality of its length and breadth and depth. She spent most of her days helping out in the galley or scrubbing the decks or cleaning the nets – a task her small fingers quickly became adept at.

The rest of the crew did as bid and kept their distance, so the nights were her own. Sometimes they were spent leaning over the rails, gazing at the coal-black roll of the ocean shot through on occasion by lines of phosphorescence flowing and fluctuating like underwater murmurations of the starlings she saw back home who gathered in the sky, wheeled and dipped in rapid formation, before settling down to roost.

She saw great rafts of eider tipping wing to wing into the water as the boat approached them, emerging twenty or thirty yards further on a few minutes later, calling to each other in eerie whistles that filled the darkness and might have seemed – to a less level-headed person than Greta – to be the calls of drowned sailors sorrowful from the depths.

On the last night, a low mist drifted across the waves, giving a damp drizzle to the air, confining Greta to the tiny cabin she'd been allotted that was barely bigger than the hard board of her bed. She sat on its edge, not tired enough to sleep, too full of what the next day might bring, the light of her candle wavering with the gentle rocking of the boat and, for the first time since leaving Shauna's she had the idea to take out the pouch and the little package in which the stringy thing was wrapped. Out it came and, stuck to its bottom, was a small scrap of paper she'd not noticed at Shauna's: a tiny article ripped from a broadsheet with a few haphazard scribbles in faint pencil upon its edges. She moved her candle closer and leant in to read them the better:

Brother Joachim/Walcheren. Grimalkin/Deventer. Golo Eck/ Ruan Peat/Loch Eck, Scotland.

The words meant nothing to her, excepting Walcheren, until she recalled that the pouch was not the only thing to have come from Fergus for she was still carrying the letters he'd given her with such urgency the morning of the Battle of New Ross. They'd been tucked into the poacher's pocket carefully sewn and concealed into the back of her jacket but so much had happened since she'd forgotten they were even there. She coloured slightly with the guilt of never having done anything about them, and knew it was probably too late to do anything about them now, but she removed her jacket and took them out anyway.

They were mere folded sheets of paper, badly creased and a little tattered at the edges, but still intact by dint of the poacher's pocket aligning with the small of her back, and she brought in the candle to see to whom they'd been addressed. The first, perhaps not surprisingly, echoed several of the names she'd just read: *To Golo Eck, care of Brother Joachim at the Servants of the Sick in Walcheren, and if not there then care of Hendrik Grimalkin of the*

Athenaeum Library in Deventer, Holland, and if not to Golo Eck himself then to Hendrik Grimalkin.

The second was slightly more alarming, being addressed to someone whose name she knew but could not understand how Fergus could possibly know it too, or why:

To Wolfe Tone, of the French Revolutionary Council in Paris, Leader of the Irish Legion of Napoleon, on behalf of Golo Eck from Loch Eck in Scotland.

She went back to the small scrap of paper and brought it right up close to the candle, the letters of the article so small she could hardly make them out with setting them to flame, some already lost to damp and wear.

Lost, the Collyb...kie, departed from Port Gl.... nd for the Continent... thereafter in a stor...aid the captain, James Fe... rom Vlissingen, 'We lost several passen...ut thanks to God's Gr... nsular of Walcheren, an... rvants of the Sick who bide ther... rsonal thanks must go to one B...ther Joachim who w... back to health aft... even now caring for... engers who did not fare so wel...

Greta sucked in her breath and laid the letters Fergus had written side by side on the blanket of her bed and next to them the tiny article, with its worn words and strange message jotted in the margin, and wondered about Fergus, who apparently knew Wolfe Tone, and maybe knew about the botched invasion of his French forces back in June, and likely too therefore, she reasoned, knowing also of the Road to Exile.

But he hadn't come to Ireland to join their cause, at least not to fight. He'd come specifically to find Peter, to ask for Peter's help in getting to Mogue Kearns, maybe as a conduit to Wolfe Tone. It was only because Peter had been arrested that Fergus ended up with Greta, got taken to Mick Malloy who had bullied Fergus into fighting at New Ross. Backbone of the rebellion and all that, but

Malloy not a man anyone refused lightly.

She'd never considered previously where Fergus had come from or why he was in Ireland or how he'd ended up, which was most probably dead, seeing as Mogue had given her his pouch. Nor had she considered the true worth of what he'd given the Cause in the form of the stringy thing, not until she and Shauna had taken a proper look, figuring out how it could be used, was maybe being used right at this moment.

A gift beyond compare and no wonder Mogue so keen to get it out, maybe the reason Fergus came to Ireland in the first place, because obviously he was more than one of the other Scots who joined the Cause, not if he was on speaking terms with the likes of Wolfe Tone.

She shook her head, unable to get to the bottom of it, but she could at least deliver his letters, or one of them at least. Walcheren, the Servants, exactly where she was heading, and now she had this Brother Joachim's name into the bargain.

Ruan was fidgety. He'd not slept well, he and Hendrik billeted in the Athenaeum Library where several rooms were kept for visiting scholars. And they were decent enough, spacious and comfortable; what worried Ruan, when he got up the following morning, was that all the correspondence passed between the lawyers here and in Scotland, all the papers that said he was who he was, and the signed document from the Servants that was witness to Golo's death, had gone up in smoke. Literally.

He hated to think he'd have wait yet more weeks, maybe months, to go through it all again, not with Golo's Last Will and Testament due any day. He'd no doubt it would be delivered here instead of to the smoking remnants of the Grimalkin house, but what if the lawyers refused to budge without the rest of it? What was he going to do then?

He certainly couldn't ask Hendrik to help out. The man appeared to have drifted off on a sea of grief the moment it became evident that Louisa – dry old stick that she was – had gone up with the house. Being young and resilient Ruan couldn't quite grasp Hendrik's depth of despair, was frustrated and impatient and made no bones about it, stamping up and down the library, hoping to indirectly shake Hendrik from his torpor.

'I'm going back up to the Singel,' he announced loudly. It was eleven o'clock, late morning, not yet twenty four hours since the fire had started, 'see if there's anything can be salvaged.'

Hendrik didn't move. He'd been curled up on one of the large leather sofas in the library since being dragged back from the Singel and deposited there the night before.

'We could really do with moving,' Ruan was saying.

Hendrik heard the words but didn't respond. They were of no consequence. Ruan himself was of no consequence. A great welter of images was swirling through Hendrik's head, twisting and tumbling, patterns forming and disintegrating, joining and separating, unpredictable as autumn leaves jumbling down a weir Their primary function was to barricade him in, fill his head so entirely that nothing else was allowed: no memories that could soak him up like ink into blotting paper; everything dispersed and therefore easier to bear, locking him down until he could cope. Better to jettison the anchor than lose the boat.

The fire of the Singel transmogrified into the last thing he'd been thinking about before he'd got the news, that thought about the bees he'd not been able to grasp coming to the fore: that mere wisp of smoke going up, not into the sky above Deventer but into the sky above Rome. A faint buzzing sound filled his ears from the thousands of bees said to have swarmed into the Palace during the papal conclave way back when – taken as a sure sign that Maffeo Barberini was their man, his family crest being a trigon of wasps; the manuscript of the *Melissographia* hoving into view – the very sound of it soothing – dedicated to Barberini by the Lynx, first known microscopic pictures of the bee, amongst the rarest manuscripts in the world.

The Barberini wasps swiftly shifted into bees to reinforce his power, their trigon seen all over Italy: sculpted into Bernini's fountains, crawling up the great serpentine columns of St Peter's, sewn in gold in its famous baldachinno, painted impossibly large on the vast ceiling of the newly built Barberini family seat at Quirinal and also, much later, on Maffeo's tomb, the *odo sanctitatus* of his decaying body drawing the stone bees back to live, or so the pilgrims – who saw them shift in the shadows of the mausoleum – swore. Drawing the bees back to life but not Hendrik. Not yet. Not yet.

Greta arrived – after several hours walking – at the Servants of the Sick, the latest in a long line of Irish to pass through its gates, it being the first outpost of safe houses on the Continental Road to Exile established a decade previously by Mogue Kearns himself.

She rang the bell and, when a monk appeared a few minutes later, she spoke the phrase Shauna had made her practice, a halting version of the Dutch, meaning *My name is Joseph Finnerty, come from Ireland on the way to France.* The monk smiled and nodded though did not reply, presumably knowing she wouldn't understand, instead indicating that she should follow as he led on. He took her directly to the Abbot who, before his entry into the Servants forty three years previously, went by the name Padraig O'Shaunessy, of the O'Shaunessy's of Cork.

'Welcome,' the Abbot said, though Greta hardly heard him for already she was taking out one of Fergus's letters, brandishing it in front of him, stabbing at it with her finger.

'I need to find this Brother Joachim,' she said slowly, also taking out the flimsy scrap of broadsheet that was hardly more than a wisp, waving it towards the Abbot's face.

The Abbot looked at Greta with curiosity.

'Will you not sit?' he asked politely. Greta sat, and then suddenly looked up at the Abbot.

'You're Irish?' she asked, forgetting to keep her voice low in her astonishment.

'Once Irish, always so,' he countered, 'no matter where we end up. And you, who are you?'

'Joseph Finnerty,' Greta said without hesitation, the Abbot noticing the studied drop of pitch, the way she pulled her ankles together, putting one foot behind the other, laying one hand upon her lap while still holding her letter up with the other. It was plain as a pikestaff to the Abbot of the Servants of the Sick – as it had not been to the skipper O'Rourke – that this was a girl. It wasn't the first time a person of the female persuasion had attempted to infiltrate their ranks on the lookout for some long lost beau, brother or father. He wasn't fooled for a moment by the ridiculously large boots that didn't in the slightest match the rest of her, but he was intrigued.

'And you're here for why?' he asked gently.

Greta dithered, not wanting to go into a long explanation about Fergus and Vinegar Hill.

'It's a bit complicated,' she said. 'But basically I'm here because Mogue Kearns said…well never mind that just now, but I've a letter to deliver to a man named Brother Joachim who bides here.'

She laid her letter and the small broadsheet cutting upon the Abbot's table.

'To Golo Eck,' he read out loud, 'care of Brother Joachim at the Servants of the Sick in Walcheren, and if not there then care of Hendrik Grimalkin of the Athenaeum Library in Deventer, Holland, and if not to Golo Eck himself then to Hendrik Grimalkin.'

And the cutting, barely legible, that described the wrecking of the Collybuckie. The Abbot took his time studying both, not immediately reacting.

'So is he here?' Greta asked, leaning forward eagerly. 'This Brother Joachim? And the other one too?'

The Abbot was not so easily inveigled into giving out information he wasn't sure he should give.

'Why do you need to know?' he asked, making Greta squirm in her seat. She grimaced, but made a choice.

'Because a man called Fergus Murtagh gave these to me to bring on and deliver, and I promised.'

The Abbot lifted his eyebrows.

'You promised,' he repeated slowly. 'And you came all this way to the Servants just to deliver a letter?'

'Well no,' Greta said, uncomfortable, thinking how well this Abbot would have got on with Mick Malloy, both able to squeeze information out of you before you were even aware you were being squeezed. 'I was kind of coming anyway. Bad times back home,' she added without going into detail, 'and Mogue told me to get out, and it was only when I was getting out that I realised that these letters... well...the fact is that Fergus gave them me and I forgot all about them till I was already on my way over, and now that I'm here...well...'

She tailed off, wondering if she'd said too much, or maybe too little, but the Abbot on the other side of the table only nodded, tapping his finger against the wood.

'So this wasn't the only letter…Fergus gave you?'

Greta swallowed, decided to come clean. This was, after all, a safe house, a link in the chain to France she meant to follow, but how to get to Wolfe Tone when she got there she'd no idea. Maybe an Abbot could do better.

'One more,' she murmured, laying it by its brother's side, the Abbot leaning in with interest.

To Wolfe Tone, of the French Revolutionary Council in Paris, leader of the Irish Legion of Napoleon, on behalf of Golo Eck, from Loch Eck in Scotland.

And now it was the Abbot's turn to be wrong-footed and unable to hide his surprise.

'And do you know any of these people?' he asked.

'Um, I don't,' Greta admitted. 'I mean I know about Wolfe Tone of course. He was supposed to get his soldiers to Ireland before Vinegar Hill to help us, but that didn't work out too well.'

She scrunched up her eyes to stop the tears that were on their way and the Abbot saw it.

'It went badly,' he said, without judgement or question.

'Very bad, Father,' Greta answered, unaware of the appellation she had used. 'Very bad. But some are still alive, and there's still some hope…'

'So you got yourself up in your boy's disguise and came here,' the Abbot stated.

Greta started visibly. She'd not expected this. She'd been travelling as a boy for so long, using her brother's name, it never occurred to her that this man, this Abbot, could see through her as if she was made of glass. She narrowed her eyes and puffed out her cheeks.

'What difference would it make, if I was?' she said stoutly 'A girl I mean.'

She might have said more but in truth she was too tired, and now she'd stopped moving her feet were hurting again. The two thick pairs of woollen socks bulking out her feet in her too big boots – boots that had once belonged to Shauna's youngest son – were damp and scratchy. She couldn't wait to shake everything off: boots, socks and pretence. She stared back at the Abbot until he smiled and held up his hands.

'It makes no difference to me,' he said after a short pause, 'but it's going to make your travelling harder.'

'Used to it,' Greta said, but her defiance was empty.

'And your name?'

'Greta,' said Greta shrugging her shoulders. 'Greta Finnerty.'

'Well, Greta,' said the Abbot amiably, 'the curious thing is that I know both these names on your first letter, and I may know how to deliver the second.'

Greta let out a breath as a rapidity of thoughts blundered about in her head. This was amazing! She wasn't all that bothered about the letters themselves but she did want to find the people they were addressed to because there was a faint chance they would know how to work the stringy thing properly, and that could mean the saving of Ireland.

'So when can I speak to this Golo person?' Greta's green eyes sparkled with an anticipation that was quickly quashed.

'I'm afraid that won't be possible,' said the Abbot. 'He's dead, has been for some while.'

'Oh for f…' Greta bit back the expletive, her cheeks going pink as she shot an embarrassed glance at the Abbot, who was smiling benignly in return.

'All is not lost, young Greta,' he said. 'Golo Eck is certainly dead, interred here in our graveyard, but he has a next of kin who will be most glad to receive your missive.'

He didn't add what he knew of Hendrik Grimalkin, not yet. He wanted to ruminate on the situation a while, see if he couldn't untangle the threads. It seemed incredible that all these separate lives had converged on Walcheren, and the Servants in particular, and although God's ways were often mysterious they were never without purpose.

'You must be tired, and hungry, young Greta. Why don't I get someone to take you to the refectory, get you something to eat? Then you can meet our Brother Joachim. In the meantime I can take care of your letters for now,' he said, 'unless you'd rather…?'

'I'd rather,' Greta replied by reflex, snatching up the letters and scrap of broadsheet, the messenger never giving up the message except to its direct recipient. 'But food now, that sounds grand.'

'Very well, then,' the Abbot said, standing and shepherding Greta out into the courtyard, summoning Brother Eustace from the goat shed because he knew the man spoke English rather well and would be keen to have someone to practice on, Brother Eustace – as predicted – delighted to oblige, twittering away like a particularly restless sparrow the moment he had Greta on her own.

'So from Ireland?' Brother Eustace began enthusiastically as he led the way. 'I know about Ireland.'

The refectory was empty, apart from a man sweeping the bristles of his broom across the floor somewhere towards the back, and Greta was relieved that Eustace seemed happy to carry on his conversation singlehanded. He sat her down, brought her some very welcome leek and lentil soup.

'Great place for missionaries, Ireland,' Eustace chattered on. 'Gave us St Padraig, and let's not forget Columba. Of warrior aristocracy he was, went over to Scotland and brought its heathen into our fold.'

He flitted off again, returning with more soup, this time with some bread and butter.

'And so you've come to see our Brother Joachim? Well, how exciting! He's not like the rest of us, you know. A soldier first, just like St Columba. Came to us in middle life. Abandoned his family in Deventer to join us.'

Greta glanced up, recognising the word, aware that the man sweeping his broom had stopped just as she had. She glanced over at him and frowned. She supposed Brothers were just as good at eavesdropping and gossip as anyone else but it didn't sit well with her, knowing too well how wrong words in wrong places could cost people dear, it going against the grain.

Brother Eustace leapt off again, coming back this time with a bowl of honey looking like liquid amber just poured from the comb. Greta couldn't remember the last time she'd had honey, let alone so good, and eagerly dipped the remaining bread in it, nodding her thanks.

'Enjoy, enjoy!' said Brother Eustace, pleased at Greta's evident enjoyment, before picking up the previous thread of his one-sided conversation.

'Deventer,' he mused. 'Such a grand place and with such history. Never been there myself, but as a Dutchman naturally I'm proud. Had one of the first proper printing presses in Europe, and is the birthplace of Geert de Groote and his Brethren of the Common Life – Protestant leanings, of course,' Brother Eustace tutted, 'but such worthy goals. They brought books to schools and libraries all over Europe, and then of course Erasmus was among their number, as was Johannes Heckius – one of Deventer's greatest sons, despite, well…I'll not go into that. But Thomas à Kempis was of the Brethren too and if one has ever read his *Meditations on the Life of Christ or the Hospitale Pauperum* – of particular interest to us, of course – well, what can one say? Such words and so well put. And then there was Adrian Dedel, another of their number before he went on to become Pope Hadrian VI…'

Brother Eustace finally drew to a stop when he noticed Greta was beginning to snooze where she sat over her empty bowls.

'Come on,' he said gently, lifting her by the elbows, depositing her in one of the small guestrooms. It was tiny, a bucket in one corner for a latrine, a small table on which was placed a jug of water for washing alongside a rough cotton towel, the rest of the space taken up by a thin straw-stuffed mattress onto which Greta gratefully subsided, tugging off her boots, pulling off her socks, before laying down and sleeping the whole night through, best night's sleep she'd had since she'd left Shauna's.

Ruan was still in the library, pacing up and down the aisle, face puckered with indecision. He'd been all set to go stamping up to the Singel to gawp and then off to the lawyers, but undoubtedly they'd already heard the news and anyway it didn't feel right to leave Hendrik on his own. He'd owed the man. If it hadn't been for him Ruan's Great Adventure would have been scuppered as surely as the Collybuckie had sunk.

He took another walk back down the library and went further this time towards Hendrik, curled and hunched within the acreage of green leather. It blew into his head how badly he'd misjudged Hendrik and Louisa on first call, and how the sudden excision of one from the other was like leaving a sentence partway said. Half-marrowed, they would have called it back home, husband and wife weaved together so closely no one saw the seams until they were ripped back to the quick, a modicum of compassion entering him to see it so starkly illustrated.

'Mr Grimalkin?' Ruan began. 'Hendrik?'

He got no more response than earlier. Hendrik was awake, eyes open, flicking from one side to the other as if he was reading, which in a way he was. The bees were long flown through the windows of his mind but they'd left the footprints of the Lynx behind them. House was gone, books were gone, wife was gone, but Golo Eck's fixation on the Lynx remained, caught like a hook inside him, a path to follow, a way to tread, a life-line to hang onto, the ragged root of a tree on a riverbank he could use to haul himself out of the surging waters that were trying to pull him under.

'Hendrik?' Ruan said again, but could see it was useless. Hendrik's mind was elsewhere.

Hendrik's mind was conjuring up the rest of the letter he'd found in the archives, filling in the blanks he could not remember, those leaves swirling again, making patterns, forcing meaning out of chaos, transported elsewhere, into someone else's life, a life that was at its start, surging with expectations and better things to come.

Having left the trees that were rocks or the rocks that were trees, Federico went to the summerhouse he called his study. He had a table there, knocked together from an old stable door he'd sanded smooth and propped on a few lengths of discarded fence posts for its legs. He'd erected several shelves to hold his books and journals, and a rough cabinet that held three badly fitting drawers. He could have asked one of the estate's craftsmen to do all this for him but there'd been a certain satisfaction in doing it himself, without anyone's knowledge, creating his secret space out there on the edge of the estate where his parents rarely went.

He lit a lamp, took out parchment, pencils, quills, ink, wax block, candle and seal and sat a while looking out of the window at the low crouch of the hills, the blue strip of sky diminishing as the sun descended below the line of his horizon to shine on different places, different continents, that had day where he had night, if Galileo – and Copernicus before him – were to be believed.

And believe them he did, absolutely and without question, knowing they were right and that he was a tiny speck upon a world that was spinning madly through space, one world amongst the many that were spinning out there just as madly as was his own, all adrift within a universe that might conceivably be without end.

Where his father's God fitted into this framework of new physics he didn't know, only that maybe He was somehow the whole of it. Like the mosaic of the Christless Entry into Ephesus in the Cesi Palazzo's hall floor, God had no need to be painted in by human hand but would be there of His own accord, implicit in every brush-stroke, every piece of glass the craftsmen made. Likewise He would be in every wandering planet, every star, was maybe everywhere all at the same time, not outside the universe but implicit in every tiny detail of it, everywhere and everything in the whole marvellous plenitude that was waiting to be explored.

He had the conviction, did Federico Cesi, that he'd been called upon to do just that: explore it and bring others with him. Believing it to be so he pulled some sheets of paper from the ream at his side, took up a pencil, and on the first piece of paper wrote four names: Francesco Stelluti, Anastasio De Filiis, Johannes Eck, Walter Peat. Beside each name he made small sketches, devising mottos and emblems, jumping up several times to refer to his journals, to his books, his stacks of letters.

His new Society, his Academy of the Lynx, was about to break forth like a chick from an egg. It might have to remain secret in these church-heavy times, at least for now, like a bride beneath her veil, but Federico Cesi was not going to be stopped, and no more would be the men who would soon join him at Aquasparta, ready, willing and able to wed his Academy to the world.

Hendrik saw the scene in front of him as if it had been given form. Present, all four of Federico's documents signed and sealed, spread upon his desk in his little summer house, and Federico Cesi looking once again out of his window into the night. *Il Celivago* – the name he'd given to himself, the wanderer of the heavens – doing exactly that, finding the bright white light of Venus hanging like a cohort to the rising moon.

It was a sign that he was on his right path; a sign that acted at a distance, traversing time and place so that Hendrik could follow it too. The leaves from the stream broke away, reconfigured, creating patterns of their own, affording Hendrik glimpses of their underlying order, a bridge between past and present on which he was stood, watching the water, watching the leaves, a sudden strong conviction that the bridge was real, that the present – *his* present – was an inevitable consequence of Golo's ancestral past.

The Abbot at the Servants had come up with a plan. It was audacious, but he'd not come upon it lightly. After Greta had left him he'd thought of little else, working all the ramifications through and through until now, in the bold light of morning, he was rather pleased with himself. He knew from Brother Eustace that Greta had not yet spoken to Brother Joachim, had instead retired directly after having eaten and had only just emerged. So much to the good, as far as the Abbot was concerned. Time to put his plan into action.

'George, Joachim,' said the Abbot warmly, as both George and Joachim were ushered into his room. 'And how are you feeling, Joachim? You look much better than even a few days past.'

'I feel it, thank you, Abbot,' Joachim said, and meant it. In fact he felt pretty good, despite the arm that was strapped across his chest from having dislocated his shoulder when he fell, not that George was having any of it.

'He should still be in his bed another week ...' George began, Joachim cutting him off abruptly. Lord knew he was grateful for George's ministrations, without which he would undoubtedly have fared far worse, maybe even have died out there by Saint Drostan's shrine, but enough was enough. The man was turning into the most intolerable kind of nursemaid, and that was not for Joachim. He was the one who tended to the sick, not the one tended.

'Not at all,' he said in rebuttal. 'Indeed I was meaning to talk to you, Abbot. I think I'll be fine to return to my normal duties any day now.' Joachim ignored the snort that came from George but smiled tolerantly adding, purely for George's benefit:

'As long as I have my helper here by my side for just a little longer.'

The Abbot nodded. He was not unaware of the devotion newly sprung in George Gwilt since his part in rescuing the survivors of the Collybuckie, nor the impact made on him by finding the body of Golo Eck and thereafter his involvement – facilitated by Joachim – of taking care of his corpse. George had even spoken a few words when Golo Eck was buried, a feat more daunting for George than anything he'd ever done, and far more than Golo's ward – Ruan Peat – had done, for by then Ruan had skidaddled, scarpering off soon as he was able to Deventer. Yet another reason – if he needed one – why the Abbot had come to the decision he had.

'Well,' he said, 'I'm glad of it, but that's not why you're here. There's someone I want you both to meet.'

There was a knock on the door and the Abbot nodded at its timeliness. Mysterious, God's ways, but occasionally just exactly when you needed them.

'Come in,' he said, and in came Greta Finnerty.

She'd been given – at the Abbot's orders – the pick of abandoned clothing from the Servants' stores. If she was put off by the fact it had come from dead people she'd made no mince of it, and had found herself a new old pair of boots that actually fitted her feet, a new old shirt and a new old pair of britches. She hadn't entirely abandoned her previous look and refused absolutely to swap her scruffy leather jacket for something more serviceable. But in she came, undoubtedly a girl this time, despite the boy's woollen bonnet on her head that hid whatever hair was underneath.

'This is Greta Finnerty,' the Abbot introduced her, Greta unabashed by the situation and looking hard at both Joachim and George, though mostly at Joachim, for it was plain by his garb and demeanour he was a Brother, presumably the one she'd come looking for.

'Greta has come all the way from Ireland,' the Abbot went on, speaking first in Dutch and then in English so all would understand. 'She's seeking our help which, as you know, is our primary duty. She's carrying the last possessions of a man who is believed to have died some while back in Ireland, a man named Fergus Murtagh, of the household of the late Golo Eck, and has letters, one of which must go to Hendrik Grimalkin in Deventer.'

Joachim drew in a sharp breath and shifted his gaze from the Abbot to Greta, but the Abbot wasn't finished and snagged the attention of all three with what he said next.

'And I need you both to accompany Greta to Deventer, make enquiries there for Ruan Peat at the library of the Athenaeum, secure delivery of one of the two letters she has in her possession. The other I can take care of myself.'

George froze, gripping the back of Joachim's chair to keep himself upright. Joachim, by contrast, was rigid as an icicle. He stared unwaveringly at the Abbot, a man he thought of as a friend, unable to fathom what he considered tantamount to betrayal. George found his voice first, at least what little he could squeeze out.

'But Joachim's hardly healed,' he protested, 'And I've never been anywhere further than three villages over. It's just not possible,'

'And yet it is,' the Abbot contested quietly, keeping his eyes latched on Joachim's. 'There's things you all need to do,' he said in his habitually calm tone. 'Greta has a duty to deliver her letter where it has been sent, which ultimately is Deventer; and Joachim could do with a little holiday from his chores. He left his family there in a manner that has never been fully resolved, and the time to do both is now. And you, George,' the Abbot went on without mercy, 'have only just found your faith and you need it testing. And here is that test. Fallen into our laps like manna. Three people, three problems, one solution. A holy trinity, one might say.'

The Abbot looked away from them all, stretching his neck, rubbing at his jaws with finger and thumb before going on.

'And I will not allow a young girl to travel across the country without protection, and when she gets to Deventer she will undoubtedly need someone to intercede on her behalf with Hendrik Grimalkin, for the probability is that Ruan Peat has already moved on.'

He had the grace to clear his throat as Joachim flexed the fingers of his free hand, the storm brewing behind Joachim's eyes plain to see.

'Can you not send anyone else with her?' Joachim spoke in a monotone. He knew the Abbot had made up his mind and that, once made, it would be harder to break than a feather going at an anvil, but he had to try.

'I could,' the Abbot said soft and slow, 'but I will not. Both you and George had the most to do with Ruan and Golo while they were with us, and if anyone has a need to speak to Hendrik Grimalkin, Joachim, then it's you.'

Decision made. No point arguing. Padraig O'Shaunessy had not spent the last forty years of his life - travelling from Cork to becoming the Abbot of the Servants of the Sick on Walcheren - for nothing. He'd earned his authority and it was not to be disobeyed.

Joachim, George and Greta set off from Walcheren to Deventer that same morning, soon as they had gathered what they considered necessary, delayed only by George having to nip back to his village to tell them what was what. Their journey was shorter and far less arduous than Ruan and Caro's had been for the Abbot had granted them monies to assist. They took a trap to Vlissingen and from Vlissingen onto a boat to Amsterdam, and from there another straight to Deventer, arriving only two days after they'd left the Servants.

Once in Deventer Joachim led the way, this being his home patch, no matter he'd left a long time ago. On the way, he'd freed his bandaged his arm, flinging it in wide circles through the air to grant it back some strength, invigorated by the sea air. It was an odd feeling for him, this homecoming, but the more they'd gone on the more the Abbot's words had taken root, and far from dreading seeing Hendrik – now the meeting was imminent, and now he'd had time to reflect on it – he was actively looking forward to it, if with trepidation. There was a jauntiness to his step as he led his two companions up the way from the river to the Brink, waving his arm at the great conglomeration of market stalls sited there as if they were all his own doing.

Greta too was chirpy as a grasshopper on a hot summer's day, fascinated by how different everything looked, how colourful, compared to back home – every shop, every building, every street, everything everybody was wearing – all was new to her, and she couldn't stop talking. George was thankful he couldn't understand a word she said, but found it oddly comforting, the chattering of this young girl and the evident thrum of adventure that energised her every movement and exclamation. They were about to leave the Brink, head toward the Singel, when Joachim placed his hand on George's arm and pointed.

'Look,' he said, and George did, just as the clock in the square struck midday and out came the woodcutter, chopping diligently.

George laughed to see it as Joachim had described, the first time Joachim had ever heard George laugh, the sound like the creaking of a robust door being dragged across the floor. A miracle, Joachim thought, hoping there were more to come, hoping that Hendrik would not send him off into the wide afternoon without even giving him the time of day. He gazed up at the odd trail of smoke blowing across the sky, reminding him there would probably be a new pope in a couple of weeks, Pius VI believed to be on his deathbed. Even in a community so far flung as the Servants of the Sick on Walcheren they'd heard the news that he was ailing badly and would most likely be dead in a matter of days. He hoped the man could hang on until Joachim got back to the Servants, for the election of a new Pope was not to be taken lightly. Prayer would be needed, there being two prime candidates to take over the role, both looking good on the outside and one maybe a nose above the other. But you could never tell. It was a time that Joachim wanted to spend amongst his own and not here in Deventer, in the very heart of the Protestant north.

'It's this way,' Joachim urged, eager to get on now that he was he was here, enjoying the easy brightness of the day, Greta and George following on his coat tails as he marched quickly on; until they turned the corner onto the Singel when all three stopped in their tracks. A great black tide looked to have been swept down half its length, seeing it to be wet when it should have been dry, and covered in dark detritus, scraps of charred paper and cloth caught upon its surface, a faint glow emanating from a heap of rubble at the next intersection down.

They could feel the heat coming from it as they approached, the corner house shrugging down from its neighbour, almost completely collapsed, hanging on by a few smoking joists that lay at uncomfortable angles above an ash-covered heap. The adjoining house was black with smoke but still standing. Across the Singel itself was the thin snaking of a pump-operated hose, a litter of buckets strewn higgledy-piggledy along its length, a small gaggle of men squatted down by the capstans of a pier that jutted out into the waters of the lagoon beyond, ready to take up arms if the fire should start up again, although that seemed unlikely.

Every hair on Joachim's body stood up and itched. Twenty four years since he's stepped along this street but he remembers every stone of it, and knows the destroyed house to be his family home. His stomach tightens, forcing his breath into short hard gasps.

'What's happened?' he managed to squeeze out, while his skin goes into a cold sweat.

'Whole place went up in a fireball yesterday afternoon,' one of the men about the capstan offered. 'One minute nothing, next it's like hell itself has come up for a bit of a look around.'

'Two dead, far as we know,' said another. 'Both women. Both...'

His voice petered out abruptly as the memory of the smell hit him and he turned his head, retched and spat, still seeing Teresa torso twitching.

'Women?' Joachim asked, a couple of the men standing up on seeing Joachim's religious garb, the rest taking no mind.

'Grimalkin's wife,' one of the standing men supplied, fiddling with the rim of the cap he'd thrust hastily off his head and into his hands as the religious approached. 'And the woman a couple of doors down. Poor sod.'

Joachim's throat was so dry it was all he could do to scratch the words out without choking.

'And Hendrik Grimalkin himself?'

'Went off to that library of his. The Athenaeum,' came the reply, Joachim gasping with relief, managing a nod because he knew about the library and of course that was where Hendrik would have gone, and where Joachim needed to go now. The stink of the burned-down house was getting right into his lungs and he turned to go, George and Greta trailing after him, Greta frowning, turning back to look at the wrecked house again, wondering what it meant.

'Mind he's just lost his wife in there,' one of the men called after them, seeing Greta's looking. 'And she's still in there somewhere, though Christ knows there'll be little enough left of her to find, if we ever do.'

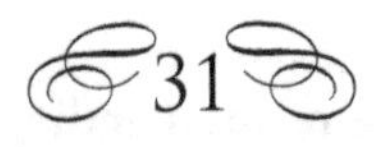

AND NOW THE ATHENAEUM

The door-bell of the Athenaeum jangled loudly, a coarse sound, like a nightjar screeching into an otherwise peaceful dawn, Ruan jumping up and running towards it as if it was about to save his life. He suddenly had in his head that it might be Fergus come to drag him from the mire and, despite the fact they'd recently got on no better than a horseradish root rubbed up against a grater, there was no one he would rather find standing there, except Golo Eck but that, of course, was impossible. He got to door before Isaac – the watchman – got there and undid the bolts, wrenched it open and stood there staggering with surprise.

'Christ All bloody Mighty,' he announced without grace or civility. 'What on earth are you doing here?'

'Is Hendrik here?' Joachim asked, pushing past Ruan who hadn't had the wit to move. Ruan jerked his head.

'Down the bottom. Hasn't moved a muscle since we got here last night. Must have the bladder of an ox.'

'Have some pity, boy,' George said sharply. 'He's just lost his wife, and in a dreadful way.'

'Can think of worse,' the words slipped out before Ruan could stop them, ending his sentence with an embarrassed clicking of his tongue.

'No use clicking,' said the third visitor, 'better bite that tongue right out of your head before you say anything else.'

Ruan took a step backwards as a young girl marched in behind George, and it was definitely a girl, despite her get up. She immediately took off her moth-eaten cap as if she'd just entered a church, releasing a short crowd of ginger spikes that shot up like hedgehog spines.

'Crikey, but that's a lot of books!' Greta said, Ruan taking a few quick paces to catch her up, his eyes latched onto her back as it swayed and swivelled as she took in the vast atrium of the library.

'You don't know the half of it,' he got out. 'If this place had gone up instead of the house it'd be burning from here till Sunday. Chuck in a few of the idiots who spend their days buried in this mausoleum and what a party that would be.'

He'd not registered she was speaking English nor that he'd replied in the same. He'd been long enough in Holland to be almost naturalised to the Dutch but was captivated by that spikey hair, wanting to put out his hand and brush his palm across it but she turned just then and pinned him with a hard, green-eyed stare.

'That's horrible. Why would you say such a thing?' she sounded angry and Ruan bristled.

'What would you know?' It was a weak comeback, and he knew it. Greta straightened her shoulders and glared at him.

'Plenty, as it happens. Ever seen a barn full of men being burned alive?'

Ruan blinked because of course he hadn't, and presumably neither had she.

'Well I have,' she said in immediate rebuttal, 'and I can tell you that you'd never want to see or hear such a thing again.'

Ruan was without words. His head had gone completely blank. The girl looked at him for another two seconds that seemed to stretch on and on, before jutting her chin at him.

'Thought that might shut you up,' she said defiantly, 'and if ever a mouth needed shutting then it's yours.'

Further down the library George was busy striking his tinder and lighting the few candles liberally placed upon the desks, at least the few that hadn't already burned down to stumps. It was only a half hour after noon but the thousands and thousands of books on their hundreds and hundreds of shelves sucked away the light, leaving the place in permanent shadow.

Joachim was standing a few yards in front of him, completely still. There was a tiny red circle on the back of his habit exactly where the arrow had struck him through. George worried for him, wanted to go to him, but understood how huge a moment this was for Joachim. He shook his head. He knew what it was like to lose a wife and wouldn't wish it on anyone, let alone in the circumstances he'd witnessed up on the Singel. Joachim must have been thinking the same thing because he took one step forward, hesitated, turned and looked at George.

'No better time,' George said quietly in response, 'and no worse. But it has to be done.'

Joachim nodded, rubbing his eyes with his fingers before moving on down the library towards his son.

'So who are you, and what are you doing here?' Ruan had regained speech and plonked himself down on the seat opposite Greta, who had chosen to keep a respectful distance from what was about to unfold down below and sat herself neatly at the desk closest to the Athenaeum's doors.

'Not sure what it's got to do with you,' she said, with such disdain that everything inside Ruan shrivelled like a salt-covered slug. Jesus, but she was annoying, getting right under his skin.

'Get chucked out of the work house?' he asked, trying to sound casual, looking pointedly at her clothes, his eyes resting a little too long on the small rise of her breasts.

'Hear they've still got places,' Greta replied, quick as a snake flicking out its tongue, 'if you're looking for somewhere to call home.'

Ruan flinched. Words a bit too close to home. He let out a breath. He'd met his match and knew it, and oddly did not begrudge it. He'd not had much contact with women, or girls – for plainly she was a couple of years younger than him – and when he had, his kneejerk reaction was to dismiss them. They'd been servants, cooks, one governess who'd not lasted a week in the wilderness of Loch Eck. But this one was different. She'd seen men burned alive in a barn, for God's sake, or so she said.

He looked at her speculatively. She was Irish, that much was plain. Different type of accent from Fergus, but a bogtrotter all the same. And then it hit him like a side of beef. Irish. Like Fergus. Like where Fergus had gone after he and Golo boarded the Collybuckie. And maybe a lifeline, a way out, especially now Hendrik was a mewling wreck and unlikely to be amenable to helping Ruan, having more pressing concerns of his own. But Fergus, maybe this was Fergus, or Fergus's way of getting a message to him, and oh God, he hoped that it was so.

'Let's start again,' he said, holding up his hands in placation. 'My name is Ruan Peat,' and was immediately gratified by the girl looking at him curiously with her wonderful green eyes.

'Is that so?' she said, same truculence, but a definite softening at the edges. 'Well then,' she added, 'then my name is Greta Finnerty, and I've come a very long way to find you and yours.'

Joachim moved down the centre of the library. Hendrik was curled up on a large leather sofa, head and knees tucked inwards, hugging himself, hands showing on either side, just like he'd done as a boy when the world got too much for him. Joachim sat down. He was finding it hard to breathe. The lung that had collapsed when the arrow hit him was not yet at full capacity and whenever he was under stress, or tried to do too much, it felt like it was collapsing inside him all over again.

'It's me, your father,' Joachim said gently.

He was desperate to put out a hand to comfort his son, now a man around the same age Joachim had been when he'd chosen to leave him. But he did not, wasn't even sure if he could. A tremor was beginning to take him over at just the effort of breathing, unable to cope with the depth of grief he was witnessing.

He'd seen it all before, both on the battlefields and at the Servants, but it had belonged to other people then, villagers for the most part, someone dying from gangrene or fever, or lost at sea. But this was Hendrik, his little Hendrik, the boy who was born with such a full head of hair his mother had gasped whilst Joachim – or Wynken as he had been back then – laughed.

'Such a strong boy he'll be because of it, you'll see,' he'd said, and he'd been right. Hendrik was never huge in body but had the most tenacious of minds, and Joachim had been so proud of him he could have burst all the while he was growing up. That's how he'd known Hendrik would save the printing press Joachim had brought to its knees, and Hendrik hadn't let him down. Had never let him down, ever. And he'd gone on to be so much more: become a scholar, an elected member of the city council, put in charge of one of the greatest libraries in Europe.

Hendrik moved. Hendrik uncurled enough to speak.

'I've no need of a father,' he said weakly. 'I've no need of religion of any kind. You don't want to hear what I think about God on this particular day, so I'd be glad if you would just take yourself off and go do your do-gooding someplace else.'

Then back up he curled, and Joachim had to bring his hands together to stop them shaking, interlacing his fingers as if he was about to say a prayer.

'You misunderstand,' Joachim whispered. 'It's not a father here with you, it's your father. It's me. It's Brother Joa…it's Wynken. Your father.'

'So what is it?' Greta asked of Ruan, pointing at the tangled mess of strings she'd turned out onto the reading table.

Ruan wasn't listening, his eyes locked on the ring that had spilled out with it – his ring – the one that had belonged to old ancestor Walter, *Il Petrogradia,* with its etching of the stone circle at Kilmartin and the rising sun. He picked it up and slid it onto his finger. Far too big, not that Ruan minded, only that he now had two very valuable rings in his possession, made more so by him having them together.

If everything went south because of the loss of the documents in the fire on the Singel then at least he had a back-up. A bit of gold never went amiss, let alone a couple of huge precious stones, and it occurred to him that with the researches Hendrik had been carrying out about the Lynx he might be able to bargain them both as a package to someone more interested in dusty old societies than he was himself.

'If you've finished being distracted by shiny things,' Greta said scathingly, 'it was actually this that I was asking about.'

She rapped at the table with her knuckles to draw Ruan's attention. She wanted to scrape the eyes right out of his head. She'd never met such a blockhead as this man was proving to be, so unlike Fergus who'd been willing to chuck himself into the Cause. She couldn't imagine Ruan doing anything like it in Fergus's place.

'What are you looking at?' asked George, coming up to join them, setting a couple of candles carefully into the empty holders by Greta's elbow.

Greta was a quick study and had picked up a few words of Dutch from listening to the exchanges between Joachim and George and asking strategic questions when necessary, and got the gist of what George was saying. She delved into her satchel, took out the folded piece of beet bag and ostentatiously flattened it on the table to catch Ruan's attention.

He took the hint and glanced at it, even as he surreptitiously slipped Walter's ring away into his pocket. Greta stiffened. She knew from Joachim that Ruan was the closest person Fergus had to family, his guardian having died, though giving no specifics; she'd been harbouring some pity for this Ruan Peat, until she'd actually met him. Right now she had no sympathy for him at all, thieving magpie that he was. He'd not even asked about Fergus or what had happened to him, not that she precisely knew.

'It's a khipu,' said the magpie, already sliding his eyes away, one hand fingering the pocket into which he'd secreted the ring, no doubt already planning to get it melted down to fill the teeth that filled his goddamned useless head.

'A...khip...u,' George repeated the word slowly as he drew up a chair and sat down between the two. 'So what's that when it's at home?'

Ruan sighed deeply, realising he was going to have to be the buffer between the two duffers on either side of him, neither speaking the same language as the other. He was pre-empted by a low rumbling coming from the other end of the library and all looked round to see Hendrik Grimalkin hightailing up the central aisle towards them, anguish sharpening his features and gait, eyes blazing like he'd the devil on his tail instead of Brother Joachim, who was hurrying on behind him, legs tangling in his habit and his haste.

Hendrik Grimalkin did not pause as he neared them, but all caught the dark fury clouding his normally passive face and saw the drawing back of bloodless lips from gritted teeth. He passed them by in a blur and moments later was flinging open the doors of the Athenaeum and marching out into the early afternoon.

George stood up abruptly as Joachim took a stumble, and was there within a moment, putting a supporting hand beneath his elbow.

'Going back up to the Singel,' Joachim gasped, plainly finding it hard to get enough breath inside him to speak. 'Couldn't stop him.'

Joachim collapsed onto the chair George had just vacated.

'My fault,' Joachim croaked. 'Told him about the Collybuckie and Golo…told him what you said, George.' He shook his head, kept on shaking it. 'Shouldn't have said that. Shouldn't have said that…'

'You've nothing untoward,' George said firmly, 'truth is what it is.'

'What happened on the Collybuckie?' Greta asked quickly, having picked out enough from Joachim's slow speech to link what he was saying to the article Fergus had cut out, and that had to mean something.

'It's a boat. George thinks Golo was murdered on it,' Ruan said. 'Thinks someone did him in while we were all being shaken to hell in that storm. But I'll say now what I said then. Why would anyone bother?'

'Jees, but you're a cold son of a bitch,' Greta snapped, flashing her green eyes at him. 'Do you ever stop long enough to think about other people? Has it never occurred to you that you're not the centre of the wheel?'

Ruan was trying to compose an answer to this egregious accusation when Brother Joachim got some of his breath back, waved an arm.

'I don't care about your bickering,' he wanted to shout but the words came out in a wheeze, as did the next. 'All that matters now is that Hendrik is running back up to the Singel like a mad man, and you're all still sitting here doing nothing about it.'

Ruan and Greta exchanged glances, and then both turned simultaneously to George Gwilt.

'Get on,' George said decisively. 'We'll follow you up.'

TO THE SINGEL ALL

Greta and Ruan needed no more telling. They stood up, kicking back their chairs, youth and adventure coursing through their veins as they ran to catch up Hendrik, who was by then already half a street ahead of them, striding towards his goal like a man in seven league boots, so focussed that every other thought had gone out of his head.

The closer he got to the Singel the tighter his focus became until he no longer saw the streets or the buildings, only the fact that he was going forward. Had to go forward. Brother Joachim – his father, Wynken Grimalkin – coming back to life was too much. He couldn't cope with it. Not with what he'd said and that Golo Eck had been murdered, because there were the leaves again in their inscrutable pattern and the Lynx whispering at his back, everything connected if only he could figure out how and why. Just needing to get back to the Singel, just needing to get back…

He got there. He saw the blackened carcass of his home and imagined the blackened carcass of Louisa somewhere inside, overwhelmed by the need to find her. Ruan bumped into Hendrik's back as he rounded the corner on a run, Hendrik looking back in irritation to see a young girl with Ruan he'd never seen before who must have arrived with his father, re-emerged from the past.

It might have seemed a miracle in any other circumstance, but not today. He'd lost the most important person in his life, a truth he'd only just begun to realise. A long lost father turning up was nothing in compare. Hendrik had a rage in him that all the waters of the Ijssel couldn't put out, just as they had failed to put out the burning ruins of his house despite being only yards from its front door.

The group of men who had been keeping watch by those waters stuttered into belated movement once one of them realised it was Hendrik Grimalkin himself who was here and not another gawper come to see the wreck. Their muscles twitched but they didn't approach him, instead looked mutely at one another when Grimalkin suddenly strode into the hot ashes, right up to his knees, and started frantically scrabbling through them, whatever search he was undertaking surely futile.

'Oh my God,' Greta whispered as she came up beside Ruan, putting a hand over her mouth, her stomach lurching, her throat constricting, her eyes involuntarily watering up.

'What the…' Ruan began, stopped from saying more by Greta lashing out and thumping him hard across his chest, pushing out all his breath.

'Shut up, why can't you!' she hissed. 'Can't you see what he's doing?'

Ruan let out a wounded breath and shrugged because no, he had no idea what Hendrik was doing. He looked like a maniac – a grey, ash-covered, ash-coloured maniac – poring through dirt and hot embers for Lord knew what.

'Oh Lord protect me,' whispered Joachim, who with George had just turned the intersection to witness his son scouring through the dead remains of his dead house for his dead wife.

'I'll get him,' George said, detaching himself from Joachim, but before he could do so a movement caught his eye and he looked towards his right, saw a small figure appearing at opposite end of the Singel. The small figure was walking, and then walking faster, and then running, and then running and calling, and then running and calling and crying and then was in their midst, ripping off his backpack but did not stop. The boy was still running and crying when he went straight into the wreck of the Grimalkin house, wading through the ashes, kicking up burning embers that tinged the air with the singing of his trousers and his hair, but still he did not stop. He went straight to Hendrik Grimalkin like an arrow from a bolt, keening like a puppy being strangled.

'Oh no oh no oh no...' the young lad did not stop until he reached Grimalkin and flung his arms about Grimalkin's waist, arresting Hendrik for just a moment from his useless task, for just long enough for him to turn within the orbit of the boy's arms and recognise his assailant.

'She's in here, Caro,' Hendrik whispered, 'and I mean to find her,' and in truth Ruan's assessment had been correct: there was madness in his eyes, and soon there was madness in Caro's. The two of them began their digging in unison, flinging out ashes with their hands, chucking pieces of wood behind them, chips of crockery, splinters of glass, the spines of dismembered books, the detritus of daily life burned down into its component parts.

It was enough to break anyone's heart and Greta couldn't stand to look any longer. She turned away, walked a few yards around the corner, towards where the back of the house would have been if it was still standing. The stench was too raw and recognisable and she was fearing she might start to blub at any moment, and the thought of Ruan Peat seeing her cry was too much.

She came to an abrupt halt when she saw the delivery hatches where coal and wood would have been thrown down into cellar below. They looked to have been blown clean off their hinges only to settle right back down again into their accustomed places, edges splintered and blackened, but intact. She put her fingers below one of them and lifted it a few inches, shifting it over its supine companion and, by doing so, could see the wooden chute off to the left, and a set of stone steps immediately beyond, heading down into darkness.

She lay down on her stomach and poked her head through the gap she had made. The first thing she noticed, once her eyes had got used to the dark, and after she'd brushed away several motes of ash that blurred her vision, was that this underground cavern was uncluttered by any fallen timbers. It had been excavated directly into the compacted ground below the house, a couple of yards of packed earth separating the two, bolstered by props and joists to keep the cellar ceiling up, keep this space cool for any foodstuffs, fuel or drink that needed to be stored down here. The house above might have collapsed but this cellar was relatively undisturbed, a dark and empty place into which Greta wriggled.

At the far end she could see where a hole had been blown into the house above, or from the house above down into this space below, seeing the black and ragged diameter and the thin lines of ash that were trickling between gaps in the soil, caught by the dark light of several smouldering patches of embers in the two foot thick joists that were nevertheless strong enough to keep the remains of the house from tumbling in.

The second thing Greta noticed was that there was a very distinctive smell down here, now she'd got half her body in. She wrinkled her nose, sniffed some more, because it was a smell she recognised from Peter's printing presses, coming from the strong solvent they used to clean away the old ink from the printing plates when it had begun to clog the presses up.

She wriggled a little further in, but there was only darkness and more of it, and into that not even Greta was willing to go. She backed her way out, wondered if she should say anything. She had an idea, but might be wrong. She thought on Hendrik Grimalkin and that young boy shovelling their way through the ashes up above like beavers going haywire. She might be right, she might be wrong, but she knew she had to say it.

She took a few minutes to pull away the remaining boards of the hatchments and then walked her way back around to the Singel. The men who had been sat over the way were now gathered in a huddle with George, Joachim and Ruan at their centre. She went to Joachim, tugged at his habit, pulling down his ear.

'Um, don't know if it means anything,' Greta whispered, 'but the cellar's pretty much intact down there, and there's a bit of a reek in it that I'm thinking is turpentine, or something very like it.'

Joachim heard the words but didn't comprehend their implication. He was finding it inestimably hard to witness his son digging through the ashes, and even more so when Caro had come out of nowhere to join in. If George hadn't been hanging onto him like a crab he would already have gone blundering in to intervene.

'What did she say?' George asked.

Joachim translated like an automaton, alarmed when George suddenly let him go, went running off around the corner, grabbing at the young girl's shoulder as he went.

'To the cellar!' George was shouting, flinging his arm to give direction to the others. 'Get round the back and to the cellar!'

The cluster of men were slow to react. By the time they'd turned the corner, following George, he was already all the way down the cellar's steps. Greta had been right, he knew it immediately. The smell was all pervasive and unmistakable. He needed a light, he needed to see down here. He went back up a few steps and shouted loudly.

'Get me a lamp, but keep it shuttered!'

The straggle of men understood the words, but no one had a lamp, shuttered or otherwise.

'Grimalkin!' George yelled. 'Get Grimalkin here!'

He'd seen something rolled against the far wall. Or rather, someone. He could see her head. Definitely a head, hair coming out in wisps from one end, boots – toes down – from the other. No time to spare. No time to wait for a light. He inched his way across the earthen floor of the cellar, hands held out in front of him in case anything was in his way that he couldn't see. And there she was. Louisa Grimalkin. Not burned up in the fire but down here all the time. George knelt and moved her gently away from the wall.

She was dead. Obviously so. No one could have survived a fire like that, not even down here. Smoke inhalation was George's best guess, for her face was drawn and contorted, her mouth a horrid echo of a smile. He stood back. He didn't want to touch her. Not his call, nor his duty, no matter what Joachim had taught him at the Servants.

'She's here,' he said, his voice quiet, no one else to hear him, until suddenly there was, the grey shape of Hendrik Grimalkin thundering down the steps and arriving at George's back.

'Is it she?' Hendrik whispered, although he already knew the answer.

'I think so,' George replied, for who else could it be?

Hendrik went down on his knees with an audible thud, George holding out his hand, keeping the man back from the body. And thank God he did, for right on Hendrik's heels came a few other men from the Singel including Pieter Dulke who had served for many years in a munitions factory supplying gunpowder, cannon balls and shells to anyone who would buy them, and knew how to survey a blowing-up with a practiced eye.

He'd managed to procure a few candles and got one lit, thereby revealing the dark halo of blood beneath Louisa's head and also a thin black line burned into the cellar's floor that led from a burned out circle in the soil to the steps that went from cellar up to kitchen. Immediately over this circle a massive hole had been blasted into the earth above. Dulke followed the black line of what he recognised to be a fuse, taking his time, undistracted by the other men milling about the cellar that had undoubtedly been constructed well, its dimensions large and admirable, the pantry alcoves dug into its walls seemingly untouched.

Men were even now taking out the foodstuffs that had been stowed within those alcoves – jars of pickles and bottled fruit, cheeses, hams, smoked meat joints, jams and chutneys. Pieter Dulke hoped these rescued vittals would be reunited with their proper owner, though he rather doubted they would, but it was not his primary concern. Instead he was looking above him, at that ragged hole, and all about him, at that line from stair to stack and, as he did so, he saw and understood what must have happened here.

He walked towards Hendrik Grimalkin, who was still on his knees, watching as George turned his wife's body back to the wall, but oh so gently, so that Hendrik could not see her face. Pieter went towards Grimalkin but it was to George Gwilt that he spoke, recognising a certain professionalism in the way George was conducting his actions.

'What can you see?' Pieter asked. George coughed, and then spoke, apparently understanding his role, and that less, in this situation, was more.

'She's one blow to the back of her head,' George said, 'and another to the side that took out an eye, and there's blood but no smoke in her nostrils, so pray God she wasn't alive when the fire took.'

Small comfort for Hendrik, but it gave Pieter another piece to his puzzle. He nodded, then placed a hand on Grimalkin's shoulder, gripped it a little harder until Grimalkin reacted, got off his creaking knees and stood up.

'There's some surmises I can put forward,' Pieter started, 'though I can't say exactly what happened, only that it seems to me most likely that someone offloaded a couple of barrels down here – one of turpentine maybe, like the lass said, because I can surely smell it too – and another keg, probably of gunpowder. They were here, see,' Pieter pointed to the burned out circle that was surrounded on its outer perimeters by small wisps of straw and several curved staves of wood.

'On the straw bales,' Hendrik whispered. 'Louisa kept them for kindling for the range.'

'Doesn't everyone,' Pieter stated blandly before pushing on. 'Seems like they laid a fuse. See here?' He pointed out the wriggly line that ran from the blackened circle to the kitchen steps. 'Probably set the fuse going there, at the bottom of the steps,' Pieter said, 'so's to make sure they'd get out in good time,' telling the scene as he saw it, 'for it's no easy science is explosives. But when it went, the main blast went straight up yonder, blowing out the soil between the joists immediately above the bales and kegs, pushing the fire straight into the house. Lots of air up there,' Pieter added as he looked upwards, 'and would have drawn the fire very quickly up and away. Which explains why this place never got much of a look-in, and why your lady here is still pretty much as she was when she was left.'

Pieter glanced at Hendrik Grimalkin at this last pronouncement, saw his face set like rock and everything about him as grey and forbidding as the ash that was filtering down from the ceiling above. He decided he might as well go for bust, was enjoying this analysis, hadn't done it since he'd been back at the Munitions Factory when he and his colleagues spent all day long blowing stuff up and figuring out ever more efficient ways to do it.

'She must've been down here when the blast took, but wasn't directly affected by it,' he said. 'And most likely wasn't aware,' he added, having taken in what George had said previously. 'Body says relaxed,' he ploughed on, 'which most likely means unconscious or already dead. Probably blown over from maybe there to the wall,' he pointed with his boot at the faint marks on the cellar floor where something prone had rolled along through its dust, eventually abutting against the wall a few foot distant, where Louisa's body lay.

A brief shudder went through his body as he thought of the other body – Teresa Arnolfini's – for fire, Pieter Dulke knew, was capricious that way: gentle one moment, inestimably cruel the next, seeming almost conscious in how it moved, as if it had a logic all its own, able to burn out one place so completely and be so ferocious it could halve a woman right through at the waist and yet leave the place it had started in – and Pieter was in no doubt that was here – with barely a scorch mark.

He caught something flickering at the corner of his vision, shifted his gaze, saw it move and change, saw that the fire, beautiful and unpredictable as it was, had read his thoughts. He looked straight up above him, at the huge wooden joists that were holding the cellar's ceiling in place over their heads and raised the corner of his lip in a smile that was teetering on admiration; and knew that the fire wasn't done, that the beams were nested through and through by several slow-burning patches of embers, consolidating and warming themselves these last few hours like a body of hornets trying to burn out an intruder. He understood too that they were just about to go up again in the reconflagration the men on the Singel had so feared, mostly likely kicked back to life by the opening of the hatchment doors and all these men moving and churning up the air about them, and that all the while they'd been down here the fire had been gathering itself, getting hotter and stronger, firing up from grey to red, from red to white, and were about to go to hell and fury.

'Everyone out!' Pieter suddenly shouted. 'Joists are going! Whole place is going to fall down about our ears any moment!'

And all the men down in that cellar looked up and saw Pieter was right and that the small pockets of embers they had glanced at previously, and had assumed were the last hurrahs of a dying fire, were burning now with a determined furiosity that was frightening in its intensity and speed. It crept down every crevasse and crack along the pathways of the wood grain and next began to leap and jump from joist to joist as if in some game whose rules only they understood.

'Get out, get out!' they all began to shout, immediately running and tumbling over one other in their panic to get back up the cellar steps.

They all funnelled towards the only exit, dropping their candles, whose tiny flames joined in the game and began to seek out the still unburned threads of turpentine that had soaked into the soil when the first barrel blew so suddenly its staves were punched out all across the cellar floor.

'Get back, get back!' they yelled, a thick press of bodies corralling at the bottom of the steps as everyone began to push and shove, all grabbing and grubbing to get themselves out, dragging others up behind them the moment they hit the afternoon air, the only ones left behind being Hendrik and George, and the already dead body of Louisa.

'I can't leave her,' Grimalkin said grimly, but it was George who was closest and so he dipped down and scooped his arms below Louisa's, Grimalkin coming immediately to his aid, grasping at her feet to take the weight and together they staggered across the cellar floor, the fire now bright and burning so they knew the way to go.

A sudden guff of smoke speckled with grit came billowing down from above, leaving them blind. But they were at the bottom of the steps now, Hendrik stumbling into the lowest, dropping Louisa's feet with the force of his ankles hitting the stone. He scrambled upwards, gained a couple of steps, got his balance, but by now the burning embers were raining down upon them both, falling onto their backs, eating their way into the seams of their coats, the worst of it on George, who was still in the body of the cellar, trying to shove Louisa on.

The smoke was getting thicker and blacker and hotter with every tiny step he took, the heat suddenly so intense George wasn't sure he could make another inch. And then his load was lightened, Grimalkin having grabbed his wife's ankles and began to haul her up the steps as he bum-shuffled up them one by one, George trying to keep her head from bumping against the stones, still pushing her up from down below although he couldn't see a thing, because by now the smoke from the cellar was heading for its own escape, going the same way they were, right up the steps and out to freedom.

A single ember caught Hendrik's hair and began to sizzle its way through all the rest, and George's trousers were burning at their ends where he'd stumbled over a couple of turpentine-soaked staves set to flame by one of the candles the Singel men had dropped. Hendrik still pulled for all his worth, heaving Louisa's body up one step at a time, George still pushing her on from down below.

Several men up above tryied unsuccessfully to grab at Hendrik, beaten back by the smoke and because his head was truly on fire now and it was hard for them to get a hold of him. Hendrik looked to George, from down below, like one of those saints in the windows of the Servants' chapel, the ones with those golden aureoles painted about them, and just for a moment he thought he could see Joachim's face there too, just behind those flames. Because of it he gave one almighty push and up Louisa went, Hendrik reaching the final step, someone smothering the flames over his head with their jacket, others pulling him on, and Louisa with him, so that George could see the last of her disappearing up into the light.

George let out a long breath, glad the deed was done, that Hendrik had got his wife back and Joachim there to see her right. His lungs were seared from the acrid smoke and could draw no more breath in. The day was there at the top of the steps but down below George was going up in flames lithe and strong, orange fire, black smoke, a tiger eating him alive. His head fell forward, propping his chin upwards on the bottom step, eyes blinking despite the lack of breath and half of him devoured, last sight a shadowy glimpse of Joachim peering down into the cellar, hands waving madly, other hands holding him back; last thought flickering through George like a sigh, the vague hope of there being something on the other side, his Maker, maybe, if Maker there was. All over for George Gwilt a millisecond later when the central joist groaned and fell, burying him beneath a ton of earth as the cellar's roof gave way and brought the house of the Grimalkins down upon his head.

WIND AND WATER, AND THOSE WAITING TO BE BURIED

Maker or no, the rain came down that night as if heaven-sent and carried on, unstinting and unstoppable, right into the following morning, dousing the smouldering, smoking remains of Hendrik's house. It filled the air around it with eerie pops and groans as it sizzled and settled, pulling itself down into the cellar below.

Wet ash was everywhere, carried by the night breeze gusting down every gap and ginnel and by the rainwater that funnelled down the central gutter of the Singel, snaking into every adjoining street, carried further abroad by people's boots right into the Brink and beyond. Small scraps of Hendrik's house carried all over Deventer, smaller scraps of George going with it.

In the library, the mood was grim. Hendrik insisted Louisa be brought in with them, and she was lying wrapped in a dust sheet on a couple of reading tables that had been hastily shoved together at the base of the library beyond the green sofas where Hendrik was keeping vigil, Caro curled up beside him, sleeping when he couldn't keep his eyes open a moment longer.

They looked a motley pair, grey as mules, ash in every corner and crevasse of their clothes and skin. Hendrik's head was almost entirely bereft of hair, his scalp the colour of boiled beef, blisters rising up and bursting, only to rise up again, Hendrik refusing all attempts to have it cleaned and salved. He wanted to suffer. He deserved it, after what Dulke had said and George had done. One night of it at least.

'So what are we going to do about Mr Grimalkin?' Greta spoke quietly to Joachim where they sat together a few tables up, the huge shelves of books towering above them, heavy giants at their backs.

'We leave him be,' Joachim replied simply. 'Death requires space, but I'll tend to both him and his wife in the morning.'

Ruan clicked his tongue.

'Should she really be here at all? It's just not right. It's not hygienic. Don't you have undertakers in this part of the world?'

Greta rolled her eyes, but was too tired to respond. If Ruan was going to behave like a child then she would treat him as such and ignore him. Joachim was more tolerant.

'It's plain you've not had much contact with the dead,' he said, 'or those they leave behind. Everyone grieves in their own way, and this is Hendrik's. If you want to be of help you could go and find an undertaker yourself, pick out a coffin. Plain but functional, I suspect, would be best.'

Ruan creased his face in irritation.

'But it's dark out there, and bloody well pouring with rain. I'm not going out in that.'

'Then hold your tongue,' Joachim said, more sharply than he'd meant and immediately regretting it, tried to soften his words. 'Why not go and get some sleep? I gather you've a room upstairs you're using.'

Ruan knew when he was not wanted – this time at least – and no more did he want to be here. He cast a glance down at the sheeted figure lying on her makeshift bier and shuddered. It wasn't natural, and if he didn't have to be here then so be it. He was off, taking quick strides up the library towards the stairs by the door that led to the upper floor, Isaac appearing suddenly from the outside, time for his shift. Ruan nodded briefly but was not about to hang around passing niceties and took his noisy way off up the stairs.

Isaac gazed after the young man, then slowly turned and carefully bolted the library's doors. He hadn't been sure whether he should come, not tonight, but he'd no one at home. He'd arrived in Deventer as one of the many Jewish refugees after the Seven Year War, his village near Lobosik destroyed by the Prussians, every last member of his family brutalised and killed in ways that didn't bear thinking about. Once safe in Deventer, he never made new friends, let alone attempted to create a new family. He couldn't stand to go through all that again, all that loss, and when he'd heard of the Revolution in France and their insidious advancement from border to border he was glad he hadn't. This library and its books and the people who visited it were all the family and social life he needed, and he thanked God for it every night when he tidied away the books left out for re-shelving, and later took a snooze in the peep-hole room. It was Isaac's favourite place in the Athenaeum – small and round, no corners for shadows, snug and safe. The perfect place.

Coming in now he wondered if he shouldn't just slip into it and close the door. He couldn't face Hendrik, would have no words, violent bereavement a private endeavour, his instinct to steer well clear; but he'd steered clear the night before and couldn't spend another night alone at home. And he was glad he'd come now, because there were two people sitting partway down the library that he'd never clapped eyes on before, and that – in the words of Ruan Peat – just wasn't right. The library at night was his purview and he took exception to anything going on that he didn't know about.

'Hello?' he said, taking a few steps towards them, stopping short as he caught sight of the draped figure lying on the desks at the other end of the atrium lit by two candles, one at head, one at foot.

Joachim stood up and came to greet him.

'It's Louisa,' he said, 'Hendrik's wife. We brought her here a while since.'

Isaac nodded. He understood. For what else should Hendrik have done with her?

'It's a terrible thing, terrible,' Isaac said slowly, and Joachim could see the old man knew the meaning of that word right down to the bone.

'I'm Brother Joachim, Hendrik's fa…Hendrik's friend,' he introduced himself. 'And you?'

'Ah,' Isaac said. 'Isaac. Night watchman. Usually tidy away the books, replace candles, refill inkwells and the like.'

'Not tonight, I fear,' Joachim replied sadly.

'Not tonight,' Isaac repeated. 'No. I see that. But if it's alright with you I'll take my usual post. Keep my usual watch.'

'I think we'd all be glad of it,' Joachim nodded his approval. And indeed he was.

He didn't know the details of what had been said down in the cellar before it had all gone to fire and burn. He swallowed, didn't want to think about George, that last sight of him being engulfed, George's face an agony of resignation, if two such words could be coupled, but Christ, that's what he thought he'd seen. But no time now for that. Time now to be a father to his son, if Hendrik would allow it. His own personal loss could be dealt with later when he was alone again, when he was back at the Servants amongst the people who knew George best. And Goerge's sons.

He let out a breath. God knew what he was going to say to them. He closed his eyes, rubbed a hand against his temples. Made a conscious decision to brush all that away. Concentrate, he told himself. Concentrate. From what he'd gathered from the swirl of men who'd come bursting out of the cellar dragging Hendrik and Louisa after them, the talk was definitely of foul doings, of deliberation, of the fire having been engineered into existence. He tried to recall the name of the man who'd come up with this explanation, but could not. A munitions expert, he remembered, someone who surely knew what he was talking about. Come the morning he'd need to try and find the man, get him here, sit him down, talk it all through.

But he was so weary, and felt like a hot wire was being pulled back and forth through his chest where he'd stretched his scars too far. He needed rest. Isaac was already walking away. He'd said his piece and was done, so Joachim turned back to Greta.

'Are you tired?' he asked.

'I'm not, but you are,' she said. 'Come on. Let me get you upstairs. There's got to be more than one room up there because this place is like the biggest barn I've ever seen.'

Joachim smiled. He liked the girl. Honest and direct, and wise beyond her years. If Ireland grew girls like her in plenty then it was a place that could only do well. He heard her stomach grumbling loudly as she stood and realised they'd eaten nothing all day, not since they'd arrived in Deventer. Fine for older bones like him, but not for a child like her.

'Sorry,' Greta said, but did not complain.

'Ask Isaac,' Joachim said. 'There must be food and drink here somewhere.'

'I'll ask,' she said. 'But first, upstairs. If I find anything I'll bring it up to you in a couple of shakes.'

Greta knocked on the door of the room she'd seen Isaac going into and entered on his call. She'd been impressed by what she'd already seen of Deventer. That place they called the Brink had been amazing, and the library was the grandest place she'd ever been. Peter would love it. And if he was still alive when she got home she swore she'd get him to the Athenaeum by hook or crook, just to see the look on his face the second he walked in.

Yet this little room Isaac brought her into had her entranced all over again. For starters it was round, and she'd never been in a perfectly round room before, and all across the white-painted walls she could see patterns – moving patterns – going from floor to ceiling like she was standing in the middle of a kaleidoscope. The roof was domed, and she'd never seen that before either, and right at the centre of the dome was a small round skylight through which she could just make out a pinch of the moon and a small scatter of blurry stars.

'It's called a *camera obscura,*' Isaac told her with pride, pronouncing the words carefully to accentuate their importance. Greta showed no hint of understanding but Isaac pushed on with his talk anyway, having said it plenty of times before. 'There's a labyrinth of lenses going from that little hole in the roof to one of the pillars right outside the Athenaeum's doors so we can see whoever is standing on its steps.'

Greta shook her head to indicate she didn't understand, so Isaac demonstrated with his hands, miming the dome and the skylight, the pillar outside the door, Greta getting the gist and giving a short laugh.

'So what's out there now? Hundreds of little midgets dancing?' she pointed at the shapes upon the walls, tracing several of them with her fingers as they quickly slid up and down the surface. Isaac smiled again.

'It's the rain, my dear. You're looking at the rain.'

Once more he took to hand demonstration, Greta picking up quickly on what he was saying as he repeated the few key words she had grasped...*rain...upside down...mirrors.* Then it was time for Greta to do a little miming of her own, but food was easy and Isaac had it in a second, leaving the round room, beckoning for her to follow. He'd not thought of this and wished he had.

This was part of his remit, to see to any visiting scholars' needs after the doors of the Athenaeum were closed for the night. Not that there were any visiting scholars at the moment, only Hendrik and this odd assortment of people he'd brought with him. Caro he'd met plenty, and Ruan Peat he recognised from once before, but now there were two others, this girl and a monk. He stopped abruptly, suddenly realising that to get to the little kitchen at the back end of the library he'd have to go pass Hendrik, and Louisa.

'Not go past,' he shook his head apologetically, shrugging and pointing. Greta's stomach was growling again and Isaac heard, held up a hand, going back into the round room and returning with the little packet he'd made up for himself – several mean lumps of rye bread, sausage and cheese and a lit candle to see her way to bed.

'Take,' he said, pushing it towards her. Greta hesitated, but Isaac pushed the packet at her again and she took it, along with the candle, smiling so radiantly his old heart jolted within his chest.

'Thank you,' Greta said, bowing briefly, and then was off up the stairs to share her meagre repast with Joachim, but Joachim was so exhausted he'd lain down on his bed and gone straight to sleep. Nevertheless, she carefully divvied up Isaac's piece and laid half of it on his bedside table and, as a final gesture, lit a candle before creeping away and shutting the door quietly behind her. She stood for a few moments leaning at the rails that kept folk from tipping precipitously over into the library below, the mezzanine like a minstrels gallery buttressed out from the library walls, leaving a gap of maybe six foot by ten at the centre. She saw Isaac moving slow and silent amongst the shelves, fitting new candles into holders, pouring ink into inkwells. And she saw the two flickering lights at head and base of the makeshift bier, the slump of Hendrik's Grimalkin's shoulders at the very edge of the green sofa, his raw read head lolling, almost touching the winding sheet.

God help him, she whispered, lifting her own head, stretching her neck. *And God help Peter and Mogue Kearns, wherever you are.*

LOUISA'S LAYING OUT, AND LAYING DOWN TO DIE

Joachim did not sleep well. Two hours in his eyelids had flickered open against his will and he was awake. The rain was tappering on the Athenaeum's roof, running helter skelter down its windows, gathering in its gutters, pouring from them into the street below.

He could smell the library beneath him, the dusty aroma of a hundred thousand musty books, the wax used to polish its floorboards and desks, the faint hint of the cigars and cigarillos the habitués used when they were studying, the even fainter hints of Hendrik's burned-down house that emanated from his own clothes. He was aware too of the tiny flicker of light to his right where someone had lit a candle on the table by his bed, a small point in the darkness. He levered himself up on his elbows, feeling a slight dampness at his chest scar as he did so. He touched it with his fingertip but when he put it to the light he saw no blood, so that was good.

He also noted the paltry offerings of food, reminding him how hollow was his stomach. Greta Finnerty. Undoubtedly she. He sent up a quick prayer of thanks for Greta before taking a small bite of bread and cheese, getting it down with several convulsive swallows, but needed a glass of water to get down anymore and so swung his legs from the bed, lifting the candle in its holder and padding his unshod way from his room and down the stairs. The noise he made was minimal, but enough to bring Isaac hurrying from his room who, on seeing Joachim, merely nodded and retreated, leaving Joachim to his own devices.

This is the hardest thing I'm ever going to have to do. God give me strength.

He went down the central nave of the library towards the bier, the candles there swaying wildly as candles always do when they're almost at their end.

Just like life, Joachim thought, plucking two new ones up, setting them solidly in the soft wax, extinguishing their fellows as he did so. *The new coming from the old.*

Hendrik was awake, sitting on the sofa, Caro curled up beside him, deeply asleep.

'Can I join you in your vigil?' Joachim asked, soft as he could, so as not to wake the boy. Hendrik stared at him a moment, but the small act of replacing the candles was a kindness he could not overlook and he nodded, waved his hand, and Joachim sat down. They shared the silence for a good while, neither moving nor speaking, until Joachim deemed it right to say what he had come to say.

'I could lay Louisa out for you, if you will allow it. It's what I do. Laying out the dead, if we've not been able to save them. A last duty, seeing them right.'

Hendrik said nothing. He'd been pondering this very aspect of Louisa's death, dreading handing her over in the morning to some stranger to strip her down, wash her most intimate parts when she was at her most vulnerable, Louisa always the most modest of women. The very idea of it was unconscionable, and yet not to have it done was even more so, a paradox that had been chasing its tail through his mind for hours, and here was a solution. Brother Joachim – Hendrik still could not think of him as anything other, keeping Wynken, the father, at a distance – but both a stranger and a familiar. Family and yet not. Another paradox. He took his time. Thought about the implications.

'Did you ever think of us at all when you went?' Hendrik eventually asked, keeping his voice low, one hand laid gently on Caro's head, fearing that any sudden movement would wake the boy. The only part of Louisa he had left.

Joachim placed his own hand involuntarily over the heart that had been so recently bruised by an accidental arrow, painful now, far more so than before, metaphorically speaking.

'But of course,' he said, in the same low monotone Hendrik had employed. 'How could you think otherwise?'

'Because you left!' Hendrik hissed, turning his face towards his father with such sudden rage that Joachim had to turn momentarily away.

'But I sent you letters,' Joachim murmured. 'Did you not receive them?'

Hendrik closed his eyes and shook his head.

'Mother would not allow me. She put them unopened on the fire the moment they arrived.'

His anger gone as soon as it had come. Loss and grief in every limb, only the warmth of young Caro here to keep him company. Caro stirred as Hendrik moved his hand across the boy's head but didn't wake. Hendrik was too tired to carry on this conversation.

'Letters are nothing,' he said shortly, 'when your father abandons your family.'

Joachim blinked into the darkness.

'I hoped they would offer explanation,' Joachim whispered,

thinking of the woodcutter in the Brink George had so delighted in. 'I hoped you would understand that…when a man has discovered…darkness, and I did, Hendrik, discover darkness in that war I went into…well, that sometimes…when a man comes out of such things…such things he has seen that no one should… well… he has to try and find the light…and for me that was the Servants. And God forgive me if I did wrong. Oh God, and my own son, forgive me if I did wrong.'

Joachim shook his head. He'd put down all those words and excuses in his letters that he now knew had gone unread. The tragedy of the situation struck father and son at the same moment, Hendrik bringing his teeth together, tightening his jaws to try to stop the tears because at last he understood.

Any day before this one he might not have, but now he was in his own darkness and had seen things he never should have seen, he understood, and a sob came from deep within him as he accepted it, lay his burning head against his father's shoulder and began a gentle weeping. He was more comforted than he could say when Joachim encircled his arm about his son's heaving shoulders, keeping him safe. Always keeping him safe, just like he'd done when he was young.

Louisa's laying out was performed by Joachim with the utmost respect and care. The clothes she had on were the only ones available for her to be buried in, so Joachim removed them, brushed them down, washed her body as was necessary before dressing her, placing the herbs he'd asked Isaac to fetch from the early morning market, between their folds.

By the time Hendrik was awake – for when he'd finally slept he slept so deeply that not even Joachim's moving around had awakened him – all had been taken care of. Louisa was there on her bier when he opened his eyes, just as he had left her, except there was no smoke or blood about her face; hair combed and braided; jaw discretely, eyelids closed – hiding the empty socket – sealed with wax, for which Hendrik was immeasurably grateful.

'Thank you,' Hendrik said to Joachim, who was still arranging the last niceties of Louisa's cuffs and collar when Hendrik got himself off the sofa.

'The coffin is on its way,' Joachim replied. 'A simple thing, pine and white satin. I hope you approve.'

'I do,' Hendrik replied. 'It's just as she would have wanted.'

'And I've been to see her priest,' Caro offered. His eyes were still swollen from his night of crying. When he'd been awoken by Joachim's comings and goings from the library's kitchen with jugs of water he'd been at first outraged and then terribly shocked and embarrassed to see Louisa naked on her bier, a nakedness hurriedly covered by Joachim throwing a sheet over her. Caro had been about to shout out into the morning until Joachim shushed him, pointing at Hendrik asleep on the sofa.

'It has to be done, lad,' Joachim said. 'Far better to do it here than anywhere else.'

Caro had subsided but was desperate to get away and Joachim gave him the perfect opportunity.

'You knew her,' Joachim said, 'undoubtedly far better than I did, so why not go and fetch her priest? She has need of him now more than ever.'

Caro left the library quick as he could on his errand. He'd hoped, when he first woke on the sofa, that the fire and Louisa dying had all been a nightmare he'd conjured up. He couldn't bear that his wonderful, warm Louisa could really be dead. He started crying again the moment he left the Athenaeum. The rain had stopped, but the smell was still there, that stink of burning coming from the Singel real and visceral, and Louisa really gone.

Greta was the next to emerge, coming bleary eyed down the stairs, short red hair all on end except for a flat patch at the back where she'd lain on her pillow. She was ravenous, Isaac's small supper from the night before nowhere near enough to fill the void.

Isaac still refused to pass Louisa's dead body to fetch food from the pantry but when he'd been sent to the market for Joachim's herbs he returned with a basket of fresh baked bread, butter, cold meats, sauerkraut, and some rollmopped herrings soaked in caper oil. All this he carefully placed on the desk closest to the door, Joachim bringing plates and cutlery from the kitchen.

No sign of Ruan yet, but he was a sleepyhead of the first order as both Hendrik and Caro knew, and both were glad of it. The last thing either of them wanted to hear this morning was one of the rude, abrasive comments that seemed to fall from Ruan's lips like stones scurrying down disturbed scree, unable to stop themselves, uncaring of any damage they might do when they landed.

Hendrik had consented to letting Joachim see to the burns on his scalp, ears and forehead. The beneficial effects of the ointment that Joachim knocked up from goose fat, tallow and herbs were so cooling and immediate that Hendrik was managing to think in straight lines, as he'd not been able to do the night before.

'I've never been one for prayers,' Hendrik said, once Caro, Greta and Joachim were gathered with him around the table on which Isaac had strewn his wares, 'but I would like to say something before we eat.' Hendrik had situated himself so he could see Louisa, unwilling to let go this last sight of her, not when the undertaker with his coffin might arrive at any moment. 'But I would like to say this.'

He took a deep breath before carrying on, the hint of a smile twisting on his lips as he saw Greta snatching back her hand at his words, the faint growl of her stomach reminding him to keep his speech short.

'What I would like to say is that I'm truly grateful for you all being here, and… for Brother Joachim especially. You have done me a great kindness,' he said, turning towards his father. 'Louisa would have hated to have been…mauled at by people she didn't know. And I know you didn't know her, but you were the next best thing.'

He was quiet for a couple of moments, his head bowing slightly before he went on.

'And there is someone else I would like to thank, someone who is not here,' he said. 'George Gwilt, who took Louisa's place down there in the cellar, and who is still down there now.'

Joachim closed his eyes. He'd not expected this. The brief exchange he'd had with Hendrik the night before, and then again this morning, had given him only the faintest glimmer of what his son had grown up to be, but to have become someone so gracious was a blessing indeed. Joachim had never questioned his calling and certainly never fully understood the impact his leaving had made on his family. He'd always assumed they were pleased to see the back of him, giving them the chance to claw back the business before he sent it toppling to the dust.

Hendrik's brief rage had unmasked this belief as a selfish and self-serving lie, one that Joachim had stuck to all these years because it made him feel good about his decision and what he had chosen to do with his life. But more than two decades later George was dead because of it, if indirectly, and Joachim regretted it with an intensity he could not express.

The silence following this pronouncement lasted only a second or two before Greta brought them all back to the here and now.

'Erm if it's alright with you, and if you've said all you've needed saying, then I'm really hungry and I'd like to dig in. Battlefields aren't going to stop coming just 'cos you wish it, and it's always best to be prepared for the one that's about to come next.'

Hendrik could not stop himself and let out a wheezy laugh, Joachim joining him involuntarily, father and son jolted from their navel gazing by this young girl who had only hunger on her mind.

'By all means,' Hendrik managed to croak out. 'Greta is it?'

Greta got stuck in immediately, nodding wordlessly in reply, and just as well for five minutes later there was a knock at the door, Isaac out of his cubby hole in as fast a flash as his old legs could carry him.

'Don't recognise him,' he said breathlessly, directing his words at Hendrik. 'Muddy boots. Filthy clothes. Definitely not a scholar. What do you think?'

Hendrik nodded. He'd already spoken to Isaac, told him no one was to be let in without his say so, library doors to stay locked and bolted. No one welcome, at least not until Louisa had been buried.

'See who it is first,' he said, and Isaac scurried off, Greta shoving as much food into her gullet as she could in case everything kicked off again. Isaac returned with someone Hendrik recognised but could not put a name to.

'Pieter Dulke,' the man introduced himself. 'Was down in the cellar last night?'

'Of course,' Hendrik remembered: the man who had stated with such conviction that the fire was no accident.

'Hope you don't mind,' Pieter went on, 'but I've done a bit of asking around...'

'And you've found something?' Hendrik asked quickly, stomach tightening with expectation and dread.

'I have,' said Pieter. 'Quite a lot, as it happens. We know when the fire at your house started, and you know what I think about the how of it. The smell the young girl pointed out,' Pieter nodded at Greta, 'and the way everything was down there…well, after that, got talking to some of the folks round about. Seems there was a delivery to your home just before – one man, two barrels on a dray cart, far as anyone can remember, and someone who saw your wife leading him in through the house with a cask loaded onto his shoulders.'

Pieter stopped briefly, looking at Hendrik, a big cog in the wheel of Deventer, someone Pieter could do with the backing of to get him back into the work he'd been lacking. What he said next was going to seal the deal, or ditch it down the nearest hole. But no point prevaricating.

'The woman who saw this heard a sloshing in the cask, took it to be ale, took that to be the reason your wife might have led the man in through the house and not got him to send it down the chute, when all the lees would have swilled up and spoiled it.'

Hendrik interrupted Dulke with a cough, a great black gobbit coming up and out from his lungs. He placed a napkin across his mouth to catch it, nodding for Pieter to go on.

'It wasn't ale, sir. I believe it was two barrels of some explosive material, that he coshed your wife so she couldn't identify him in the unlikely event she escaped the following explosion. He set them on the straw bales for maximum burnage, got a fuse lit and then got out smartish. Several people reported a man rushing off down the Singel on an empty dray at about the same time, when there was a God Almighty bang…'

Hendrik coughed again, put his napkin up against his face. So, as he'd expected then. A fire set deliberately, his house the target, Louisa surely not the intended victim but rather himself and probably Ruan Peat too. The straight lines in his mind became fluid, snaking left and right. He was remembering something, something he'd read about the Lynx – always the blasted Lynx, as Ruan would have said if he'd been here, but the blasted Lynx all the same. And Caro's book. He couldn't pin it down, it hovered in the background like a bee about a flower, a niggling remembrance of a document he'd come across, a name he'd stumbled over; a name he'd heard before, something Ruan – of all people – had at some time mentioned. He couldn't grasp it, couldn't get those lines in his mind back to the straight.

'Did you get a description of this man?' Hendrik asked, Pieter happy he could deliver a positive answer.

'I did,' he answered. 'Several of the folk I spoke to commented on it. Tall and skinny, foreign looking, Spanish maybe, or Italian or Greek. Dark hair, bad skin, like he'd an almighty case of the smallpox when he was young.'

Greta stopped stuffing food into her mouth, and not because the rolled-up herring she'd just tried was a little disgusting, but because – as Joachim translated this conversation for her – she realised she'd seen someone very like that herself. Not here, certainly, but at the Servants: that man pushing about his broom at the back of the refectory the afternoon she'd arrived, the man who'd paused at his sweeping when the food-providing Brother Eustace mentioned Grimalkin and Deventer in the same breath. Battle had been in her blood ever since she'd started off with the United Irish, and battle said *don't ignore coincidence, look for connections, look for the hidden string that ties two disparate events together.*

'I saw a man like that back at the Servants,' she started to say, Hendrik's head swivelling towards her, both halted by another knock at the library doors, and Isaac didn't need to ask about it this time because here was the undertaker with his coffin and its bearers and Louisa's priest coming in on their tail. Everyone stood up, hung their heads in solemn silence, everyone except Ruan who chose that moment to come thumping down the stairs.

'What's the what?' he asked loudly as he turned the corner, his eyes immediately latching onto the table, apparently oblivious of the coterie of men making their way towards Louisa's body.

'Food!' he said enthusiastically. 'And thank God for it. I'm absolutely starving!'

'Young man, desist,' Joachim said sharply and Ruan raised his head briefly before swiftly lowering it again as he caught sight of the coffin. Not even Ruan could sit down and eat when a coffin was on the move and a body about to be nailed inside.

Hendrik had wanted to keep the funeral ceremony small and quiet, but this was not to be. The moment the coffin, with Louisa in it, was processed out of the Athenaeum, men and women started falling into step behind. Hendrik Grimalkin was well known in Deventer, and news of the untimely death of his wife in such tragic circumstances had spread fast and wide.

By the time the coffin arrived at Louisa's church the latter was bursting at its seams with the great and the good, the not so great scrambling in behind them to squash themselves into the gallery, the latest arriving spillage of curious and well-wishing bystanders clustering about its doors and pathways.

Hendrik was dismayed at the throng, but Joachim and Greta were stalwart and indiscriminate in clearing people out of his way, Ruan and Caro standing at his back like inanimate shadows. Louisa's priest had never been so proud as he was this day and didn't want to let slip such an opportunity for addressing the most important people in Deventer. Because of it he chose to use the occasion to further his own preoccupations, indulge in a little grandiloquent oratory, stretching his theological beliefs against the Protestant bounds he was not altogether comfortable with.

The service, therefore, was longer than usual, strewn through with many references to biblical exegesis and the patristic books the pastor had studied throughout his long preaching life and, once done – everyone breathing a sigh of relief that all was nearly over – he led the largest congregation he'd ever had out to the cemetery, there to give his final closing words, that were undoubtedly Catholic in their leaning, just as he was himself.

'On this sad day,' he said, once at the graveside, 'we must remember not only all those who have passed over, and the one we are burying today, but also that we must send up our prayers for the fathers over in Rome who have a far greater decision to make than we will ever be tasked with, soon to be in conclave, given the duty of electing the next man in line to be given Saint Peter's Keys. For although we here, in the Low Lying Lands,' he was quick to add, 'may only be a small part of the Greater Nation of Christ and not driven by the bells of Rome, their decision will affect us all. Be in no doubt of that, my children, nor that every one of your prayers will be heard and counted and must be used to push that conclave towards the right decision for the greater good of the entire church, ourselves included.'

And in those words Hendrik got his revelation. The niggle that had been at the back of his mind, the name he knew he knew but couldn't latch onto. Straight lines. By God, but he could but see them now: fishermen chucking out their strings and hauling in a catch they'd not expected, Golo Eck doing the same, hooks chucked out into the world with awful consequence, the foremost of which was Louisa being dead so piteously soon after Hendrik had reclaimed her and she had reclaimed him.

Straight lines converging here in Deventer; parts were missing here and there – exactly how and by whom Golo had been murdered, exactly why his own house had been set on fire – but straight lines nonetheless, originating in the same place. Only thing needed doing now was to get back to the Athenaeum and find their source.

Without any warning, Hendrik Grimalkin interrupted the priest's matherings right as he was going into the *earth to earth, ashes to ashes* part of his speech as the coffin was lowered into its grave.

'My apologies to the church!' Hendrik shouted, fighting to keep his voice under control, 'and to those of you who have chosen to attend the funeral of my wife. But this is not the time for me to be standing idly by and so I am going to cut things short. Food and drink, ladies and gentlemen, will be available for all in the Golden Globe in the Brink, but myself and my fellows will not be there. We have work to do, plots to uncover, and mark my words, friends, vengeance will not be far behind.'

He bent down and scooped up a handful of loose earth and cast it onto Louisa's coffin, every soft pattering of it heard in the stunned silence that followed his unprecedented outburst. Hendrik did not wait for any reaction, merely turned and strode away from the crowd who parted like the Red Sea before him, Caro and Greta tripping along behind, Joachim grabbing at Ruan's arm as the latter grimaced and hesitated, plainly wanting to head for the Golden Globe with the rest.

The crowd sucked closed again once Hendrik's small party had passed, their excited whispers growing into clamour and crescendo, immediately thereafter breaking into small groups, no matter the pastor's exhortations for them all to stay, ignoring him, flooding away like a tidal bore from the graveside to the Brink and from there to the Golden Globe where they fell upon the feast that was going on someone else's tab, rumours and theories abounding, everyone thrilling with having been present on this most unusual of days.

There was only one man who did not follow the ebbing tide of the graveyard gaggle as they eased themselves excitedly away towards the Brink. He took a quieter path, a more silent street, Hendrik Grimalkin's words at his heel like a pack of vengeful hounds, wondering what the Jesus Hell he'd got himself him into, and how the Jesus Hell he could get himself out.

GEORGE AND THE GUILDSMAN

Hendrik went down the Athenaeum's main aisle like a rat down a sewer, Caro beside him, worrying at the dark bubbles of blisters on Hendrik's head now that Joachim's liniments had dried up in the meagre day's sun. Greta was next in with Joachim and Ruan, Isaac bolting the doors behind them.

'What the hell does he think he's doing?' Ruan grumbled, soon as he'd breath to do so, putting his hands to his sides to stop the stiches. Greta and Joachim had no idea, but weren't going to say so in such blunt terms. They hung around for a few minutes until Hendrik re-emerged from the basement, dusty as a sandman, arms filled with papers held in place by his chin, reaching the nearest desk and spilling them out, starting frantically to burrow through them, scanning first one document and then the next.

'Hendrik,' Joachim said, reaching out a hand but not touching Hendrik, who was totally focussed on his task, whatever that might be.

'It's in here somewhere,' Hendrik mumbled. 'I know it is. I saw it. When I was following up Golo's notes in Caro's book.'

Ruan rolled his eyes. So it was all about the Lynx. That figured.

Obviously obsession was catching. He shook his head.

'Jesus, man,' he said, exasperation in every syllable. 'It's just a load of old crap written by a load of old men a couple hundred years ago.'

Hendrik lifted his head sharply and fixed Ruan with a look he recognised. This way led to madness. He'd seen it in Golo and knew there was no arguing with it. He held up his hands, turned away, intending to have at the food he'd not had the pleasure of getting acquainted with earlier. If he couldn't get to the Brink then this was the next best thing.

'Don't you ever get sick of being an idiot?' Greta was standing in his way with her hands on her hips.

Ruan coloured, not with embarrassment but anger.

'You don't know what it's like,' he replied sharply. 'God damn bloody blasted Lynx is all I've ever lived with and look what it's led to: Fergus disappeared, Golo dead, Louisa dead, George dead. Christ knows why the rest of us aren't dead too.'

Greta narrowed her eyes.

'What do you mean?' she asked, stopping Ruan with that fist again.

'I don't mean anything,' Ruan shouted crossly, everyone looking involuntarily in his direction, 'just an awful big coincidence we were all almost crushed to death by a couple of boulders when we left Loch Eck, and that everyone connected to the Lynx is getting bumped off, including your monk over there, who's obviously been shot through by something or other. Can see the blood from here, front and back. So who's the fool now?'

Greta stared at him, then dropped her arm and let Ruan pass. Straightaway he went to the desk with the food, sitting himself morosely down on one of the chairs but not immediately eating anything. Hendrik looked at Joachim, and Joachim looked back at his son.

'Is this true?' Hendrik asked softly, dropping his eyes to his father's chest and seeing there a small round splotch of blood.

'A fowler's accident,' Joachim said, embarrassed to have his weakness so publically announced, immediately covering the spot with his hand. 'An arrow that went astray.'

'And when did this arrow… go astray?' Hendrik asked.

Joachim swallowed. He didn't want to remember the day he thought he was going to die, nor how profound his fear had been despite his faith.

'About three weeks ago,' Joachim murmured, Hendrik unexpectedly nodding his head.

'About the same time I was sending letters off to Golo's lawyers for Ruan and getting some answers back,' Hendrik said. 'About the same time I began looking hard into the history of the Lynx.'

'But what of it?' Greta asked, alerted by the name of the Lynx popping up again, the mention of Fergus jolting her, reminding her why she was here in the first place, about to take out the letter when Ruan – as usual – interrupted.

'Never mind that,' he said, suddenly standing up and turning towards her. 'Who the hell are you anyway? And what the buggeration does any of this have to do with you?'

Greta's turn to colour now, because he was right. She'd never explained herself to anyone since she'd arrived, although Joachim knew the gist. There'd simply been no time. She was about to launch into her defence when Hendrik held up a hand.

'Enough,' he said, the schoolmaster back in his voice, glancing at the untidy heap of papers on the desk, but they could wait.

'Everyone sit,' he commanded, and everyone did, only Hendrik standing, towering above them all.

'Let's try and get everything straight,' he said, thinking of those lines again and the gaps in them. 'Let's start with you, Ruan.'

Ruan let out a breath but didn't say anything.

'What are these boulders you mentioned?'

Ruan shrugged.

'Bit of trouble on the way down to the Holy Loch,' he said, wondering why he'd bothered to mention it, why in the heat of the moment it had tumbled from his lips. 'One bloody great rock near rolled us all down the ravine, second one came down soon after.'

'And that didn't strike you as odd?' Hendrik asked.

Ruan shook his head. 'Why would it? It'd been raining, like it always rains up there. Makes for landslides all the time.'

'But it impeded your journey?'

'Not as much as the buggering ferry being holed,' Ruan replied quickly and then slowly looked up, pushing one hand over the other, cracking his knuckles, making both Greta and Joachim wince, 'and before you ask, no. I didn't think much of that either, because that's just every day up there in the wilds. Things go wrong, things take a while to fix and then they're fixed and everything goes on.'

Coincidences, Greta was thinking, *and more of them.*

Hendrik nodded. 'And all this held you up by how long?'

'A few days,' Ruan said. 'But the Collybuckie was still in dock, captain had got sick so sailing was delayed.'

'And if he'd not been sick and if the sailing hadn't been delayed?' Hendrik persisted.

'Then we wouldn't have been in that blasted storm!' Ruan said hotly.

Hendrik blinked slowly. 'That's not what I meant. I meant that…'

'I know what you meant,' Ruan interrupted. 'I'm not an idiot,' he cast a quick withering glance at Greta. 'What you're saying is that someone was deliberately trying to stop us leaving Scotland

and yes, if the landslide hadn't slowed us down and if the ferry at the Holy Loch hadn't been holed and if the Collybuckie hadn't still been at anchor, then I reckon we'd've been stranded in Port Glasgow another couple of weeks. Get more tickets sorted. Find out what was going where and who would take passengers close into anywhere near Deventer and over to Ireland too.'

'A couple of weeks,' Hendrik said, splaying his fingers out on the table as if to make a point.

'But it's all nonsense!' Ruan remonstrated. 'Random accidents! Next you're going to tell me that all that guff Golo went on about his mail being intercepted was true too!'

He could have bitten off his tongue, because it was plain to him that everyone about the table seized on this latest piece of information as if it was a revelation of the first order.

'Oh for God's sake,' he muttered, but subsided quickly enough. Let them make of it what they would. Conspiracy theories were not for him. Let him get his goods and gear and the moment Golo's Will arrived he'd be out of here. He rubbed his fingers on his nose and looked at Greta, who had put her two elbows on the table and was resting her chin on her hands.

'I think there's something here I might be able to add,' she said. 'Ruan, why did Fergus come to Ireland, and not with you and Golo?'

Ruan held out his hands in a quick gesture before dropping them onto his lap.

'It's just more of the same,' he sighed. He was sick of being dragged back into all this Lynx shit again and was keen to shift the focus but knew the only way to do that was to get it all said and done with when, with any luck, the rest of them would understand at last how ludicrous Golo's plans had been.

'The old Lynx Library was split early doors after Federico Cesi died,' he said, 'a small part to Ireland, a small part to Deventer, most going the Albani collection that's ended up in Paris, brought back from Italy by Napoleon, and that last part's due up for auction any time now.'

Maybe already gone, he was thinking, which would make all of this moot.

'And?' Greta prompted.

'And,' Ruan went on, injecting as much tedium into his words as he could, 'everyone knows France is full of mad revolutionaries who don't know the difference between the Scots and the English, and so Golo needed some good will on his side, hit on the idea of sending an Irishman in his place.'

'Wolfe Tone?' Greta asked quickly, sounding interested.

'No,' Ruan answered, surprised, never having heard that name, looking hard at Greta. 'That wasn't it. It was the man who had the Irish bit of the library. He'd agreed to be their agent at the auction in Paris. That's why Fergus was sent to Ireland, first to make sure his collection really had come from the Lynx, second to make sure he wasn't mad as the rest of them. Took my ring with him as down-payment,' he muttered, before adding what he'd only recently learned. 'No one realised the whole place was being hacked to bits in the middle of some stupid war.'

Greta's intake of breath was audible.

'Some stupid war?' she said slowly, her voice sharpened to such a point Ruan could feel it almost physically digging into his flesh.

'Well,' he blustered. 'I didn't mean that exactly…I just meant we didn't realise how bad it was, all that stuff in Ireland.'

Greta jumped to her feet and would have throttled Ruan there and then had not Joachim stood up behind her and pinned her by the elbows to keep her back. Hendrik hadn't said a word throughout this brief exchange, but when Joachim stood up he saw the second red splotch of blood at Joachim's back, heard the creaking of his ribs and intervened.

'Enough!' his voice was hoarse but loud enough to make everyone stop moving, all except Isaac who came out of his room to make sure everything was alright. That everything was not alright was obvious and for a moment Isaac dithered, but withdrew almost immediately on seeing the look on Hendrik Grimalkin's face which meant Hendrik was out of whatever tunnel he'd been in and back to himself again. Enough for Isaac, who retreated to the safety of his eye-spy room and left them to it.

'Let's concentrate on the salient facts here,' Hendrik said.

'And Ireland is not one of them?' Greta spat, thinking of the men who'd already died, and more of them dying maybe this vey minute.

'Of course it's important, Greta,' Hendrik said, his voice back to calm waters. 'But it's more important at this moment that we figure out what is going on here, how it all ties together, and I think I have some of it at least, if everyone will sit down again.'

Greta subsided, as did Joachim, his face grimacing with the pain of having moved so quickly, a look that did not pass Hendrik by. He was going to have to come to terms with Joachim being his father and Joachim having turned into someone else, but that time was not now.

'I have a theory I would like to put to you all,' Hendrik said, once order was re-established. 'Ruan, you said early doors that Golo was murdered whilst on board the Collybuckie.'

'I never said that,' Ruan replied, grumpy and disgruntled. 'I said that was what George Gwilt told me.'

Joachim was about to speak on George's behalf but a swift glance from Hendrik stopped him, Joachim never been so in awe of his son: authority in every measured movement. He'd have made a great Abbot if he'd been so inclined.

'Let's take it George was right,' Hendrik went on. 'Let's take it that someone tried to stop you getting on the Collybuckie, but by good fortune you got on it anyway and then, by bad fortune, you were caught up in a storm and someone took advantage of it.'

'I looked for him,' Caro piped up quietly. 'He didn't like being down under didn't Golo, being with loads of other people, especially not with it being so dark and the boat turning somersaults.'

Hendrik turned towards Caro and placed a finger beneath Caro's chin, lifting it so the boy had to look at him.

'So you saw Golo, during the storm?'

'I did and then I didn't,' Caro replied, such misery and regret in his voice that Greta moved her hand and laid it on the boy's shoulder, understanding how it was to know someone was in trouble and not be able to help them.

'I tried to find him,' Caro whispered. 'I knew he would be out there on deck. We all did. He hated being under. But all the lamps had blown out by then and I was only up a few minutes when I was suddenly over the side and in the water, and would've drowned if Mr Peat hadn't hauled me in.'

Hendrik blinked, partly for the bleakness of Caro's description of his last moments on the Collybuckie, spent in his desperate search for Golo Eck in the middle of a storm, partly because it seemed that Ruan had for once done something good for someone other than himself.

'And then you landed up at the Servants,' Hendrik stated, Caro nodding.

'I wasn't there very long,' he said. 'Had to take one of the passengers to Middelburg on account of him not knowing the lay of the land. You remember Signor Ducetti, Mr Ruan? I mean, who wouldn't? Fat as a giant dormouse he was, and we both dragged him onto the raft, remember?'

Ruan nodded. Of course he remembered. The man had been an arse of the first order, hardly let up talking the whole time they were plunging in and out of waves the size of houses, but Ruan had to admit he'd kept them all going with his inane banter, his ability to laugh at his own stories, making them chortle with him like madmen, hysterical with their fear and the fact that someone could carry on a non-stop stream of anecdotes despite the fact – or maybe because of it – that at any moment the lot of them might be upturned into the churning waters and never seen again.

'Ducetti,' Hendrik repeated quietly, 'and you're both absolutely sure that was his name?'

'Of course,' Caro and Ruan answered in the same moment, looking at Hendrik, seeing the sudden darkness on his face.

'And I saw him on my way back from Arnhem,' Caro added. 'I almost forgot to say. I saw him on... my...way...back...'

Caro's voice slowed, halted, came to a stop, cheeks going red and then white and then green as he tilted off his chair and threw up on the floor beside him, the rest of him following so he was on his hands and knees like a dog that has swallowed a bone the wrong way. Greta was off her seat and down beside him, heedless of the thin string of vomit that was coming from the boy's mouth, and the rest of it into which she knelt.

'What is it, Caro?' she said, gently as she could, patting a hand on Caro's back as he coughed and retched, coughed and retched.

'Kept me from the barge,' Caro hiccupped. 'Kept me at the inn overnight. Got me to tell him all we'd been doing...in Deventer... oh my Christ Saviour...'

He retched again before he could get any more words out because, just like Hendrik, his lines of comprehension had suddenly crossed and he understood.

'I told him!' Caro wailed, the sound of a fox in pain in the middle of a dark night in the middle of nowhere and with nowhere to turn. 'And he kept me there! He told me! He told me he was repaying me a favour and I never understood!'

There was no consoling Caro, who fled the company and flung himself onto the green ocean of leather sofa where Hendrik had spent his grieving hours.

Greta got to her feet.

'I can't understand why he's so upset,' she said.

'I can,' Hendrik said grimly, 'and I think Ruan might be able to provide some answers, if he's a brain in his skull worth tapping into.'

It was a cheap shot, Hendrik regretting the words immediately, but Ruan didn't react because he too was beginning to see a pattern: Ducetti on the raft telling them of his great trading feats in Italy and Amsterdam and how he and his nephews had been in Port Glasgow to set up yet another shop, how there was just the scrape of a possibility they could have been the cause of the falling boulders and the holing of the ferry. What he couldn't understand was the why of it, how Golo could possibly have been any threat to them. And why set Hendrik's house on fire?

He could see how Ducetti could easily have talked Caro so casually into spilling out the details of how they spent their days in Deventer – Ducetti being a man who could talk the guts out of a dying donkey – and was aware that had it been a normal day they would all have been in the house at the time the fire had started, having just partaken of Louisa's lunch. The only reason it hadn't been a normal day was precisely because Caro wasn't there to do her bidding.

Usually he would have ferreted Hendrik from the library in time, come looking for Ruan too, who was normally to be found mooching about the Brink, visiting various pawnbrokers and jewellers trying to ascertain what he could get for his ring if he had to sell it, maybe dropping into the Golden Globe or one of the other taverns scattered liberally about the square, spending a precious coin from his fast diminishing supply on a drop or two of ale.

'Ruan?' Hendrik prompted, and Ruan let out a breath, irritated by Hendrik treating him like a student he was coaxing towards the answer to a logic problem.

'I get it,' he said sharply. 'The Ducettis, big store owners. Italy, Amsterdam, Glasgow. I get they might possibly have had opportunity, I simply don't get the why.'

'Store owners?' Greta asked. 'What kind of store?'

'What the hell does that matter?' Ruan shot back.

Greta shrugged. 'All grist to the mill.'

'Importing artefacts and armaments, I think,' Ruan complied testily.

'What kind of armaments?' Joachim's turn to ask a question.

'Oh for God's sake!' Ruan snapped. 'How the hell am I supposed to know? Crossbows, daggers, hunting gear, that kind of thing, from what I remember the man saying while we were being tossed about like a bad salad on a raft that was damn near breaking up in the middle of a God Almighty storm!'

Hendrik looked at Joachim, who had closed his eyes briefly. Store owners who sold armaments, *store owners who would be obliged to demonstrate their goods; assistants, sons or nephews young and nimble enough to climb trees and let off arrows...*

'But why?' Great asked, unconsciously echoing Ruan's earlier question. 'Why any of it?'

Hendrik did not answer, instead started going through the documents again; now he knew what he was looking for his eyes flicked and filtered, his paper-fluent fingers fluttering through the mass until he found what had previously eluded him.

'Because,' he said, holding up a sheaf of documents, 'of these.'

STARS ALIGN

'What are they?' Greta and Ruan asked in unison, exchanging angry glances with one another to have spoken the same question in the exact same words at the exact same time.

'They're letters,' Hendrik said, 'written from the Lynx to the Master of this library who was of their ranks. And they're an explanation of sorts, the first informing him of the death of Federico Cesi…'

'Frederick whosit?' Greta interrupted.

'The founder of the Academy of the Lynx,' Ruan answered, as much to his own surprise as everyone else's. A knee jerk reaction. All that information drummed into him over the years that he'd hardly paid attention to and yet there it was, taking up valuable space in his head that he would have preferred it would vacate for facts more important.

'Go on,' Hendrik said, and Ruan did, parroting out the words he'd been taught.

'First scientific academy in Europe,' he said. 'Federico Cesi, Francesco Stelluti, Johannes Eck, Anastasio de Filiis and Walter Peat. Founded August 17th 1603, met on Christmas Eve later that year to establish their constitution: Eck the Master, Cesi, Stelluti and Peat chief counsellors, de Filiis the secretary. One for all and all for the Lynx, the all-seeing eye; their aim to study nature in all its component parts, figure out why the world is as it is and what makes it tick.'

Greta raised her eyebrows and looked at Ruan with curiosity; not such an empty vessel after all then, though obviously he went to great lengths to hide it.

'All got secret names and emblems,' Ruan went on, flinging his two rings out upon the table. 'Look here. First one's Golo's, from his ancestor Johannes Eck – *L'Illuminato* – a moon at quarter lit by the sun; second is mine, from Walter – *Il Petrogradia* – emblem: the stone circle at Kilmartin and the rising sun.'

'So the ring I brought with me really belongs to you?' Greta asked, understanding now why Ruan had snatched it up the moment she'd produced it, wondering why he'd not said anything about it at the time, wondering when was going to be a good time to tell him that Fergus was most likely dead. Ruan sighed.

'That's what I'm telling you. All great pals, those five men, stuck together their whole lives through, even after Cesi's bastard father had the lot of them kicked out of Rome on charges of heresy and Eck formally exiled for trying to convert Federico to Protestantism which was ridiculous, considering he was a rabid Catholic, which is why he left Deventer in the first place. But it was never forgotten that Cesi and his pals had Johannes Eck sprung from prison, where he was serving out a sentence for beating to death his apothecary over some dispute or other. Not to mention the fact that the other four were a few years older than Federico and there were hints of more than brotherly love going the rounds.'

Ruan took a breath, unaware of the stunned silence into which he had poured his words.

'What then?' Hendrik asked. He knew a fair amount about the Lynx from his burrowing through the archives for the last few weeks, but the way Ruan spoke was so un-academic, so immediate, it made it all very real.

'What's to say?' Ruan answered. 'The others scattered over Italy, except for Eck who always had itchy feet. He went barging off across the whole of Europe to drum up support for the Academy. Came back to Deventer briefly, but was exiled again for being too Catholic. Went to Scotland with Walter, who tickled him pink by taking him to Loch Eck, loving symbolism and symmetry like they all did, not that there's any connection with the name. Gaelic one side, Dutch the other, but enough to make Johannes build a house there. Golo's house.'

My house now, the thought flashed through his head, not that he ever wanted to see it again.

'All small stuff so far,' Ruan went on, 'and they carried on publishing, including some by Johannes Eck, like his pamphlet on the Nova of 1604 and his fever book...'

'My God!' Joachim interjected. 'But I know that work! *On the Plague, and why it has particularly spread through the Low Countries, and how to treat it.* I used it to treat you, Ruan. It's my medical bible, so to speak. The author being Johannes Heckius of Deventer, Lincean Knight, though I never understood what that meant before.'

He took a couple of deep breaths to steady himself. In went the woodcutter and out again. From darkness into light. Symbolism and symmetry. Ruan had hit it bang on the head. 'I'm sorry,' he said. 'Please go on, I didn't mean to interrupt, it's just...'

Coincidences upon coincidences, as Greta might have said.

'Well, like I said. Small potatoes,' Ruan picked up the thread, 'but then Galileo came to Rome to show off his telescope, and

Federico and his pals threw a massive banquet for him, promised to publish his more controversial work, persuaded him to become a member, which he did. Fifth living member, because by then de Filiis was already dead.'

'Why did you never tell me any of this before?' Hendrik asked mildly. 'You knew I was looking into the Lynx, carrying on where Golo left off…'

Ruan cast Hendrik a look and Hendrik let out a breath, understood, held up his hands, because of course Ruan wouldn't have said anything, precisely because Hendrik was carrying on where Golo had left off and wanting nothing to do with it. Hendrik felt like pulling Ruan inside out to learn all else he knew. He had an idea how it could all have culminated in the fire on the Singel, but first he needed to get a few facts straight in his head, explain a few things yet unpuzzled out.

'Thank you, Ruan,' Hendrik said. 'So before I say what I'm going to say, I need to emphasise just how important the Lynx were, despite the fact they've been subsumed by silence. Back then they did what hadn't been done before; they were in the right place at the exact right time, and served to connect the greatest minds in Europe, from Scandinavia to Spain, mostly because of Golo's ancestor, Johannes Eck. Including Galileo, as Ruan rightly said, who valued them highly enough to style himself a Lincaen Knight on all his correspondence and in the frontispieces of his books. They changed history in their way, and would have changed it far more if Cesi hadn't died when he did.'

'You mean *The Dialogue*,' Ruan put in, with a small sigh. 'Golo went on and on about that. About to publish Galileo's *Dialogue on the Two Chief World Systems* when Cesi kicked the bucket, all hold put on publication, his wife having better things to think about and all their six children dead in infancy, so no one to carry on the flame.'

Joachim grimaced to hear such tragedy spat out so flatly, but the young were young, after all, and scarcely understood such loss. He looked over at Hendrik, amazed all over again. Hendrik had no surviving children any more than Cesi had but, like Cesi before him, he had survived and thrived and made an extraordinary life for himself. Master of the Athenaeum of Deventer, no less.

'Yes, Ruan, that's what I mean,' Hendrik said, unaware of his father's scrutiny. 'Because if Federico hadn't died when he did then the Lynx would, in all likelihood, have obtained license to publish that particular work. Don't forget that Cardinal Barberini was a member of the Lynx from the start, his whole family very well connected in the church, made a Pope in 1623: Urban VIII.'

'Um, sorry to be a bit thick,' Greta put in, 'but I've never heard of any of these people. Who's Gali…well, whatever his name is. And what's so important about him and what he wrote?'

'And you called me an idiot,' Ruan barked out a laugh, swallowing it half-way through, pinioned into immobility by the hard green stare from Greta that both repelled and fascinated him in equal measure.

He wondered if Fergus had ever witnessed it, and how they would have laughed and joked about it in earlier days, Fergus's grizzled face so vivid in his mind that for a moment he neither heard nor saw anything else. The bald fact was that he missed his old crosser of swords and the companionship they'd always had before crossing swords was all they did. His fault, he knew. He just hadn't been able to stop himself. The closer they'd got to Golo finally embarking on his bid to resurrect the Lynx, the more impatient Ruan had become to leave that godforsaken square of moor Johannes Eck had been so enamoured of, and that impatience had found its primary target in Fergus because the only other person in the house was Golo, and to spit his venom at

Golo was unthinkable, even to Ruan Peat.

'I never asked,' Ruan said, leaning forward now, looking into those green eyes, 'how it is that you came to have my ring, how you got it from Fergus.'

Greta swallowed. She'd been in tougher situations than this, but it didn't feel like it.

'Because he joined us...briefly anyway. He went to fight in the battle of New Ross, which didn't go too well. He gave me letters...'

'Why the hell didn't you tell me this before?' Ruan exploded, jumping up and staring daggers at Greta who flinched beneath his scrutiny. 'Is he dead? Are you telling me he's dead?'

'I don't know for certain,' she admitted quietly. 'But after Vinegar Hill and me getting his pouch...well, I just supposed...'

Ruan turned his back on the lot of them and moved a few yards away, eyes wet, heart hammering every last shred of hope gone from him that Fergus was still alive, guilt creeping over him, knowing that if he'd not been so spiteful to Fergus then maybe Golo wouldn't have sent him to Ireland to keep them separated. Then Fergus would still be alive and maybe Golo too, if Fergus had been on the Collybuckie to protect him. Grief was creeping through his bones like honey fungus, strangling the life out of him unseen, so deep below the surface he was only just grasping it was there at all.

He missed the following conversation between Hendrik and Greta, caching up only at the end when Greta was summarising what she thought she'd understood.

'...so back then no one knew that the world went around the sun and not the other way round?'

'Precisely so,' Hendrik nodded.

'And your Galileo loon was one of the first to make the case?'

Hendrik nodded again.

'But the church didn't like it, because as far as they're concerned we're the be all and end all of creation.'

'It's changed a little now,' Joachim put in. 'But not, sadly, entirely.'

Greta took this comment on board and went on.

'So if Federico hadn't put on the timmer-breeks when he did the Lynx would have put out Galileo's treatise a lot earlier than actually happened?'

'You've caught it,' Hendrik said. 'And that's why I'm saying what I'm saying. If Cesi hadn't died in 1630 then he'd have broadcast Galileo's Two World System under the Lincaen imprint which, at that time, had the backing of Maffeo Barberini who was by then the Pope.'

'And if that was the case,' Joachim added, keen to impress his son with his liberalism, 'then the Copernican view of the world would have been accepted many years before it was, and Galileo would never have been put before the Inquisition in '32 when he actually published …'

'And never have been put under house arrest for the rest of his life,' Hendrik finished for his father. 'And you can imagine the implications of that.'

Greta couldn't.

'Big?' she offered.

'World-changing,' Hendrik said, smiling the first proper smile since Louisa had died, his head entirely taken up with the Lynx and what they could have, should have, achieved, if the only the sole source of their funding – Federico Cesi – hadn't died.

'The scientific enlightenment,' Hendrik expounded, 'that we are experiencing right now could have happened a couple of centuries earlier, Galileo and his fellow academics free to pursue their work without the persecution of the church; and that's why Golo's mission is so important. This hidden corner of our past needs bringing into the light, its legacy fully known, its traditions upheld and carried on.'

'Not that everyone would choose for that to be the case,' Joachim stated soberly, bringing everyone back to the present tense. 'And presumably you see some points of cause and effect …'

Hendrik nodded. 'I do, and there's another letter here explains why. After Federico's death the correspondence with the Athenaeum Master continued, mostly, Ruan, you might be interested to know, coming from the hand of Walter Peat himself.'

Ruan blinked, turned back, sat down, picked up Walter's ring, turning it carefully in his fingers. Golo had letters too, all written by Johannes Eck to Walter, who had apparently bided for several years in Johannes' house before latterly settling several miles to the west going towards Kilmartin, the place with all the ancient stones that were mimicked on his ring. That Walter must have replied, written his own letters to both Eck and other people, had never occurred to him. Hendrik paused briefly, looking at Ruan, nodding once before going on.

'Mostly he talks about other members of the Lynx, what they were working on, how Galileo was faring under hourse arrest, how they'd devised a method of communication with him even after all his correspondence was being raked over by Inquisitionary aides keen that he not be dispersing his heretical views. But one letter is of particular relevance to us now,' he announced, pulling a yellowing page from the sheaf and holding it up, 'because it tells us something of what Galileo – and a few of his more outspoken followers – underwent.'

Joachim was aware of this period of his church's history.

'You mean torture,' he stated soberly after a couple of seconds.

'I do,' Hendrik nodded, 'one practitioner of the art, as Walter puts it, being far more enthusiastic than his fellows, and that man's name was Lorenzini Ducetti.'

From down below them Caro – who had apparently been listening – let out a wail thin and shrill, like a titmouse in the morning, getting up from the his sofa and running past them all up the library towards the door, his hand gripping hard on the hilt of the knife Ducetti had given him. Greta was on Caro's tail in a second, Isaac coming out of his cubby-hole as Caro reached the door, fingers already scrabbling at the heavy bolts, trying to draw them back, nails splitting and drawing blood as he went at them with all the fury his small body could muster.

'That man! That man!' he was shouting. 'I'm going to kill him dead! Stone dead, I tell you!'

Greta reached him, put her arms about Caro's waist trying to pull him away, Isaac wheezing up beside them both, stopping all escape by withdrawing the huge iron key from its lock, slipping it into the leather workman's pouch that hung from his belt.

'Come on, lad,' Isaac said, soothingly, no idea what was going on but recognising sore distress when he saw it. 'Come on now.'

Caro desisted, his hands falling uselessly to his sides as he recognised the futility of his plan, which had been to run all the way out into the afternoon and on and on and on, right out of Deventer, right back to the inn where he'd last encountered Signor Ducetti, where that man, that traitor, that murderer, had greeted Caro like a long-lost friend.

AND MORE INTRIGUE YET TO COME

'I'm sorry,' Caro whispered, curling himself into a chair beside Greta, Isaac coming with him, placing himself at a discreet distance behind the rest but unwilling to let Caro out of his sight, Joachim and Hendrik still on their feet, shocked by the boy's abrupt reappearance. That he'd been listening all the while to what they'd been saying was evident, though in truth they'd forgotten he was there at all.

'Shush now,' Greta said, patting the boy's arm, understanding his reaction, remembering back to old Owen and his fire and her own thoughts then of murder.

'Alright then,' Hendrik said, subsiding into his seat, Joachim following suit. 'But Caro, you're right. I do believe the Ducetti family might be behind everything that has been going on.'

'But for why? And why now?' Ruan asked quietly. 'They could have killed Golo at Lock Eck if that was their plan.'

His face was paler than usual, his fine features pinched at the edges. The Lynx had always been a fairy tale as far as he was concerned, Golo's mad obsession, nothing to do with him or the real world - except that now it was. Golo, and Fergus – probably –

dead because of it. And now Walter Peat had been introduced into the mix as a real live actual person, his ancestor, his blood, someone for whom the ring Ruan had previously been so contemptuous of had been specifically designed for, worn on his finger… a puppet on an ancient stage suddenly come to life.

'Because of the enclave,' Joachim said quietly, shaking his head, closing his eyes, everything clearer now, including the attack on him back at the Servants: a tactic probably intended to bring Hendrik running to his dying father's side, stop him digging any further into the Lynx on Golo's behalf, at least for a few more weeks, unaware that father and son had not communicated with each other for twenty four years.

'Exactly,' Hendrik nodded, echoing Joachim. 'The enclave are sitting right now, just as the priest reminded us at Louisa's graveside. The present Pope is sick, sick enough for everyone to believe he is about to shuffle off his mortal coil. So bad that the cardinals were told several months ago to prepare for the worst, think of his prospective successors, rake through their pasts, make reckonings of who they are and where they have come from and, if they are elected, whether their familial history will bear the scrutiny that will inevitably follow.'

'I don't get it,' Greta said, wrinkling her nose. 'What do you mean, the enclave? And what's it to do with anything?'

Hendrik laid out Walter's letter on the table before him.

'You're a Catholic?' he asked Greta.

'I am,' she said stoutly, 'but we don't take sides like that anymore. Not since the Uprising. Altogether we are, Catholics, Protestants and Dissenters.'

Hendrik smiled, as if this should always have been the case.

'But you haven't heard of the enclave sitting?'

'We haven't,' Greta said, 'but we've had other things to think about.'

Like New Ross, for instance, and Vinegar Hill, and me running the country up and down and over the sea to here.

Hendrik nodded, as if she'd spoken these last thoughts out loud and made a great truth of it.

'Quite right,' Hendrik said. 'For the plain fact is that people like you, Greta, and me, live in a world that is unstable, constantly shifting, the sitting of the enclave hardly of great import to us. But for others, for the families connected to the forerunners for the post of Pope that is not the case. They stand to make a great deal of money on the outcome.'

Joachim was shocked. The sitting of the enclave was of the greatest importance to him and his order, and to every other order of monks the world over.

'But how can you say that?' he asked.

'Because it's true,' Hendrik said sadly. 'You people live in a bubble,' no rancour to his words. 'You live in seclusion, away from the rest of us, forgetting how we live. You forget too that the election of a new pope has little relevance for the quotidian; of far more importance to most of Europe now is the revolution that has just shaken France root and branch, and the enormous implications it is having for everyone who lives close by its borders. Whatever the French are doing is of far more significance that a load of old religious electing another old religious to be dressed in white and given a papal tiara, a staff and told he is the most important person in the world.'

Joachim dropped his gaze. Hendrik hadn't wanted to be so brutal, but honest to God he needed to get this point across, because this was the nub of his argument.

'To us here, today,' he said, 'around this table, what everyone needs to understand is that one of the two forerunners for the enclave to consider is one Cardinal Eduardo Ducetti, because if he beats off the opposition and is elected then the rest of the Ducetti family stand to do very well out of it. Very well indeed. Once – if – he is elected then all well and done. The Pope is infallible. But a public revelation that a previous member of the family took great pleasure in torturing heretics – particularly heretics who had previous Papal support, like a member of the Lynx, like Galileo himself – well. That would not go down well at all.'

'All for the matter of a few weeks,' Joachim whispered. 'Stopping Golo in his tracks, murdering him when the opportunity arose, setting fire to your house in the hope of putting an end to your researches once and for all…oh Hendrik! I can't tell you how sorry I am.'

'It's not your fault,' Hendrik said with bitterness. 'It's no one's fault but the Ducettis. Our problem now is trying to prove it.'

Silence then, as everyone digested the plain truth of it.

'Um, everyone?' Greta was the first to speak, the first person to not only see the stratagem in what had been presented but a further stratagem in how they might proceed. She'd not spent the last few years with the United Irish without learning something of attack and defence and the means with which to combat both.

'Don't know if you're all forgetting but just before the undertaker came and all that, well, we was talking about a man that was seen?'

Pieter Dulke's description of the man with dark hair, the one who looked foreign, with bad pock marks on his face.

'Well,' Greta went on, 'I was starting to say then that I think he was at the Servants – or someone very like him – sweeping floors he was, but stopped his sweeping the second the Brother I was with mentioned Deventer.'

Caro fluttered into life beside her.

'She's right,' he said, trembling all over, the need to fight coming back into his veins like a flame enlivened by the wind. 'And it was

Signor Ducetti sent him back with me! Said he needed succour, a place to stay…'

And then someone spoke who no one had even realised was there: Isaac, standing in the shadows beyond Caro's chair, listening intently, and reacting now with concern and some trepidation.

'Excuse me, sir, Mijnheer Grimalkin,' Isaac was loathe to interrupt but had to speak up.

'If you've anything that can help,' Hendrik said, 'then now, please God, is the time to say it.'

'Excuse me,' Isaac said again, embarrassed, hoping he wasn't about to muddy the waters or add to Hendrik's burdens, for Christ knew that was the last thing he wanted. He swallowed, cleared his throat, embarked on the longest speech he'd ever given in his life.

'It's just that I spoke to Pieter Dulke earlier, and he sort of caught me up on what's been going on and, well, I don't know if I should say so, but there was a man very like the one you're describing who was here at the library, a few weeks back. He wanted in, to study he said. But all he had with him was a certificate from the Guild of Silver and Copper Workers for his credentials which, as you know, is by no means enough to give the man entry, so I sent him away. Told him to apply in writing, as is usual. But it strikes me now that of all the options open to you, Mijnheer, maybe the Guild would be a place to start.'

Hendrik peered into the shadows in which Old Isaac was hiding, Old Isaac who had been here for years and years and years, for as long as Hendrik could remember. Old Isaac, who knew every in and out of the library and the way it worked. He should have thought to ask him sooner about any unusual happenings but it would have been like asking the walls themselves, such a fixture was he.

'Oh Isaac,' Hendrik said warmly. 'But where would we be without you? Thank for this, thank you a hundred times.'

Hendrik was already on his feet, looking at the clock face set into the wall above the Athenaeum doors and that it was showing ten minutes to six. Ten minutes to get to the Guild House before it closed for the night. He moved abruptly, grabbing Isaac's face between his hands, kissing him swiftly on one cheek and then the other.

'Thank you old friend. I'm leaving now. Lock the doors and batten down the hatches. No one in unless it is one of the people you see here with me right now. No one, do you understand?'

Isaac nodded, dumbfounded, but Hendrik was already on the move.

'Joachim,' Hendrik commanded, 'stay here with Caro. Greta and Ruan, with me.' *Pick the strong ones*, his mind was telling him, no matter that one of them was Ruan Peat. Hell, let Ruan come on anyway; this was as much his fight as Hendrik's, and tossing it up for discussion was not an option. Off Hendrik went, up and away down the library aisle on a run, only thing stopping him being that he had to wait for Isaac to puff up after him and put his key in the lock, set this mystery and its machinations free.

GUILDSMEN, GOLO, AND SLIP-SLIDING EELS

The House of the Guild of Silver and Copper Workers was just off the Brink, Greta running fast on the wet cobbles now the rain had started up again, trying to keep pace with Hendrik Grimalkin who was racing ahead like a hare with a hound on its tail. Ruan was somewhere behind her, at least she thought he was. She didn't bother wasting time looking back to find out. They'd only minutes left to get to the Guild before the place closed up for the night, and Hendrik certainly wasn't going to wait until the morrow.

The Brink was deserted, all street stalls packed up for the night the moment the rain came down. The big clock was already striking the hour of six, its woodcutter coming out on obligation before swiftly departing. Greta was alarmed to hear Hendrik shouting, *We're going to be too late! We're going to be too late!* before suddenly diving into an alley at the top right of the plaza.

And they were too late, or almost, for the Guildsman's gatekeeper already had his key in the lock when they reached him, Greta and Hendrik dripping with the rain, sweating from exertion, hardly able to draw a breath. But Hendrik was well known in Deventer, by name, if not by sight, more so because of the Singel fire and the funeral earlier that day, and once Hendrik told the man who he was the gatekeeper reopened the door and let them in.

'An Italian, you say? Ducetti?' the man asked, as Hendrik breathily laid out his request. 'And how long has he been registered with us?'

Hendrik shook his head.

'I don't know that information,' he said. 'Try a few weeks back, maybe more. Last residence most likely listed as Amsterdam. Maybe Scotland.'

His desperation was so obvious that the gatekeeper did not demure. He opened the huge Registry of Guildsmen and ran his finger down the line of names.

'Ducetti?' he asked again..

'Ducetti,' Hendrik said, spelling it out for the man, wanting to wring his neck, take the register and do his own looking.

'Ah,' the man hesitated after turning a couple of pages. 'I think I have it. Yes, it's here. Registered himself six weeks back as a tradesman from Rome who also has premises in Amsterdam, and was looking to set up shop here in Deventer.'

Hendrik was impatient at the Guildsman's slow hands and lurched forward, turned the register around, reading for himself the name and address given there in scratchy writing. He thanked the man briefly and was already heading away.

'It's only just down the road,' Hendrik shouted to Greta as he scarpered back out onto the street, seeing Ruan standing there scowling, the rain falling hard and heavy, splashing about his head and shoulders.

'Come on! Come on!' he urged his companions, and they were off again, a few minutes later were at the Guildsman's hostel, Hendrik going banging his fist on the reception desk because there was no one was behind it, the whole place seeming quiet and deserted, no sounds of men moving around in the upstairs rooms or milling about the common dining area. A few moments later a weary looking woman emerged from the small vestibule behind the desk.

'Yes?' she asked. 'If you've forgotten your key then you'll have to wait for the night manager. If I've told you all once, I've told you a thousand times.'

'Ducetti,' said Grimalkin. 'We're looking for Luigi Ducetti. Second floor, room 27.'

The woman regarded them without curiosity.

'He isn't in,' she said shortly. 'None of `em is. All took a kind of holiday on account of that big man's wife's funeral. All lording it up, they are, at the Golden Globe, at that poor man's expense.'

Hendrik stopped moving and Greta saw his shoulders sagging. Unexpectedly it was Ruan, who had come in behind them, who took up the reins.

'This is Mijnheer Grimalkin himself,' Ruan said. 'And we have need to see inside that man's room. Could you possibly oblige us?'

The woman perked up at this nugget of news, studying Hendrik Grimalkin with great interest.

'Not supposed to give out the gentlemen's keys,' she said, 'not without the manager's say so.'

'For God's sake, woman,' Hendrik was so angry he was about to boil over and the woman harrumphed, but disappeared back into her little room and returned a moment later with the key.

'Up the stairs, second floor, third on the right,' she said. 'But mind you don't leave any mess while you're up there. I've a job to keep,' she added and, as an afterthought, 'I'm very sorry about your wife, Mijnheer Grimalkin. Very sorry. A horrible way to go. Horrible.'

As if Hendrik needed reminding. But they were soon away from this dreary woman and her dreary life, off up the narrow wooden staircase, one floor, two floors, heading down the dank and low corridor with its many tiny rooms. It did not take long to find the one that had been painted with a large 27 upon its door.

Back at the Athenaeum, Isaac was sitting in his peep-hole room. Everything was calm, almost normal. The monk Joachim, who it turned out was also Grimalkin's father, had not looked in good shape, very pale and started coughing up lacy splatters of blood. Never a good sign in Isaac's view, so Isaac took him upstairs and made him comfortable.

He double-checked all doors and windows were closed and locked before returning to his peep-hole room, where he saw to his great shock a man standing dithering on the library steps looking uncannily like the one Hendrik had gone haring off after. Very like him, Isaac squinted, but not quite. Something about him was different, his stance maybe, his height, his breadth. Whatever it was, it had Isaac unnerved. And the man was just standing there doing nothing, obviously hesitating about whether or not to ring the bell, and so Isaac went out of the peep-hole room and whispered down to Caro. He didn't like to disturb the lad, for Caro was plainly in some deep pit of his own making, but Isaac needed verification.

'Caro, get yourself here. There's something I need you to see. Or rather, someone.'

Caro was slow to respond but got himself up and joined Isaac in the peep-hole room, Isaac pointing out the images on the wall of the man standing obligingly motionless on the Athenaeum's steps just below the portico, to keep out of the rain.

'Do you recognise him?' Isaac asked Caro. 'Is that the same man you took back to the Servants?'

Caro gazed at the walls of the round room, confused by the upside-down image, bending over and screwing his head around to get a better look,

'Is that him?' Isaac asked again, Caro nodding grimly, straightening up ramrod stiff, hand on the hilt of his knife.

'It's him,' he said. 'No doubting it.'

'What should we do?' Isaac asked sucking in his breath. 'I could let you out the back, go and fetch Mijnheer and the others...'

'No,' Caro said, not about to let this opportunity slip, not after what this man had done, and before he knew it a plan was ready formed in his head. Nothing like vengeance to sharpen the mind. He might be young, but by Christ he had scores needed settling.

'So here's what we need to do,' he said, spelling it out, Isaac dithering, but not for long, not at the sight of the knife Caro had unsheathed from his belt and the look in his eye. It was two against one after all, and so Isaac did as the boy bid and moments later brought out the large iron key from his belt and turned it in the lock, began to draw back the bolts.

Hendrik opened the door to room 27 and stepped inside. The place was spartan in the extreme. A thin bed took up most of the floor space, with a rickety set of drawers pushed into one corner, a small desk and chair fitted into the other below a dirty window maybe two foot square, looking out over the street leading up to the Brink, if anyone could see through the grime and the damp and splintered shutters that hung from their hinges. The place was altogether so depressing that Hendrik wondered how anyone could stay here more than a few days, yet the Guild Book made clear that this Luigi member of the Ducetti family had signed in six or so weeks before.

There was a niggle in his head – for if the man had been in Deventer all this time he couldn't possibly have been at the Servants when Greta was there, and if he had been at the Servants then how could he have set the fire on the Singel? He needed to ask the old crone downstairs what tabs she kept on her lodgers, if any, find out his comings and goings, when he had been here and when he had not. Easy enough to appear to be in one place by paying the rent up front, but not so easy to be in two places at the same time.

He looked about him for help. There wasn't much in the way of belongings: some clothes spilling from the chest of drawers, a haversack pushed clumsily below the tiny planked bed whose mattress was so dilapidated Hendrik could see the horsehair poking through the thin sheets. The bedding on top looked fresh enough, free of lice and fleas, and the water bowl and ewer on top of the chest of drawers newly filled, the floor swept clean of dust and detritus, the lamp newly filled: a brief surge of admiration for the woman on the desk – if this was part of her job and not another's – that she kept the rooms so well-turned for the young gentlemen she had spoken of earlier, who she so plainly rather despised.

Greta was running her hands through the clothes in the drawers, Ruan tugging the haversack out from underneath the bed, so Hendrik went to the desk. It was of the kind children had at school, with a lid and therefore a compartment hidden underneath it.

'Nothing,' Ruan said, riffling through the haversack which was entirely empty, save for a crumpled and torn piece of paper in one of the side pockets that he nevertheless took out and tried to uncrease.

'Nothing here either,' Greta added, her search of the drawers without discovery, except that this man was nowhere near as good at darning his socks as Shauna was of Donal's.

Hendrik lifted the lid of the desk, saw a couple of letters lying there and picked one up, reading it quickly. Only a brief missive giving directions to the hostel and the Guild, the other giving a list of the route of towns and rivers a man would have to take from Amsterdam to Middleburg on the Walcheren Peninsula. Middleburg was the place Caro had taken Signor Ducetti after the wrecking of the Collybuckie, from where Caro had brought back his kinsman who'd stayed on sweeping floors at the Servants for no apparent reason.

Hendrik spotted the corner of another piece of paper below this route-list and picked it up, the shock of its contents parting his lips though no words came out, for here was no letter; here instead was a complex table of calculations and experimental inputs and out-goings, with gunpowder on one axis, liquid turpentine on the other, and a single X where the two lines of the graph optimally met.

The bolts that had been drawn at the Athenaeum Library doors had been pulled back.

'No deliveries, thank you,' Isaac said, eying the hand-pulled drey that stood behind the stranger standing on the steps.

'But it's just beer,' the man said, looking pathetic and sodden, making a show of shaking the wetness from his hair, squeezing some of the water from a corner of his jerkin.

'All deliveries round the back,' Isaac stated. 'Always been so, always will.'

'I'm new,' tried the black haired, pock-marked stranger. 'Just been told to dump it off and then I'm away. Got a wife expecting. Got to get back soon as I'm able.'

'Round the back,' Isaac said again.

'Can't you make an exception, just this one time?'

Isaac hadn't been in any doubt but now he knew for certain. Good Dutch, but accented in the exact same way as the man who'd been here before, not the same man, but one very similar.

'Wait,' he said, closing the door in the supposed tradesman's face.

'Ready, Caro?' he whispered.

'Ready,' came the reply.

Isaac opened the door again.

'Just this once then,' he said, beckoning Luigi Ducetti in.

'Proof at last,' Hendrik said softly, holding up the piece of paper he'd fished out of the desk, Greta and Ruan coming forward.

'Um,' Greta interrupted, 'not to put a dampener on things, but what does this prove at all?'

'That they know how to blow things up, Goddamit,' Ruan said.

'Well yes,' Greta said, placing a small finger on the piece of paper. 'But they sell armaments and presumably stuff that explodes, so all it really proves is that he knows his trade.'

Ruan watched Greta's finger on the paper and heard the certainty in her words, and thought abstractly that she probably knew as much about blowing things up as this Luigi fellow. And then he had a brainwave.

'But we know where he might be,' he said quickly. 'At the Golden Globe, like the concierge told us. Surely it's worth a try?'

Luigi Ducetti was not at the Golden Globe. He was at that very moment bringing the first of his two barrels into the Athenaeum Library. He'd been seriously apprehensive about them trying the same trick twice and had told his brother as much, but as usual Ricardo overruled him.

'It'll be easy,' Ricardo assured him. 'Just make sure you get the first barrel in and I'll do the rest.'

'But what about the watch-man?' Luigi remonstrated, his stomach flipping with fear. 'They're sure to have doubled up on security.'

'Stop fussing, brother,' Ricardo had said. 'Just do as I say and it'll be easy.'

But easy it had not been, not any of it, not for Luigi at any rate. His heart had almost stopped when he'd sent that boulder down the hill, very nearly crushing those people stone dead – horse, cart and all. He'd only meant to cause a landslide, block their path so they would have to turn back.

He'd been so terrified he'd had to lean against that second boulder before he could move, and when that had accidentally gone down too he'd trouble breathing, let alone running, his legs giving way several times. But the money Uncle Federigo had promised them was ridiculous.

'And lots more like it, lads,' Federigo had assured them, 'and the second that old fool of a pope has gone to the blue beyond, cousin Cardinal is sure to be elected in his place. And nothing to stop us then, nephews, nothing.'

But there'd been so much to stop them ever since, Luigi thought bitterly. Federigo killing the old man on the boat wasn't the half of it, though Ricardo had been mighty impressed. And by God, but the stories Federigo had told them about that night – about the way the boat had dipped and swung in the waves, the boards groaning and screeching, the wind tearing the sails from their runners and masts with no more trouble than plucking seed from ripe sedge.

'It was howling like the biggest pack of wolves you've ever heard,' Federigo told them, 'and when I rolled Golo Eck into the waves I near went in after him. It was only by good fortune that the pipsqueak came yelling for the old man right at that moment and some sailor heard him, turned around just in time to grab me before I went over too, the wind slapping us down so's we were crawling like slugs on our bellies; and when I saw the last lifeboat go over the side, swinging like a hammock, crashing down into the waves, there was nothing left to do but to fling myself in after it and hope for the best. But if I'd died, boys, I'd've died knowing I'd seen you right, with Golo gone, and everything with him.'

But everything hadn't gone with Golo Eck, Luigi knew, though he was always the slow one: good with his hands, good with all the metal-working and making replicas of the ancient armaments that brought in so much trade to uncle's shops, but not so good at thinking. Never so good at that, and he tried not to think now, tried not to think on what Ricardo and Federigo were going to do once he'd got his barrels safely stowed side by side in this huge library. His back was aching with the effort of carrying the first one down the hallway. The place was so much bigger than it looked from the outside and was dark, like crawling into a conch shell, except for a small circle of lamps and candles somewhere further on down.

'This way,' said the old man who'd finally let Luigi in. And this way Luigi went, until about halfway to his goal when he felt a terrible pain in his buttock, enough to have him screaming, the barrel clattering to the boards, rolling a few yards down before slamming into a table and coming to a stop.

And there Luigi was, down on the floor, trying to figure out what the hell had happened, trying to curl up about himself to get his hands to where the pain was so bad he knew he wouldn't be able to get up again, warm blood oozing down his legs like it would never stop. He looked up, and saw the shadowed face of a young boy and the glint of the knife he was brandishing, the blade whistling through the air as he swished it from side to side, the boy moving as if to straddle him, stab at him again with the knife that Luigi recognised, because he'd made it himself.

'Steady lad,' came a voice. 'Killing folk ain't our business, not at all. No matter what a man's done.'

The lad cast Luigi one more murderous glance before desisting, and down instead came Isaac's mottled hands, pulling Luigi up to sitting – which was excruciating – forcing the wound to open and stretch and bleed, making him cry out in pain.

'It's nought more'n'a scratch,' said Isaac, 'just a bum-cut that'll bleed like buggery, but you'll live.' He hauled Luigi to his feet, dragging him the ten yards to the leather sofa and depositing him there. 'One more move, one more squeak out of you,' said the old man, 'and I swear I'll not stop the lad the next time.'

Luigi didn't move, didn't squeak, but lay his head down upon the cool green leather, oddly glad that everything was over and no more would be asked of him.

'Oh my Christ, forgive me,' he whimpered, realising it was the end of the line for Luigi Ducetti, completely unaware that his brother had taken advantage of the commotion to dodge himself inside the library, bringing with him the second, lighter barrel – held against his chest with his smithy-strong arms – depositing it quietly on the floor as he slowly, silently, pulled the bolts to, closing them all in.

BROTHERS BETRAYED

They got to the Golden Globe in the plaza to find the place heaving, Hendrik having previously organised for food and drink to be available to his wife's mourners, both the Athenaeum Board and the Civic Council adding their own contributions; the outcome being that the great and good of Deventer had had a bit of a party, particularly once they'd understood that Hendrik himself was not going to join them, for no party can really go with a swing if the grieving widower is in attendance.

They'd gone on late into the afternoon before returning home, and now the place was filled to bursting with apprentices and guildsmen – whose watering hole the Golden Globe was by default – hoping to take advantage of any tab that was left, of which there was plenty.

A loud singing match was going on as Hendrik, Greta and Ruan got to the door, the tables outside filled with carousers; it soon became apparent that to find one black haired foreigner amongst the many was not going to be an easy task. Nevertheless, they forced their way in, Ruan taking charge because he knew the place and knew the manager, got him buttonholed in a corner. Once

Ruan had introduced Hendrik the man apologised profusely.

'It's all rather got out of hand, Mijnheer,' the manager said, his face red and sweaty, clothes a little awry, it being the first time in several years he'd had to help out manually at the bar alongside his usual staff, so great was the surge of customers hoping for free drink. The tab, he told them, had only just closed, so generous had been not only the Mijnheer but the Board and the Council and many others sad for his loss, the revellers staying on anyway to blow what little money they had on what had become for them all an unexpected holiday.

'I'm so sorry,' he repeated several times, 'that such a sad occasion has become a rumpus, but we can't turn away trade. You know how it is, Mijnheer, you know how it is.'

Hendrik did know, although he despised every person in the tavern at that moment, was focussed on his goal.

'It's no matter,' he told the manager. 'No matter at all. I'm happy my wife's death has occasioned such gaiety.'

The manager of the Golden Globe cringed, pronounced himself ready to do whatever Grimalkin asked.

'We're looking for a man, maybe of Italian extraction,' put in Ruan. 'Dark hair, bad pox scars on his cheeks, kind of foreign looking.'

It wasn't a great description but, despite the crush of men about the bar and the swamp of all the others about the tables, the manager drew his staff together and asked them of such a man.

'I think you must mean one of the Ducetti brothers,' piped up one of his helpers, a girl so young it seemed to Hendrik barely decent she worked in a place like this.

'Where are they?' he asked. The girl waved a hand.

'Often in,' she said, 'this past while anyways. Sometimes together, most often not, and sometimes with their uncle who ate about the most I've ever seen one man eat.'

'But are they here now?' Hendrik persisted, a note of desperation to his voice, the singing of the men outside on the plaza almost drowning out his words. The girl didn't answer straightaway, instead sent her eyes roving over the crowd.

'Don't see `em,' she said. 'And now you mention it, ain't seen neither hide nor hair of either for a good half hour since.'

Isaac was feeling good, in fact was feeling grand. He had the perpetrator of the Singel fire – the killer of Louisa Grimalkin – right here and now in his library and no way for him to escape, the only thing to do being to prevent Caro from finishing the man off before the others got back.

'So,' he said to his captive, feeling like he thought he always would have if he'd ever caught up with the Prussian officer responsible for annihilating his family and village. No sympathy, no care that his blood was seeping into the green sofa, even if it would be Isaac's duty to clean it later on. Isaac had a few words ready, when Joachim appeared by his side causing Luigi to shrivel involuntarily as the blood drained from every extremity, a feverish jumble of whispered words falling from his lips as he attempted to cross himself.

'Oh my Christ, my Saviour...Lord, deliver me in my hour of need. Please don't send me to the dark place or consign me to the flames...'

Isaac and Caro were mighty puzzled; Brother Joachim, seeing the awful fear in Luigi's eyes, put two and two together.

'You didn't kill me, son,' Joachim said quietly. 'You may have tried but you didn't succeed, for here I am. Flesh and blood, just like you.'

Luigi gawked, then began to stutter out a few words over and over.

'I..I..didn't…know…I didn't know. P…please don't j…judge me, Brother, please don't judge me…'

Joachim's turn to be bewildered, recognising genuine confession and terror when he heard it; logic dictated this was the man who'd shot at him and presumably, therefore, had attempted to murder a houseful of people in the Singel fire. But how could a man so loaded with guilt, so abjectly pathetic, have come to do such things? Something was wrong, something badly out of kilter. He knelt down next to Luigi.

'Tell me everything. Forgiveness is only be a breath away.'

Ruan, Hendrik and Greta began to push their way back out of the tavern, but not before a couple of hot-blooded apprentices noticed one of their number was a girl, and stood up to block their path.

'Now what's a pretty young slip like you doing here?' one asked, puffing out his chest, adjusting his hat to what he thought was its best advantage.

'Come to give the boys a treat?' his companion slurred, the leer in his voice turning Greta's stomach.

'Out of my way,' Greta said, trying to push past him, but the first man caught her about the neck and slobbered a great kiss on her cheek and before Ruan knew what he was about he lifted his fist and smacked it hard into the side of the man's head, grabbing at Greta's arm as he did so, manhandling her through the throng, the closest of whom were beginning to stand at the spectacle and starting to cheer. The struck man staggered back a step before being shoved forwards again by his outraged companions so he stumbled directly into Greta's back, Greta spinning on her heels, eyes flashing.

'You will all desist!' Hendrik shouted. 'It was my wife who was buried today, and she whose life you are supposed to be celebrating, and you repay her by what? By all this?'

The manager noticed the commotion and was terrified. One word from Hendrik to the Council and he would be shut down the very next day. He rushed forward and took the young drunkard in an arm-lock he'd not had to perform for years.

'I'm so sorry, Mijnheer,' he said, shoving the miscreant hard onto the floor, cracking his cheekbone as he went down. But Hendrik wasn't listening. Hendrik came up on Greta's other side and together he and Ruan marched her through the crowd without further incident, the three of them spilling outside and past the tables before Ruan let her go.

'Are you alright?' he asked, his heart thumping wildly in his chest.

'No thanks to you,' Greta said, brushing hard at her sleeve as if Ruan's hand had defiled it. The shaky tone of her voice belied her words, and Ruan knew it the moment she swivelled her eyes towards his. 'Was just about to flatten him myself,' she said, some of her usual defiance creeping back in.

'I don't doubt it,' Ruan replied. 'We should've drawn up fighting plans before we went in there.'

Greta snorted and let out a brief laugh. 'You and who's army?'

'Don't think I'd need any more than you,' Ruan gave his riposte and then immediately turned the colour of a ripe cherry to have given her such a compliment and couldn't get out another word.

Ricardo moved swift and silent as a stoat in the night, keeping to the darker edges of the library far beyond the small circle of light. He could hear his brother talking – always the weak one.

They looked alike, did Ricardo and Luigi, always had, especially at a place like the Servants, wearing habit and cowl, none of the Brothers paying much attention to their floating population of travellers and lay helpers.

Easy then for Luigi to accompany Caro back from Middleburg – their prearranged meeting place – at his uncle's behest, keep tabs on Ruan Peat, trailing him and Caro to Deventer, volunteering a bit of useful information when it turned out the threat wasn't coming from Ruan Peat but the man he'd been sent to for help.

'He's Brother Joachim's son,' Luigi had faltered, at which news Ricardo ground his teeth, gathered Luigi up and off they went for Walcheren, new plan in place, Luigi slipping back into his previous role with no one any the wiser that he'd ever left. Ricardo took over every now and then to study Joachim and his habits, taking his chance, taking his shot, sending out a letter to tell Hendrik his father was dying. He had presumed Hendrik Grimalkin would come running from the protection of his library to his father's side, when Ricardo would pick him off like a crow silhouetted against the sun, Luigi stopping at the Servants so no one would suspect; several days of Ricardo twiddling his thumbs, avoiding George Gwilt's savage interrogation of anyone and everyone he could find, and no evidence yet of Grimalkin rushing to his father's deathbed; not that Joachim had actually died, at least not yet.

Good plan, bad result; Ricardo back to Deventer quick as he could, leaving Luigi to inform him immediately Hendrik got there or Joachim actually croaked. But the blasted Joachim hadn't croaked, and the news of his near death hadn't even slowed Grimalkin down, and time was running out. Loads of it back in Scotland, but not now, the old stick of a scunnered Pope keeping on inconveniently reviving.

Two weeks delay is all we'll need, Federigo had said at the start; two weeks turning into three and then four and now six, and all the while the danger to their family growing.

Just get rid, Federigo had sighed eventually, leaving the details up to Ricardo, Ricardo happy to obey. Fire on the Singel and all that. Another good plan, more bad luck. All resulting in Ricardo being here in the Athenaeum, his brother caught banged to rights, about to squeal out everything.

But sentimentality be damned; brother or no brother, if push came to shove Ricardo was the cuckoo in the nest who chucked the other siblings over the edge in order to survive. No accident that Ricardo had signed himself in as his brother in the Guildsman's book; no accident either that he'd sent Luigi in with the first barrel, astonished Luigi got as far as he did, not so astonished when Luigi was stuck by the kid with his knife.

All good for Ricardo, giving him the distraction he needed to slip in like an eel, only thing perplexing him was where all the main protagonists had got to. Hendrik's words at the graveside – the ones Luigi had been maundering about – could only have meant they'd all come rushing straight back to the library. Ricardo presumed they were either down in the stacks or up in their beds, for where else could they be?

Either way, the bolts were drawn, the library locked down. Luigi was obviously not going to get out of this, but hey ho. He'd always been expendable. All the more profit for Ricardo and Federigo, the Ducetti name about to fly high across Europe and in the South Americas, anywhere the Catholic root had taken hold: Eduardo Ducetti soon the new Pope who would maybe take the name of Urban, like they'd joked about, just to chuck all that long-forgotten Lynx crap right back in its face where it belonged.

CONFESSION AND CONFUSION

'At least we know there's two of them, and the uncle too,' Greta said, once they'd extricated themselves from the Golden Globe and all the grabbing hands it had contained. She glanced over at Ruan, her feelings of his intervention on her behalf decidedly mixed.

It wasn't the first time she'd ever been accosted, not by a long chalk, and she was thinking back to that time just before she'd got to Peter's when she'd got so angry afterwards with that beggaring flea. If Ruan had been there then she'd have been glad of it, although undoubtedly if he'd intervened then he'd have been strung up from the nearest tree or sliced in two by a sword. She'd no great liking for the man but she had to admit he had a fine looking head, and it would have been a shame for him to have lost it.

'And presumably they're still in Deventer, or were a half hour since,' Ruan added, as they made their way towards the fountain at the centre of the Brink to wash their faces, sit down to regroup despite the drizzle the previously beating rain had shrugged itself into.

'Except they might not be,' Hendrik said, dejection in every syllable. 'If they've got on one of the barges they could be up or downstream several miles by now, and we've no idea where they might be heading.'

The incidents at the Golden Globe had depressed him deeply, and he couldn't think straight. 'Half an hour is a long time,' he added. 'They could be anywhere.'

'But they've no idea we're onto them,' Greta countered brightly, 'so why on earth would they be running?'

'She's right, Hendrik,' Ruan said, smiling briefly at Greta above Hendrik's bowed head, a smile not returned. Jesus, but the girl was infuriating and yet, annoyingly, he found himself thinking about her fingers and as he did so his own fingertips brushed against the small crumpled piece of paper he'd found in the haversack's pocket back at the Guildsman's hostel. He brought it out, fixed his attention on it so he did not have to think about Greta.

The paper was worn and torn by being folded over on itself numerous times but there, in one corner, he saw a barely visible impress looking very like the crest of the Cesi Family Estate. It didn't mean much. It certainly wasn't the proof Hendrik had hoped to find, but it was a connection and connections, Ruan was dimly beginning to understand from this whole fiasco, were what mattered.

'We should take what we've learned back to the library,' he said, neglecting to mention his small discovery, not wanting to get anyone worked up about it, especially not Hendrik.

Ruan was ravenous, needed to get some food down his gullet before lying down and getting some proper sleep, preferably with Greta by his side – a random thought that came out of nowhere, but so strong in its conviction that he went a merry pink, shocking himself – making him bluster on about not leaving poor Caro alone; Caro, of all people, and a trite sentiment that nonetheless both Greta and Hendrik agreed with, all three peeling themselves from the fountain's steps and heading away from the Brink.

‘It started about eighteen months back,’ Luigi was saying through clenched teeth, eyes fixed on Joachim, at that gentle face, the one who had forgiven him the deed he hadn’t done, but had undoubtedly precipitated. ‘We were in the shop in Amsterdam when our uncle came in, said your Golo Eck was going to start the up Lynx again.’

He twisted his head to sip at the glass of grappa Isaac had given him. A couple of sips wasn’t going to make everything go away, but it kept at bay Luigi’s almost uncontrollable impulse to weep.

‘And?’ Isaac prompted, refilling the glass. He didn’t think the man had any fight in him, but a man filled with strong drink would be far less of an opponent than one without. Luigi swallowed, and went on.

‘Uncle Federigo had been sent a letter by his cousin with some paper or other from the Cesi Estate, and he was spitting mad because of it. He’s always had a temper. Whipped us black and blue when we were kids and got even the tiniest thing wrong. Anyway, he said that no way was he going to let the Lynx start up again, not now, because if it did it was going to cause trouble.’

‘What kind of trouble?’ Isaac pushed him on, filling up the glass again, the man having drained the previous one in a single, grimacing gulp.

‘I don’t really know,’ Luigi said quietly. ‘Just that it was going to cast our family in a bad light and that if that happened the Cardinal wouldn’t stand a cat’s chance of getting elected Pope because of it, or even be given one of the more important posts in the Vatican if someone else was elected instead of him.’

Isaac sucked air in through his teeth and looked at Joachim kneeling beside Luigi, mopping away some of the blood with a cloth he'd fetched from the kitchen. He had the notion he was witnessing the physical manifestation of a biblical parable: the way Joachim was tending to the man who, by all accounts, had tried to kill him. He wished he had the same capacity to forgive with such grace and ease instead of having lived a life with bitterness at its core.

He glanced over towards Caro, who was staring intently at their prisoner, hand hovering over the knife lying idle on the table beside him, ready to take it up again if he detected the slightest subterfuge or lie. Isaac moved his head, narrowed his eyes, looked beyond the small circle of light that encapsulated them all, certain he'd detected a small twitching in the shadows.

But surely no one else could be here with them.

Isaac's thought was subsumed immediately by the enormity of his neglect as he realised in that split second that yes, yes there could be, because although he'd shut the door behind this interloper he hadn't bolted it, and hadn't turned the key.

'The door!' Isaac shouted, standing up, dropping the grappa in his haste, Caro springing up as the glass bottle shattered, reaching for his knife, aghast to see a hand other than his own getting there first. Next thing he knew the blade was up against his throat, slicing through a couple of millimetres of skin, deep enough to draw blood, sharp enough to make Caro gasp and stand as still as he could, the knife's keen point a whisper away from the vein pulsing in his neck.

'No need to worry, folks,' said the man who had Caro pinioned against his chest. 'The door is locked and bolted. No one in, no one out, not unless he has the key, and I'm the man who has it.'

Isaac was horrified. How could he not have done such a simple thing as securing the doors the moment the object of his and Caro's plan came into the library? Almost more shocking was how similar the man holding the knife to Caro's throat was to the one on the sofa. Brothers without a doubt, two halves of the same nut. Maybe even twins of the sort who aren't quite identical, but identical enough.

Isaac's old body sagged with self-recrimination and anger at his own neglect. This library was his life and now both it, and Caro with it, were in danger because he hadn't had the nous to turn a single key in its lock and secure it back into his pouch.

'Get up the way,' the man holding Caro commanded Isaac. 'Roll down the other barrel. It's by the top end near the doors, and no point doing anything other or this young lad here will no longer have a throat through which he can breathe.'

Isaac was sweating profusely. He cast a quick glance at the sofa but couldn't see Joachim, and if he couldn't see Joachim then maybe this new attacker couldn't see him either, so some hope yet, enough to propel him forward on shaking legs, appalled at the awful panic in Caro's wide eyes as he passed him by, a thin-beaded necklace of blood beginning to encircle his throat from that single point of contact with the blade, Caro's eyes following Isaac as he went.

If he could have swapped places with the boy he'd have done so in a heartbeat, but there was no possibility, Isaac trapped like a wasp in a bell jar, beating its head repeatedly against the glass to find a non-existent way out. He could maybe try to save the boy or he could maybe try to save the library – for he was in no doubt what those two barrels signified – but he could not do both.

Isaac had blithely assumed the war was over once he and Caro had the Luigi fellow in hand, but they'd been outmanoeuvred with humiliating ease. He'd often wondered how his family, his village, had reacted when the Prussians came stamping down their streets declaring – as they'd done in other Jewish enclaves – that they were vermin, fit only to be swept from life and land. And now he knew. Powerless then, powerless now.

He moved slowly, desperately looking about him for a solution but none was to be found. They were three against two, at least if Joachim was a Brother who would fight and Isaac couldn't count on that, but even so the enemy held all advantage because he hled Caro. Back in the bad old days Isaac had merely been the goat-herd who'd answered a Prussian officer's casual request for directions, and the results had been catastrophic.

This time round he swore he would do better. If he died from the consequence of his own actions, of his not seeing to the locking of the library's doors, then that was fine with him, but not Caro. Absolutely not Caro. The man holding him must have an exit strategy and Isaac had to persuade him to take it without taking Caro with him.

He reached the top of the library, the second barrel, and came to a stop.

'Get it rolled down here,' commanded Ricardo. 'Get it rolled down next to the other one, and be quick about it.'

Ricardo was excited, he had half an erection as he pressed himself up against the young lad at the thought of the fireworks to come. He wasn't sure where Hendrik Grimalkin was, but no matter. Get rid of the library and get rid of Hendrik's researches was Ricardo's reasoning – and Hendrik himself, if he was hidden in here somewhere – putting paid to any further poking about in his family's private affairs. So all good, as far as he was concerned, and Federigo would surely agree with him and pour on him the money so frequently promised but not yet seen.

Isaac looked with longing at the closed door of the peep-hole room, the place he'd felt safe these last twenty odd years. He still had a heel of bread in there and a corner of really good ham that had been slathered over with molasses and honey, cooked for hours and hours in pastry to keep its juices in: a protector that sealed in the good, kept out the bad, just as Isaac had done for the Athenaeum – apart from tonight, when it really counted.

He took a step behind the barrel, readying himself to push it on down the library, taking one last look at all the shelves, at all the books he loved like family, and had to swallow down his tears. He couldn't bear that it was all going to be destroyed because of him. His eyes came to rest on Luigi who was, at that moment, levering himself up with difficulty from off his sofa, his head poking out from its depths. Isaac paused, foot on the barrel, ready to get it going, and saw that Luigi was winking – and winking desperately – with his one visible and blood shot eye.

Ruan, Hendrik and Greta got to the library and went up its steps. They didn't bother knocking, knowing Isaac would be in his peep-hole room as ordered, ready to let them in. But apparently Isaac was not, because the door did not open. After a couple of minutes they glanced at one another and at the closed doors, wondering what the hold-up was. Possibly Isaac had gone to relieve himself, but surely he would have put Caro or Joachim on guard in his stead. Hendrik frowned, but Ruan did not. He'd been emboldened by his recent encounter in the Golden Globe and keener still to impress Greta, so he took a step forward and began to hammer the flat of his fist upon the wood, shouting out for Isaac and Caro, but no answer came.

'Not much time,' Ricardo Ducetti said grimly, hearing the banging on the door – possibly the Grimalkin man at last, who seemed to have seven lives – the point of his knife digging a little deeper into Caro's neck as he tensed, ready for action.

'You,' he commanded,' meaning Isaac, 'get that barrel down here now, and I mean now. And Luigi, stop lollygagging about and bleating like a stuck pig. We've work to do. Get those barrels opened and let's be gone.'

Luigi moved slowly, dragging one leg behind him as he moved, the blood from his wound dripping onto the floor with every step. He didn't want to obey his brother but he knew Ricardo well enough to know he would slit the boy's throat soon as he would sneeze. He also realised, dullard as Ricardo believed him to be, that Brother Joachim was still hunkered behind the sofa, Luigi having shoved his head down the second Ricardo made himself known.

He didn't want to be here – Christ, he'd never wanted any of this, not the way it had gone. Unlike his brother or his uncle, or even cousin Cardinal Eduardo de Ducetti, as he styled himself, Luigi was a true believer and dreaded besmirching his soul's passage to Heaven any more than he'd already had. He'd been a coward, he knew, and needed a miracle to get himself out of the shit he'd been tossed into, but Joachim had given him exactly that: the miracle of forgiveness, maybe not for what he'd actually done but that was alright. It was forgiveness just the same.

He wished he'd been able to stay at the Servants, would gladly have stayed there for the rest of his life for there was peace there: no brother or uncle to drag him under. If he ever got out of this, then that's where he would go – to the Servants. He winced at the pain of his moving but got to the first barrel, soon had its nozzle opened, the turpentine coming out in a mere trickle because of the angle at which the barrel was leant, an angle Luigi deliberately did not correct.

Then came Isaac, rolling the second barrel down the library, bringing it to rest against the first as Ricardo ordered. Once again

Luigi did has he was bid and loosened the tap, the gunpowder flowing out briefly but soon clogging and coming to a stop, Luigi trying to block it from his brother's sight. Unsuccessfully as it turned out, Ricardo clicking his tongue, seeing exactly what the problem was.

'You bloody idiot,' Ricardo growled at his brother. 'You need to shift them into a better position, get everything flowing properly. Thank Christ one of us has a brain. Here,' Ricardo added, pulling out his guildsman's hammer and chisel from his workman's belt, slamming them down on the table, the knife once more digging another millimetre further into Caro's neck as he did so, unintentionally nicking Caro's windpipe, making Caro wriggle, making him release a thin squall that almost broke old Isaac's not so slowly pumping heart. Ricardo tightened his grip on the boy.

'Keep still,' he ordered, and Caro did, although he was crying freely now and having some difficulty breathing. Luigi limped forward to take up his brother's tools, seeing the wet shine on the boy's face, knowing he was in serious trouble. The hammering on the doors had not lessened, nor the calls for Isaac and the boy to come and let whoever was out there in.

Luigi had a pain all of his own and maybe because of it, or maybe because of the boy's unnerving mewling, he had a sudden and immediate awareness of his surroundings and of all the books that were about him and all the knowledge they contained, all the stories they could tell, all the things he might have learned if he'd ever been given the chance; and he also saw the faint figure of Brother Joachim creeping away from the sofa towards the Athenaeum's kitchen, his face peeping out around the corner of the stairs that led down to the second depth of the library, a face that was round and white and as filled with shadows as a moon half risen.

Vacillation now for Luigi Ducetti, his miracle on the move, his soul getting heavier and dirtier with every step Joachim took away from him. He picked up the hammer. He picked up the chisel. He looked up at Isaac, and saw his chance.

'Something's wrong,' Ruan Peat was saying. 'Where the hell is Isaac?'

Greta was jittering beside him like a cricket on a hotplate, and soon they were both pounding their combined fists upon the great wooden doors, trying the huge iron circles it had for handles. Ruan had the sweat of panic on his hands, on his neck, and looked at Hendrik for direction, but Hendrik closed his eyes, hands loose against his chest, unable, Ruan thought, to weather yet another imminent disaster.

'There must be another way in,' Ruan said. 'Hendrik. You have to help us. Is there another way in?'

Hendrik opened his eyes at the question and Ruan saw he was right. Hendrik had given up. Hendrik had done all he was going to do. Hendrik had lost so much he couldn't contemplate losing any more, was finding it difficult to function, and oddly Ruan understood. The ties binding him to the world were also suddenly dissolving, as they had for Ruan with Golo gone, and Fergus too; no freedom in that loosening, only fright and foreboding. In Ruan's case, there was an urgent need to kick back against the man or men who had taken them from him. He'd been set adrift in a new world like he'd always wanted but everything in this new world was wrong, excepting Greta, who suddenly brought that world back into focus.

'There has to be a delivery door round back,' she said and Ruan knew she was right.

'Hendrik,' Ruan pleaded, his throat constricting, the next words hardly more than a whisper. 'The delivery door. Is there a key? Do you have a key?'

The moment stretched. The moment ran on into infinity, until Hendrik spoke, dull and flat.

'Around the back down the ginnel, duplicate key beneath the water trough in case of emergency. In case of emergency...' Hendrik repeated slowly before leaking out something approaching a hysterical laugh, Ruan not hearing, already setting off , Greta just behind him, Ruan gripped by the unfamiliar notion that he had a purpose for the first time in his life.

Luigi put chisel and hammer to first one barrel and then the next, releasing their contents freely out onto the wood of the Athenaeum's wood-planked floor. The ensuing smell of turpentine was strong, the scent of gunpowder raw and redolent, and Ricardo was momentarily bewitched. Luigi saw it, lurched forward, throwing the hammer and stabbing the chisel at his brother's chest, all of his years of denigration and insult going into that single thrust which was nevertheless feeble but so unexpected that Ricardo took a step backwards on impact, dragging Caro with him, pushing the knife further into Caro's throat, the sudden spurt of blood making Ricardo's hand so slippery that he let go the knife and Caro with it as he struggled to regain his balance.

Caro crumpled to the floor, Isaac moving immediately to the boy's side. Luigi toppled over beside the two of them, his gesture of defiance having drained what little strength he had left. Ricardo, looming above his brother, recouped in seconds, grabbing the chisel from the floor, stamping on Luigi's useless out-flung hand, giving his useless brother a hard kick in his useless belly that sent Luigi sprawling.

'So now we have a development,' Ricardo said, loud and harsh. 'One turncoat brother, one ancient handyman, one boy bleeding to death. And so you can all go to hell together in the merry blast, but not I, not I.'

He snatched up a lamp from the nearest table and took a few steps away from them, calculating how far he would need to go before he could chuck it into the vicious mix of barrel spillage and get out alive.

'Don't do this, Ricardo!' Luigi was terrified. His brother's kick had sent him right into the pool of turpentine and he was soaked in it and Jesus, whatever he'd done in his life and however bad it had been, surely not even Ricardo would let him die like this. But apparently Ricardo would, because his only riposte was to smile and raise his arm, chucking the lamp right into the thin-fingered spreading out of the turpentine as it snaked here and there down the central aisle, following the differing grains of wood and the lengths and knots of the planks.

The lamp landed with a crash and a small whooshing as the edge of escaping turpentine caught, Luigi lying between Ricardo and the barrels that were a few yards further up from him, yelling and rolling, trying to crawl away as it went straightaway to flame. It rushed towards him at such a speed that Luigi knew he could not get out of its way in time; but his brother paid him no mind and didn't stop to help him. He instead ran on towards the very back of the library and down the short corridor that led to the kitchen area, straight for the door he knew deliveries were always made to, key always this side, heading for escape.

Ruan and Greta were almost there, Hendrik summoning enough gumption to follow them but was slow and uncoordinated, slipping on the wet cobbles, going down hard, cracking his shoulder bone as he went, twisting his spine. Greta heard him go down and turned back but Hendrik Grimalkin held up a hand, didn't want any help. House burned down, Louisa dead, and now the Athenaeum itself under threat. He couldn't cope with it. He lay down his head on the wet cobbles and switched himself off. Let life go on without him, because he couldn't do it anymore.

'Go,' he whispered, and Greta nodded and did exactly that.

Isaac's old heart was torn in two, or maybe three, if that was even figuratively possible. The man who'd thrown the lamp was getting away and the flames from it were racing towards Luigi who'd tried to do the right thing and was now about to go up like a torch because of it. Caro's blood was pumping between his fingers in a tiny fountain, and then again there was the overriding need to get the barrel of gunpowder out of the way of the oncoming flames so they weren't all blown to smithereens.

Only one choice. Abandon the dying child in the hope he could save them all and so Isaac threw himself forward and kicked at the barrel of gunpowder, sent it rolling down the library with as much strength as he could muster, a grey streak left behind like a fuse line as it went; then straightaway back to Caro, who might peg at any moment, taking off his coat, wrapping it tight about the boy's neck to stop the bleeding, no chance to help Luigi, his boots alight, him howling as the fire moved from leather to socks to flesh, tears streaming down his face, heart almost stopping as a terrifying figure appeared out of the gloom, lunging towards them all.

‘Christ save me…’ Luigi whispered, believing this to be the devil come to take him. But it was not the devil. It was Brother Joachim, habit halfway over his head and then off, flinging it fast over Luigi’s legs, wrapping him tight, rolling him over and over. The action put out the immediate flames but not the ones that were surrounding the two of them like a fallen halo as the wax polish on the floorboards gave them sustenance and reason to grow, snaking and curling towards the mother load of the tipped-over cask of turpentine whose contents were seeping slowly and inexorably in all directions, including towards its brother barrel of gunpowder a few yards away, like calling to like, maybe a minute or so left before they were all blown to hell.

Ruan and Greta arrived at the back door of the Athenaeum. Ruan tried the handle but it was locked, Greta going straight to the trough to fetch the second key as Ruan took a couple of steps back, getting ready to kick the door in if it was not found, when the door opened of its own accord and out came a man who went at them like a bull, head lowered, fists out, bowling into Ruan, knocking him over, punching hard at Greta’s face as she tried to intercept him before running for all he was worth into the falling night.

Isaac saw Joachim tumble Luigi over and over and out of the way of the burning pool of spirits. There was a still a creep of flame over Luigi’s upper legs like you got on the top of a plum pudding that has been soaked in brandy and set alight. Worse still was the plight of Caro, blood pumping, face white, lips going blue. Isaac pulled himself and Caro back into the shadows, upturning a desk as he did so, pulling it over them for shelter. It was a bad decision because by doing so he inadvertently let slide off the surface the candle that was on it that joyously joined the mayhem as it fell.

The candle found its own path towards the victims who were not yet alight at which point Isaac folded himself about Caro, bringing up his legs about Caro's own, likewise shielding his shoulders, body and head with his own in the faint hope that when he burned he might be able to keep Caro at the kernel of it, and somehow safe.

Ruan was up on his feet in a moment, a little dizzy from the knock his head had taken as he tumbled to the ground but he wasn't going to let that stop him. He grabbed at Greta and missed, couldn't understand how, and tried again, missed again, unaware that he was seeing double.

'For God's sake, get on!' Greta shouted, seeing Ruan's flailing arms coming towards her as she hoisted herself up on one elbow, her right eye already swelling and closing from Ricardo's fist and a knee going the same way from how she had gone down. She saw the confusion in Ruan's eyes and saw too, in that single second, a determination she'd seen many times in many men's faces before they went into battle when they were so fired up they were ready to do or die and, God help her, she took advantage of it. She didn't know what was going on in the library but she figured it was urgent and so she sent him on.

'Jeez, man. Ruan,' she urged, 'never mind me. Get inside. Do what's needed to be done.'

And Ruan did. He left Greta and he left the yard and he ran through the open kitchen door and up the few step into the library proper and what he saw scoured away everything he thought he knew, his double vision clearing and giving such an immediacy to the scene that it was like stepping into another world. The library was burning. The floor of the main aisle was licked about by flames; Joachim was there, strangely denuded, trying to drag another man up the way, Isaac and Caro hunkered down beneath a table and one of them was bleeding, no doubt about that, the blood beneath them bright and visceral.

In between the two misshapen groups was a small wall of fire coming up from the library's floor, waxing and waning as if it was breathing, heading for the dark hulks of two barrels, one maybe ten yards further up than the other, barrels just like the ones he knew had been in Hendrik Grimalkin's house.

'Everybody out!' he shouted. 'And I mean everybody. Isaac, Joachim, drag your charges out by their heels if you have to, but get them out!'

Ruan started running like a madman around the library, grabbing up several buckets of sand meant for the stubbing out of the cigars the visiting scholars were so fond of. He hurled their contents over the floors and the wall of flames that were gathering in strength, heading without compassion or diversion towards two barrels, one goal. The sand hit but did not extinguish the flames, merely moved them to one side or another, the draft from Ruan's movements apparently exacerbating them so they jumped and spat, making the situation all the worse and far more dangerous.

In desperation Ruan did the single most heroic thing he'd ever done in his life and side-stepped the small ocean of creeping flames, tried to tighten the nozzle from where the turpentine was still dripping and, when he couldn't stop it, indeed only made it worse with his fiddling, picked the barrel up, groaning with the weight and size of it and half ran, half staggered with it back down the length of the library and out through the kitchen door, its contents all the while freed up by his jiggling and jogging so the nozzle finally gave, began to pour its contents freely down his back as he ran with it.

Once out of the library he heaved the barrel far as he could into the yard beyond. He didn't wait to see what became of it, merely turned and ran back into the Athenaeum, screaming at Joachim and Isaac to get a move on, not understanding why they were hauling their respective burdens towards the kitchen and not the fastest and safest way out which was through the doors at the front. But he wasted no time and went on up the library, as inexorable as the flames that seemed to be all about him, still low-lying but high enough.

Ruan ran through the knee-high flames, ignoring the singe and sear of his clothes and boots, the thin line of fire that was creeping up his back where the turpentine had sketched out a rudimentary route; reaching the second barrel and hauling it upwards, although it was already beginning to snap and burn. How he had the strength to do it he never knew, but have it he did and he took it up, hoisted it upon his shoulders, shuffling and staggering with its weight. His nostrils filled with the fumes of turpentine evaporating from his coat, the growing sensation of heat upon his back as the flames began to take hold of both coat and barrel. But he did not let go, would not give up.

He got down the library's length, stumbled down the last few steps into the kitchen and out through the open door, stepping straight into the spilled puddle of turpentine gathering between the cobbles from the splitting of the first barrel that had broken as it fell, Ruan's heart hammering so hard he could hear it. He understood that any second now he was going to go up like a tar-dipped brand and would most probably die here in this yard but Jesus, he could see all the others scattered about him: Joachim, for some undetermined reason in his singlet, dragging a man across the cobbles, Isaac leaning over Caro who was pale as a swan, Hendrik Grimalkin – who had managed to crawl his way down the alley and was leaning up against the post of the wall trying to haul himself to standing and Greta Finnerty crawling towards Hendrik on hands and damaged knee, and that was the last spur he needed.

'Out of the yard!' he yelled. 'Everyone out of the yard!'

He couldn't hang on for long because by now his sleeves and the back of his coat were burning and he could feel the heat mere millimetres away from his skin, but he kept that barrel upon his shoulders until he saw from his peripheral vision that all were out. Then his legs went of their own accord the few yards towards the water trough, kept there for the tradesmen's horses' use, and dropped the barrel in. It hit the edges but was too wide to touch the water and the wood did not cease its burning, indeed seemed invigorated by the rush of air occasioned by the fall.

Ruan staggered backwards as the flames suddenly took on new life, about to lunge forward, try to scoop the water from the trough onto the staves with his bare hands when someone grabbed at his shoulder, pulling off his coat, hauling him bodily, if lopsidedly, out of the yard and behind the wall.

It was Greta, her face grimy and with one eye puffed up to the size of a duck egg.

'Enough, Ruan Peat,' she commanded. 'You've done enough, and we need to get out of here before it blows.'

RESOLUTION AND SOMETIME REDEMPTION

And blow it did.

Moments later the back yard of the Athenaeum Library went up like the greatest fireworks show Deventer had ever seen, the sound of the explosion bouncing and reverberating from eve to eve, from street to street. It brought Deventer's inhabitants running from their houses, fearing the French had finally arrived and were laying the city to siege.

It blew Greta and Ruan off their feet. They were fifteen yards down the street but were showered cruelly with the stones and bricks of the Athenaeum yard's retaining wall that came at them like shrapnel. Both were floored, clinging to one another like shipwrecked sailors as they were rolled along the cobbles, winded and then elated as they lay like upended beetles when once all had settled, laughing hysterically to find themselves still alive and relatively unscathed. Not so hysterical when they found themselves side by side with Caro, shielded by Isaac during the blast, but not doing well.

'Come on, Caro,' Isaac was saying. 'Come on, lad. Just stay calm, just keep still and I'll have you fixed up in a moment.'

Greta recognised the noises Caro was making as he tried to breathe, a task that was obviously getting more difficult by the second, his lips already turned a ferocious blue.

'We have to stick a pipe in him,' she said, disentangling herself from Ruan and rolling over onto her knees, wincing with pain as she did so.

Isaac shook his head. A pipe? What kind of pipe? What was the girl intending to do? Lucky for Caro, Ruan understood. He fumbled in his pockets and brought out a pen, thrust it quickly into Greta's hands. She swiftly pulled out the nib and broke off the top, draining the ink and then pulled her knife from her belt and jabbed the point of it deftly into the hollow of Caro's naked throat before Isaac could stop her and after it went the tube of the pen, and then Greta blowing gently, once, twice and again, Caro's heels tapping at the ground as his body shook, as Greta blew again and again at regular intervals, until his lungs started to move again of their own accord and he relaxed, lips and skin resuming a more normal hue as the oxygen returned to his blood.

'Done it for piglets a hundred times,' Greta said, by way of explanation as she rocked back on her heels. 'Had this sow once, always bore her litters blue.'

She winced, becoming aware of numerous cut and grazes sustained during the explosion and then narrowed her eyes, knife in hand, having noticed Luigi a few yards up and recognising him: the man at the Servants, the man she blamed for all this. Joachim was crouched beside him, grey and curled like a hedgehog newly rolled from the fire, ears ringing, inexplicably holding Luigi's head in his hands.

Greta got up, her bad knee almost giving way – almost, but not quite – staggering towards the enemy; she wanted to fillet Luigi like the wet fish he was. She instead settled for sending a very unladylike fist straight and hard into his face, breaking his nose with a horribly audible crack.

'See you?' she said, breathing hard, sheathing her knife. 'That's barely a pennyworth of what you deserve.'

Luigi moaned at the impact of her fist and Joachim looked up swiftly to complain at the injustice but Greta didn't see it, pain and exhaustion coming over her in a wave that had her bum-down on the cobbles, Ruan stumbling up beside her and gently scooping her up, arm muscles stretched and strong from the barrel-carrying, getting her to the nearest wall against which he gently propped her, the two of them sitting side by side, backs against the stone. Two disparate people emerging from a battle won.

The library was saved; the low-licking fire inside soon extinguished by the men and women of Deventer running to the fountain in the Brink with every bucket, pail, pan and chamber pot they could lay hands on, and within half an hour of the explosion in the yard it was doused and done, long dark streaks and shadows burned into the wooden floors and up the legs of several tables, shelves and chairs to mark its passing. These latter were taken outside in case they harboured embers that might yet burn – as had happened with such terrible consequence at the Grimalkin household – and sitting on them were all manner of sightseers and rescuers, all chattering like excited starlings about their part in saving one of the most important institutions in the town.

Barely a one of them had thought of it that way before, let alone gone inside its walls, but today the Athenaeum was the emblem of their collective resilience, of clawing back what had almost been lost to unnamed and unknown assailants. Let the French come, because if they did this was what they would get: a town ready to rise up and fight for their own. The town of Deventer was theirs, as was everything and everyone in it, and they were damned if anyone was going to take anything from it anytime soon.

Help was soon at hand for Caro too, several women easing him from Isaac's cradling arms, the pen sticking up like a thorn from his neck, quivering with every shallow breath he took. The beeswax from Isaac's coat had done a good job by its melting, thereby sealing the edges of the wound and stopping the blood. He was in a desperate state but alive, and alive an hour later when Deventer's most experienced surgeon arrived to sew him up properly. The man went on to extract shards of wood and stone from Greta, Ruan and Isaac; tended to Hendrik's shoulder, dressed the worst of the burns on his head.

Hendrik's hair never grew back except in tufts, and the tips of his ears remained melted and deformed, but he was glad of it – a constant reminder of his guilt. He would accept no external exculpatory explanations of why he had so suddenly shut down that evening. He couldn't understand it himself, or clearly remember it.

Up one minute, down the next, like Ruan and Caro on their raft during their black night at sea. And with them had been Federigo Ducetti – the architect of all their misfortunes – who had killed a man one minute and the next was buoying up the other surviving souls on the raft with a bravery that bordered on altruism. A curate's egg of a man then, like most were; a complex, contradictory tangle of motivations and emotions.

Hendrik raised his eyes to the dark sky above Deventer now that the worst was past. If Joachim's God really was up there, looking down in judgement, he wondered who would be found wanting at the final trumpet call: him or the Ducettis. If it hadn't been for

Ruan Peat the library, and all its collective knowledge, would have been razed to the ground with Hendrik not lifting a finger to save it. In the face of adversity he'd simply gone to bits, abnegated all responsibility, preferring to lie like a dog in his ditch. And for that he would never forgive himself.

Hendrik swore an oath, as he sat there that evening outside the library that he would put heart and soul, every remaining breath he had, into the resurrection of the Lynx. And heart and soul and every breath he did: firing out letters to every journal and broadsheet he could think of, promissory notes of donations soon pouring in from every corner of Europe, the Enlightenment getting up from its knees and starting to run.

The punishment of the Ducetti family was another matter entirely, and neither good nor fair. Ricardo disappeared like a ferret down the ginnels and side streets of Deventer, never to be seen again. Plainly he'd gone straight to Amsterdam for, by the time the authorities there were alerted, the store was discovered to have been entered, the safe open and empty, and some very valuable and easily transportable items missing from the inventory. Federigo Ducetti played his hand differently, remaining where he was, still at the inn where Caro had left him, carrying on business as usual; surprise his main defence.

No, he didn't know where his nephews were or what they had been doing in Deventer.

And no, he'd never heard of the Lynx, whatever that might be.

And yes, by all means he would accompany the arresting officers back to Deventer and offer what help he could in wringing a confession out of Luigi, the only member of the family to be actually apprehended in the middle of a murderous attack. *The poor boy was always slow,* he volunteered in Luigi's scant defence, *and undoubtedly his brother was the mastermind, but where was Ricardo? Federigo had no idea. Try Amsterdam,* he suggested, *or possibly even Rome.*

That Rome was the last place Ricardo would go was a moot point, news of the Lynx Affair quickly travelling abroad down rivers and canals, trade routes and pilgrim trails, and when Rome heard of it Rome was mighty displeased. It wasn't the worst scandal to hit the Papacy – there was at least one every century: Pope Pius IV executing the nephews of his predecessor Paul IV in the 1560s; the notorious nepotism of Cesi's beloved Maffeo – Urban VIII – that led to the inglorious but happy rioting in the streets when he died in 1644; and now this, right at the end of the 1700s.

That a member of the enclave – a man a hair's breadth away from Papal election – could be connected even so tangentially with the plot that had unravelled in Deventer was not taken well. As luck would have it, the ailing Pope had revived enough to have the enclave dismissed, for the time at least, but Cardinal de Ducetti would not be asked back again. No longer was he in the running for anything but a mean post as far away as the Vatican could get him, despatched to South America as soon as they could bundle him onto a ship, his name scrubbed from their records and never spoken of again.

His connection to the man who had begun the entire fiasco was never uncovered, the secretary of the Aquasparta Estates of the Dukes of Cesi smiling broadly every morning to think of the tidy nest egg he'd been given by the Cardinal for the information passed on about Golo Eck and the Lynx.

Of all the Ducettis, it was the one who did the least who shouldered the most blame, Luigi mouldering in a dirty prison cell in Deventer where the untreated burns on his legs became rotten and gangrenous within forty eight hours, at which point enter the prison surgeon – barber and tooth-puller by trade – who took one look at the blackened mess of flesh and bone and rubbed his hands in glee.

'Have to chop them off,' he said, unrolling his band of dirty tools, glad of the practice but needing more: Luigi's howls and screams echoing about the Brink for almost a full hour as his legs were sawed and then hacked through mid-thigh; a bottle of bad brandy an ineffective anaesthetic; flesh tied and stitched in unpretty, preinfected stumps. Luigi emerged the other side of his surgery into an ever narrowing tunnel of increasing agony.

His amputated limbs were taken in plain view: severed into sections, tumbled into a large bucket in the corner of his cell, collected later that day by a pig man – friend of the barber – to add to his slurry. Brother Joachim was appalled at the unnecessary butchery for, if left intact, Luigi would have died soon enough and in far less pain, not this half-a-man tumbling downhill at breakneck speed towards his death, tortured by every breath.

Joachim tried to make him more comfortable, wiped the comingling sweat and tears from Luigi's cheeks, pushing pillows below the grotesquery of his stumps.

'Thank you,' Luigi murmured, Joachim closing his eyes, the injustice almost unbearable; plain as a pikestaff Luigi had done nothing worse than send a boulder tumbling down a cliff meant to slow folk up, holing a ferry, following a plan he neither properly understood and never endorsed. Federigo had chucked Golo overboard with his arms bound, not that it could be proved; Ricardo had been the one to impale Joachim and also doing for Louisa in his attempt to get rid of Hendrik.

Not that Hendrik's neighbours cared for the difference between the brothers, preferring to plump for the one in custody who looked kind of like the man running off so quickly with his empty dray. It seemed to Joachim that Justice had taken an ill-advised holiday and was nowhere to be seen.

He administered Last Rites. He said prayers. He felt Luigi's fingertips tapping at his arm as he knelt beside Luigi's pallet.

'Will…God have mercy…on my soul…do you think?' Luigi whispered, Joachim placing a hand lightly on Luigi's forehead. No sweat there now, and no tears, only that strange dryness to a person's skin as the body pulls its resources inwards in a last desperate gambit to draw in another breath.

'I know He will, Luigi,' Joachim softly said, 'and it will not be long. Remember, my friend, that suffering is of this world not the next. Keep your faith and all will be right.'

But it wasn't right. It could never be right. Not George, nor Luigi, not any of it.

And it would trouble Joachim for the rest of his life.

'Can you tally any of it?' Joachim asked Hendrik later that day, Hendrik shaking his head.

'If you can't,' he said sadly, 'with God on your side, then what chance do I have?'

Joachim grimaced, Hendrik immediately apologising.

'I'm sorry. I didn't mean that badly,' casting a quick smile at his father. 'Remember that old proverb of mother's? The one she used when I complained I'd been hard done by?'

Joachim's turn to smile. 'I do,' he said. '*Justice becomes injustice, one man given two wounds when he barely deserves one.*'

'Harsh words then, harsh words now,' Hendrik commented. 'But with Luigi…well…where to start…'

'Is there nothing you can do, Hendrik?' Joachim asked, 'nothing to at least get this Federigo fellow clapped in irons? Or get Luigi's name cleared?'

He looked about the library where his son spent all his days and now his nights too, Hendrik living in one of the upstairs rooms. Plans had been put to him of getting his house rebuilt with monies from the Common Good Fund of Deventer, Hendrik quashing them from the start, stating that he absolutely wouldn't countenance living on the Singel, certainly not on the same spot Louisa had died.

An exact parallel to Wynken Grimalkin returning from his war of mud, mist and fog in Lobosik, forced into violence not of his making, both giving atonement for that violence ever since: Wynken to the Servants to become Joachim, Hendrik to his library and the Lynx.

'Anything at all?' Joachim asked again, watching his son drum his fingers on the desk, obviously thinking hard; another moment; another few beats of his heart.

'If there is then I can't see it,' Hendrik eventually said. 'Ricardo registered as his brother with the Guild so the paltry evidence we uncovered in his room all points in the wrong direction. As for the uncle…well, it's out of my hands. He's been let go. Due to leave for Amsterdam tomorrow. But believe me, if I had it all to do again I would have done it differently.'

Joachim frowned.

'How so?' he asked. 'What on earth could you have done to make a different ending?'

Hendrik gazed up at the large window in the upper echelons of the Athenaeum's western wall. He loved that window, it's ancient glass mellowing and yellowing the afternoon light, suffusing the interior of the library as it might have done a holy place, a cathedral maybe.

'I should have been the one to rescue the library, not Ruan,' Hendrik said quietly, 'but before that I should have gone to the Servants. I should have hurried to your side as they expected, then none of the rest would have happened.'

Joachim was puzzled. 'How could you respond to an event unknown to you?'

'Because I did know,' Hendrik said simply. 'What would have been the point of it if I didn't? A letter came to me at the Athenaeum purporting to be from your Abbot telling me things were badly with you. I didn't pursue it because plainly it was a hoax. No Abbot would have written such an untutored letter. I had no idea…no idea…and I don't understand why the Servants didn't send me a real missive telling me you were so incapacitated…'

Joachim bowed his head.

'They didn't send anything because that's not our way. Not until a Brother dies. When we enter the Order we shrug off our former lives until our lives are actually over.'

Joachim suddenly stood up, almost shouted as the realisation hit him.

'But surely that letter is absolute proof of ill intent! Proof of the Ducetti's involvement! The handwriting? Can't we match it to Ricardo's from the Guild Book?'

'We can't,' Hendrik sighed, turning back to the window and the light, 'because I threw it away. There was nothing to keep. Nothing of any meaning.'

A few moments of silence as Joachim took this in, thinking that of course it would be so, *nothing of any meaning*, for why would his abandoned son keep anything of him, especially something so obviously dubious.

Joachim sat down slowly.

'Does it have to be like this, between you and me, I mean?'

he asked, looking at Hendrik, seeing his gaze fixed on the large window, the amber light falling on his son's uplifted face. 'Can we not term a truce? Can we not begin again? We've lost so much, Hendrik, you and I…'

The light was fading to the west, the sun dipping below the horizon, shadows falling over Hendrik as another night stepped in lightly on the heels of another day.

Life, he thought, is so fleeting, so temporary, its anticipated duration not to be relied on – Louisa was proof of that – and Joachim was right. They'd lost so much, the two of them. Why not wipe the slate clean and start again? *Tabula Rasa.* Father and son reunited.

Louisa would have been pleased about that.

42
AND RIGHT BACK AT YOU

Deventer & Ireland 1799

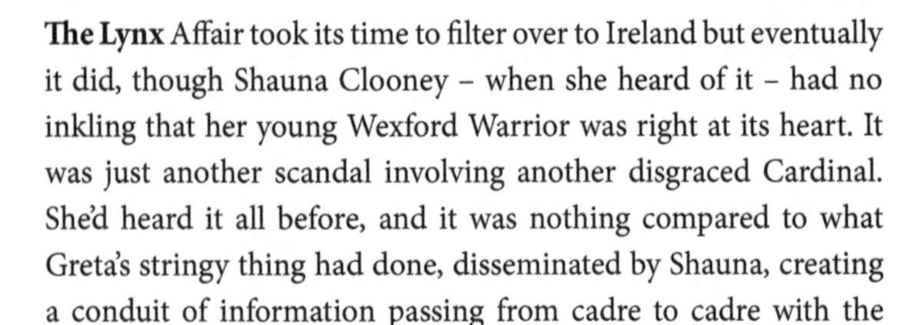

The Lynx Affair took its time to filter over to Ireland but eventually it did, though Shauna Clooney – when she heard of it – had no inkling that her young Wexford Warrior was right at its heart. It was just another scandal involving another disgraced Cardinal. She'd heard it all before, and it was nothing compared to what Greta's stringy thing had done, disseminated by Shauna, creating a conduit of information passing from cadre to cadre with the Loyalists being none the wiser, the only shame of it being that it had come so late in the day.

Vinegar Hill had been the last real stand of the United Irish, the sporadic skirmishes afterwards mere charades of the real thing. Not that Shauna cared overmuch, for it had given her the one piece of news she valued above all else: that her younger son had survived, away over the sea like Greta to join Napoleon's Irish League, safe for the moment at least.

The Irish would rise again like they always did and next time round might have a better chance because of Greta, the pouch of whose shorn hair Shauna looked at every morning, crossing herself in thanks the girl had chanced across her path.

Old Owen often thought of Greta too, or rather of that perfect boy, that perfect boy with his perfect green eyes and the spikes – oh the spikes – of his perfect red hair. If Owen had seen Greta as she looked now his ardour would have quelled in an instant. Gone were the boy's clothing and cap; gone the bandages about her chest; gone the clumpy boots and thick socks needed to fill them out; laid aside was her brother's battered leather jacket.

She was a young woman again, looking all her eighteen years, no longer needing to hide in plain sight, nor appear younger than she was. She might not be beautiful, but she had everything else going in her favour – strong face, round cheeks, square jaw, small hands, and a smile that could set the world alight, or Ruan's world at least. He could hardly bring himself to look at her without his heart dancing a tarantella.

'Hells bells,' he whispered when she came into the library decked out in a simple green dress and dainty boots – just a few of the items donated by the members of Louisa's Sewing Circle. They'd offered her several pretty bonnets but Greta had refused them. Enough was enough. She'd spent the last several years in dirty jerkins and trousers and already felt odd and constrained in this new garb; a bonnet looking like a bird's nest thrown together with a posy of silk flowers was a step too far.

Even so, the transformation seemed as much of a miracle as Ruan had ever seen, and the letter he'd just fetched from the lawyers slipped from his fingers. No matter. He knew what it was: the copy of Golo's Will. Any day previous to the attempted blowing up of the library he'd have been spitting like a pole cat, absolutely raging at its contents: *half of Golo's estate to Fergus?*

He would have ranted and raved, kicked his heels into the dust and sworn bloody murder at how unfair life was, how badly mistreated he'd been, cursing every last one of the hoops he was going to have jump through because of it, like how was he going to prove Fergus was dead, and how long it was going to take for anyone to verify that Fergus had no family but him and Golo. And come to that, was there any other extant family over in Ireland? That was going to take a couple of years and a lot of money to track down.

But all that was gone. Swept away. Ruan, at the grand old age of twenty, grown up overnight, the veils of his youth torn away, seeing life for what it was: precious and precarious, unpredictable at best and downright dangerous and deadly at worst, no clue given when your time was up. Whatever was going to happen was going to happen, but what had happened to him in the few days since he'd saved the Athenaeum had shifted his world view. And now, seeing Greta, it was being shifted all over again.

'Cat got your tongue?' Greta asked, Ruan struck dumb by her latest incarnation.

He was unaware that he seemed a different person himself: restrained and polite, offering his help wherever it would matter most, instrumental in getting the library back to working order: scouting Deventer for the workmen needed to replace the damaged floor and furniture, gathering together the few scraps of Walter's letters that had survived fire and water, as if a couple of lines of writing out of context would be sufficient to condemn the entire Ducetti family to hell.

'So you got Golo's Will then?' Hendrik asked, looking up briefly as Ruan came in before reverting back to the large piece of paper spread out on the desk before him.

Once a scholar, always a scholar. Some things could not, would not, should not change, at least not for Hendrik. He'd been witness to an experiment many years ago when a man of vision had turned the ordinary into the extraordinary. He'd placed a bowl of mercury at the bottom of a well and had a boy down there to stir it gently and, come the night, the man entertained his fellow scientists – Hendrik amongst them – with an experience beyond compare.

The swirling mercury had acted as a telescopic reflector so that they saw a hovering depiction of the night sky a few yards above the well; present but inanimate; a will'o'the wisp that had shape and form but no mass. Hendrik never forgot it, indeed it was what inspired him to install the peep-hole room in the Athenaeum. And he had his own miracle to entertain his own guests now.

'Join us,' Hendrik invited Ruan and Ruan sat, abandoning the lawyer's letter without a second thought, wanting only to gaze on Greta, at what she had become, the promise of the tight-clad bud suddenly blossomed into a flower that defied categorisation. He wanted to stare at her, take it all in, but every time he raised his eyes she was looking at him and so he dropped his gaze again, listening to what Hendrik was saying.

'We found out something very interesting while you were away,' Hendrik began. 'And strangely enough it has to do with you, and with Golo and Fergus.'

Ruan stared hard at Hendrik but Hendrik did not look up, his long fingers moving slowly about the sheet of paper he had in front of him on the desk, Ruan's interest piqued because he'd seen something similar before: that mucky beet bag Greta had brought out of her satchel when she'd been banging on about the khipu.

'Greta noticed something,' Hendrik went on, Ruan's heart annoyingly jumping at the mention of her name, making him glance involuntarily towards her, her rounded cheeks, her curling hair…

'She saw the khipu,' Hendrik drew Ruan's attention back, 'when Fergus first showed it to her cousin Peter and then later to Mick Malloy.'

Peter. Her cousin then, so not some long lost lover, and thank God for it.

Ruan tried to concentrate.

'But it's different now,' Greta added, and at the sound of her voice Ruan could take no more. He stood up suddenly, swiping the lawyer's letter up from the floor just for something to do, reverting for a moment to his old persona.

'And so what?' he blustered. 'It's nothing. It'll be the Lynx again, a whole crate of rubbish that should've been thrown on the fire years ago.'

The hurt he saw in Greta's eyes floored him. He sat back down, turning the lawyer's letter over and over in his hands, wishing he could take back those words, take back everything he'd ever said about the Lynx, his understanding of their purpose and importance only just having crept into his consciousness like a tide runs through the polders on a low slung beach.

'Ah,' Hendrik went on, undisturbed by Ruan's theatrics. 'But you don't know what Isaac found in the stacks. A copy of the *Mellisographia...*'

'The folio the Lynx dedicated to Maffeo when he became Pope,' Ruan reacted as if someone had struck his knee with a hammer, the lore of the Lynx soaked into him right down to the marrow. 'First ever depiction of a bee studied under a microscope, sign of the Barberini family name. But isn't it very rare?'

Ruan sounded so uncharacteristically enthusiastic that both Greta and Hendrik lifted their heads and looked at him. Same black hair, same pale face, but gone was the scepticism they were so used to seeing, replaced by a keen interest that was enchanting.

'It is, my young sir,' Hendrik replied happily. 'I'm impressed by how much you know, though I suspect what I'm about to tell you is of a different order. I assume you know the Lynx used the khipu to communicate messages between themselves and latterly between themselves and Galileo, once he was under house arrest?'

Ruan closed his eyes because of course he knew; those men so fond of their codes and cryptograms, their rings, secret names and emblem; obscurely heartened to realise he was still a part of it way down the line, wearing Walter's oversized ring on his finger. He wondered how he would have been cast if he was there at the first: probably *Il Ignorami, Il he-doesn't-give-a-cuss, Il he-doesn't-even-know-Latin-well-enough-to-get-his-own-monniker-right.* He was kidding himself. He would never have been invited into their inner circle as Walter had been. *Il Ignorami*, and deservedly so.

'Yes,' Ruan said quietly, in answer to Hendrik's question, opening his eyes, looking with longing at Hendrik, eager now for answers. 'And yes, I know I've been the most abominable ass for the most time I've known you, but please believe me when I say that I'm curious now.'

Hendrik smiled broadly at the expression on the young man's face, seeing there what Golo and Fergus always had before Ruan became so insufferable, so intolerant of his confinement in the house on the shores of Loch Eck.

Just a boy growing up, Hendrik thought, *kicking at his bounds,* forgiving Ruan all that had gone before, saddened that neither Golo or Fergus were here to do the same.

'I'm glad of it,' Hendrik said, and meant it. 'But what you may not know,' Hendrik went on, 'is that Fergus and Golo had a working theory of how the Lynx adapted the khipu for their use. Not the way the Incas did it obviously, for it's highly unlikely anyone will ever be able to solve that particular conundrum. But the Lynx?

Well, we now have it chapter and verse. Or rather Caro had it in his book, and a very interesting little book it is too, Caro.'

Caro beamed. He would have nodded his head if he'd been able, but his neck was strictured and immobilised by the tightly bandaged collar the surgeon had applied so his stitches could heal correctly. He'd also been directed not to speak for a couple of weeks. It was a small price to pay for Caro who knew how close he'd come to dying, still feeling the coldness that had crept over him as Isaac held his strong fingers to his throat, still hearing the words Isaac spoke to him: *Come on lad. Just stay calm, just keep still and try to breathe.* Which was what he'd been doing ever since: keeping still, trying to breathe.

Most of his life had been spent balanced on a knife edge on board one ship or another, be it a whaler, fisher or tramper like the Collybuckie, and he'd always understood it could end at any moment. But now, because of all the bizarre things that had happened, Caro could actually envision his life stretching on and on and on, and all because Golo Eck had given him a book. Without it, without Golo, Caro could never have started his life again.

'It…was…the bees,' Caro croaked, unable to stop himself, smiling all the more when Hendrik and Greta tutted at the same time, absurdly glad that not one, but two people cared enough for him to do so.

'The bees it was,' Greta took up the reins. 'Golo hid a little picture show in the corners of the pages of Caro's book, like the flicker books you sometimes see where usually there's a lady undressing…'

Hendrik coughed.

'Quite,' he said shortly. 'Just like that, except this one had a far more important message to impart than a small boudoir thrill. It was giving us direction, guiding us to its source. It's long been known that *Apis Mellifera*, to give the honey-bee its correct name, are masters at communicating information amongst the individuals of a hive, mostly to do with the whereabouts of food sources. And that's precisely what the Lynx were doing with the khipu: communicating information. The little flicker book Golo created for Caro shows us a single bee hopping from flower to flower, each flower's stem having a different twist in it, sometimes two, with a letter or word beside each one…'

'Just like your beet bag,' Ruan said, suddenly aware he'd not looked away from Greta since she'd spoken.

'Just like my beet bag,' Greta replied, dropping her eyes as she remembered Shauna leaning over the table in her little cottage, remembering Shauna's kindness, wondering if Shauna had ever made use of the rudimentary khipus they'd created from scraps of leftover wool, if Shauna had ever had word about her sons.

'And much more,' Hendrik added animatedly. 'And so much more. Your Golo, Ruan, was a genius! How he worked it out I don't know, but it's all here. Like Caro said, it's all about the bees. They're dotted throughout the pages like doodles; a shorthand, if you will, for how the khipu works. Undoubtedly Golo would have made proper records that were lost with him, but luckily for us we still have the gist here, namely that he realised the Lynx were highly likely to have kept detailed notes of their conversations – natural list-makers all – and would be consistent, in their own idiosyncratic way. Every message passed between themselves and between themselves and Galileo – amongst others – jotted down so that in later, less judgemental times such as ours, they could all be revealed and understood.'

Il Ignorami – emblem: an ostrich buried in the sand right down to its feet – was beginning to catch up. No wonder Golo had been so keen to acquire the lost library of the Lynx in Paris and Ireland.

'But that could be huge,' Ruan said, leaning forward, elbows on the table, mind skewing away from Greta, concentrating on the task at hand because it really could be huge if they found the last conversations of a man as famously ground-breaking as Galileo talking to the Lynx. It could open the doors of Galileo's mind and let the world blow in.

'Huge is the word,' Hendrik said, with not a small amount of glee, 'and I have the proof of it. It's been here all along – lost until today perhaps – but not in Paris, nor in Ireland, not anywhere but right here in the Athenaeum, lying like a corpse within a tomb…a coda tacked into our rebound copy of the *Melissografia*…'

Greta interrupted, leaning forward, placing her hand on Hendrik's arm.

'That's all well and good,' she reminded him, 'and maybe there's some fantastic new idea that Galli-whatsit told them, ready to be revealed, but you've forgotten what we were supposed to tell Ruan…'

Hendrik reined himself in. She was right. It could wait. Science might be about to be unbounded but it wasn't going anywhere. It was going to take days yet, weeks, maybe even months to go through the lists in the coda and get it all figured out – every conversation the Lynx had ever committed to the khipu with Galileo and others besides. But there was one message that couldn't, or shouldn't, wait.

'Quite right, my dear, quite right,' he said. 'The Enlightenment is only just beginning and we have all the time in the world to explore it, but for Ruan the enlightenment is now.'

Ruan sat quite still. He'd no idea what to expect, no idea how any of this could involve him. The lawyer's letter was abandoned once more, his hands clasped together on the table, sweat prickling on his palms.

‘It’s Fergus,’ Greta said quietly, taking her hand from Hendrik and placing it over Ruan’s, feeling the slight jolt that went through him as she did so and oddly pleased for it. ‘We said before how I thought the khipu looked different from when I first saw it with Peter and then Mick, and so it was. I didn’t realise it before at Shauna’s, I don’t know why. Maybe because it’s only now everything’s come to a stop I can look back and see it all as it was. And it’s different, Ruan. I know it. Fergus changed it. Maybe before he went into battle at New Ross or maybe afterwards, but I know he changed it, and because of the letter he sent to Mr Hendrik here, we know he changed it for you.’

Ruan’s blood drained away like water from a lifted sod of peat. All the anger he’d ever felt for Fergus had long since dissipated, grief at his loss taking its place. He knew he’d been the spoiled child, favoured over Fergus for as long as he could remember and for no better reason than Ruan having been descended from Walter Peat. Two siblings shoved into a nest not their own vying for Golo’s favour, but Ruan always superior in his claim because of Walter. Blood calling to blood; the Ecks and the Peats always entwined, just as Golo had said.

Greta’s touch tethered him to the world, bringing back to him the last words he’d had for Fergus before they left Scotland: *You’d be nothing but a couple of muddy footprints without Golo, you and your da. Ever think on that?*

His throat tightened. He swallowed. He was close to tears. Such cruelty in those words, aimed at the man who had practically raised him, who had taught him, tried to show him not only the world of Golo’s obsession but the myriad opportunities that lay beyond. Ruan let out a short sob. He couldn’t help it and couldn’t hide it.

He was suddenly seeing himself as others had these past few years: an ungrateful little sod so self-involved he believed the world owed him a living, assuming he was more important than any shelf-load of books left behind by the Lynx. That this wasn't the case was now so self-evident all Ruan could do was shake his head in sorrow.

Il Ignorami finally disinterred from the sand. Golo had been right all along. The Lynx really did have something reveal to the world and just when Golo was on the doorstep of it, ringing the bell, about to be let in, the hell-damned Ducetti family had stopped him dead. Literally.

'Ruan?' Greta asked. 'Are you alright?'

That hand again, warm fingers resting anxiously over his own. Almost too much to bear.

'You said Fergus gave you a letter for Hendrik?' he whispered. 'What did it say?'

Hendrik nodded at Greta.

'You tell him.'

And Greta did.

'A fair bit that concerns you,' she said softly, 'but basically he repeats what he encoded in the khipu now we've figured out how the Lynx and Golo worked it and that is this: *To Ruan Peat,' Greta quoted, 'to my friend, my family, I leave everything. FM.'*

Too much for Ruan Peat, his shoulders never broad, and out came the tears held in far too long and out and out they came once they'd started, a blubbing drain in a rainstorm. Hendrik winced at Ruan's meltdown, too close to the bone, got himself up, took himself off. He left Greta stranded by the wreckage blinking in alarm, one arm held out about Ruan's shoulders but never quite touching, waiting for Ruan to subside which he soon did, folding in on himself, all dignity gone. The only thought in his head was that he might as well have stripped himself bollock naked and paraded through the town of Deventer, because if he had he couldn't have felt more exposed than he did now.

'It's alright,' Greta said gently, patting his hand, moving her arm, resting it on his shoulders. 'It's alright.'

The humiliation of Ruan Peat complete.

SINGING THAT OLD SONG

IRELAND, 1799

Shauna's Young Wexford Warrior disembarked at Rosslare and set herself on the path to Vinegar Hill, going by carriage this time, reaching it late the following evening.

It was later still when she found the small litter of scrub and gorse she'd been seeking, the cairn tumbled by time and weather but notable, if only to her. She pulled away the remaining stones one by one, and there it was: dirt-ridden, chain rusted into nonexistence. She licked a finger and brought up the tiny silver cross on its tip, laid it bare, folded it into a square of linen and placed it in her pocket to nestle against the blood flakes of Mogue Kearns.

'Alright, Greta?' Ruan asked, Greta turning her face towards him.

'Quite alright,' she smiled. 'Only one thing left to do.'

Ruan took her hand, drew her up and together they began to walk up the hill, reaching the blackened stump of the windmill as the sun began to sink, the slim crescent of a new moon rising out of the east, just as the old rebel song had it, the song of the United Irish:

Beside the river the dark mass of men were seen,
Shining weapons above their own beloved green,
'Death to every foe and traitor, and Hurrah, my boys for Freedom'

And the rising of the moon. Just as it was doing now. Bodies gone, earth drinking in the blood of the dead to its own purpose, swallowing their flesh the same way, filling the craters carved by hooves and boots, shell and canon, burying bones, abandoned weapons and farm implements that had not months before been pilfered for better use. A new moon rising above Greta, a new earth beneath her feet. A new life waiting to be lived.

Shauna came out of her door as the horse trap drew level with her gate, holding up a freckly hand to shield her eyes from the sun, watching the young couple alighting, presuming they'd stopped for directions or maybe some refreshment on their journey.

The pale young man lifted down the girl who had such a glory of red hair curling about her head. What on earth she would find to give them she couldn't think. She'd a few eggs of course, and milk, and could maybe throw a bannock or two upon the fire… and then her mouth dropped open as she recognised something about the girl, about the way she moved. She didn't dare believe it. She rubbed her hands furiously in her apron and began to shake her head.

It can't be, she thought. *It absolutely can't be.* And then the girl spoke.

'Shauna!' Greta called, starting down the path towards Shauna, tripping on her skirts, falling headlong into the dirt only to have Ruan come up behind her and pick her up, set her back on her feet again.

'Should have kept her in trousers,' he said wryly, not that Shauna heard for she was already running towards Greta, seizing her from him, engulfing her Young Wexford Warrior in her arms.

'Oh my Lord, girl, I can't believe it! Oh my Lord, but you've come back! I can't believe you've come back!'

They sat for a long while in Shauna's kitchen, Shauna catching Greta up with the news.

'It's not good,' she told Greta. 'All dead, or almost. Philip Roche, the man who took command after Bagenal Harvey? Well, he didn't last long. Hanged with eight others in Wexford, back end of June. And Cornelius Grogan? You mightn't've known of him – High Sheriff of Enniscorthy – executed a week after the battle of New Ross, and early doors July John Kelly too, along with Father Murphy and James Gallagher.'

'Bagenal Harvey?' Greta asked, hoping he hadn't escaped completely after his skulking away, leaving the men on Vinegar Hill in the lurch.

'Got as far as the Saltee Islands with John Colclough but was betrayed, as befitted, ' Shauna said, like Greta having no love for the man. 'The two of 'em brought back to Wexford and strung up like chickens.'

Greta nodded, took a breath before asking about the men who meant most to her.

'And Mick Malloy?'

She was thinking on all the fearless stands he'd taken, his squinty eye looking down on her, his all too rare smiles, his many kindnesses to her over the years despite his ferocious reputation. Shauna shook her head.

'Missing. No word on him, nor on Harry Docherty, nor Gerry

Monahan. All have to be dead.'

Greta swallowed, absorbing the bad tidings. She'd hoped for better but had always feared the worst

'And Mogue Kearns?' she asked, dreading what she would hear.

'I'm sorry, lass,' Shauna said in response, 'but he's gone too. But you'll be glad to know he got off the Hill that day, hid out in Killoughram Woods so I heard, got fighting fit again until he got arrested a few weeks later. Hanged in Edenderry, twelfth of July last year since…'

'Anyone else?' Greta whispered. 'Anyone survive at all?'

Shauna smiled and patted Greta's shoulder. 'As a matter of fact some did, and one of them was your Myles Byrne. The boy you told me you grew up with.'

Greta let out a breath and thanked God for it. But Myles Byrne? Of all of them she'd have thought he'd have gone under – such a hothead and a go-doer all the days she'd known him.

'But how?' she asked, astonished.

'Went over like you,' Shona said. 'Went over to join the Frenchies. And didn't go alone. Took my youngest with him, so he did.'

Greta coloured, hung her head.

'I should have asked,' she said quietly, 'about your sons, I mean. That should've been my first question.'

'Don't you fret, darling,' Shauna placed a finger below Greta's chin and lifted it up so their eyes met. 'And don't you be sorry, because if it hadn't been for you and those…knitted things…the name of which I've forgotten, well, if hadn't been for you and them I'd never have known a thing. I can't tell you what a Godsend they were in the last few months after the Hill, messages flying here and yonder. We mightn't have won, Greta, and Lord knows we haven't, but we'll rise again, and when we do they'll give us certain advantage.'

Ruan had been sitting back all this while, taking everything in. The little Greta had told him of what went on in Ireland had never seemed quite real. Even her pilgrimage to Vinegar Hill hadn't swayed him. Only when she started pointing out the pitiful places she'd slept, the miles she'd trudged, had he caught a glimmering of the true extraordinariness of Greta Finnerty.

The litany of men dead and executed – men Greta had known and fought beside – shocked him to the quick. And now the khipu was kicking in too – that old cats-cradle he'd once blithely consigned to the rubbish bin of history along with the rest of the Lynx. Who knew it could have an actual practical use? Well, Greta and Shauna obviously, sitting at this very table, planning how an ancient Incan artefact could be adapted to save Irish lives on a used beet bag, of all things.

'Can I ask you something, Shauna?' Ruan slipped his words into the silence left between the two women.

'But of course, Ruan. What is it?'

'Did you ever hear anything,' he said, 'of a man named Fergus Murtagh?'

Shauna looked towards Ruan, and the smile he got from her was so absolutely unexpected he moved back slightly in his chair.

'But of course, my dear boy,' Shauna said brightly. 'I thought everyone knew! I thought at least that Greta did. Has she not told you?'

Ruan shook his head, glanced at Greta, who shrugged her shoulders. She'd told Ruan everything she knew of Fergus which wasn't much, except that he'd fought briefly at New Ross and presumably died. This was part of the reason they'd come over here together – her to her home to find out what had happened to Peter, Ruan to find out about Fergus. Shauna Clooney laughed like a lark on the wing.

'But he's our great hero!' Shauna explained, giving the party line because that was the only line she knew, the same line Mick Malloy had given out to all and sundry: build up a legend, give the men some fire in their bellies before the last big push.

'Well, it went like this,' Shauna went on, oblivious to Malloy's machinations, never contradicted. 'Fergus was the only one who volunteered to go after Bagenal Harvey, which was when he got caught; but if he hadn't got caught then Mick Malloy would never have found that nest of Loyalists in Scullabogue and they'd have been on Malloy's men come the morning; and if that had happened then Malloy would never have got to Vinegar Hill, and if Malloy had never got to Vinegar Hill then your Mogue Kearns, Greta, would never have made it out alive. And neither would the Scotsman's Bauble and our stringy thing, so think on that! Fergus Murtagh is a hero, son, an absolute hero, and don't you ever forget it.'

Ruan drew in a deep breath and let it out again. Fergus, a hero. He nodded agreement and never did forget, those words running through the rest of his life like a root going down and down until it could go no further. He cleared his throat.

'It's called a khipu,' he said softly, 'that bit of Fer… the Scotsman's Bauble that helped you. It's called a khipu.'

'A…khipu…' Shauna repeated the word once or twice, before turning back to Greta, unimpressed. 'And now, young lady, I want to hear the rest; what happened after you left here, and how you met this handsome fellow. I knew you would have adventures, didn't I say it at the time?'

Greta smiled and began her tale, starting with the sea, then the Servants, how she got to Deventer where her and Ruan's stories dovetailed. Ruan nodded at appropriate intervals but wasn't really listening. He had in his head the sight of a slender bodied, sharp eyed lynx stalking the mountains of the Pyrenees, the northern forests, the snowy plains of Scandinavia and – long, long ago – the wilds of Scotland too. Maybe it had licked at the waters of Lock Eck, left its paw prints in the mud on which Johannes Eck built his house. Ruan's house now, thanks to Fergus and the khipu. Legally binding, given the contents of the letter he'd sent to Golo care of Hendrik Grimalkin.

Everything connected, from beginning to end, from when Federico Cesi first puzzled over rocks turning into trees – or trees turning into rocks – and enlisting his band of merry men to help him explore the puzzles of the universe; lines of men linking down the years, lines of footprints in the mud leading on the one from the other until here Ruan was. He had a sudden longing to return to his homeland, take Greta to the stones of Kilmartin depicted on Walter's ring, fitted now to his finger along with Golo's moon at quarter, given light by the shining of the sun.

L'Illuminato: the Illuminated One; what Johannes Eck had been to Federico Cesi; what Greta had become for Ruan – not that he'd plucked up the courage to say it out loud; the one who sees, who pours light into your darkness, revealing the world for what it truly is. The lesson of the Lynx finally learned and never abandoned, not by Ruan Peat.

Only open up your eyes, he thought, and see.

A journey started, one he hoped he wouldn't have to take alone; he looked at Greta, head bent towards Shauna as they talked quietly and privately of places, men and battles he had no knowledge of; but that was fine. *Il Ignorami* could wait. A few hours or days here and there were of no consequence; he would wait until the time was right and then he'd ask her.

New moon rising, new world unfolding at his feet.

Just one word from Greta to make it the best it could be.

HISTORICAL NOTE

The Accademia dei Lincei was founded in 1603 by Federico Cesi when he was eighteen, against the express wishes of his god-fearing father who went out of his way to try to destroy it. The initial four members were all under twenty six: Francesco Stelluti, Anastasio de Filiis, Johannes Eck (also known as Johannes Heckius or van Heeck) and Federico Cesi. Walter Peat, though, is entirely fictional. The details about Aquasparta and the fossilised wood are all well documented, as is the dispersal of the Lynx Papers following Federico's death in 1630.

Federico did issue his founding members with rings, emblems and secret or Academic names as given in the text. And they did use cryptographic forms of writing to communicate with each other, which further fuelled Cesi's father's paranoia about their activities, and convinced him that Johannes Eck, in particular, was trying to convert his son to Protestantism. A bizarre charge, as Eck was keenly Catholic and had left Protestant Deventer precisely because of it, but nevertheless Cesi's father had Eck accused of heresy. That Eck was also in prison, convicted of murdering his pharmacist, is also true, as is the fact that it was Cesi and his companions who convinced the authorities that he was a valuable enough medical man and scientist to be released into their care.

Galileo came to Rome in 1611 and Federico Cesi laid on a huge feast for him, after which Galileo went on to join the Lynx and had many of his most important works published by their press, including the infamous letters that ended with him accused of heresy. He was born in 1564 and died twelve years after Cesi did , Cesi dying young, in 1630 and Galileo twelve years later in 1642, by which time he was still under house arrest and the supervision of the Inquisition, and also by then almost completely blind.

Cardinal Maffeo Barberini was indeed a great supporter of Prince Cesi and the Lynx, and also of Galileo in his early days, before the Copernican Hersey declaration of 1616. He became Pope Urban VIII in 1623, and Cesi's and Stelluti's monogram on bees was dedicated to him as stated, and was the first printed book to include illustrations taken from microscopic observations. The *Melissagraphia* is one of the rarest books in the world today, only two known copies are still in existence.

After Johannes Eck was ejected from Aquasparta by Cesi's father he travelled all over Europe, including Spain, Germany, Sweden and Scotland recruiting members and correspondents for the Lynx, and also wrote the book on treating the ague and fever that blighted much of the Lowlands, as Joachim is posited as using.

As far as the United Irish goes, I have kept true to as much of the history as possible, including the battles mentioned, New Ross and Vinegar Hill amongst them. Peter Finnerty (1766-ish to 1822) was a real person, a famous journalist keeping the fires alight for the United Irish and their fight against English oppression with his press in Dublin. He was imprisoned in the spring of 1798 for seditious libel, following his paper's condemnation of the judges who had William Orr to death. He was defended by John Philpot

Curran, a well-known lawyer and later a judge; despite this he was sentenced to two years in prison, during which time he stayed in correspondence with various United Irish supporters, including James MacHugo, a tobacco trader (and possible smuggler) who acted as liaison between the United Irish of Loughrea and Dublin.

Peter later came over to England where he was imprisoned again in 1811 for several articles written about Lord Castlereagh's treatment of Irish prisoners, which led in turn to a campaign to have Finnerty freed, a petition signed by many of the good and the great, including the poet Lord Byron. Finnerty was also invited to accompany the English Army when they took up against the French in Walcheren, with disastrous results, thousands upon thousands of men dying of disease before lifting a finger to fight.

The khipu (or quipu or qipu) was indeed an Incan method of recording numbers and statues and the details of taxes. Approximately six hundred are extant today, and although no one knows exactly how they encoded information there has been enough study done to be almost certain that it was managed by a complicated system of numbers, using the knots, beads, colours and patterns as described. And the Lynx truly did have a fascination with South American history, and Mexico in particular, compiling a great monograph on the subject, so it is not such a great stretch that they might have come across a khipu or two – after all, the Incan Empire only finally fell in 1533, when the Spanish murdered their last ruler. And the Lynx was started in 1603, so all is possible…

If you enjoyed *The Legacy of the Lynx*, you might be interested in *Deadly Prospects* by Clio Gray, a historical crime novel which will also be published by Urbane Publications in February 2017.

Extract from *Deadly Prospects* by Clio Gray

Part 1

Storofshvoll, Iceland

8.43 a.m. September 2nd 1855

The air smelled of snow, though Lilija Indridsdottir doubted it could be so, for surely it could not fall so early, not when the ground below her feet was so warm she'd taken off the clogs she'd been wearing and slung them on a string about her neck. She looked for the dog, who was nowhere to be seen, wondered why there were no chickens pecking and chafing about the yard. She went out to the cattle to give them their feed, found them all snorting and snuffling together at the back end of the paddock, apparently unwilling to come forward as they usually did to greet her, remaining there even when she'd lugged out and loosened several bales of summer straw, scattering it enticingly about their feeding trough.

'Hi!' she shouted in encouragement, and 'Hi!' again, but the usual scrum was unforthcoming, and the cattle stayed resolutely where they were, milling about as much as they were able in the confines of the crowd from which they seemed unwilling to break free, hooves pawing restlessly at the mud and spilt faeces, bodies jittery and jumpy, eyes large and white-rimmed when they raised their heads. Something must have spooked them; she understood this, and looked around her, but saw nothing out of the ordinary – no strangers, no foxes, nothing. She shrugged, and left them to it, went off towards the rye field to inspect the stooks. Even at this distance she could see the huge flocks of greylags and pink-footed geese that had settled upon the field, milling and moving restlessly, rustling like the wind through autumn leaves. At their farthest end was a line of whooper swans, white necks erect, yellow bills upturned, their melancholy calls soon drowned out by the increasingly shrill crescendo of the heckle and cackle that was beginning to break out amongst the geese as they stirred and shuffled and yet did not take to wing. Again she looked about her, looked up into the sky, searched for eagles, for harriers, for anything that might have given all these animals such alarm.

Her eyes traced the lines of the hills that surrounded the valley, and then she saw it, saw the great dark burst of ash that was coming out from Hekla's summit, rising like a thundercloud, bright flicks here and there of burning embers and pumice, moving and dancing in the currents made by the heat that was coming up from beneath. She stared at the silent spectacle, a quick short gasp escaping her lungs as her blood began to thud beneath her skin, her mouth as dry as the straw she had just loosened for the cattle, her hands shaking, moving involuntarily towards her throat. The darkness moved as she watched it, grew and spread, went up in a great plume above Hekla's craggy neck, a sound like breaking thunder just then reaching her ears, and that was when she ran, her clogs flying off from her neck on their string as she covered the ground, realising only now why it felt so warm beneath her feet, cutting her soles on the stones and gravel as she ran and ran, the sounds of her livestock now unbearable, the shrieking of the cattle, the grackling of the geese which all of a sudden rose up and shook the air with the concerted effort of their wings, went up as one, went as a throng, before starting to separate into desperate single ribbons as one phalanx met another, and the superheated ash began to darken their outspread feathers, caught their wings alight as they tried to navigate the unfathomable darkness that had descended upon them with no moon, no stars to guide them, and one by one, they began to fall out of the sky.

Lilija Indridsdottir did not stop; she heard the plunking of birds hitting the ground all about her but could not see them. The sun had disappeared, and her world reduced to twilight in a moment, the only light coming from the embers that had embedded themselves into her clothes, into her skin, and from the bright halo about her head as her hair began to singe and then to burn. She could no longer see the path that led down to the village, but was pushed on by her own blind momentum headlong into a rock that broke her foot with its contact; she heard the crack of her bones even as the impact knocked her sideways, sent her off into a skid further on down the hillside, sliding into something warm and wet as cattle-shit, though she could smell nothing except the sulphur of Hekla exploding somewhere up above her, and knew now why the old folk called that mountain the gateway into hell.

Birds were falling indiscriminately all about her, all kinds, not just geese, but sparrows too, buntings, larks, thrushes, many still alive as they hit the ground, though not for long. A swan crashed down two yards to her right, neck bent and contorted like a gorse root in the hearth, tail feathers flaming, ash- blackened wings still beating, beating, as it tried in desperation to clear the ground, its white burned into black, its flight turned into immobility. Lilija reached out a futile hand towards it, but stopped mid-stretch; she could hear a kind of arrhythmic thumping and struggled to understand this new thing, the message of the beating drum, and then the sweat broke out upon her forehead, making grey rivulets through the ash there as she realised what it must be. She struggled to stand but could not, and instead flailed out with her hands, caught her wrist on a boulder and began to drag herself towards it, heaved with all her might to gain its protection, curled herself up tight against its solidity, beneath the slight overhang, an acorn trying to squeeze itself back inside its cup. And then they came, several score of steers and milkers broken free from their paddock, stampeding headlong away from the farm, down the hill towards the river. She could feel them coming, feel their movement in the ground, in the soil and in the bones that were shuddering within her skin, and then they were on her, passing over her in a chaos of tangled legs and panicked hooves, several tumbling as they hit the obstacle of the rock scree, crashing into their neighbours, tripping up the ones that came on behind. A hoof caught Lilija on the shoulder with the strength of a sledgehammer swung onto a fencepost, smashing a clavicle, breaking an elbow, and she whimpered as she tried to pull herself further inward, terrified by the burning of the ash, the thickening dust, the mud scooped up by the fleeing cattle, the snorts and bellows of those still running, the anguished screams and cries of those that had been brought down, and she felt the weight of them all around her as they crashed into the earth, felt her world breaking a little more with every fall.

In the river beyond the village, seven fishing vessels had not long been pushed from the pier to take advantage of the outrunning tide. Above the creaking of their oars, of wood on water, of ropes being pulled through badly oiled winches, sails rising up into the wind, the sailors heard other sounds, and looked up to see the vast cloud that was spewing out of Hekla. It came at them with the speed of an avalanche, a great black tongue unfurling down the mountain towards them, wiping out the morning as it blackened every stone, every field, every roof, every blade of grass, doused the day completely, subsumed them into night. Every man on every boat began to shout, to call out incoherent instructions or pleas, some tugging at the rudder ropes, unable to gauge direction, sails coming crashing down as knots were left incomplete, untied, everything unravelling, and soon came the crash and splinter of wood on wood as one boat ploughed into another, forced a third into what they called the Shallows, a sandbank at the river's middle where the tide insisted on depositing tree boles, rocks and boulders, after every winter's storm.

The air about them thickened, darkened, and men began to fling themselves into the water, lashing out for bank or pier, hurled on by thoughts of wives or children, treasured livestock or possessions, the water beginning to crust about them, sizzling and boiling with the fling of molten rocks, scalding their arms, their faces, the ash clogging their clothes and hair and lungs, weighing them down, narrowing their vision, constricting their breath. Into the cauldron went Lilija's brother, tripping up the man they'd called the Bean Counter, who went headfirst in behind him.

And then above all the pandemonium, the crack of wood, the panicked shouts, the clashing of oars, the splashing of men in the water, the crashing of unsupported rigging, above it all there came another sound as of a bell at the starting of its tolling, a bell so vast, and its peal so low, that it came first as a vibration, making the smoother surface of the downstream water begin to shiver as the air compressed and began to move in gusty, unaccustomed ways, pocking at the sails that were still erect, growing in strength, as every tolling bell will do, until the noise of it was vast enough to become the whole world, as if every boulder on every hillside had begun to shift and roll, as if the earth itself was roaring. Hekla yawned and then was woken, breathed out another mighty exhalation, a new turret of burning ash that rose then fell towards its southern slopes, spat out a tarred-black rain that leached the light from the sky, swallowed the sun; released it, grey and greasy, for seven long and weary months into Storofshvoll's future, vomiting out the last plume of ash from its cracked and broken summit, the last eruption of Hekla, at least, in the lifetime of Lilija Indridsdottir and her village.

September 2nd 1855, it had started. Nine o'clock in the morning, almost to the second.

April 5th 1856, when the last plume died. Seventeen minutes past three.
Storofshvoll grey as granite, an uninhabitable tundra, everything buried beneath half a year of Hekla's winter-compacted ash.

~

Spring-time, early 1859
Three years now since the eruption, three years with no more ash but plenty of storms, welcomed where they had once been cursed, sweeping away the worst of the loose ash with their wind and their rain and their ice and their snow, lifting it up in great black maelstroms and carrying it out to sea, dropping its dark ruin onto Scotland, England, France and Spain, wherever the winds took their way.

Tiny pinpricks of grass were beginning to struggle up through the new grey soil; previously buried farmsteads began to re-emerge roof tile by roof tile, timber by timber, then wall by wall, an inch of plank here, a foot of plank there, as they were washed free by wind and rain, storm and spate, as ice and snow gave way to successive springs, and the small brief blooms of the intervening summers.

Another spring, this time in 1860, and now several of the original, surviving villagers returned, began to dig out the old homesteads in earnest, abandoning those too badly damaged, concentrating their excavations on the few that appeared intact and airtight, hammering away at the outer crust with picks and shovels until they had broken through the pumice casing, finding a chink, a window, a doorway, inside. And when they finally gained ingress, it was like walking through the interior of a blown egg, a going from day and into twilight, out of noise into utter quiet. A thin layer of ash covered every surface, every boot that stood by every door, every coat that had been slung on every hook, every piece of fish that still lay in the smoke-holes dug into the inglenooks by long-dead fires, every piece of fur and blanket that lay on every bed, every pot and pan that hung from every hook in every ceiling, every cheese and jar that stood on every shelf in every pantry. All was as it had been before, yet had undergone a subtle transformation, a kind of quiet sleeping, a hibernation that felt as if it could have gone on without end, and gave the eerie sense that it belonged to an entirely separate world that was neither waiting for, nor wanting, anything to change.

The men who crashed into these silent worlds felt like stomp-pigs, large and loud, intolerably intrusive, and they did not stay long, at least not the first time. It was the women who came in later who broke the spell of these abandoned burrows, stirred them up with their brooms and cloths and dusters, brought in great pails of water and washing soda and wiped away the secret lives of these abandoned rooms and replaced them with their own normality, brought in with the noise of toil and graft, their clicking knee-joints, and the scrub, scrub, scrubbing of their brushes.

Amongst these women was Lilija Indridsdottir, a lopsided version of the woman she had been before, with one shoulder angled towards the sky, the other dipped towards the ground, right arm stuck in an awkward crook at an elbow that gave her no mobility, her left foot splayed, every bone broken in it and badly mended, flat as a frog's. She'd not been able to help with the harder work, and spent most of her hours down at the pier, sorting through what had been salvaged from the boats that had been wrecked upon the shallows, bones and possessions and trade-wares entangled as if in a beavers' dam, encased in a shell of ash that only the ever-flowing water of the last few years had been able to breach.

The population of Storofshvoll had been more than decimated, and less than a tenth of its surviving members elected to return; all others chose to stay where they had taken refuge with outlying relatives, or had already migrated into Reykjavik where they had decided to make their new home. The ones who chose to return and stay spent all their time repairing pumps, harrowing fields, digging out old crop cellars, living on whatever sacks of grain, dried peas, beets and roots had been found beneath the old houses they had managed to excavate from the ash, still preserved, just as they had been five years before.

At the end of the summer of 1860 these few survivors, Lilija amongst them, moved back into what they had dug out of the ruins, broken and blackened constructions they unimaginatively christened the New Storofshvoll, and made their own constitution, the basic tenet of which was Give help where help is needed.

And there is no better foundation on which to build a new society, no matter how small.

The citizens of New Storofshvoll came across some disturbing sights during the following months of excavation, especially when they began to dig out several of the farms on the outlying slopes of the village, where the ash from Hekla must first have fallen; they found people inside them, friends and relatives, who had been unable to get out in time, who had been suffocated, baked alive, by the smoke and ash that had poured in through their open windows, through open doorways, down chimney flues, through cracks in the roof, gaps in the wall joists.

One such family was discovered huddled in a heap in the middle of the room, bodies and clothes intact and discernible, eyes closed, arms around each other's shoulders. The outside men who had dug into this desolation did not speak, but withdrew by common and tacit consent and retreated, one of them taking up a wooden tablet from the pile they had ready, someone taking his knife from his belt and carving out the names into the wood of those within, before hammering it into the ground outside, and moving on. Maybe one, maybe more, of these men would return later, anyone related to that lost family, or a neighbour who had known them well, to shovel in as much ash as they could through the windows or doors they had opened during their earlier expeditions, trying to make of it more of a burial, more of a grave, than it already was.

It was different with the bits and bobs of bodies they discovered tangled in the wreck-heaps stranded on the Shallows, because they were only scraps of bone and tatters, flesh and clothes having long since been devoured by sea or fish, or by the acid of the ash that had plummeted down upon them. Nothing much of the remains of those who had been on the boats marked out one man's body or belongings from another, so instead the decision was made to collect together every bone, every rag, every button, every scrap of paper, of leather, everything collected at the edge of the site of the new cemetery, the old one having disappeared without a trace.

It fell to Lilija Indridsdottir, with her gammy shoulder and splayed-out foot, to sort through this pile of dead men's detritus, a fortuitous decision, because it had been in her barn that the man had bided, giving her and her brother a bit of extra rent, a bit to gossip about, and also because she was the only person in the whole of the world who knew where he'd been going, and why, on the morning the sky had exploded.

She had puzzled over the old battered travelling case when she unearthed it from her pile of rubbish, scrutinising its rusting edges, its balding leather, wondering why it seemed so familiar. It took her several minutes to realise it had belonged to the man they'd called the Bean Counter, on account of his habit of tramping up and down the coast, visiting villages and towns, ticking off who went to this church, who went to that, how many and how often, scribbling down any other, older beliefs any of them might still hold to, the tales the old women had of ghosts, of the huldufolk, who supposedly lived beneath certain stones, guardian spirits who took the forms of birds or bulls.

Counting beans, was what they'd said of him then, that man who went around their island country counting souls, adding everything up for some purpose they didn't know. But he'd been a nice old stick, she remembered, and she pondered about this bag and what to do with it, remembered what the old Bean Counter had said when he'd told her he was finally leaving.

'Where will you go next?' she'd asked him, and he had sighed deep and low, shoulders sagging, looking as tired as if he had just dragged his own cross to Rifstangi from the Holy Land itself.

'Home,' he had said, and she remembered that the deep crease between his eyes had softened as if he was about to smile, though he did not.

'Home,' he'd said again. 'If home will still have me.'

It struck her back then as such a very sad and lonely thing to say, and now, five years on, it seemed all the worse because she knew he had never even got out of the harbour, that he had never gone home, that he had gone down with Anders and all the rest on the boats that had been boiled into the river when Hekla had done her worst. And she felt for him, for this stranger, for this man she had hardly known, and for the family at the home he had never managed to reach. And so she took hold of his case that had been dragged from the Shallows, wedging it awkwardly against her bad shoulder so she could get at the rusty clasp with her one good hand, managed to snap it open from its rust without much fuss.

'Well now, Mr Bean Counter,' she murmured as she opened it up. 'Let's take a look. See if there's anything left of you inside.'

Clio was born in Yorkshire, spent her later childhood in Devon before returning to Yorkshire to go to university. For the last twenty-five years she has lived in the Scottish Highlands where she intends to remain. She eschewed the usual route of marriage, mortgage, children, and instead spent her working life in libraries, filling her home with books and sharing that home with dogs. She began writing for personal amusement in the late nineties, then began entering short story competitions, getting short listed and then winning, which led directly to a publication deal with Headline. Her latest book, The Anatomist's Dream, was nominated for the Man Booker 2015 and long listed for the Bailey's Prize in 2016.

'Surprisingly,' Gray says, 'The Anatomist's Dream - although my eighth published novel - was amongst the first few stabs I made at writing a book. Pretty appalling in its first incarnation (not that I thought it at the time!) it was only when I brushed the dust off it a few years ago that I realised there really was something interesting and unusual at its core that I could now, as a more experienced writer, work with. The moral being: don't give up. The more you write, the more self-critical you become and the better your writing will be because of it.'

Clio has always been encouraging towards emergent writers, and founded HISSAC (The Highlands and Islands Short Story Association) in 2004 precisely to further that aim, providing feedback on short listed stories and mentoring first time novelists, not a few of whom have gone on to be published themselves.

'It's been a great privilege to work with aspiring writers, to see them develop and flourish,' Gray says. 'There can never be too many books in the world, and the better the books the better place the world will be.'

URBANE